"Do you enjoy the theater, Miss Chevillon?" asked Jason Moreland. "Perhaps you would do me the honor to accompany me to a performance?"

"I'm sorry, I couldn't possibly," Denise said. It was one thing to receive an ex-slave trader in one's home, but to go out in public with him—that would be impossible.

She glanced at her mother, then at her father, hoping that one of them would provide her with an excuse for her blunt refusal. When they did not, she said, "I haven't been well, Mr. Moreland. The crowds—"

His blue eyes told her he knew she was lying, but he only said, "Then perhaps I might take you riding. I'm sure that a quiet drive in the fresh air would be beneficial."

Denise rose to her feet. "I don't wish to go anywhere with you, at any time."

She did not know then how much things would change. . . .

Fawcett Gold Medal Books
by Diana Haviland:

THE PASSIONATE PRETENDERS 13810-0 $1.95

THE MORELAND LEGACY 14038-5 $1.95

THE MORELAND LEGACY

Diana Haviland

FAWCETT GOLD MEDAL • NEW YORK

To John K. Payne

THE MORELAND LEGACY

THIS BOOK CONTAINS THE COMPLETE TEXT OF THE ORIGINAL HARDCOVER EDITION.

Published by Fawcett Gold Medal Books, a unit of CBS Publications, the Consumer Publishing Division of CBS Inc., by arrangement with The Bobbs-Merrill Company, Inc.

ISBN 0-449-14038-5

Printed in the United States of America

10 9 8 7 6 5 4 3 2 1

BOOK 1

Chapter 1

Denise Chevillon slammed the door behind Tilda, the little black girl, who had fled to her room to escape her mistress's angry outburst. Tilda had left Denise's white organdy dress flung carelessly over a chair, and, although the organdy was the only presentable dinner dress Denise had left, she didn't bother to hang it up. Instead, she shrugged and tossed her head, so that her dark red hair fanned out around her face. Her gold-flecked brown eyes were stormy and rebellious.

She would not be wearing the white organdy tonight, for she had no intention of taking her place at the dinner table, no matter what Papa had said.

She turned from the door and walked swiftly across her bedroom to the window overlooking the garden. It was early autumn, and here in Charleston the air was still warm and damp. To Denise, the view of the high-walled garden, serene in the twilight, with its live-oak trees trailing Spanish moss, its tea olives and banana shrubs, was comforting. She was able to smile a little, remembering Tilda's headlong flight; if the girl had not been so new at her job, she would have known that although Denise might be hot-tempered and strong-willed, there was no cruelty in her nature. Her anger was always brief and was usually quickly followed by remorse.

Poor Tilda was saddled with the work that back at Riverview would have been divided between two slaves. On the other hand, Tilda was better off than many of the freed black girls who roamed the streets of Charleston in this autumn of 1868; she had a roof over her head and a clean bed to sleep in. She wasn't forced to sell herself to the Yankee soldiers in exchange for food and lodging.

Denise's thoughts, not wholly appropriate for an unmarried girl of eighteen, were interrupted by a knock at her bedroom door.

She turned from the window to face Mama, who, seeing that her daughter was wearing only her camisole and pantalettes, threw up her hands in despair and assumed an injured look Denise knew all too well.

"Denise, how can you dawdle this way, when I told you hours ago that we're having company for dinner? And what's your dress lying on that chair for—how could Tilda have been so careless?"

"Don't blame Tilda," Denise said. "I told her I wasn't coming down to dinner. I guess I lost my temper and scared her out of the room."

"I should think you did. I heard you at the other end of the hall. It wouldn't surprise me if Mr. Moreland heard you, too, although he's down in the library with Papa—"

"I don't care if Mr. Moreland did hear me. Mama, what on earth could have possessed you to allow a man like that into our home for dinner?" The gold-flecked eyes were narrow with renewed anger. "Have you forgotten that the man used to be a slave trader?"

Before the War, no slave trader had ever been received by the female members of a planter's family. Instead, he conducted his business with the master of the house, while the ladies politely ignored his existence. To the coastal aristocracy of Charleston, slave trading was a regrettable necessity which was left to the males of the household or to their overseers.

For Papa, with his rigid code of social behavior, to

suggest that his wife and daughter entertain Jason Moreland in their Charleston townhouse was unthinkable. Even now that the Chevillon fortune had been swept away by the War, the slaves set free and the plantation ruined, Mama continued to lecture Denise and her sisters about the importance of the family name.

It was therefore incredible that Mama should say, "Mr. Moreland is no longer a slave trader—he deals in lumber, and is a shipbuilder, too. Times have changed, Denise. At any rate, Papa expressly requested that you come down to dinner this evening."

Although times had changed, Denise reflected, Papa's word was still law; that was plain. Under ordinary circumstances she would have submitted without question, but in this case she knew she had to make Mama understand why submission was impossible.

"If you knew how I felt about Mr. Moreland, surely you would make an excuse for me."

"How you— You've never even met the man."

"Not . . . formally, Mama, but I have seen him. And he's seen me, and I can't, I won't face him again."

Quickly she told Mama what had happened three years before, when the Chevillons had still been living at Riverview, their plantation upriver from Charleston. It had been a hot, humid day, with low-lying gray clouds that promised rain. She had returned from a ride on Fury, her black stallion, and had gone into the house, relieved to be able to take off her riding habit and her undergarments and to slip a light wrapper over her thin chemise.

"I was brushing my hair, Mama, when I heard the sound of carriage wheels in the drive. We hadn't had visitors at Riverview for so long, and I thought it might have been one of the Dupré girls. I didn't stop to think how I was dressed—I ran out onto the balcony outside my bedroom and looked down.

"A man was getting out of a carriage. He wouldn't have noticed me, I suppose, but I was leaning on the railing of the balcony, and a piece of that wood carving broke loose —it fell almost at his feet. Then he stared straight up at me."

"That was quite natural, wasn't it?"

Mama's soft voice was sweetly reasonable, her round dark eyes completely guileless.

"Yes, I suppose so, but—it was the *way* he looked at me. Any gentleman, seeing me dressed like that, would have looked away at once, but Jason Moreland—he stood there, staring at me, as if—as if he—"

Although Denise had recognized instinctively the meaning in the man's cool, appraising stare, she had no words with which to describe it. And Mama, taking advantage of her confusion, asked, "How could you have known the man in the drive was Jason Moreland?"

"Addie told me. Mr. Moreland had sold her to Papa a few years before."

"I see." Mama picked at a thread in her lace handkerchief. "Well, no matter, Papa wants you downstairs, and you must start dressing at once." She looked around. "Tilda—oh, where has that girl got to?"

"It doesn't matter. I'm not—"

"Oh yes, you are," Mama said firmly. Then, changing the subject, as she always did when conflict was in the offing, she said, "I wonder if the white organdy is the best choice for this evening. The lace is so frayed. There's the gray silk, of course, but perhaps that makes you look too—I mean, white organdy is more girlish, more—"

"Mama, surely after what I've told you, you can't expect me to meet Mr. Moreland again."

"You never have met him, not formally. He will certainly behave like a gentleman here, at our dinner table."

She fanned herself with her handkerchief, and the faint scent of her lily-of-the-valley perfume reached Denise. "My head is beginning to ache," she said. "I do hope I won't have one of my spells tonight."

"I hope not. But, Mama, about dinner. I must ask to be excused."

"Denise, I don't like to hear you speak in that tone. You sound stubborn and opinionated. Gentlemen find those traits most distasteful in any lady, and particularly in a young girl."

"What does it matter?" Denise pushed her heavy red

hair back from her forehead with an impatient hand. "Chances are I'll be an old maid, no matter what tone of voice I use. And so will Lucille and Madelaine."

"Don't say that! Don't even think it!" Mama sounded genuinely horrified. "Of course you and your sisters must marry. Why else did I scrape together every penny to send Lucille and Madelaine to visit our kin in New Orleans? If only I could have provided them with new clothes. And then, of course, there's the matter of dowries— But I've always done the best I could for my daughters, and I—" For a moment Denise thought Mama was going to cry. Her round chin quivered, and she dabbed at her eyes with her scented handkerchief. Then, with a swift change of mood, she brightened. "We may soon have all the money we need, though. If Papa's business dealings with Mr. Moreland go well, it could change everything for us. I don't understand a thing about business, of course, but it has something to do with all that timber out at Riverview."

"What I don't understand is why on earth Papa's business arrangements with Jason Moreland—whatever they may be—depend on my coming down to dinner."

"Papa knows what is best for all of us. You must trust his judgment."

All at once, Mama's plump shoulders sagged. "You don't know what life can be like for a spinster, Denise."

Although Denise was used to Mama's conversation, her habit of abruptly changing from the subject under discussion to another that seemed to have no connection, she was still startled now.

"A spinster," Mama was saying, "is the most pitiable creature on earth, living on the charity of relatives, doing those dreary errands no one else wants to do—taking second best.

"It was bad enough to be an old maid before the War, but these days it's so much worse. Which of our relatives is in any position to offer charity to one spinster, let alone three? No, Denise—for you and your sisters, marriage is the only way."

Denise looked closely at Mama, and a frightening suspicion began to fill her mind.

"Surely you can't think—not Mr. Moreland. Mama, I

know the War has changed many things for us. We have no slaves to keep Riverview producing—we can barely afford to keep this townhouse, to pay Addie and Tilda—but even so, you and Papa can't possibly expect me to—" She clenched one hand around the other to steady herself.

"Don't upset yourself, dear," Mama said quickly. "Papa only wants you to dine with us tonight, and to be your own sweet, charming self. If this business about the timber can be settled, Papa will have enough money to plant a new crop at Riverview, to rebuild the house. Think of it, Denise. Everything the way it was before—" Mama's voice trembled and her round dark eyes were bright with tears. "Except that Louis won't be here."

Louis, the only son. Mama's favorite. The tall, dashing young man Papa had thought would carry on the Chevillon name and add to the wealth and splendor of Riverview in the years to come. Louis, who had died of his wounds in a northern prison camp during the second year of the War.

Denise could not face the agony in Mama's eyes, even now, when she mentioned her son's name.

"Please don't cry," she begged. "I'll go down to dinner. I'll even try to be agreeable to Jason Moreland, if you and Papa want me to."

She threw off her wrapper and stood in her ruffled petticoats, her high, rounded breasts half-revealed by her ribboned camisole. Her shoulders were white and smooth, her neck long and slender.

"Denise, I do believe you're the prettiest of my girls," Mama said, hurrying to the chair to bring Denise the white organdy dress.

It wasn't until later, when she was descending the stairs, that Denise found herself wondering whether that was why her parents had sent her sisters to New Orleans and kept her here in Charleston to meet Jason Moreland.

Although beeswax candles were in short supply, the mahogany dining room table was bright with their glow. Somehow Addie had managed to prepare an acceptable meal in spite of the inflationary prices that made food shopping an ordeal in post-War Charleston. There was jambalaya, okra daube, and, for dessert, tipsy pudding.

Denise found herself darting quick, secret glances at Jason Moreland. He was not at all what she had expected.

When she had seen him from the balcony outside her room at Riverview, she'd noticed only that he was somewhat over six feet tall, with wide shoulders and an arrogant stance. Now, looking at him across the candle-lit table, she saw that his hair was black and that it curled crisply across his broad forehead. His skin, tanned a deep bronze, made his eyes appear a deeper blue by contrast.

She had expected that his voice would be loud and coarse, with perhaps that hateful New England twang that could be heard in the streets of Charleston so often these days. Instead, he spoke in quiet, pleasant tones.

"I'm looking forward to our trip upriver tomorrow, sir," he was saying to her father.

"I fear you will find Riverview sadly changed," Mama said. "Nearly all our servants ran off at the end of the War. The Yankee troops stole everything they could lay hold of, and then set fire to the house. We were fortunate to have this townhouse here in the city to shelter us."

The Yankees had commandeered the townhouse to quarter their troops in during the War, and Denise had often wondered how Papa had managed to get it back for his own use. Even at eighteen, she had come to realize that her father, despite his high-flown sentiments about honor and family pride, could be something of an opportunist when necessary.

"Yes," Mama was chattering on, "Riverview is quite different now. Those few servants who remained—the old, the sick, a few of the children—are barely able to take care of themselves. They have their own little vegetable patches, of course, and there are plenty of fish in the river. Still, it worries me. They are just like children, really, and we can't take care of them as we should."

"All that may soon be changed, my dear," Papa said, an optimistic ring in his voice. He hadn't sounded like that for so long, Denise thought.

"It will be, Mr. Chevillon," Jason Moreland said. "You'll see. It requires only the investment of a good supply of capital. Rice, indigo, lumber—all those are important commodities. And, in the long run, you may find that paid field hands are more efficient and more profitable than slaves."

Denise felt her cheeks growing hot. Of course a Yankee would feel that way. How could it possibly be more profitable to use paid laborers instead of those who worked without wages?

"But forgive me," he was saying. "Such dull matters cannot possibly be of interest to the ladies."

"You're quite mistaken," Denise said. "I should very much like to know how we can get along without our servants, especially now, with the Freedmen's Bureau filling our darkies' heads with all sorts of foolish notions. But I suppose that you, as a Yankee, are in sympathy with the Freedmen's Bureau, Mr. Moreland."

"Denise, that's quite enough," Papa's voice was quiet, but the steely undertone silenced Denise. From earliest childhood she'd been taught that courtesy to a guest was essential, no matter what one's personal feelings might be.

But Jason Moreland did not seem to be offended. "I must confess that the education and improvement of the Negro are not matters of concern to me, one way or the other. I only feel that his labor should be used in the most profitable way." He smiled at Denise. "And to set the record straight, Miss Chevillon, I'm not a Yankee. My parents were English. I spent my early years in Liverpool, and after that—"

"Yes, Mr. Moreland?" Mama leaned forward.

"I went to sea at twelve. I've been in many parts of the world. At present I live in New York City, but only for business reasons. So you see, Miss Chevillon, I'm not, properly speaking, a Yankee."

"Indeed, Mr. Moreland, your background is no concern of mine."

Denise expected another reprimand from her father, and a stern one, but Jason Moreland intervened. "Perhaps one day it may be," he said quietly. Before she could answer, he went on smoothly, "Do you enjoy the theater, Miss Chevillon?"

"I—I don't know. I've never been to one."

"Then I would very much like to take you. There will be a small touring company here next week, I'm told. Perhaps you would do me the honor to accompany me to a performance."

"I'm sorry, I couldn't possibly," Denise said. It was one thing to receive an ex–slave trader in one's home, but to go out in public with him—that would be impossible.

She glanced at her mother, then at her father, hoping that one of them would provide her with an excuse for her blunt refusal. When they did not, she said, "I haven't been well, Mr. Moreland. The crowds—"

His blue eyes told her he knew she was lying, but he only said, "Then perhaps I might take you riding. I'm sure that a quiet drive in the fresh air would be beneficial."

Denise rose to her feet. "I don't wish to go anywhere with you, at any time."

Mama looked horrified. "Denise, I'm sure you don't—Mr. Moreland, she—she's not herself—this dreadful heat we've been having—"

Jason Moreland waited for Mrs. Chevillon's fluttering voice to grow silent.

"No matter," he said. "I will ask you again when your father and I return from Riverview. Perhaps by that time the weather will be cooler. And you will have changed your mind."

"Papa, I won't do it!" Denise could not believe her own temerity in standing up to her father this way. She was in his study, after their dinner guest had departed. Mama had slipped off to bed with one of her "spells."

"You will do exactly as I say, Denise. When Mr. Moreland and I return to Charleston, if he asks you to go out with him again, you will go."

"But why?"

"Because he is in a position to help me—to help all of us. I thought your mother made that clear."

"She did, but—I don't like him, Papa."

"In this case, your likes and dislikes are not important. Now will you please go to your room, Denise? If Mr. Moreland and I are to get an early start tomorrow, I'll need a good night's sleep."

Papa's voice became less stern. "Believe me, child, we know what is best for you—Mama and I."

"Yes, Papa."

But even as she answered in the only way possible for a dutiful daughter, she thought, I'll go driving with Mr. Moreland, just once, but I'll make him sorry he ever asked me.

Chapter 2

Denise sat beside Jason Moreland in the gig, a smart new vehicle with bright yellow wheels and a soft black leather seat. He flicked the whip, and the lively chestnut cob started off at a brisk trot.

Charleston lay in a brilliant blaze of afternoon sunlight; the heat moved like a heavy tide along the narrow streets. Only the gardens gave a promise of shade. "Perhaps we'll get a breeze down by the harbor," Moreland said. Then he added, "Not going too fast for you, I hope."

Denise shook her head. With another companion, one of her own choosing, she would have enjoyed the drive. "I like a fast horse," she said.

"I should have known. I remember seeing you, that day at Riverview, galloping along at top speed, taking one fence after another."

Denise stared at him in surprise. "But you couldn't have seen me, not until I came onto the balcony—"

She faltered under his steady sardonic look.

"And a lovely sight you were, out there on the balcony,"

he said, his blue eyes sparkling with amusement at her embarrassment. "But I did see you before that, quite by chance. I was driving up the River Road when I got my first glimpse of you. You were riding a big black brute of a hunter, and wearing a green riding habit. The veil on your hat had come loose and was whipping out behind you."

She turned her face away to avoid his eyes. Under his mockery was an intensity that made her uneasy. "I knew I had to see you again," he continued, "although I wasn't sure how I'd manage it. You solved my problem when you came out onto the balcony and nearly hit me with that piece of woodwork."

Denise's gloved hand tightened on the handle of her small rose-colored parasol. "I would prefer that you forget the incident."

"No, indeed. It's one of my fondest memories. You, with that red hair loose around your bare shoulders, and your wrapper falling open. Your skin like ivory. . . . You were a little on the thin side, as I recall, but I—"

Fury crackled through her. "You talk like a slave trader still," she said.

"I do have a keen eye for a female's selling points, if that's what you mean. Though, indeed, narrow hips were never a selling point; they're thought to be a sign of a poor breeder." He shrugged. "No matter, I'm not in the slave trade any longer. I'm in shipbuilding now, and a few other highly profitable ventures besides. You'll have no need to be ashamed to me."

"I should not be ashamed of you in any case, Mr. Moreland, since you're nothing to me."

"Not now, perhaps. But I'm going to be. You know that, don't you?" He stopped the gig. "Don't you?" he repeated.

"I've no idea what you mean."

"I see. I thought perhaps your father had told you."

"Told me what?" She looked out over the harbor, unable to meet his eyes.

"Your father has given me his permission to marry you, Miss Chevillon."

Denise began to tremble, so that the parasol shook in her hand. "I don't believe you. Papa wouldn't—Please take me home. At once."

"We haven't finished our drive. You haven't even given me a chance to propose to you."

Denise stood up. Jason Moreland put a hand on her arm and drew her down beside him again. "Surely you're not going to walk home. No respectable southern miss is safe on the streets of Charleston, I'm told. Not with all these Yankee soldiers about."

He was right. How she hated the sight of these arrogant Yankee soldiers and their wives. She knew, too, that some of the gaudily dressed women with the soldiers were not their wives, but those fancy women who had flocked to the city after the army of occupation. How dreadful if, unescorted, she were to be mistaken for such a woman. Better to endure Jason Moreland's company for a bit longer.

"I'll take you home in a little while. First, we'll go down to the harbor."

"But I—"

"You don't want your father to think we've quarreled, do you? It would displease him."

She remained silent as they started off again. There was a slight breeze blowing in from the harbor. It cooled her burning cheeks, and she would have found it pleasant but for Jason Moreland's company. And for the memories of war that were more vivid down by the sea.

There was Sullivan's Island, where the first fortifications had been built, where dashing young Confederate officers like her brother Louis had gone out to war with the same careless air as if they had been riding to a ball.

In those early days of the War, boats from Charleston had landed on Sullivan's Island with cases of champagne and claret and boxes of fine Havana cigars for the pleasure of the officers of "The Live Tigers," "The Palmetto Guards," and "The Marion Scorpions." Those young officers had been so sure the War would be over in a few months. . . .

"Please, can't we drive back?" she said.

They started off again, but instead of driving home, he

turned in the direction of the Race Course—scarcely more cheerful than the view of the harbor, she thought. At one time it had been quite different, with splendidly dressed Charlestonians flocking to the Race Course to enjoy the sport. But during the War, the Race Course had been used as a prison for captured Yankees, many of whom had died there. The South hadn't had enough provisions for its own army, let alone for prisoners of war. Even now she could not help feeling guilty when she read the inscription over the entrance to the small enclosure that served as a cemetery. "The Martyrs of the Race Course," it read.

Then she reminded herself that her own brother must have suffered, too, before he died in a northern prison. And the rest of her family, even now, faced a bleak future because of the War, unless—

"Mr. Moreland, are you going to go into business with Papa? Will he be able to rebuild Riverview, to plant a new crop—"

"It's quite possible. But I shouldn't have thought you were interested in business."

"I'm not. I mean—I only want everything to be the way it was before."

"I'm afraid that will never happen. But your family can be comfortable and prosperous. They can have all those luxuries I'm sure they've missed."

"It isn't a question of luxuries, Mr. Moreland. These last months, we've been without decent clothes, without enough food—" Her hand flew to her lips. How shameful to have lost control, to have forgotten her breeding, her mother's training, the unwritten law that one must never admit those harsh facts she had just blurted out.

"It's no disgrace to be hungry, Miss Chevillon. Until I was twelve years old I rarely went to sleep with a decent meal inside me. Often I didn't have a roof over my head, either. When I remember those days back in Liverpool, all I can see is myself, my mother and my brothers being put out of some wretched lodging house." His voice turned harsh, and his eyes looked past her. "I'm sure the sun must have shone from time to time, but looking back, I can see only the dirty wet streets, the bunch of us soaked to the skin, my mother carrying the youngest, and the rest trailing along like a pack of gypsies."

"And your father—"

"Dead. He was a seamen in His Majesty's Navy. Flogged to death for striking an officer. My mother was left with four children and no money—no home—"

Denise looked at this tall, powerfully built man seated beside her, wearing a fine broadcloth suit, a starched and ruffled shirt, and light gray satin vest. She tried to imagine him as a small boy, homeless and half-starved.

"I didn't profit by my father's unhappy experience," he was saying. "I went to sea when I was twelve."

"You were in the navy, then?"

His mouth, full-lipped and sensual, became a thin, hard line bracketed by two deep creases.

"I shipped out on a merchantman, bound for the Ivory Coast." His tight smile did not reach his eyes. "That was my first introduction to the slave trade."

Her distaste must have shown in her face, for he asked abruptly, "Tell me, are all southern ladies as hypocritical as you?"

"What do you mean?"

"My dear Miss Chevillon, your father's plantation was worked with slave labor. Your brother died fighting to preserve slavery. Yet, when you learn that I started in the slave trade as a boy, you look shocked, thoroughly disapproving."

"It's not the same thing. I mean—"

"What *do* you mean? You probably don't know. No matter. Under all your silly conventional ideas, I suspect you may have some honesty, perhaps even a little intelligence—"

She made a small, angry sound, but he went on calmly, "I've always liked honesty in a woman, and even some intelligence, for that matter. But you have another quality—a most desirable one, to my mind."

"I don't care to hear—"

"I sense that somewhere beneath that veneer of charming innocence are the passions of a real woman."

"You are insufferable."

"Why? I've just paid you a compliment. And now—"

With a swift movement he took her parasol from her hand, snapped it shut and tossed it to the floor of the gig. The next moment his arms were around her, holding her against him. His lips came down and covered hers, gently at first, then, as she struggled to turn her face away, more insistently.

She had been kissed only a few times before, and those had been decorous kisses, given to her by respectable young Confederate officers who were going off to war. Jason Moreland's kiss was completely different; his lips were hard and demanding. He bent her back until she lay across the seat, and he kept her pinioned with the length of his hard body. His lips moved until her lips were forced apart, until she felt the touch of his tongue. The pounding of her blood in her temples made her fear that she might faint.

She realized at that moment that she was afraid of him, and that her fear had nothing to do with convention. She feared the emotions that he aroused within her, strange new emotions that she barely understood. That was why she had avoided him, why she had tried to avoid being alone with him.

He released her so suddenly that she fell back across the seat, her face upturned to the blaze of the afternoon sun. The heat of the sun seemed to have entered the very center of her being. She tried to turn away, but Moreland's blue eyes held hers, and she saw in them what she had never seen in any man's eyes before: hot, naked desire.

He bent and touched his lips to her throat. His tongue traced a line of fire to her shoulder, half-bared where the ruffle of her bodice had slipped down. Through the light fabric of her dress, she could feel the touch of his hand on her breast. That touch brought her back to cold sanity. She had never been alone with a man like Jason Moreland before, and for one terrible moment she wondered whether she would be able to control him.

Although her ideas of what his intention might be were vague and undefined, they were nonetheless frightening. Whispered conversations with her sisters and with friends had given her confused, monstrous ideas of what happened "after you were married." She gave a strangled cry of pure terror.

Jason Moreland took his hands away. "All right," he said. "Nothing's going to happen—not now." He picked up her parasol and handed it back to her. "You needn't look so uneasy, Miss Chevillon. I assure you, you're quite safe from futher advances—until we're married, at any rate."

"I'll never marry you. I don't care what Papa may have promised you. I'll never—"

"Oh, yes, you will." There was cool mockery in his smile. "What's more, if I can judge by your responses a few moments ago, you'll enjoy being married to me."

In the years that followed, when Denise looked back to that golden autumn of 1868, it seemed to her that the time between that afternoon when Jason Moreland first kissed her and the moment when she uttered her marriage vows was a blur of activities, confused and hectic. Before the War, a courtship had been a leisurely process, but now all that had changed. So much had to be crowded into the days between early September, when Jason Moreland announced his intention to marry her, and late October, when the wedding was to take place.

Denise's sisters, Lucille and Madelaine, had returned from New Orleans in a flurry of excitement. Even as Denise went through the preparations for her wedding, Mama and the two older girls were busy buying clothes and packing trunks for a trip to France.

There was no longer any need to make desperate efforts to find suitable husbands for Lucille and Madelaine with the help of the Chevillon relatives in New Orleans. Now, provided with suitable dowries and splendid new wardrobes, they could have their choice of suitable young Frenchmen from good families. Mama had dozens of relatives in Paris who would welcome her and her two daughters, under the circumstances.

Although of course there had been no open discussion of the matter, Denise was well aware that the money for the trip to France, her sisters' dowries and their new clothes had all come from Papa's share of the business he had set up with Jason Moreland.

Denise was surprised to find that neither of her sisters was scandalized by her forthcoming marriage. Indeed, Madelaine sounded downright envious when she discussed Jason with Denise.

"He is handsome, you know. And there's something about him, a kind of energy and vitality." She sighed. "Those men we met in New Orleans, the ones who'd been through the War, all had an air of defeat, of hopelessness about them. They were charming and polite, but they were living in the past. Jason Moreland's different. He's looking to the future, planning what he'll do next month, next year."

Denise stared at her sister, who was tall and slender, with the high cheekbones and long, elegant neck that were characteristic of all the Chevillon women. "Perhaps you should marry him," Denise snapped. As the date for her wedding drew closer, she had found herself growing more nervous and short-tempered.

Madelaine said quietly, "He didn't ask me." She looked closely at Denise. "Don't you love him at all?"

"Well, I—" She couldn't answer, nor could she meet the searching look in her sister's soft brown eyes. "That is, he—"

"He loves you, doesn't he?"

"He wants to own me, if that's what you mean."

Madelaine gave a little gasp and put a hand on Denise's arm. "That is a terrible thing to say. It sounds as if you were . . ."

"Say it."

"One of those quadroon girls in New Orleans, the kind men used to buy and keep in the houses on Rampart Street."

"Perhaps Mr. Moreland sees me that way. He used to be a slave trader, you know."

"I think that is best forgotten," Madelaine said gently.

"Yes, by all means let us forget it. Mama and Papa have. The prospect of Mr. Moreland's fortune has quite driven it out of their minds." Denise felt a growing tightness in her throat, and all at once her bitterness changed to wild, uncontrollable weeping. Madelaine embraced her, holding her close, as she had done when they were children. "You don't have to marry him; you can break the engagement, even now."

"The wedding is only four days off." Denise gained control of herself, fumbled for her handkerchief and wiped her eyes. "Besides, think what it will mean to you, to all of us, when I'm the wife of Jason Moreland."

"I don't care. If you hate him so much, you can't marry him."

"I don't hate him. I—Maddie, I don't know how I feel about him. He frightens me, and yet I . . ." How could she possibly tell her sister how she felt about the man who was to be her husband? She didn't understand her own feelings. There were times when the thought of being Jason Moreland's wife repelled her, when she wanted to run away and keep on running. But then there were moments when, lying in bed, before drifting off to sleep, she remembered his embrace that day at the Race Course. She felt again the warmth of his mouth, the shocking intimacy of his kiss. When his hand had closed around her breast, she had experienced a sensation as violent as it was mystifying, a tingling sensation that spread from her breast to other hidden parts of her body, those places that no nice girl even thought about. "He frightens me," she repeated hopelessly.

"Perhaps that's natural," Madelaine said. "But after you're married, you'll feel differently, of course."

"Will I? If only I could be sure."

But even as she spoke, she knew that she would go through with the wedding. Madelaine had offered to forego her lavish dowry if accepting it meant that Denise had to marry a man she didn't love, and because of her very generosity, Denise could not allow her to make the sacrifice. Madelaine could not be permitted to go through life as a spinster. As for Lucille, small and pretty, with her melting amber eyes and mass of soft coppery curls, she had something of Mama's helpless, fluttery quality. She would need a husband to care for her in the years to come.

And Mama herself was flighty, perhaps, and selfish in many ways, yet filled with genuine grief over the loss of her only son. The trip to Paris would take her away from her bitter memories—for a year, at least. When she returned to Charleston, it would be in triumph. She would have found husbands for Madelaine and Lucille, and Riverview would be a place of gracious elegance once more. Denise was well aware that Jason Moreland had bought acres of timber, had hired freedmen to do the cutting and to build a sawmill on the River Road. The timber would be used at his shipyards up North. Both her father and Moreland would profit from the venture.

Her marriage to Jason would save them all from the disaster that threatened to overwhelm so many of the families they knew. And maybe she would be able to find some happiness for herself as a result of the marriage. She and Jason Moreland would live in Charleston, but she hoped he would spend time up North looking after his business interests. She managed to conjure up a vague but agreeable picture of herself, taking her friends for rides in her carriage, inviting them for tea, playing hostess at dinner parties. . . .

Two days before the wedding the house was filled with relatives who had come to Charleston from New Orleans, Savannah, Cape Fear and Asheville. Now, late on this warm October afternoon, Denise watched Mama and Tilda as they unpacked her trousseau.

"Oh, how lovely!" Mama ran her fingertips over the nightdress and negligee that had just been taken from a large, shiny white box and spread out on Denise's bed.

The two garments were made of champagne-colored satin, to set off Denise's dark red hair and to emphasize the warm specks of gold that gave her brown eyes their curious fascination.

Until now she had worn only the simple cambric gowns that were suitable for an unmarried girl, virginal nightdresses that covered her from chin to ankles. But the satin gown on the bed was cut low, with a deep V-shaped band of lace set into the bodice, so that when she wore it her breasts would be half-revealed. She thought of Jason Moreland's blue eyes, of the desire she had seen there. "Put it away—put all these things away, Tilda."

Her voice was shrill and uneven.

"Darling, what's wrong? You look a bit flushed."

"It's so warm. I feel as if I were stifling."

"The air is heavy," Mama agreed placidly. "Perhaps it will rain tonight." She walked to the window to open it wider.

"Oh, dear, there's Mr. Moreland's gig turning the corner. Put on a fresh dress, dear—that new organdy with the violets on it."

The air was even more oppressive when Denise accompanied Jason Moreland into the garden. He led her to a bench near the wall, in the shadow of a huge live-oak tree. He watched in silence as she arranged the skirt of her new organdy dress around her, but his eyes were appreciative.

"You look cool, in spite of the weather," he told her. "You're a little pale, though. Perhaps all these preparations for the wedding have tired you."

"No, indeed, Mr. Moreland."

"Look here, we're going to be married in a few days. Can't you start calling me Jason? And I'll call you Denise. After all, you won't be Miss Chevillon much longer."

"As you wish."

"You sound like the sweet, submissive wife already. I wonder if you will be. Denise, there are certain matters concerning our future that must be discussed, and this is as good a time as any. Where we'll live, for instance."

"I thought we would live here in Charleston, until Riverview can be made ready."

"I was afraid you had some such notion. Riverview was a fine house, Denise, and will be again, but it's not my home, and it never can be."

"Then where—"

"We will live in New York," he told her. "No, wait—let me finish. I know you love Riverview, and I'll have no objection to your coming back for a visit from time to time."

"A visit! But my family is here, and my friends."

"Your mother and sisters will be leaving shortly for France."

"But I—"

"Denise, I've always wanted a home of my own, where I would be master."

"We could build a home here in Charleston."

He shook his head. "I have already built a home for us. It's not quite finished yet, but it will be by early spring. I engaged the finest architect in New York to design it, and I've ordered furniture from Europe." He took her hands in his. "Wait until you see it."

She tried to pull away, but his hands tightened around hers, while his eyes willed her to see his vision, to share it. "Mooncliff is a mansion, and you will be its mistress. My sons will be born at Mooncliff."

"No. My life is here—"

"Your life is with me." His voice was hard, commanding. "Surely you've been taught that a wife's place is with her husband. My business interests are in the North, and that is where we'll live."

Only then did she realize how much she'd counted on making a life for herself here, among the people and surroundings she knew. "You have interests here, too," she said.

"Your father can see to those, with the help of a good overseer and a hard-working manager for the sawmill. Now we won't discuss this any further. Immediately after the wedding we'll leave for New York."

"Right away?"

"One of my ships will be waiting in Charleston harbor. After the reception, we'll go on board." His eyes brightened with enthusiasm. "She's a schooner, a real beauty. When we land in New York, we'll go to the Fifth Avenue Hotel—I've already reserved their finest suite—and we'll stay there until Mooncliff is ready for us."

He sounded so firm, so sure of himself. Denise remained silent, staring into the shadows that had descended over the garden, trying to imagine her future life in a strange northern city. Jason put his hands on her shoulders and turned her to face him. "I know this comes as a surprise, but once you get used to it, you'll—"

"What does it matter to you whether I like New York or hate it? What do my feelings mean to you? You own me, or you will in a few days, and that's all you care about."

His hands tightened on her shoulders, his strong fingers biting into her flesh through the thin fabric of her dress.

"That's enough, damn it! You make it sound as if I—"

"As if you were a slave trader?" She glared up at him, her eyes narrow. "Why not? You're buying me, aren't you?"

He released her, and she drew back, frightened by his look. In the still, charged air that presaged a storm, the odors of the tea olive and banana shrubs in the garden were overpowering. She felt dizzy, unable to take a deep breath, not sure whether anger or fear was causing her heart to pound in this odd, irregular way.

"You little idiot," he said. "Do you really think that if I only wanted to buy a woman's body, I'd have to marry her? Don't you know there are hundreds of beautiful young quadroon girls down here in Charleston, in New Orleans—all over the South—who are trained in the arts of pleasing a man? I could buy any one of them if that was all I wanted."

"What do you want, then? Surely you don't expect me to love you?"

"You think that would be impossible?"

He took her in his arms, pressing his mouth down on hers. One of his hands twisted in her luxuriant hair, forcing her head back.

His lips moved to her throat, warm and caressing against her soft flesh. Although she was dimly aware of his fingers opening the buttons of her bodice, she did not try to pull away. Her hands pressed against his shoulders, not to repulse him, but to draw him closer. She felt the heat of his body, the hard muscles of his broad chest, the rhythm of his breathing.

His hand moved under the flimsy cotton and lace camisole; his fingers touching her skin, stroking, pressing gently.

She moaned softly as she felt the tingling sensation

spread downward to her loins. Her body arched, as if with a will of its own, and she thrust herself against him.

She heard the low rumble of thunder, far away, and at the first flash of lightning illumining his hard, tanned face, she came back to reality, shocked by what she saw in his eyes.

Big drops of rain were falling now, soaking through her dress, molding it to her body. She tried to rise, but he held her a moment longer.

"You see, Denise, it's not impossible; you can learn to love me. And you will."

Chapter 3

The ballroom, which occupied most of the third floor of the Chevillons' townhouse, was filled with guests. The musicians in the gallery at one end of the ballroom struck up a waltz, soft and lilting, as Jason Moreland led his new bride out onto the floor.

Denise looked up at the man who had been her husband for less than an hour, trying to read the expression on his face. Pride was there, and a sense of satisfaction.

"You and your sisters are the best-dressed women here," he said softly, as he whirled her around the polished floor. "And your mother, of course. She looks quite splendid in that purple taffeta."

She found his words irritating. "No one else was able to afford new clothes for the wedding; you know that. I'm surprised so many guests accepted invitations at all, considering—"

"Considering you married an outsider, a carpetbagger—a man whose family hasn't lived here in Charleston for three generations. Don't look so flustered, Denise. I've told you I admire honesty in a woman. Particularly if she's as beautiful as you are."

"You like my dress?" She was relieved to change the subject.

"You look lovely," he said. "I like that. I want my wife to be the best-dressed woman wherever I take her. When we get to New York, you are to buy yourself whatever clothes you like. I don't suppose you have anything in your trunks suitable to a northern winter."

"How could I have, since I didn't know we were going North until a few days ago?"

A sardonic smile touched his lips briefly. "With all your other reservations about marrying me, I thought I'd better keep that piece of news for the last," he said. "I trust you're getting used to the idea of living in New York."

The tempo of the waltz quickened, and Jason's arm held her firmly as he whirled her through the crowd of dancers, her ivory skirt billowing around her.

In a year when other southern brides had to be content with wedding gowns handed down from mothers or sisters, or with made-over ball dresses from pre-War days, Denise had ordered a splendid new dress. Seamstresses had come to the house and had sewn day and night to complete it in time for the wedding. The full satin skirt was trimmed with white lace, and the bodice was cut low, with full, puffed sleeves. Before the dancing had begun, she had removed her voluminous veil of white silk tulle, with its wreath of orange blossoms, and had given it to Tilda to pack away. She had no personal maid, but Jason had assured her that it would be no problem to hire a French or Irish lady's maid when they arrived in New York.

Denise had never had a white servant; the idea was strange to her, but she supposed she would get used to it. She told herself that she would have to get used to many alien ideas, now that she would be living in the North.

"You look very thoughtful," Jason observed. And when she did not answer: "Perhaps you'd like to stop dancing. We might take a walk in the garden—"

"No," she said quickly, remembering their last walk in the garden, his ardent lovemaking and, worse still, her startling response to his caresses. If they had not been interrupted by the thunderstorm that evening— A hot blush started at the base of her throat and moved upward. She hated this weakness that revealed her feelings as clearly as if she'd spoken them aloud. Jason, she had already learned, was a man who caught every nuance of her expression.

She tried to draw away, but his arm was like iron, holding her against him, and she could feel the pressure of his hand at her waist. He had large hands and heavily muscled arms. She thought there was something almost brutal in the look of his big-boned frame.

She remembered that in the romantic novels she'd read the hero was always tall and slender, with long, tapering fingers. Jason was tall enough; indeed, he towered over her father, and most of the other men in the room, but under the fine broadcloth suit his body was like the body of one of the field hands who used to work the acres at Riverview.

Her face grew even more flushed at the thought. It was indecent to think about a man's body this way, even though the man was now her husband. Yet in a few hours she would be sharing a bed with Jason Moreland. She tried to put the thought out of her mind, to lose herself in the beat of the waltz, in the swift, whirling movements that left her a little dizzy.

It was plain that the guests were enjoying themselves, and Denise knew that her wedding and the reception had come as a welcome relief from the dreary day-to-day grind of their lives. Festivities such as this one were all too rare in the South in 1868. While the elders sitting on the sidelines here in the Chevillon ballroom might still be preoccupied with their everyday problems, the young girls were making the most of this chance to dance, to flirt, to meet eligible young men.

Denise was pleased to see her sisters dancing by, in their new gowns. Madelaine looked regal in a dress of mauve satin, her hair arranged in a becoming chignon ornamented with mauve velvet ribbons. Lucille was obviously having a wonderful time, tossing her copper tresses and laughing at whatever her partner might be saying to her at the moment.

Mama sat enthroned on a striped satin and mahogany love seat, her taffeta skirt spread out around her. Denise saw the proud, complacent look on her face. And why not? Her youngest daughter had made a most successful match. With a little luck her other two daughters would do even better, finding husbands who were not only wealthy but socially eligible as well.

Papa was very quiet, as he had been for several days. Denise wondered whether he was having second thoughts about her marriage. Perhaps his satisfaction at being able to rebuild his fortune was somewhat dimmed by the knowledge that he had sold his daughter to seal the bargain.

As for Denise, she was not yet sure what this marriage would mean to her. A few times since she had become engaged to Jason, she had listened to Mama's half-hearted attempts to prepare her for "the duties of a married woman." But such sessions had not gotten very far. Mama would end by stammering slightly, then remembering an appointment with a dressmaker or a milliner. The lecture would conclude with Mama's reassurances that Denise would surely be a good wife and obey her husband in all things. Now, as Denise looked up at Jason, she realized that, with or without Mama's little lectures, she would have no choice; Jason would be master of his house, and of everyone in it.

Once more she thought of that house and its strange name—Mooncliff. Since she'd first heard the name, she had repeated it over and over to herself, trying to imagine what it would look like. A curious name—romantic, surely, but eerie, too. Jason must have chosen the name, as he had chosen the land and the type of house he wanted to have built on it.

He had made these choices before he had proposed to her. Had he, then, been so sure of her answer? And had he decided to marry her after catching a brief glimpse of her three years before at Riverview?

Perhaps he had decided to come South to choose a bride and had selected Denise purely by chance, because of his business with her father. Maybe another girl, young, pretty and of good family, would have suited him as well. Not a very flattering thought, to be sure, but Denise, under her veneer of romantic idealism, was something of a realist. She accepted the idea that Jason probably did not love her. He had never said he did. He had spoken of a house and of the sons she would give him. But if he didn't love her, he desired her in a purely physical way; of this she was certain. What would he expect of her now that she was his wife? Would she be able to satisfy him?

A few hours later, when Denise went to her room to change into her traveling costume, she was still tormented by these questions. Jason was almost twice her age, and a man of considerable experience. A few nights ago he'd spoken of the quadroon girls of New Orleans who were "skilled in the arts of pleasing a man." What were those mysterious arts, and how did one learn them? She shivered slightly. Jason did not appear to be a patient man, or a kind one.

She had reached the door of her room, but she stopped short on hearing her sisters' voices. They must have come to help her change her clothes and to say goodbye to her in private.

"If only she'd waited," Madelaine was saying. "She's known Mr. Moreland only a few weeks."

"Maybe she was afraid to wait," Lucille said. "Jason Moreland's a good catch—you can't deny that. All that money. And a fine big house in New York and—"

"Lucille. You talk like a Yankee."

"It's true, all the same—he is a good catch. I know he's not a gentleman. Or even a southerner. But things like that don't seem to matter anymore."

"They do," Madelaine said firmly. "They always will. How can Denise be happy with a man she scarcely knows, a man who used to sell slaves to Papa? In the old days we wouldn't have had a man like that at our dinner table."

"I know, but—she's better off than the Dupré girls, isn't she? Iola Dupré had to marry the man who used to be their overseer, that horrible red-faced Irishman. And poor Coralie is going to marry a widower old enough to be her father, with five children of his own. Denise hasn't done badly." She giggled. "Even you've said you think Mr. Moreland is handsome."

"Suppose he is? Is that all that matters? Lucille, none of us knows anything about Jason Moreland. What kind of family does he come from? How did he make all that money during the War?"

"You worry too much," Lucille said lightly. "Madelaine, just think, in a month we'll be in Paris. We'll be meeting young men, going to parties, maybe even—"

Denise, standing outside the door of her room, wasn't concerned with Lucille's dreams of future glory. All she could think of were Madelaine's words:

"None of us knows anything about Jason Moreland."

She was married to a stranger. In an hour she'd be leaving her home, her family and friends, to go with him to New York, to live in a house called Mooncliff. . . .

At sunset, the swelling tide floated the *Enchantress* out of the harbor. From the quayside the calls of farewell still echoed on the air, and in her mind's eye Denise could see her family waving to her, although they were now lost to view. How many years would pass before she saw them again?

The breeze ruffled her hair now, and she put up her hand to make sure her small hat was firmly anchored to her head. The hat was a frivolous affair of pale yellow straw, trimmed with jade-green ribbons. Her traveling dress, of delicate muslin, was whipped around her by the wind so that the full skirt billowed out, then flattened against her body.

Jason had left her as soon as they had come on board, to make sure that the cargo had been properly stowed by Captain MacKay, a stocky, bearded New Englander. Denise was somewhat taken aback to learn that Jason had used the schooner to bring down a full cargo and that he had loaded on another cargo in Charleston for the return voyage. He was being practical, she admitted; nevertheless, his actions made the honeymoon trip seem all the more a kind of business transaction.

"And that's what it is," she told herself.

Jason came to join her at the rail, and she raised her

head, pressing her lips together to keep them steady. He must not know the depth of her unhappiness, her fear of the future.

He put his arm around her waist, pointing out to sea with the other hand. "Fort Sumter," he said quietly. She fixed her eyes on the pile of mortar, stones and sand that had played such an unforgettable role in the War. From the center of the pile a flagstaff rose, and on top, the Stars and Stripes floated in the breeze. The flag of a conquering nation—and she was one of the conquered.

The setting sun turned Charleston harbor into a sheet of burnished steel. She looked away and saw that Jason's eyes were searching her face intently.

"Denise, you're not crying, are you?"

"Certainly not," she snapped. "The sunlight on the water is so bright—"

But the sunlight did not explain the tightening in her throat, the sinking sensation she felt as his arm tightened around her.

"Perhaps you'd like to go below," he suggested. "I think you'll find our cabin to your taste."

She hesitated.

His eyes were sardonic as he interpreted her hesitation. "I still have a few things to see to here on deck," he said. "I'll just show you to your cabin. Bathsheba will see to your comfort."

She stared at him blankly.

"I wanted to surprise you," he said. "Bathsheba's a mulatto woman. She approached me on the wharf a few days ago and begged me to take her to New York. She has a husband there, a freedman she hasn't seen for years. She has no money, but she has had experience as a lady's maid, so I offered her passage in exchange for her services."

"Thank you," Denise said. "But I thought—you said something about my having a French or an Irish girl for a maid—"

"And so you will, when we reach New York. But in the meantime you'll need someone to brush your hair and perform all those other little services a gently reared southern lady requires."

She decided to ignore his sarcasm, grateful that he had gone to the trouble of making these preparations for her. In all her life Denise had never undressed herself, put away her own clothes, or brushed her own hair.

He took her arm and helped her down the steps leading to the cabin. "You'll find it unusually spacious," he was saying. "It took some doing, I can tell you."

He unlocked the door, and Denise caught her breath in surprise and pleasure. The cabin was most attractive, with a fine Turkish carpet on the floor, a small carved desk, a chest of drawers. The bed was larger than the one in which she'd slept at home, and it was curtained in embroidered silk.

Bathsheba, a tall, thin mulatto woman with a spotless white turban and a starched apron, was unpacking the small trunk that held those items set aside for the voyage. Her movements were quick and competent. At Denise's entrance she paused, curtseyed, and then went back to her duties.

"I had Bathsheba fix a tray for you," Jason said. "You didn't eat anything at the reception."

He brushed his lips across her cheek, turned and left her alone with her maid. Some of the tension flowed out of her at this brief respite. But she found that she had no appetite for the supper Bathsheba offered her.

She looked at the delicately browned breast of chicken, the fluffy biscuits, the bowl of grapes and peaches, and the bottle of wine arranged on the silver tray, and although she hadn't eaten since that morning, she felt no hunger at all. She pushed at the chicken with her fork, then poured a glass of wine. Sipping it, she relaxed slightly.

The movements of the ship were becoming more pronounced, and Denise hoped she wouldn't be seasick. She had never been to sea before, but she had heard dreadful stories from those of her friends who had. Gradually she became aware of the many strange new sounds that were a part of the ship: the creaking and shifting of timbers, and a noise like the crack of a pistol, which she later learned was caused by the wind as the sails were unfurled.

"What nightdress will you wear, Mrs. Moreland?"

Denise started and looked around before realizing that

Bathsheba was addressing her. The new name had an alien, disturbing sound. "I don't know— Oh, yes, there's a satin gown in the trunk somewhere, with a lace inset."

Bathsheba found the nightdress and the matching negligee, laid them out on the bed, and helped Denise undress. The satin felt soft and soothing against her skin. Then the maid took the pins from Denise's hair and brushed the thick waves down over her shoulders to her waist.

"Sure you don't want no more supper?" she asked, preparing to leave the cabin.

"No—I'm not hungry."

"Another glass of wine, then?"

Denise shook her head. "You may go now, Bathsheba." She hoped her voice sounded calm and controlled.

The maid picked up the tray. "Good night, Mrs. Moreland," she said.

When the door had closed behind Bathsheba, Denise paced the floor of the cabin. The swinging lamp on the wall cast huge flickering shadows. The motion of the ship was making her a little dizzy, and she sat down on the bed. She forced herself to study the pattern of the embroidered silk curtains.

There was a rap at the door and the grating of a key in the lock, and then Jason was inside the cabin. He strode to her side, sat down next to her and took her in his arms.

She closed her eyes and felt her whole body go rigid as a stone statue. She did not try to pull away, but neither did she respond. Her eyes remained shut even as he drew her down on the bed and kissed her. Then he released her, and she heard him moving about the cabin. She opened her eyes for an instant, saw him unbuttoning his shirt and turned away, her face to the wall. If only Mama had been more explicit; if only she had some idea of what to expect.

After what seemed like hours, Jason was beside her, his voice quiet and even. She sensed the passion in those soft tones, however.

"Don't turn away from me," he said.

Obediently she moved to face him. "And take off that robe, or I will."

Her fingers fumbled with the tiny satin-covered buttons, and she slipped off the robe, letting it fall to the floor.

"The nightdress, too."

Again she obeyed, this time more slowly.

He held her in his arms. "Don't fight me, Denise," he said.

"I'm not. I—"

His lips covered hers, cutting off whatever else she was going to say. She felt terror, but mingled with it were the first stirrings of desire. It was like that night in the garden, only this time she knew there would be no drawing back.

"Jason, please be patient with me. . . . I don't know what to—to expect . . ."

He lifted his face away from hers. In the light of the swinging lamp, his eyes, startlingly blue against the tanned face, were remote and unreadable.

"Surely, Denise, you must know something about marriage." His mouth curved in a sardonic smile. "I thought all well-brought-up young ladies spent hours speculating on the joys of the married state. In the most ladylike terms, of course."

Fear gave way to hot anger. "Don't you dare laugh at me, Jason Moreland. Can't you see how I—"

"Yes, I think I'm beginning to see. You're afraid, aren't you? You're not just pretending, as I thought you were."

Unwilling to admit the truth of his words, she turned her face away, setting her teeth in her lower lip. Her body was tense and unmoving.

To her surprise, he touched her face gently with his hand, running his fingers along her cheek. "I didn't know," he said softly. "Seeing you that day back at Riverview, I thought how it would be when we were married, but I couldn't have known how lovely you were. No, don't turn away. You have the most beautiful body I've ever seen. It was meant for pleasure, for loving."

His hands moved over the swelling curves of her soft skin, with none of the haste or violence she'd feared. Only when he began to stroke her delicately rounded thighs did she cry out softly; he silenced her with a slow, lingering kiss. Her muscles relaxed, and her arms went around him.

His hand, still moving, caressing, parted her thighs with an easy movement. His fingers found the center of her being. Her feeling of outrage at this shocking intimacy gave way to a slow current of desire, a fierce pleasure unlike any she had known before. Her parted legs began to tremble, and her body arched upward.

He laughed softly. "I knew you'd be like this," he said.

Then he was poised above her, and she felt the weight of his body, holding her against the bed. "No, wait—please—"

"Don't play games with me," he said harshly. "You're ready—"

She tried to push him away, but he gripped her wrists, forcing her arms down at her sides. A sharp thrust of pain made her cry out; the sound echoed in the small cabin, then was lost among the other noises—the creaking of the ship, the thundering of the sails as they filled with the night wind.

She awoke before dawn. Jason lay beside her, sleeping peacefully, his powerful body relaxed, one arm bent under his head. Sitting up in bed, she waited until her eyes became accustomed to the shadowy cabin, then got up to retrieve her nightdress. Her movements woke her husband, so that when she got back into bed beside him and before she had time to put the nightdress on, he reached for her.

"You're awake early, my love," he said. "If you're so eager to enjoy the pleasures of marriage again, I'll be happy to oblige."

"I was cold," she said. "I got up to get my nightdress."

"Surely that flimsy thing won't keep you warm. Come here."

He put his arms around her and drew her against him, and in spite of herself she found that she was pressing against him. "This time it will be better for you; you'll see," he told her.

As it happened, he was right. But afterwards, she could not repress a sense of shame. How could she have given herself to him with such abandon, unable to hide her need of him? She wasn't in love with him, and she was sure he didn't love her. And yet in one night he had stripped her of her modesty, had changed her from a gently reared young virgin to a shameless creature without restraint.

So long as she had been able to tell herself that their

marriage was a simple business proposition, that she had become his wife because her parents had demanded it, she could preserve her dignity. Now that pretense was gone, and, knowing Jason Moreland as she did, she was afraid that he would use his knowledge of her weakness as a weapon against her in the years to come.

Chapter 4

The *Enchantress,* her canvas spread to catch the stiff November breeze, moved out of Lower New York Bay, through the Narrows, into the Upper Bay, docking at South Street on the tip of Manhattan. After he had given Captain MacKay last-minute instructions concerning the disposition of the cargo, Jason escorted Denise ashore.

She turned for a last look at the three-masted schooner.

"Look well," Jason said, and she thought she could catch a touch of regret in his voice. "She's one of the last of her kind. It won't be long before steamships drive sailing vessels like her off the seas forever."

"You speak as if it were a woman."

"Ships are always called 'she,' " he said. "I suppose that's because they're often capricious and hard to handle. But men love them for their grace and beauty."

Denise searched his face. Could he be declaring his love for her at last, in this roundabout way? But he caught the look and laughed.

"I suppose you'll have fond memories of the *Enchantress,* my dear."

"I found the voyage pleasant," she said primly. "We were fortunate not to run into bad weather this time of year, I suppose. Indeed, Captain MacKay said—"

"I'm not referring to our sailing conditions, and you know it."

"Jason, really, there's no need—"

When her mother had lectured her on a wife's duties, Denise had never imagined the pleasure a bride could find in marriage. In the course of the voyage to New York, Jason had initiated her little by little into that pleasure, and she had found herself responding. Her passion did not match his, but nevertheless it startled her, revealing a side of her nature she had not known existed. No real lady should be so ardent, even after marriage.

Her troubling thoughts were interrupted as Bathsheba came off the ship and stood a little distance away, looking in their direction. The mulatto woman held a battered straw suitcase that Denise suspected contained all her personal possessions.

Jason took charge of the situation. "You're leaving us now, Bathsheba. I suppose you have the directions for finding your husband's shop."

"Yes, sir," she said, curtseying.

Jason took out his wallet and counted out a few bills. "Mrs. Moreland found your services satisfactory," he said.

"Yes, indeed," Denise said.

"Good enough." He turned back to Bathsheba. "Take this, and good luck to you."

The woman did not giggle and shuffle with pleasure as Denise had seen the Chevillon slaves do when they were given an unexpected reward. Instead she held herself erect, raised her head and looked squarely at Jason. "There's no need to give me money, sir. You gave me free passage."

"Take it," he ordered brusquely, putting the bills into her hand and closing her fingers around them. "You'll find this an expensive city in which to set up housekeeping. And you'll surely want warm clothes for winter."

"Thank you, sir." She took the money, folded it and put it into the bosom of her calico dress with care. She curtseyed again. "Goodbye. Goodbye to you, Mrs. Moreland, ma'am."

Carrying her straw suitcase, she turned and left them, hurrying off along South Street, pushing her way through the crowd of stevedores, teamsters and porters. The docks were piled high with cargo, and the crisp air was filled with the shouts of busy men, each of whom seemed bound on an errand of the greatest urgency. It was noisy and hectic, and a bit frightening. Denise moved closer to Jason. "I hope she finds her husband. With this crowd—"

"Bathsheba will manage, I'm sure."

"I've never seen a black woman quite like her," Denise said. "It was almost as if she considered herself the same as a white servant."

"Damn few white servants turn down cash, in my experience," Jason said. "Besides, in the eyes of the law, she is the same—she's a free woman, remember."

"There were free women of color back in Charleston," Denise said impatiently. "But they were different. They—"

"No doubt. You'll find many things here in the North that will take some getting used to."

The breeze from the harbor tugged at her dove-gray cloak, and she pulled it more closely around her. "It will surely take time for me to get used to the weather. Is it always so cold here?"

Jason laughed and put his arm around her. "You think this is cold? Wait until you go through your first winter up here in New York."

"I've heard it's quite beautiful—snowflakes swirling through the air. . . ."

"It's well enough, if you have warm clothes and hot food inside you. And a roof over your head." His voice was harsh, and she guessed that he was remembering his poverty-ridden childhood in Liverpool. Then she saw his eyes brighten.

"Ah, there's our carriage, my dear." He led her through the crowd to a fine closed carriage, sparkling with fresh paint and polished metal. It was drawn by a team of matched bays that had been curried until their coats shone like satin.

"Does this belong to you?"

"To us, my dear. I hope you like it." Jason helped her inside, the coachman flicked his whip, and the carriage moved off, to merge with the heavy stream of traffic surging northward through the city.

"When we're settled at Mooncliff, you'll have your own riding horses," Jason said.

"How wonderful. It has been so long since I've ridden a good horse. Those of our horses that weren't taken by the Confederate Army were captured by the Yankees. Fury—that black stallion I was riding the day you first saw me at Riverview—we even had to let him go."

"Just as well. Listen to me, Denise. You'll ride, since it gives you pleasure, but you'll have a gentle horse, suited to a lady. And when you become pregnant, you won't ride at all."

Denise gasped audibly. No gentleman ever used that word in the presence of a lady; instead he said "in the family way" or "in an interesting condition."

"What's wrong? You're not pregnant already?" Jason demanded.

"Of course not. How could I be, so soon?"

"It's perfectly possible. Particularly considering your shameless abandon during all those nights of the voyage."

He was taunting her, as she had dreaded he would. Anger ripped through her. "How dare you? As if you gave me any choice, when you—"

"Now, my dear, don't try to pretend that I raped you every night of the voyage. Surely you're more honest with yourself, if not with me."

His use of the word "pregnant" had been bad enough, but that other word— "Your foul language is no more than I might have expected," she said. She set her jaw and pressed her lips together, then turned her head to look out the window of the carriage.

She did not understand Jason at all. One moment he could be generous, considerate, even sensitive to her feelings; while the next, he could take pleasure in shocking and humiliating her.

"Forgive me, Denise. But now that we're married, I find your maidenly vaporings ridiculous."

"I don't know what kind of women you consorted with before you met me, but—"

"That's just as well," he said dryly. "Nevertheless, a

woman doesn't have to be a harlot to take pleasure in lovemaking, and if it pleases her, why not admit it?"

"Please, can't we talk about something else?"

"Of course," he said agreeably. "Let me give you a guided tour of the city. There—that's Union Square. And that big building is Tiffany & Company. They have the largest and best collection of jewelry in the country, so I'm told. I'll take you there one day and let you choose any bauble that pleases you."

She kept her eyes fixed on the view beyond the carriage window, refusing to answer. How could a piece of jewelry compensate for his mockery, his deliberate rudeness?

As if unaware of her displeasure, he went on smoothly, "Now, this is Broadway. That's Arnold, Constable & Company over there—a most fashionable store. You'll be spending a great deal of time there, I've no doubt."

"I have enough clothes," she replied icily. "You've been more than generous."

"Your father paid for your trousseau, my dear."

"With the money you advanced him."

He chose to ignore the challenge behind her words. "As I told Bathsheba, New York is cold in winter. You'll need more than those dainty muslins and organdies you brought from Charleston to keep you warm. I want you to buy furs and velvets, the finest woolens. . . . That store there is Lord & Taylor. There's always a crowd around their show windows."

Even in her present angry mood, Denise found herself looking with interest at those glittering windows with their magnificent displays. She was not the only one. Many well-dressed ladies clustered around the windows, while others bustled in and out.

"Everyone is in such a hurry here," she said. "And the crowds! I don't believe I'll ever get used to such noise and speed."

"Of course you will. And, at any rate, you won't be living in the city forever. As soon as Mooncliff is ready, you'll move out there. You'll find it quiet enough, with only the sounds of the wind and the river."

She shivered. He took her hand. "Feeling a bit homesick, aren't you?"

She pulled her hand away and shook her head. "I'm not a child," she said stiffly.

"Perhaps you are, in some ways." He sighed. "You know, I hated Liverpool with a passion when I lived there, but when I went to sea, I found that I was sick with longing to go back to those wet, dirty streets."

"But you *were* a child, then. You said you were only twelve."

"I was a man," he said. "Once I'd signed on for my first voyage, I was treated like any other member of the crew. More harshly, perhaps, because I wasn't big enough to fight back." He broke off. "We were talking about you, Denise."

"But I want to know more about your childhood," she said.

"Your wifely interest is touching."

"And your sarcasm is—"

She broke off as their carriage drew up in front of a handsome white marble building that occupied a full block between Twenty-third and Twenty-fourth streets.

"Here we are," Jason said. "The Fifth Avenue Hotel. We'll spend the winter here."

Denise had never been inside a hotel, and she caught her breath, impressed by the opulent surroundings. She was grateful for Jason's arm, the solid strength of it, as he guided her across the spacious lobby, lavishly decorated with frescos. Well-dressed men and women strolled about, or sat talking on the plush chairs and sofas.

Denise noticed that several of the people in the lobby stared at her.

"I can see that this cloak is light for such a chilly day," she whispered to Jason. "But I do wish people wouldn't look at me as if I were peculiar or—"

Jason laughed. "You're a very beautiful woman, Denise. You'll have to get used to attracting attention."

At the desk, she stood watching while Jason signed the regiser. "Mr. and Mrs. Jason Moreland." How strange it looked, even after these first weeks of marriage.

"So happy to have you with us, sir—and you, Mrs. Moreland. I trust everything will be to your liking. If there is anything you need, you have only to tell me."

Denise nodded, somewhat overwhelmed by the greeting and anxious to reach the privacy of her room. All at once she felt self-conscious about her status as a new bride. Her embarrassment wasn't eased when the clerk said to her husband, "I trust you and your bride had a pleasant voyage."

"Very pleasant, thank you."

The words were commonplace, but Denise had the feeling that Jason was remembering every incident of their honeymoon voyage, and she clenched her hands, hoping that a blush would not betray her.

She forgot her embarrassment on the way upstairs, however, when for the first time in her life she stepped into a metal cage and found herself being drawn upward. "It's an elavator, my dear. This hotel had the first elevator in the country, although I understand there are a few others now." She clutched at his arm. "Don't worry, it's quite safe," he assured her, as the small, creaking cage carried them upward.

After the porters had brought their trunks and the bellboy had shown them around the suite, Denise and Jason were left alone. "I wish I could have brought you directly to Mooncliff," Jason said. "But there is still some work to be done in completing the house, and much of the furniture hasn't arrived yet."

"I'm sure I'll be comfortable here," she said. The suite consisted of a parlor, a bedchamber with a great carved walnut bed, a dressing room, bathroom and water closet.

"I'll arrange with the management to provide a personal maid for you during our stay," Jason was saying. He took her arm and drew her into the bedroom. "Right now, though, I'll help you undress."

"I have no intention of— It's the middle of the day—"

He pulled her against him. "I've never heard that there was any law against making love in the daytime."

He lifted her in his arms and carried her to the bed. With swift movements he undid the buttons and ribbons that had kept her imprisoned in yards of muslin and cambric. She found herself wondering whether he'd done this for other women in the past. And, if so, what had they been like? Had they too been filled with this curious blending of desire and shame?

"Jason, draw the draperies—"

"I like to look at your body in the sunlight. Your skin is the color of warm ivory, and so smooth to the touch . . ."

His fingers slid over the curves of her naked body, stroking, probing, withdrawing. He pressed his face against the swell of her breast, so that his next words were muffled.

"Perhaps you would like to undress me, Denise." Then, as she stiffened in his embrace, he added, "I assure you, my clothes are simpler to remove than yours." He raised himself from her. "Your modesty disappoints me." He began to unbutton his shirt. "I'll do it myself, then—this time."

That evening, as they left the elevator together and went toward the dining room, Denise tried to make herself forget the hours she'd spent with Jason in the huge carved walnut bed. She dreaded the thought of sitting through dinner with him, of the way he was sure to remind her, with every word and look, of what had happened between them only a few hours before. He relieved her fears, however, when he told her, "We'll be dining with Captain MacKay and his wife." No matter how he might mock her in private, his behavior before other people was impeccable.

Captain MacKay was not a loquacious man, but his wife Rosalind filled the gaps in the conversation, rattling on in a rather high-pitched voice, commenting on the dresses of the women at the surrounding tables. Mrs. MacKay was obviously delighted with her elegant surroundings, pleased that her husband's employer thought her suitable company for his new bride.

"Indeed, I'm sure you'll like New York, Mrs. Moreland," she was saying, "and if there is anything I can do to make your stay in our city more agreeable, you have only to ask."

"That's kind of you," Jason said before Denise had time to answer. "I'm afraid I'll be busy much of the time, and my wife knows no one here. If you would accompany her to the shops, advise her on choosing a suitable winter wardrobe. . . ."

As Rosalind MacKay expressed her complete willingness to make herself useful, Denise studied the woman with interest. She seemed an unlikely mate for the dour New England captain, and Denise was sure that she could not be called a lady, at least not by Charleston standards.

Although Denise guessed that Mrs. MacKay was in her late thirties, her complexion was as pink and glowing as a young girl's. Could she possibly be wearing rouge? Back in Charleston, the only women who wore rouge were the prostitutes who had followed the Yankee troops into the city. How dare Jason choose such a woman to be her companion, to accompany her on shopping trips—and without even consulting her first?

"I'm fitting out the *Arcturus* for the next transatlantic crossing," Jason was saying. "Captain MacKay will be in command. We'll both be busy down at the docks, so I have no doubt that Mrs. MacKay will have some free time to show you around New York."

Before Denise could speak, Captain MacKay broke in. "The *Arcturus*. That floating frying pan."

"I know your feelings about steamships, Captain," Jason said calmly. "In some ways, I share them, but as I told my wife this morning, the time will come, and soon, when sailing ships like the *Enchantress* will be relics of the past. A sailing vessel, even the fastest of the China clippers, is no match for a steam-driven ship."

"I don't agree," MacKay said stubbornly. "The *Flying Cloud*—"

"The *Flying Cloud* was a beauty in her time. But every sailing ship wasn't like her. The *Nubian Queen* . . ."

Jason stopped speaking, and Denise saw that he was looking past Captain MacKay, past all of them. His lips were compressed in a thin, hard line. An uncomfortable silence fell over the party. Even Rosalind MacKay made no attempt to cover the awkward moment with her chatter.

Jason drained his wineglass. "I beg your pardon, Denise—and yours, Mrs. MacKay. This is no place to talk of business. If you'll make your selections, I'll give the waiter our orders."

Denise stared at the long, impressive menu unseeingly. "Jason, what was the *Nubian Queen*? Was she one of your ships, or—"

He turned to look at her, cold anger in his eyes. She flinched. How could she have provoked such a violent reaction with a simple question about a ship? For one terrible moment she had the crazy feeling that he was about to strike her.

"It doesn't concern you." She shrank from the fury behind those words. In the few weeks of their marriage, she had experienced the many changes of his mood, but she had never seen him like this.

It was Rosalind MacKay who eased the tension. "My husband never wants me to concern myself with his business, either," she said. "You'll get used to men and their crotchets, I've no doubt." She looked at the menu. "I'm going to have this turtle soup. I'm told the cuisine here is quite out of the ordinary, Denise. You don't mind if I call you Denise, do you, my dear?"

Denise said: "No, of course not." She was grateful to Mrs. MacKay for reducing Jason's outburst to the status of a common masculine foible, although it was plain that, like Denise, she realized it went far deeper than that.

Jason was making an obvious effort to relax. He poured another glass of wine and drained it, then leaned back in his chair. But the lines that bracketed his mouth were as deep as two scars. And there was a peculiar metallic glint in his eyes that frightened her.

What had happened to him aboard a ship called the *Nubian Queen*? She'd heard that life at sea could be harsh; hadn't he told her that his own father had been flogged to death for insubordination? She shivered. Perhaps Jason, too, had incurred the wrath of a superior officer long ago. She had never looked at his body, not even when they were in bed together; she had no way of knowing . . .

She felt her face go hot, and she raised the huge menu so that it shielded her more effectively than a fan would have done. She found that her appetite had disappeared completely.

"If you fancy some particular dish that isn't on the menu, the chef will be happy to prepare it for you."

She started at the sound of Jason's voice, then ventured to take a quick look at him. His face showed no stress now.

"I—I'm not very hungry."

"Nonsense, my dear. This hotel is famed for its food. Or are you, perhaps, concerned about getting a bit plump? Don't worry, I've always favored plump women."

"Most men do," Rosalind MacKay said complacently. She herself had ample curves, although her waist was still trim.

Denise was not thinking about Rosalind's figure, or her own, for that matter. She was still brooding about Jason, and she wondered if someday—when they'd been married a long time, of course—she'd be sufficiently at ease with him to keep her eyes open when he made love to her.

During the days that followed, Denise came to realize that she had much to learn about love and marriage. Rosalind MacKay, who accompanied her about the city on endless shopping trips, as well as on visits to the theaters and fashionable tea shops and on drives through Central Park, was not the least bit reticent about sharing her wealth of experience.

At first, Denise was shocked and embarrassed, but gradually her curiosity outweighed her modesty. Mama had told her nothing useful about the married state, only that she was to obey her husband and satisfy his needs in a dutiful manner. Rosalind was far more outspoken.

One chilly gray November afternoon, the two women were riding back to the hotel in Denise's carriage; they had spent the morning shopping at Lord & Taylor. Denise has still not become accustomed to the brisk northern climate, and she sat wrapped in a new cashmere cloak, her hands buried in a sable muff, one of her most recent purchases. A number of shiny white boxes were piled on the carriage floor.

Rosalind MacKay had been most helpful in guiding Denise to the best shops and advising her on what was being worn in New York City that winter season. The dress Denise was wearing now, with its tunic of mauve satin-faced serge and its matching underskirt, elegantly trimmed with a pleated flounce and purple velvet ribbon, had been ordered under Rosalind's watchful eye. Denise knew the garment was most becoming; Rosalind had proved to be a useful companion, as well as an amusing one.

Although she had lived in New York City all her life, Rosalind was still fascinated by the sights around her and eager to share her knowledge of the city with Denise.

"Over there, my dear, that's Wallack's Theater. All the best plays are performed there. Perhaps we can go to see one soon. It will give you a chance to show off your evening clothes—" She broke off abruptly and raised her pale eyebrows. "My goodness, look at her."

Denise, following the direction in which her companion pointed, found herself staring at a plump dark-haired woman who stood in front of the theater. The woman was dressed in a dark red velvet Watteau-Casaque walking suit, with a yellow silk underskirt. Although obviously expensive, it was far too gaudy for good taste, as was the woman's hat, adorned with red and yellow plumes.

"She must be an actress," Denise said. "No respectable woman would dress that way."

Rosalind laughed. "More likely she's a madam. New York is full of them. And they make enough moeny to dress to the nines."

"But I thought—I've never seen such a person—don't they remain at—at home in the daytime?"

"You *are* innocent. Why, my dear, you've probably dined at the next table to one of those creatures, right in your hotel. And as for the fine shops, where do you suppose they buy their clothes?"

"I never thought about it. It's horrible, isn't it? They shouldn't be allowed to mingle with decent women. They—"

Rosalind adjusted one of the curls that fell over her shoulder. "They serve a need, those women. If you ask me, there are far too many respectable married ladies who are responsible for the prosperity of—the other kind."

"What on earth do you mean?"

"It's always seemed to me that if a married lady took the trouble to keep her husband happy, he'd have no need to visit— Now, don't look at me like that. It's the truth."

Denise wanted to change the subject, but her curiosity kept her from doing so. "I don't understand. If a woman submits to her husband's demands, what more can she do?"

"Some women are so prim and proper that a husband hesitates to make certain demands," Rosalind said bluntly.

"I remember—when Jason and I first met—he once said something about—about the quadroon girls of New Orleans. He said they were 'skilled in the arts of pleasing a man.' "

"No doubt they are," Rosalind said dryly. "But there's nothing they can do for a man that his wife can't learn to do—if she's willing to forget her modesty." She went on, warming to her subject: "The truth is, lots of married women don't really enjoy that part of marriage. They like the rest of it—being called 'Mrs.' and having a man to support them, to offer respectability and security. But they don't take pleasure in making love."

"Do you?" The quesion popped out before Denise could stop herself, but Rosalind didn't seem to mind it.

"Of course I do. I was married before, you know. My first husband was an official at the Custom House. He died quite suddenly, during a typhoid epidemic.

"I met Captain MacKay only a few days after. I'd gone to the Custom House to collect poor Albert's personal effects from his desk, and Captain MacKay was there on business, and he was so kind, so understanding. He insisted on taking me back to my home, and I asked him to stay for tea, and then—everything happened quite naturally, after that."

Her meaning was obvious, and Denise once more found curiosity warring with embarrassment. Curiosity won.

"Your first husband had only been—gone—a few days, before you . . ."

"That's right." Rosalind sighed as she smoothed a blond ringlet with her finger. "I was a little surprised myself. But I can't get along without a man, you see. Even now, when Benjamin is away at sea, I feel like I'll go crazy, all alone in that big bed." She laughed. "Of course, when he comes home from a voyage, we make up for lost time."

Denise thought of her own shame at those moments when she desired her husband, when her body, on its own, demanded satisfaction. Was it possible that there was no need for shame? That her feelings, if not common, were shared by at least a few other married women?

"Marriage takes a lot of getting used to, the first time," Rosalind was saying. "And your husband—" She broke off, looking down into her lap.

"Go on. What were you going to say?"

"Only that Mr. Moreland is—well, sometimes moody, isn't he?"

Denise realized that Rosalind was only hesitating because Jason was, after all, Captain MacKay's employer. Rosalind obviously had no wish to offend that employer's wife.

"You're thinking about that night at the hotel, the first time we all dined together," Denise prompted her. "Jason's conduct seemed strange to me, too. Why should he have been so furious, just because I asked him about that ship— the *Nubian Queen*?" She searched Rosalind's face anxiously. "Do you know? Did your husband tell you afterward?"

Rosalind shook her head. "No. He refused to discuss the matter."

"So did Jason. And that night, after we went back to our suite, he . . ."

Rosalind's blue eyes were alight with curiosity, and she leaned closer. "Do tell me. What happened when you were alone that night?"

"He was very quiet," Denise said slowly. "I tried to talk to him, but he sat by the window, drinking one glass of brandy after another. I've never seen him drink so much."

"Oh, dear! He didn't become . . . intoxicated, did he? Men can be so frightening when they've had too much to drink. They're not themselves at all. . . ."

"He wasn't violent, if that's what you mean. I almost wish— But he only sat there, not looking at me, not speaking. Then later he got up and went out by himself. He wouldn't tell me where he was going. I waited up until after midnight; then I went to bed. It was nearly dawn when he returned."

"And then?"

Denise felt hesitant at sharing the intimate details of her marriage with another woman. But maybe Rosalind, with her greater experience, would be able to explain Jason's odd behavior.

"He came to bed, of course. But he—he didn't touch me. For the first time since our wedding, he didn't . . ."

"Such things do happen, from time to time," Rosalind assured her. "Even the most ardent husband—"

"But the next day," Denise hurried on, embarrassed by her own frankness, "he insisted on driving with me to Tiffany's, and he bought me a diamond and emerald necklace."

"Well, in that case, I'd say you have nothing to complain about. You must show me the necklace, my dear."

"It's in the hotel safe, but I promised Jason I'd wear it on the night of the housewarming ball at Mooncliff. You and Captain MacKay will be there, of course."

"When will that be—do you know?"

"Sometime in February, Jason says. There's still some work to be completed on the outbuildings, and a great deal of furniture ordered from France and Italy hasn't arrived yet. The gardens, of course, will not be laid out until early spring."

"It sounds magnificent. Like a castle. And the name, Mooncliff—so romantic, and yet a little strange, don't you think?" She shook her head. "I shall miss you when you're living all the way out there, on the banks of the Hudson."

"You'll be coming out to visit us often, I hope," Denise said. She realized, for the first time, how lonely her life would be after she and Jason moved out to Mooncliff. He would spend much of his time in New York City or traveling on business, but how would she fill her hours?

From the little he'd said about the house, Denise had gathered that it was far from even the smallest town and that there would be no neighbors close by, no one for her to talk to except the servants.

"You must have Mr. Moreland bring you into the city quite often," Rosalind was saying. "Otherwise you'll go mad with boredom. I must say, it seems strange to me, moving a new bride out to such a lonely place."

"I don't suppose I'll have time to be lonely—or bored," Denise replied defensively. "At least, not after I'm— That is, Jason plans on our having a large family."

"Good heavens! I've had two, and they're quite enough. I adore Emmaline and Sabrina, of course, but it is a relief having them off at school. Children can complicate life so much." She paused and looked more closely at Denise. "You're not in the family way already, are you, my dear?"

"No—at least I don't think I am."

"Don't you know for sure?"

"I haven't been getting sick in the mornings. And my waistline's as small as it was before I got married."

"You are naive, aren't you?" Rosalind leaned closer and in plain terms told Denise the simple, almost infallible way a woman could be sure she was going to have a baby.

"It's all well and good for a man to want a large family," she added. "He doesn't have to get horribly swollen and unsightly and go through hours of labor at the end of it all. I didn't have a bad time, either—not like some women I've known. But still, after having two babies, I made up my mind that was enough."

Denise stared at her companion, feeling thoroughly confused. "You said you enjoyed—that is—" She took a deep breath and plunged ahead. "If you sleep with a man, how can you avoid having babies?"

"There are ways."

"But Jason wants children—"

"Give him a couple of sons, then. He'll be willing to settle for that, I should think. Only country women have a baby every year."

The carriage stopped in front of the fashionable tea shop where Denise and Rosalind were to have lunch. There was no question of continuing this line of conversation, and their talk shifted to Denise's plans for the housewarming. But for days afterwards Denise found herself brooding over the fascinating information she had picked up from Rosalind MacKay.

In the following weeks Denise discovered that she was losing her self-consciousness about her relations with her husband. Rosalind's matter-of-fact attitude toward marriage made Denise less ashamed of her response to Jason's lovemaking. Although he was gone during the days, immersed in his business dealings, she felt a growing closeness during the hours when they were together.

She was still somewhat troubled by the prospect of moving out to Mooncliff, but now she was able to share her misgivings with Jason. "It's such a long way from the city," she said one evening, when they were alone in their hotel suite.

"I prefer it that way," he replied. "A man's home should be completely apart from the place where he conducts his business."

"But I like New York—"

"You like what you know of it—the theaters, the fine shops, this hotel. There are many places in New York you've never seen—you don't even know of their existence—and you will never will, if I can help it."

"You make those places sound quite thrilling, in a sinister sort of way."

"You'd find nothing thrilling about the slum dwellings of the Five Points, my love. Or the dives on Water Street, or—" He stopped abruptly. "You're a child, Denise." He smiled indulgently. "That's part of your charm." His lips brushed her cheek. "You won't be lonely at Mooncliff, I'll see to that."

"But we can have visitors, can't we?"

"Of course. And we'll have parties, as often as you like. I want to show my beautiful wife to the proper society, in a setting that will do her justice—Mooncliff."

Jason waited until February to take Denise to see her new home for the first time. They started out early, and although the wind was sharp and chilling during the steamer trip up the Hudson, the pale spring sunlight held the promise of warmth later in the day.

Nevertheless Denise, who was still not accustomed to the northern climate, was glad she had worn her sable-lined cloak. She drew the hood over her head so that the dark fur framed her face, and she settled back against the leather seat of the surrey Jason had hired after they had left the steamer at the Rhinecliff landing.

He pointed out the larger and older village of Rhinebeck on the hill two miles east of the landing, and the purple frieze of the mountains on the opposite side of the Hudson. "Those are the Catskills," he said. "The old Dutch settlers had a lot of legends about them. They said trolls lived up there, and gnomes and wizards." He laughed, but Denise could manage only a faint smile.

She thought that there was something eerie about the isolated road they were driving along, with its steep, wooded hills, not as tall as the mountains across the river, but desolate and strewn with rocks. She could not help remembering the moss-covered live oaks, the slow-moving yellow rivers of her own Carolina low country; by contrast, this stretch of the Hudson Valley looked grim and forbidding. Here, except for the dark pines, the trees were gnarled and leafless.

But she reminded herself that it was still early spring; later this region surely would take on a more inviting color, with willows, maples and elms in full leaf and plants flowering along the riverbank.

"Maybe we should have waited for better weather," Jason said. "We may be in for some rain before the day's over. No matter; there are several pleasant country inns along the way."

He smiled at her, his eyes bright with an almost boyish enthusiasm. "I was impatient to show you our new home, and now that the river has thawed . . ."

"You mean it's frozen solid in winter?"

"Of course. The people around here use it for a highway; they travel on the river in sleighs during the cold months, and ice yachting's becoming a popular sport. Wait until you see the ice-yacht races."

Denise began to respond to his mood. She was excited at the prospect of seeing her new home, the home she and Jason would share, where their children would be born. Moving closer to Jason, she took pleasure in thinking of the family they would have. Is it possible I'm falling in love with him? she wondered.

But wasn't it necessary to know a man completely

before one could love him? She sighed, realizing that there was still much about Jason she did not understand, moods she could not fathom.

Still, at this particular moment, seated beside him in the surrey that was now ascending the steep curve leading to Mooncliff, she was surprisingly happy. She *would* learn to appreciate her husband's fondness for this stark, rocky landscape, for the river that was ice-locked in winter, the distant mountains that for part of each year would be hidden in snow. Together they would make a life here.

Chapter 5

The gardener hurried from the stone gatehouse to open the huge iron gates, and Jason drove the surrey through. He leaned over to ask the man, "Have you finished it?"

The gardener nodded. "Yes, sir. I believe you'll find everything as you wanted it."

Jason turned the surrey onto a narrow road that twisted upward between two lines of bare trees. "What has he finished?" Denise asked.

"You'll see."

The sun had disappeared, and Denise felt a chill breeze from the river.

Another half-mile up the road, the surrey turned sharply, and the house came into view. "There it is," he said, with unmistakable pride. "Mooncliff."

In the years to come, Denise would never forget her first sight of her new home. It was different from any house she'd ever seen. Instead of a classic Greek Revival house like her beloved Riverview, she saw a massive structure of gray stone, like a baronial castle, with towers, turrents and spires and dozens of narrow and peaked mullioned casement windows. She had read in *Harper's Weekly* of his style of architecture, which was called Hudson River Gothic. Houses like this one were springing up along the banks of the Hudson, built by the newly rich who had made their fortunes in the War. Lonely, isolated mansions, shrouded by the swirling mists of the river valley. Houses inspired by the medieval castles of the Old World, complete with the trappings of the English nobility.

"I . . . don't know what to say. It's . . . very large, isn't it? And splendid."

"You like it, then."

She knew how swiftly Jason's mood could change, and she did not want to criticize the house, did not want to spoil the holiday atmosphere of this day.

"It's a fine house, Jason. I don't believe I've ever seen one quite like it."

Looking at her husband's face, she realized that the house represented the culmination of his dreams, the tangible symbol of his success. And he was presenting it to her as a knight might have presented some magnificent battle trophy to his lady.

"It's beautiful, Jason. I shall be proud to be its mistress."

Obviously satisfied with her response, he got down and helped her out of the surrey. "We've no servants yet," he explained. "The gardener's wife has been doing the necessary houskeeping chores. When we're settled, you will hire a proper housekeeper and the rest of the staff. I'll see to the coachmen and grooms."

He turned a key in the lock, and the huge front door of solid oak swung open. Jason led the way inside. A heavy hanging bronze lamp had been lit, but the rooms beyond the hallway lay in shadow, as did the hallway itself, with its black and white marble squares. Denise was struck by the chill of the house, and by the silence.

Jason led the way down the hall. The walls were of paneled dark mahogany, and the tall, narrow windows were set with panes of colored glass: deep green, indigo, garnet; even on the sunniest days, the light would be somber here.

"I had these paintings sent from Europe," Jason said,

hurrying Denise along. She was able to catch only a confused impression of a series of large canvases framed in gold.

"On the right is the ballroom. I've ordered the chandelier from a French chateau," Jason said. "It hasn't arrived yet. And here's the library."

He stopped to open a pair of tall sliding doors. Denise saw, in the gloom, walnut and velvet chairs and love seats, a high-backed chair of leather, a mantelpiece of marble, and rows and rows of books. "All from England," Jason said. "Crates of them, bound in leather."

"I didn't know you were fond of reading," Denise ventured.

"I haven't read them. I don't even know what they are. I told the architect to use his judgment. They make a fine showing, though, when the room is lit up; the bindings are green and gold—to match the draperies, you see."

Denise said, "It's . . . a handsome room. The whole house is . . . impressive." But she felt the alien atmosphere close around her like a damp, chilly garment.

She thought longingly of Riverview, filled with the warm scent of flowers, the voices of the family, of visitors and slaves. She had no time to brood, however, for Jason hurried her along the hallway, past the great staircase with its carved mahogany newel-posts, to the back of the house.

He opened a pair of stained-glass doors. "This is the terrace," he said. "It will run around the back and both sides of the house. It's not quite finished yet, but I gave orders that the workmen should take the day off. I wanted just the two of us here."

The terrace was shrouded in fog, and although Denise could not see beyond it, she heard the wind from the river and the lapping of the water against the rocks below the cliff.

Jason had turned to look at the house, but Denise moved forward to catch a glimpse of the land beyond the terrace. She had an eerie sense that she stood at the edge of the world.

The fog swirled around her, damp and chill, and then she heard a harsh cry from Jason and, a moment later, his steps pounding across the flagstones. His arm was around her, holding her in a hard grip.

"My God!" he cried. "I told you—the workmen haven't finished here. The wall isn't completed."

"I don't understand."

"You could have walked right off the side of the terrace and onto the cliffs in this fog," he said. "The river curves around the land here, you see, like a crescent. In places the cliffs are quite steep."

The knowledge of the danger she had so narrowly escaped came to her, and she began to shake with fear. He held her close to him. "It's all right now," he said, his voice soothing as he stroked her hair. "You're perfectly safe."

"It's as if we're standing at the edge of the world."

"And so we are," he said. "Our own private world."

She moved closer to him, as if to shut out the sense of desolation his words had evoked. He spoke reassuringly. "Wait until the house is completely furnished and properly lit, with fires in all the fireplaces and servants moving about. And the terrace here will be bathed in sunlight all summer, with dozens of potted shrubs and plants."

Denise was silent, trying to see the house as Jason was describing it, trying to shake off the chill feeling that clung to her like the shifting fog.

"Speaking of shrubs and plants, I have something to show you," he said, leading her back into the house. "This is the morning room, and here . . ." He flung open a glass door, and Denise caught her breath.

It was like stepping into some tropical fantasy world, where the air was warm and moist and heavy with the scent of countless flowers and shrubs. Although three sides of the conservatory were walled with glass, the view of the terrace was almost completely cut off, for a tangle of lush green vines and towering broad-leaved plants and flowers covered every wall. Her eyes were dazzled by the colors: crimson, purple, gold.

"I thought perhaps you might miss the growing things you had down South, so I had this built for you, and I told the gardener to have it ready for your first visit."

"Oh, Jason, I— It's beautiful." But more than the

loveliness of the surroundings had moved her, had caused her throat to tighten. "How good you are to me. How thoughtful and—"

"You little fool, don't you know that all of this is for you? The whole house, everything . . ."

He put his hands on her shoulders, under the cloak, and her lips parted to receive his kiss. Then he swung her off her feet and carried her to a low rattan couch at one end of the conservatory.

He laid her down on the couch and opened the cloak so that it lay beneath her. Then, swiftly, he began to undress her.

"Jason we can't—not here."

"We're alone in the house. I told you. . . ."

In a few moments she lay naked on the soft sable of the cloak, and as she moved, the fur was delightfully smooth against her bare skin. She couldn't resist moving slowly, sensuously, glorying in her own primitive sensations.

Overhead a vine with huge purple flowers released its rich, provocative scent. A few of the blossoms drifted down to rest on her breasts and thighs. Jason brushed them away, and she shivered with pleasure at his touch.

The warm, moist heat enveloped them as he began to make love to her. She smiled, remembering the terrors of her wedding night, her embarrassment during the early weeks of her marriage. Now all her doubts and fears had melted away, and she was possessed by her need for this man, her hunger for his touch.

On the drive back to the boat landing, the clouds turned darker; the northeast wind tossed the trees, hurling branches across the road. They were approaching the town of Rhinebeck when the icy rain began to fall. "We'll stop as soon as we—"

Jason broke off as a falling branch struck the road directly in front of the surrey. The horses reared and plunged, so that Jason had all he could do to bring them under control. Denise saw the heavy muscles of his shoulders grow taut as he gripped the reins and fought the frightened animals back to a trot.

"That building up ahead," Denise said, a little breathlessly. "Is that a tavern?"

"Looks like it. Yes. We can wait out the storm there. And have dinner, too."

As they drew up before the tavern, a stableman hurried out to take charge of the surrey and the horses. Jason lifted Denise from the high seat and carried her up the path to the tavern door, for pools of muddy water stood along the path, and Denise had worn her white kid slippers.

Although her feet remained dry, the rain had begun to soak through her cloak before Jason could get inside. A plump, fair-haired woman—the landlady, Denise guessed—bustled up to greet them. "A bad day to be out on the road. Let me take your cloak and hang it to dry."

After they were settled at a round table in front of the fireplace, she went on: "There's a fine saddle of lamb, just roasting. Or duck, if you'd prefer. And maybe some good fish chowder to help take the chill off your bones."

"That sounds fine to me," Jason said. "All of it. We haven't eaten since early morning."

The landlady nodded and hurried off. Denise spread her skirt around her, grateful for the warmth from the fire. She realized that she was famished.

Neither she nor Jason had thought about food back at Mooncliff; they had been too preoccupied with other matters. Remembering that timeless hour in the conservatory, the purple blossoms lying on her bare body, the soft sable beneath her, and Jason's arms holding her, she felt a glow of tenderness.

She realized that she no longer resented Jason's power to arouse her deepest emotions. Instead she was grateful to him for having swept aside her fears, her false modesty; for having made her a woman. She took pride in her power to satisfy this man who knew so much more of life than she did.

Now, sitting across the table from him, she smiled at him, and she knew from the look on his face that he too was remembering their lovemaking. He leaned forward and took her hand. He was about to speak, when an icy gust of wind swept in through the door, heralding the arrival of another guest.

The man who stood just inside the room was tall and spare; his dark suit and coat were wet with rain. He removed his beaver hat, shaking off the drops. He began taking off his coat, then stopped and stared at the table where Denise and Jason sat. Denise had become accustomed to having men look at her these last months. She knew that her elegant, modish clothes drew their attention, but she was also aware that she herself had changed. Her face had a new radiance, and her body had taken on lush curves; her waist was still as trim as ever, but there was a new fullness to her bosom.

But in a moment she realized that the stranger was looking not at her but at Jason. She saw Jason's eyes narrow, saw a tension take hold of his body under the stranger's fixed look.

A moment later the man came over to their table.

"It is you, then," he said. His voice was soft, well modulated. A man of some breeding, Denise decided. His face was long and narrow, with high cheekbones and thin lips. "Captain Moreland," he said.

"Mr. Moreland now," Jason corrected him. "I hadn't thought to see you again, Doctor Buchanan. It's been years—"

"Eleven years," Buchanan said, his eyes never leaving Jason's face.

Denise made a small movement, feeling faintly uneasy, sensing an undercurrent she did not understand in this chance meeting.

"My dear," Jason said to her, "may I present Doctor Andrew Buchanan. Doctor, this is Mrs. Moreland."

Doctor Buchanan looked at her, then back at Jason. "My congratulations." He gave Denise the ghost of a smile. "Your husband and I are old shipmates. I was ship's doctor when he made his first voyage as master of his own vessel."

"Indeed," Denise said. "Won't you join us, Doctor?"

"Thank you, ma'am." He turned to Jason. "I shouldn't wish to intrude, however."

"Not at all," Jason said. His voice was easy, but

Denise sensed a hollowness, a lack of warmth in his manner. "We've just now ordered dinner. The landlady can set another place—"

"Thank you, no. My dinner is waiting for me at home. I only stopped here because of the storm. I should like to drink a toast, however. Call it a bridal toast. A little late, perhaps—"

"No, indeed," Denise said. "Jason and I have been married only a little over three months."

The doctor signaled the landlady and ordered two large mugs of hot rum and a glass of sherry for Denise.

"You were always partial to rum, as I recall," Jason said after the drinks were brought. "Demerara was your favorite, wasn't it?"

"You have an excellent memory, Captain—Mr. Moreland." He raised his mug. "To a very lovely lady," he said. "And to a most fortunate man. But then, you were always lucky."

Jason smiled tightly. "I make my good fortune, Doctor. I decide what I want—and I take it."

"Yes, of course." Doctor Buchanan raised his mug and drained it in silence. Denise was a little startled at the speed with which he finished the drink. Almost at once he signaled for another. Jason shook his head when the landlady asked if he too wanted a second drink.

"Yes, Captain Moreland, you make your own good fortune. I'm not likely to forget that. And now I'd like to propose a toast to another lady. I've not forgotten her, either." He raised the mug. "I give you—the *Nubian Queen*."

Denise caught her breath and glanced uneasily at her husband, remembering the last time she'd heard that name. She tensed, waiting for the explosion. She saw the lines around Jason's mouth deepen, and his eyes grew bleak. But he raised his mug and said, "As you please, Doctor. The *Nubian Queen* it is. Although I believe she's better forgotten."

"You've been able to forget her, then?"

"I've been occupied with so many business ventures over the years. Shipbuilding, lumber mills, real estate—

there's no profit in brooding over the past. I tried to convince you of that, long ago."

"I remember; back in Havana, it was. I was burning with fever, half out of my head, and I remember your talking to me, telling me— No matter. I suppose I should be grateful to you for getting me on my feet again. Or should I? A nice point— I've never been able to decide whether to thank you for what you did or to hate you for not letting the fever do its work—"

Jason slammed his mug down on the table. "Stop it, man! You're not making sense. Here you are, alive and well—back in your profession I suppose—"

"I have a small practice over in Staatsburg and in some of the neighboring towns," Buchanan said. "I've tried to put my skill to some use." He drained his second mug and signaled for a third. Jason had pushed his drink aside unfinished. He looked at the mug in the doctor's hand. "I trust you're not on your way to see a patient now, Doctor."

"I'm returning from a call, as a matter of fact," Buchanan answered. "And I'd best be on my way home," he added. "Elspeth may be worried. The storm—"

Denise sensed that Jason's last remark, his implication that the doctor was not sober enough to treat a patient, had hit home. She felt sorry for Buchanan. His face had a haggard look, and she thought about what he had said to Jason moments before: that he wasn't sure Jason had done him a favor by coming to his aid during his bout of fever back in Havana.

Jason's voice broke into her thoughts. "How is Elspeth?" he was asking. "Your daughter must be a young woman now."

"She's eighteen. She was away at school until a few months ago. Now she keeps house for me. Not a very exciting life for a young girl, I'm afraid. But it's good to have her with me."

"You never remarried?" Jason asked.

Doctor Buchanan shook his head. Once more an uneasy silence descended, so that Denise became aware of the sound of the rain lashing against the windows of the tavern. The wind seemed to have died down, however. The storm should pass soon.

"Jason and I were on our way back to the city when the storm broke," Denise said, feeling the need to make polite conversation, to smooth over the tense silence between the two men. "We had driven out to see our new home. It's called 'Mooncliff.' "

"A splendid establishment, I'm sure."

"Yes, indeed. I'd never seen it before, and I found it—overwhelming. When it is finished, Jason and I are giving a ball, a housewarming. That will be the last week of this month." Remembering the doctor's mention of his daughter Elspeth and the lack of excitement in her life, she added, with the courtesy that had been part of the training of all the Chevillon girls: "You'll come, of course, and bring your daughter. I'm sure she'll enjoy herself."

"That's impossible, Mrs. Moreland." Doctor Buchanan's voice was harsh. He drained the mug in front of him.

"I don't understand."

"Forgive me. My answer was a rude one, I'm afraid. What I meant to say was that a doctor's time is not his own. An unexpected call—"

"I see. But at least you'll try to set the evening aside, won't you?"

"I really don't think—Elspeth's been away at school all these years. She's not used to fashionable balls."

"All the more reason you should bring her. It will be a perfect opportunity to introduce her into New York society."

"By all means, come and bring your daughter," Jason said. But there was no warmth in his invitation; rather, it sounded to Denise as if he were challenging Buchanan.

The doctor rose, bowed to Denise, and said, "I thank you for your kind invitation, Mrs. Moreland." He turned to Jason. "And you, Captain," he added.

After he had gone, Denise watched her husband in silence, deeply troubled by the chance encounter. What was there about the ship called the *Nubian Queen*, that the very mention of her could do this to Jason? She felt she had to know. She was his wife. She had a right to share not only his present and his future but his past as well.

"Damn Buchanan," Jason said softly. "I never thought

to see him again. Certainly not to have him at Mooncliff." He turned on Denise, his eyes hard with anger. "Why the devil did you invite him?"

Shocked, she could only stammer, "I thought—I assumed—you seconded the invitation—"

"You gave me no choice, once you'd made such a point of asking him and his daughter. What right had you—"

Denise felt a slowly rising anger that matched her husband's.

"I am mistress of Mooncliff. It is my house as well as yours, isn't it?"

They were quarreling. Only a few hours before, she had lain in his arms, had given herself over completely to his lovemaking, had gloried in the new-found closeness between them. Now, once more they were enemies.

"All right," he was saying tensely. "You've had your way. You've invited Buchanan and his daughter to Mooncliff. There's no more to be said on the subject." He looked at her coldly. "Now, if you've finished your dinner, we should be starting on our way."

The trip back to Manhattan through the damp, fog-shrouded evening was a miserable one. Denise wrapped herself in her cloak and tried to relax, but the sight of Jason's profile, hard and unyielding, made her unhappy. She was half-afraid that, after he'd brought her back to their suite at the hotel, he might go out alone for the night. Instead he prepared for bed in silence, and she did the same.

Only when they lay together, side by side, not touching, did she make an attempt at conciliation.

"Jason, I'm sorry; truly I am. Please try to understand my feelings. I'm your wife, and yet—you only want to share your success with me. You give me every luxury, but you treat me like an empty-headed child."

"You are a child in many ways, Denise."

"That's where you're wrong. Perhaps I was a child when you met me, but I've changed, truly. You've made me change, Jason. I'm a woman now, a woman who loves you—"

She heard the sharp intake of his breath, and a moment

later he drew her close to him, put his arm around her. Her head rested on his shoulder.

Encouraged by the gesture, she went on: "It's because I love you that I want to share your life. I know there are things in your past that are harsh and unpleasant. But if you've suffered, if you've known pain or hardship, I want to share those things, too. I have the right—"

The arm beneath her head shifted. "No, you don't," he said. "There are matters no man talks of with his wife. My past is my own. Don't be a fool. Don't pry and probe; don't destroy what we have now . . ."

He turned to her and held her so tightly that she could scarcely breathe. She welcomed the violence of his embrace. As she gave herself up to the hot tide of passion, she told herself that the present was all that mattered.

Chapter 6

Denise sat at her dressing table in her bedroom at Mooncliff. Fantine, her newly hired French maid, put the final touches to her coiffure. Then the girl fastened the diamond and emerald necklace around Denise's long white neck, working with quick, deft movements.

Fantine was well trained and competent, her references impeccable. But Denise was remembering the black maids she had had back at Riverview, girls who had grown up on the Chevillon plantation, who giggled and chattered as they helped her dress. She could not help wishing that one of them were with her now.

There was no point thinking this way. Not tonight, when she was preparing for the great ball, the beginning of her new life with Jason at Mooncliff. It was useless, too, to wish that Papa and Mama and her sisters could be here. Only a few days before, Denise had received a letter from Mama, filled with a glowing account of life in Paris.

"I know you will be as pleased as I am when I tell you that dear Madelaine has just become betrothed to the elder son of the Marquis de Saint-Méran. As for our little

Lucille, she has had a number of offers, and it is my hope that soon she too will make a suitable match."

Mama then went on to describe the social scene in the French capital and the growing influence of the Empress Eugénie on the political life of the nation as well as on its fashions. Denise learned that although some Parisian ladies still wore crinolines, the style was on its way out, and that high-crowned hats, with long streamers down the back and plumes falling over the chignon, were all the rage.

"How I wish I could see you on the night of your house-warming ball. Do write and describe everything, my dear. . . ."

Denise, rising from her dressing table, made a mental note to write to Mama soon and to tell her about the splendid ball gown she was wearing tonight. The bodice of apple-green faille accented her beautifully shaped high breasts and her small waistline; the full skirt billowed out around her. A delicate point-lace overskirt and a train of pale green faille completed the costume.

She would describe it all to Mama, and more, she would try to make her see Mooncliff as it looked tonight. The house had come to life, with the glow of gaslights, the glitter of chandeliers and the scent of flowers brought by the hundreds for the occasion. As she went out into the hall, she heard the hired musicians softly tuning their instruments.

Halfway down the stairs she paused as she saw Jason standing in the hall below, looking up at her. His look of admiration, of pride in her, was so plain, and when she reached him he took her arm with a gesture of triumph. She was aware that he still thought of her as a prize, a possession he had won, rather than as an equal. She would learn to accept this, as she had learned to accept so many other things about him that had disturbed her: his moodiness, his dark flashes of anger, his refusal to allow her to share his past.

They took their places at the foot of the stairs, just outside the entrance to the ballroom, and moments later the sound of carriage wheels in the drive and the hurrying foot-steps of the caterer's staff told her the first of their guests were arriving. Although she felt a surge of excitement and anticipation, she was able to greet each arrival with the poise and graciousness that were the product of years of training.

What would Mama think of her guests, the men Jason knew through his far-flung business dealings, and their wives and daughters? She forced the unwelcome thought to the back of her mind, knowing perfectly well that few of these people would be socially acceptable according to the rigid Charleston code.

In New York in this spring of 1869, fortunes were being made overnight. Money was the only passport needed for social acceptance. Back home in Charleston, people were proud of their origins; they knew the lineage of all their friends and acquaintances, back to the days of the great land grants from the English kings. Here, in this northern city, Denise had been surprised at the reticence of her new friends when they were asked about their families and their beginnings.

The women seemed to live only in the present; most of their talk revolved around the newest play, the latest fashions from France, plans for a townhouse on Gramercy Park, a summer place in Saratoga or Newport, a tour of Europe.

When Denise had questioned Jason about this, he had urged her not to probe into the affairs of their new friends. But from reading the newspapers she had learned how many great fortunes had been made in the past few years by war profiteering, how many were now being made through speculation on land, railroads and gold.

Now, as the great hallway became more crowded and the hum of conversation rose to a fever pitch, Jason introduced her to such noted figures as Jay Gould, a quiet man with dark, shrewd eyes; and his partner, the ebullient Jim Fisk, whose scandalous exploits and flamboyant manners would surely have made him unwelcome in any respectable home in Charleston.

At least Mr. Fisk was not accompanied by his mistress, the beautiful but notorious Josie Mansfield. Even Jason, for all his freewheeling ways, knew that his wife would not have received Josie, who lived openly in sin and who had the added stigma of having been divorced. Even in this, the "Age of Flash," as the period was coming to be called by the journalists who condemned it, some things were still out of the question.

Although Denise tried not to notice the way Mr. Fisk's bold eyes swept over her, lingering appreciatively on her high, rounded bosom and small waist, she was relieved to turn from him and greet the next guests in line, Doctor Andrew Buchanan and his daughter Elspeth.

"We're so pleased you were able to come, after all," Denise said.

The doctor's long, thin face looked even more haggard than it had on their first meeting, and Denise thought she caught a faint odor of rum; and his eyes were a shade too bright. But he spoke quietly. "Your home is splendid, Mrs. Moreland." He looked about him with a glance that took in the marble floors, the Oriental carpets, the glittering chandeliers imported from Europe. "Splendid," he repeated.

Denise turned to greet his daughter, knowing that the girl would probably feel a little unsure of herself, since this was to be her first ball. "What a charming dress," Denise said.

She was quite sincere, for although Elspeth Buchanan's white tulle dress was simple compared with the dazzling costumes of the other women, it suited her perfectly. She was not a pretty girl by the conventional standards of the day, for her cheekbones were too wide, her chin too narrow and pointed. Her eyes were blue-gray; the look she gave Denise as she thanked her for the compliment was direct and composed.

The opening bars of a waltz floated out into the hallway from the ballroom beyond. Elspeth's eyes brightened, and Denise was pleased that the girl had been able to come—life with her father could not be very lively for her.

A little while later, Denise and Jason were in the ballroom after greeting all their guests. The musicians, having completed a medley of waltzes, had shifted to the livelier notes of a polka. Denise found pleasure in the feeling of Jason's arm around her, the pressure of his hand at her waist. Their eyes met in a long look of shared closeness, an acknowledgment of their mutual desire; even here, in this huge, crowded room, she felt the awareness of the hours they had spent alone, and for one crazy moment she found herself wishing they could leave right now, could run upstairs, hand in hand, to lie naked together in the great canopied bed.

Jason's mouth curved in a smile, and she realized that something in her face must have betrayed her hunger for him. His arm tightened around her. "Later, my love," he whispered.

All at once, Denise found the scent of the flowers banked around the ballroom overpowering; the glittering chandeliers overhead blurred. She floated in the arms of her husband on a dizzying tide of triumph. But at midnight, when dinner was announced, she felt somewhat relieved to be able to sink into a velvet chair at one end of the room. The doors between the ballroom and the supper room had been thrown open. Many of the guests gravitated in the direction of the buffet tables.

"I'm not very hungry," she told Jason. "Perhaps a glass of punch . . ."

"I'll get you one," he said. He moved off through the crowd, pausing briefly here and there to exchange a few words with a guest.

Denise sat back in her chair, arranging her skirts around her, fanning her flushed cheeks with the ostrich-feather fan she carried. A moment later, Rosalind MacKay came over and seated herself beside her.

"My dear, it's so marvelous—this house—I've never seen anything like it—"

"Thank you," Denise said. "You're having a good time?"

"Oh, yes, but my poor feet—these new slippers—thank goodness for supper—my husband's gone to get me some refreshments—the tables look perfectly splendid—that piece of ice sculpture in the shape of a sailing ship is positively inspired—"

"That was Jason's idea, and the steamship sculpture, too. I haven't seen them yet."

"Of course, you were busy receiving your guests. But

you must come and look at them now. There are waves sculpted in ice, tinted blue. Come along, Denise."

Although Denise had thought the idea of the ice sculptures somewhat overdone, a little vulgar, she couldn't help catching some of Rosalind's enthusiasm. She reminded herself, as she had so many times during the winter season in New York, that she must accept her husband's standards in entertainment, in friends. If Mooncliff did not reflect her personal tastes, she could make certain changes in the house and its furnishings little by little. Tonight, the night of the first ball at Mooncliff, was his triumph; everything should be done according to his wishes.

"I shouldn't think you'd want this here to remind you—"

As Denise approached the buffet table, she saw Doctor Buchanan making a wide, rather uncoordinated gesture in the direction of the sculptured sailing ship that glittered under the lights of the chandeliers. "That's enough, Buchanan," Jason was saying.

But the doctor ignored his host. "What's wrong, Captain Moreland? Afraid I'm drunk—afraid I'll talk too much? Maybe you're right. Maybe that's my trouble—always talk too much—"

Denise caught a glimpse of Elspeth's face, white and strained, her lips compressed as she tried to maintain her composure. But when she spoke her voice was quiet, respectful of her father in spite of his condition. "Father, perhaps we should leave now."

Denise felt her throat tighten with pity for the young girl.

"You're right," Doctor Buchanan said in a tone loud enough to cause several of the guests to turn and look at him curiously. "Never should have come. Never should have brought you here, Elspeth."

"There's no need for you to leave, Miss Buchanan," Jason said quietly. "Your father and I will go into the library. I'll have a pot of strong coffee sent in—he'll be all right."

"All right?" The doctor laughed harshly. "Of course. You'll take care of everything, won't you? As you took care of everything on board of the *Nubian Queen*?"

Jason put his hand on the other man's arm. The supper room had grown silent as, one by one, the guests realized that something quite out of the ordinary was happening between their host and his drunken guest. "Come with me," Jason said, and it was less an invitation than a command.

"Still giving me orders, Captain Moreland?"

"I've told you, I'm not called Captain Moreland any longer—"

"Forgive me," Doctor Buchanan said with drunken politeness. "You've given up the title of Captain—you're a man of business now, with a fine house—a palace—and a beautiful, gently reared wife. Tell me, does she know the kind of man she married? Does she know that this mansion was built on the murders of helpless men—" He swept his arm in another wide gesture, his hand brushing the ice-carved sails, so that the ship swayed dangerously.

"Not only men, either," he went on, his words echoing through the high-ceilinged room. "There were women, too—one with her baby in her arms— Remember how she begged you to spare the infant, even if you killed her? She spoke the language of her tribe, but you didn't have to understand the words; you knew what she meant—any human being would have known."

The doctor's voice was hoarse, choked with grief. "Only you're not human, are you, Captain? Not weak, not vulnerable, like I was. I took refuge in the cabin below, but you stayed on deck; you watched living human beings thrown into the sea, screaming for mercy—"

Denise stood very still. She wanted to run, to escape that harsh, accusing voice that was directed against her husband, but she could not move. What was Doctor Buchanan saying? Of what unspeakable crime did Jason stand accused?

"You've said enough," Jason told him. "Now you're coming with me."

Jason put a guiding hand on Buchanan's arm, but the doctor pulled away, a look of revulsion on his haggard face.

"My daughter and I are leaving, Captain Moreland. I should never have allowed her to enter this house. There is a curse on your Mooncliff. Can't you feel it? What sort of life do you think you will have here, you and your wife, and those who come after you? Will you be able to sleep soundly at night?" He closed his eyes for a moment, as if to shut out a vision of hell. Then he opened them again, looked straight at Jason. "I've not had one night's peaceful rest since that day on board the *Nubian Queen*. I heard the cries of those dying slaves, heard the sound of their bodies striking the water—"

"You're mad." Jason's face had gone white, and he spoke in a voice Denise did not recognize.

"Perhaps I am. But you'll come to share my madness in the years to come. You'll hear those cries, too. They'll haunt you. You and your children and their children. You have built a house over the bodies of the dead. I do not envy you, Captain Moreland."

Doctor Buchanan turned and strode out of the room; the guests parted to let him pass, as if he carried some nameless contagion. Elspeth, white-faced and trembling, hurried after him.

Jason did not move. He made no attempt to follow Doctor Buchanan and Elspeth but remained staring after them, the lines around his mouth deeper than ever.

Denise wanted to go to him, to put a hand on his arm. She was his wife; her place was beside him. She took a step forward, then stopped, unable to speak, unable even to reach out to him. Between them rose a vision of unspeakable horror. There in that luxurious supper room, with its blazing chandeliers, its heavy-scented roses in silver vases, the vision intruded between Denise and her husband. The deck of a slave ship. The cries of living human beings thrown into a tropical sea. At Jason Moreland's orders.

She looked at his face now, at the hard, set lines, trying to see the man who had held her in his arms, the man to whom she had given herself night after night. The man who only an hour ago had danced with her and had whispered, "Later, my love."

She searched his face in desperation—and saw only the face of a stranger. Unable to endure the lengthening silence, she picked up the train of her skirt and fled, stumbling a little on the polished floor, seeking the sanctuary of her own room upstairs.

But halfway down the hall she was forced to stop. The tightly laced stays under her gown cut off her breath, so that she gasped for air. Little motes of light swam before her eyes, and she wondered if she was about to faint. Then she heard the footsteps behind her, felt the hand on her arm. "Denise—"

"Let me go, Jason."

"Where?"

"My room—anywhere—"

"Have you forgotten our guests?"

"What do they matter? What does any of this matter?"

"It matters to me." His voice was cold, expressionless—a voice she'd never heard before.

A stranger's voice, her dazed mind kept repeating. *A stranger's touch, this hard hand on my arm.*

"If you come back inside with me now, our guests will dismiss the whole incident as the ravings of a drunken lunatic. I've already told those who were close enough to hear the whole thing that Buchanan is a sick man—that he never should have come here. That much is true, at any rate. But I need to have you beside me for the rest of the evening, or there's bound to be ugly gossip. Those things he said about me—"

"The things he said—were they true? I have to know, Jason."

"Not now. Whatever may have happened eleven years ago, it's done, it's over."

"But murder—he spoke of murder."

"That's enough." Jason's hand tightened on her arm in a brutal grip that sent a hot dart of pain shooting into her shoulder. She cried out and tried to pull away.

"You're not to mention the incident again. And you're not to turn and run like an hysterical child."

The pain in her arm sent a wave of sickness through her.

"Don't. You're hurting me—"

He loosened his grip slightly, but at the same time turned her around. "That day at the inn, you said you wanted to be a real wife to me, to share everything—not only the triumphs, the luxuries—"

"Yes, but I—"

"Then prove it. Come back inside and act as though nothing had happened."

"Please, Jason, don't ask me."

"I'm not asking you. I'm telling you what you will do."

For a moment she thought he might strike her. But he only put an arm around her waist and led her back into the supper room. A number of guests were looking in their direction, and her breeding, the fruit of Mama's careful training, made it possible for her to blink back the tears, to hold her head high.

Rosalind came forward, her face flushed, her pale blue and turquoise plumes nodding over her elaborate coiffure.

"Is there anything I can do?" she asked in a soft voice, so unlike her usual high-pitched tones that Denise was startled.

Jason was silent for a moment. Then he said, "Yes, there is. Go into the ballroom, if you please, and tell the musicians we'll resume the dancing in a few moments. Tell them to play that new dance everyone's talking about."

"The German?"

"That's it. Those who wish can remain here and continue their supper. The others will have something else to interest them."

"Yes, indeed," Rosalind said. "It's quite daring, the German. I'm told the Reverend Henry Ward Beecher is planning to preach a sermon against it."

"That's good," Jason said. "It should cause a bit of a flurry, then." He looked down at Denise. "You need not take part in the dance if you don't wish to. Afterward, however, we'll have more waltzes, and I'll expect you to dance with any of our guests who should ask you."

His voice was quiet and respectful, but there was no mistaking the steely determination behind his words. Rosalind hurried to give his orders to the musicians. Moments later, the rollicking strains of the shocking new dance could be heard.

Although all the female guests pretended to be scandalized, Denise saw them, one by one, give in to the demands of their partners and begin moving toward the ballroom. Many of the older ladies stayed behind, preferring to linger over the pleasures of the supper table, to enjoy their lobster thermidor, sherried oysters, braised pheasant and veal julienne.

She heard a large lady in a magnificent dress of purple velvet say to another lady, "It's really quite daring, the German. A gentleman may take all sorts of liberties with his partner in the figures of the dance. Shall we go and watch?"

"Very well, my dear. As soon as I've finished this marvelous pheasant."

Denise could not believe that her guests had already forgotten the terrible scene that had taken place here in this room only a few moments ago. Whatever Jason had said, whatever excuses he had made to smooth over the incident, surely there would be talk. Even her presence here, outwardly calm and composed, could not make these people forget the shocking accusations Doctor Buchanan had made.

Rosalind, having returned from the ballroom, was standing beside her, holding out a glass. "It's brandy. Drink it, Denise. It will help you to get through the evening."

At least Rosalind understood her feelings, and that was comforting. Jason was Captain MacKay's employer, of course, but Denise felt sure that Rosalind's concern for her was genuine.

"Can you eat something now?" Rosalind asked. "A little of this delicious lobster salad, perhaps? Or an ice?"

Denise shook her head, feeling a sickness in the pit of her stomach at the mention of food.

She looked at Jason, who had moved a little distance from her and was now deep in conversation with Jim Fisk and two other men whose names she could not remember. She heard a few words of their conversation: "the Gold Exchange," "the Curbstone Brokers," and "Erie stock." Business talk. Her husband was using this ball, this magnificent house, as he was using her: to facilitate his business dealings.

She noticed that a number of the guests were looking at her, some with pity, others with avid curiosity; and who could blame them? But many of the others, oblivious or indifferent to what had taken place, were strolling back to the ballroom to take part in the German or to watch the dancers.

Denise rubbed her arm where Jason had gripped it, and then, seeing the direction of Rosalind's gaze, she covered it quickly with her fan. She was sure it bore the marks of his fingers, red now, but soon to turn black and blue.

When the German came to its riotous conclusion and the orchestra began a waltz, Jason left Fisk and the other men and came to escort her into the ballroom.

How was it possible that she could move lightly and gracefully to the sensuous beat of the waltz, her lips fixed in a tight little smile, when Jason's touch, the closeness of his body, repelled her so?

She was relieved when Jim Fisk asked her for the next waltz. He was an excellent dancer, for all his thick, heavyset body, and his conversation, easy and impersonal, was what she needed now. It was possible to make the correct replies to his questions as to how she liked New York, whether she was adjusting to the northern weather; to thank him for his invitation to his Grand Opera House; and to assure him that she and Jason would be pleased to attend.

Later she danced with Jay Gould and found herself wondering how two such opposite types as he and Fisk could be partners in business. Gould was quiet, almost to the point of rudeness; she had been told that even with members of his own family he had very little to say. She understood that it was unusual for him to attend social affairs such as this one, and under other circumstances she would have found his attendance at her housewarming ball flattering. Now, in a shell of misery and apprehension, she could only set herself to the task of getting through the seemingly endless evening.

It was nearly three in the morning when the guests began to leave. They stopped to tell her what a wonderful ball it had been, how much they admired her new home.

People whose names she could not remember said that she and Jason must dine with them; must accompany them to the theater, the opera.

Denise stood in the high-ceilinged hallway, smiling and nodding like a mechanical doll. She heard herself saying all the expected things.

"So delighted you could come. . . ."

"So pleased you had a good time. . . ."

"Indeed we should like to join you at the theater. . . ."

"Perhaps we will be able to come to Saratoga next summer. . . ."

She heard one of the women remark that it was starting to rain. Another said it was only a drizzle, that the sky would soon clear. But Denise, hearing the rising shriek of the wind from the river below the cliffs, shivered and knew a growing fear.

It was nearly four in the morning when she and Jason stood alone in the hall. The caterer's staff had departed; the gardener's wife, who had acted as temporary housekeeper, had returned to her cottage. The gaslights had been turned low, and the hall was alive with flickering shadows.

"Come into the library, Denise."

She drew back. "I'm very tired. I want to go to bed—"

"Not yet. We're going to talk first."

He took her arm and led her, unresisting, into the library at the back of the house. A fire burned in the marble fireplace. The dark red portieres were drawn against the wind and the rain.

"Sit down," he said, and took his place beside her on a leather sofa close to the fire.

"You did well tonight, Denise. I was proud of you. The ball was a success."

She looked away, feeling a throb of pain in her bruised flesh where he had gripped her arm after Doctor Buchanan's outburst. A slow sickness stirred inside her at the memory of the doctor's accusations.

She should have known what Jason was really like; perhaps she *had* known all along and had kept the knowledge at the back of her mind. Perhaps—the sickness stirred more violently—perhaps she had found the secret, hidden knowledge of his capacity for cruelty exciting, stimulating—

She fixed her eyes on the leaping flames in the fireplace.

"Look at me," he ordered her.

She shook her head. He put his hands on her bare shoulders.

"Look at me," he repeated, and this time she obeyed. His blue eyes were hard in the firelight.

"You want to know it all now, don't you? You want to hear everything."

"No. Not now."

"Don't turn away. That day at the inn, the day you met Buchanan for the first time, you said—what was it? You wanted to share my past. To be a real wife, as you put it. Have you forgotten?" He shook her lightly. "Have you?"

"No."

"All right, then. You shall share it—all of it. You want to know if those things Buchanan said about me are true, don't you?"

"I—Jason, you didn't kill those slaves. Only tell me that, and I won't—"

"I'm sorry, my dear. What Buchanan said is true. I was responsible for the deaths of some fifty slaves—men, women, children. I was the captain. I gave the orders. Mooncliff, the fortune that built it, was founded on murder."

Chapter 7

In the quiet of the library, the splitting of a log in the fireplace cracked like a pistol shot. It was raining hard now, the heavy drops pounding against the long windows. Denise wanted to free herself from Jason's hands on her shoulders. She wanted to run to the nearest window, fling aside the velvet portieres, and draw the clean, rain-drenched air into her lungs.

"I've shocked you, haven't I?" Jason demanded. "But there's no reason for you to feel as you do."

"No reason? You tell me you were responsible for the deaths of innocent people, and then you say there's no reason?"

"You knew I'd been a slave trader—you reminded me of the fact often enough. But it didn't stop you from becoming my wife."

"I had no choice in the matter," she said. "My parents forced me."

"Perhaps. But, once you got used to the idea, you were a willing wife, even ardent."

"I didn't know the truth about you. Now that I do, it makes me sick to remember that I ever—that we—"

He took his hands from her shoulders and pushed her away.

"You *are* a hypocrite, aren't you, my dear? You may have objected to marrying me at first, but you did it. You lived in luxury, knowing how I'd started my fortune. And why not? Your own father was a slave owner before the War. Your precious brother died defending the right of the southerners to own their slaves. Riverview flourished on slave labor—"

"How dare you compare yourself with Papa and Louis? How dare you ask me to share your guilt?" Her voice shook with anger. "We didn't mistreat our slaves at Riverview. Even the field hands were well treated, cared for when they got sick. Papa had a rule that no child should be sold away from its mother—indeed, he never sold a slave at all unless it was absolutely necessary."

"Never flogged one either, I suppose."

"We had an overseer."

Jason's mouth twisted in mockery. "Of course. And the overseer was not received at your table, any more than a slave trader would have been. You were shielded from the uglier side of your 'peculiar institution,' weren't you?"

"I don't know what you mean."

"Simply this: you never stopped to ask yourself where your slaves came from, how they were brought to Riverview, what was done to them before your Papa bought them." His eyes, cold with contempt, held hers.

He rose abruptly, towering over her, his shadow enormous against the wall. "How much do you know about the slave trade, Denise?"

"I don't—such things weren't talked about—"

"Take the Middle Passage," he went on in a hard and inexorable voice. "That was the part of the slaving voyage where the blacks lay jammed like cordwood between the decks. You know nothing about the Middle Passage, do you?"

"I've just told you—"

He continued as if he had not heard her interruption.

"The trade was rotten enough before the abolitionists

got to work—Wilberforce and those other soft-hearted, ill-informed idiots. After the trade became illegal in England and over here in America, slaving was infinitely worse. For the blacks and for the crews of the slave ships, too."

"Why?"

"Before the trade was outlawed, an experienced captain could bring the slaves up on deck as often as he wished, for light and air, for exercise. Afterwards, when the blackbirders took over the trade, it became a smuggling venture. The cargo had to be kept chained below any time there was the slightest chance of being overtaken by patrol boats."

"And your ship, the *Nubian Queen*—"

"She was a blackbirder, a Baltimore brig, one of the fastest afloat. She had to be, to outrun and outmaneuver the British Navy's patrollers."

Jason walked to the fireplace and leaned an arm on the mantel. Denise felt something dark and sinister stirring in the shadows of the quiet, expensively furnished room. She watched the firelight flickering on Jason's face as he spoke.

"My first voyage as captain. I was twenty-five at the time. By then, most of the older captains didn't want any part of blackbirding, regardless of the profits. The risks were too great."

"I don't understand."

"A blackbirder was subject to the same penalties as a pirate."

She looked at him without comprehension.

"Hanging, my dear wife. That was the extreme penalty, of course, but there was also the risk of capture, trial, and a long term of imprisonment."

"Then why did you—"

"I wanted to make a fortune the fastest way I could. There were still shipowners willing to put up cash, secretly of course, to buy and outfit a blackbirding vessel, and to pay her captain generously—if the voyage was successful. Smug, respectable hypocrites—not unlike you, love—who could stay safely at home while men like me took the risks.

"And then, of course, there were gentlemen like your

father who were quite willing to buy fresh stock for their plantations, knowing that the slaves had been brought in illegally. A nice point of morality, I've always thought."

"How can you speak of morality, when you've admitted—"

"Forgive me, my dear. I was telling you about the voyage of the *Nubian Queen*. You still want to hear about it, don't you?"

She looked away, confused, unable to answer. She was afraid now of what she might hear, but she knew that before this night was over, she would have to know the truth about the man she had married.

"I was to bring the cargo of the *Nubian Queen* into Havana to be sold. Later the slaves would be taken to markets in the South, to plantations like Riverview." He smiled ironically at her. "You've told me your slaves were treated reasonably well. I'm not surprised. Slaves were valuable, particularly after the trade had been outlawed. A cargo like mine could bring eight hundred thousand dollars in Havana—if we didn't lose too many blacks through disease during the Middle Passage, of course. That's why Doctor Buchanan sailed with us. He did what he could to keep the blacks healthy in spite of the atrocious conditions below decks." Jason shrugged, but his eyes were troubled. "It was then that he started drinking, poor bastard. Who could have blamed him? How could he have gone down into that filth and stench without blurring his senses with rum? He was a sensitive man, God help him. A man with a conscience."

"But he sailed with you."

"He was desperate. He had been practicing medicine only a few years when he'd become involved in a scandal. A young woman from a prominent family had been indiscreet. Buchanan was called in to help her out of her difficulties and to avoid a scandal." Jason raised his eyebrow and looked quizzically at Denise. "You do know what I'm talking about, don't you?"

"Yes, I think so."

"Well, then, the young woman had come to Buchanan too late. He did his best for her, but she died, and he had to leave Glasgow in something of a hurry."

"And you offered him a way out."

"More than that. He was a widower with a young child, Elspeth. She was living with relatives, a pious, tight-fisted bunch who would have tossed her out into the street the moment Buchanan's support money failed to arrive. He thought that with his share from the voyage he'd be able to take her away from those people, to come here to America and set up a new practice. Make a fresh start." Jason shook his head. "Poor miserable bastard."

Denise realized in some corner of her mind that Jason had never used such language in her presence before. Now he seemed determined to force her to see him as he really was. And to accept him for what he was.

"We loaded a prime cargo on the West African coast," Jason was saying. "We managed to avoid the patrols, British and American. Of course, we lost some of the blacks during the Middle Passage, but no more than I'd allowed for. Even when slaving was still legal, Parliament allowed for a two percent death rate."

"How horrible," Denise said.

"I suppose it was. . . . During the first part of the return voyage. I was filled with triumph, with a sense of—invincibility. I was captain of my own ship for the first time. It gives a man a godlike feeling. I was in control of every life on board the *Nubian Queen*. And I was on my way to making my fortune.

"The winds were with us. The ship handled well. And then, five days before we were to put into Havana, I found out that I wasn't invincible, after all."

His eyes were bleak and his mouth clamped together in a thin, hard line. He turned away from the fireplace and returned to sit beside her. He did not try to touch her.

"Early that morning, Doctor Buchanan came to my cabin to make his report. He told me that typhus had broken out among the slaves. Four had died during the night. Twelve more were seriously ill. He suspected that they had typhus, too—he couldn't be sure. He said something about an incubation period. We'd have to wait ten to fourteen days before we'd know how many of them had been infected."

Denise shivered and drew as far away from Jason as

possible. The pieces of the puzzle were falling into place now. Jason Moreland, young, ambitious, and hardened by life in the Liverpool slums and the voyages he'd made aboard other slaving ships. Bent on making a fortune, any way he could. Faced with the loss of that fortune, there was only one possible decision he could have made.

"You murdered those slaves. You killed sick, helpless people to hold on to your share of the profits."

"It wasn't like that. Try to understand. The choice was not clear-cut. Typhus spreads fast, you see. I'd seen people die of it, even back in Liverpool, but on a slaver— The living, the dying and the dead—all jammed in together, lying in their own filth, because there was no way—"

Denise made a small choking sound. "I—don't want to hear any more."

"You're only hearing about it; remember that. I lived with it day and night. And I had to make the decision. If I waited too long, all the slaves might die, and my crew as well. They were no more immune than those miserable blacks."

"But there must have been some other way, something else you could have done instead of—"

"Oh, yes. I could have put in at the nearest port, without regard for its nationality. I could have risked jail or hanging for myself and my crew.

"Or I could have tried to find an uninhabited island and set the infected slaves ashore there. But in the meantime, there was the risk that other slaves, or members of the crew, would have caught this disease. I did what I had to do—the only thing I could have done under those conditions."

Denise covered her face with her hands, but Jason took her by the wrists, forcing her hands down, so that she had to look at him.

"I had the slaves brought up on deck, the lot of them. Poor devils, they thought they were being brought up for air and exercise. I'd already given Buchanan his orders. He knew what he had to do.

"He picked out those slaves who were obviously infected, and those who showed only the early symptoms. There were fifty altogether."

His eyes were fixed on her face, but he was looking not at her, but deep within himself.

"It was close to sunset, I remember. The air was soft, and the clouds, down at the horizon, were already rose and gold. Night comes on quickly in that part of the world. I allowed Buchanan to go below after he'd carried out his orders. I didn't try to stop him."

"Jason, Doctor Buchanan spoke of a woman and her baby. He said she begged for mercy."

As if he hadn't heard her, he went on, "There was the danger of a slave mutiny, of course. But I'd taken the precaution of arming members of the crew. They had orders to shoot at the first sign of trouble."

"The woman, Jason! The woman with the baby."

"She was infected, and there was an even chance that the child— I had a couple of the hands bring a chain, a heavy one. They threaded the chain around the legs of the slaves who were to be thrown overboard. When the slaves were linked together, I gave the order. They went over the side, all of them. The crewmen lifted them over the rail, and then came the screams and the noise of the bodies striking the water. It got dark fast, and we headed for Havana under full sail."

He turned on her then, demanding, "What else could I have done?"

"I don't know," she whispered. Her eyes burned and she felt once more the dull throbbing pain in her arm. She looked down at the dark bruises left by Jason's hand. Then she stood up.

"Denise, wait! I—" He held out his hand to her.

She evaded him, afraid that if he touched her now, however lightly, she would lose control. Far back in her mind, memory stirred: her sister Madelaine, saying, "We don't really know anything about him."

I know now, she thought dully as she crossed the library and went out into the hall; I know about Jason now. She picked up her heavy skirts and ran, like a hunted creature, along the deserted hall and up the stairs, to seek refuge in her bedroom.

But even there she was not alone. Fantine, her new maid, was waiting to help her get ready for bed.

"A splendid ball, Madame. I took the liberty of watching from the landing. The lights and the music. Never have I seen anything so fine. . . ."

The woman's eyes, jet-black and deep-set in her long, thin face, now sparkled with vicarious excitement. "And the ladies, so elegantly dressed. None looked as beautiful as you, Madame, if I may say so."

"Thank you, Fantine."

The obvious exhaustion in her voice put an end to Fantine's chatter. But although the maid was silent, and although she was quick and deft as she helped Denise off with her dress and her lace-trimmed undergarments, and as she fastened the buttons on the satin nightgown, the ritual seemed to take forever. Denise watched the maid putting away the emerald and diamond pendant, the earrings and bracelet, all gifts from Jason.

But when Fantine picked up the hairbrush, she said, "Don't bother. I'm very tired."

"It will take only a few moments. I will just take the pins from the hair, so, and now . . ."

Denise closed her eyes and allowed Fantine to take down the elaborate coiffure, to brush the dark red hair over her shoulders with swift, firm strokes.

After the maid had left the bedroom, Denise remained seated in front of her dressing table, her face buried in her hands. She was tired and drained of feeling, and yet she did not want to go to bed. She was afraid of the nightmares that might haunt her sleep, with the memory of Jason's words still fresh in her mind.

If only she had not invited Doctor Buchanan to the ball tonight. But she might as well say, if only she and Jason had not met the doctor at the inn that afternoon a few weeks before.

"I've got to stop this," she told herself firmly. "I must get some sleep. When I'm rested I'll be able to think clearly."

She rose from the bench in front of the dressing table. Turning, she gave a frightened cry. Jason stood in the doorway.

Stronger than her exhaustion was her feeling of revulsion, her need to get away from him. She moved toward the door, but he had already stepped inside the room. He closed the door behind him.

"You can't sleep here tonight." She didn't plan the words; they came by instinct.

"Don't be foolish. You're my wife, no matter how little the idea may please you at the moment."

She took a step back, but he was beside her in a few long strides. "Denise, listen to me. I didn't want you to hear about that part of my life, certainly not the way you did tonight, but it's done. You know now. And you'll have to live with the knowledge, as I have."

"I can't. I should have known what you were; I should have guessed, but I—"

His arms went around her. "Don't talk now. Just let me—" He drew her close, his mouth pressed against the loosened masses of her hair. She tried to free herself, but he was too strong. "I need you. I've never said that to any woman before."

She knew that he was asking in his way for her understanding, her acceptance of him, no matter what he had done in the past. But it was too late. Nothing he could say or do would cause her to forget what he was.

His lips found hers, but she felt only disgust and a frantic need to escape. She struck at him with her fists and twisted against his arm. He only held her more tightly. Her fingers curved, and her long nails raked the side of his face.

She heard him swear. He released her, but only for a moment. Then he lifted her off her feet and threw her down on her back across the wide canopied bed. In the flickering light from the gas lamps she saw the long, livid weals that ran from his cheekbone down to his jaw. She had put those marks there.

A wave of panic swept through her. Always before, he had shown her some tenderness, even during their most passionate moments. But from her first night with him, she had sensed that there was another side to his nature, a cold ruthlessness just under the surface.

Tonight he had reached out to her, and she had rejected him. She knew that he was not a man who would accept such treatment from any woman.

She tried to rise from the bed, but he held her there. She closed her eyes, and felt him fumbling with the buttons on the bodice of her nightgown. His fingers were shaking as he grasped the lace that edged the top of the gown. With one motion he tore the gown apart down to the waist.

Chapter 8

Denise stirred and opened her eyes to the gray, wan light of the February morning. For a few moments she lay very still, listening to the rain that lashed against the bedroom windows, the high thin wailing of the wind from upriver. Slowly she struggled back to consciousness, thrusting away the memory of her nightmare.

It must have been a nightmare, she told herself.

Then, as she moved her body and ran her fingers over her aching flesh, as she pushed back the blanket and saw the ugly bruises on her breasts and thighs, she knew with certainty that she had not dreamed the horrors of the night just past.

She turned her head and saw that the sheets were rumpled, and that Jason's pillow, with its elaborately embroidered case, had been flung to the floor.

Her head ached and her eyes were swollen. Even the faint gray daylight filtering into the room was painful to her. She listened for the sounds from Jason's dressing room, off the bedroom, but she could hear nothing; the hallway, too, was quiet.

"I must get away, right now," she told herself.

The thought of spending another night under this roof was not to be borne. She looked around for her nightgown, and saw it, a heap of torn satin and lace, lying on the Brussels carpet. She remembered the sound of the fabric as Jason had ripped it apart.

He had used her as if she'd been a street woman. He had forced her to submit to indignities she had not even imagined before. She pushed the memories to the back of her mind.

She sat up in bed. Fantine would be coming in soon, and Denise would not let the maid find her bruised and naked, cowering under the blankets. Somehow she got to her feet, stifling a cry of pain, and found herself a new nightgown and a long-sleeved, high-necked robe. Only when she had put them on did she return to bed and ring for Fantine.

The maid answered the bell quickly. She carried a tray which she placed across the bed. She poured a cup of steaming coffee.

"Madame is awake early," she said. "What would Madame like for breakfast today?"

In spite of her impeccable manners, Fantine knew something of what had happened last night; Denise was sure of it. She went scarlet as she watched the maid bend and pick up Jason's pillow, punch it lightly to fluff it up, and return it to its place on the bed. A moment later, Fantine caught sight of the torn nightdress, and Denise cursed herself for not remembering to hide it.

At Riverview, she recalled, the house slaves had known and gossiped about the most intimate details of their masters' lives. Denise was sure that it would be the same with the servants here at Mooncliff. Fantine's sharp black eyes, shiny as patent leather shoebuttons, would not miss a thing.

Pride came to Denise's aid. She raised her head, looked the maid straight in the eye and silently dared her to indicate, by the slightest gesture, whatever she might be thinking. Then she forced herself to take a sip of coffee and to ask quietly, "Did Mr. Moreland have breakfast downstairs?"

"Yes, Madame. He left for the city some time ago. He

said to tell you he would be home for dinner this evening at eight o'clock. I have the menu for tonight's dinner, if you would like to look at it." The maid shrugged. "It is not my place to comment, but—"

"Go on," Denise said impatiently.

"Perhaps you will give some thought to hiring a proper housekeeper. This Mrs. Hackett does her best, no doubt, but she has had no experience in a great house like Mooncliff. And that farm woman she hired to help with the cooking—a disgrace, Madame." She took a piece of paper from the pocket of her starched white apron. "Only look at this, Madame. Cold salmon mousse, on such a day as this." She sniffed. "Probably left over from last night's buffet supper."

"We'll . . . discuss it another time . . ."

"Forgive me, Madame. Naturally, Madame is fatigued. The great ball last night—"

Denise looked sharply at her maid. Fantine's long, narrow face under the ruffled white cap was bland and expressionless.

"There is time, of course, to choose a proper staff," Fantine said quickly. "I would be happy to make a few suggestions, if Madame wishes."

No doubt, Denise thought. The woman was obviously angling for a position of power in the household; perhaps she saw herself as housekeeper, directing a large staff.

But there would be no need to choose new servants. All at once, Denise knew that the running of Mooncliff would not matter to her. She would not stay here another night. She would never remain as mistress of Mooncliff, a house built on cruelty and death.

Her lips tightened as she thought of Jason, who had gone off to take care of business in the city. How like him that was. He would be down at the waterfront all day, no doubt, at one of his warehouses or out on the docks. Perhaps he would look over a ship and consider buying it to add to his growing merchant fleet, or examine a cargo to be bought or sold. He would have forgotten what had happened between them last night, or would at least have dismissed it from the front of his mind. When he returned home, he would expect her to sit at the dinner table, dressed in one of the expensive gowns he had provided for her. Would he also demand that she make polite conversation? And later, when they went upstairs together, would he try to—

Denise put down her coffee cup and nausea stirred inside her. Fantine looked at her, a knowing smirk on the sharp, thin features.

"Madame is not feeling well? Perhaps a few dry crackers . . ."

Denise shook her head. "I'm not hungry. I—"

"Not for the hunger, Madame. For the—how do you say—sickness in the morning?"

Denise felt a wave of white-hot anger sweep through her.

"I'm not pregnant!" she said, forgetting that a lady should always use a more delicate expression to describe that condition.

"Forgive me, Madame. I did not mean to offend."

She dismissed Fantine abruptly, but after the maid was gone she found herself thinking, "Dear Lord—suppose I *am* pregnant!"

She tried to count back over the days of the month, tried to remember the things Rosalind had taught her about he symptoms of pregnancy. If she was pregnant, she must have conceived during the last few days; that was certain. But during those days before the ball, Jason had been in Connecticut, at a shipyard there. If she was pregnant, it had to be the result of the night just past. Surely she would not be having morning sickness this soon.

But even if her nausea had been caused by other reasons, she could still have conceived last night. Oh, no—not last night. Horrible to think of her child, conceived in hatred, born of rape. Her child. And Jason's.

Damn Fantine for putting the idea into her mind! "I won't be pregnant. I won't." She forced herself to concentrate on the details of her escape from Mooncliff. She would leave before Jason came home tonight.

Perhaps Rosalind MacKay would give her shelter long enough for her to make preparations to return to Charleston. Denise realized with a dull feeling of surprise that she had very little money of her own. Of course Jason supplied her with pocket money, but he himself handled any larger sums. He paid for her clothing, the food she ate, everything.

She felt a hysterical laugh welling up in her as she looked around her magnificently furnished bedroom. All this luxury was hers, yet her purse probably held no more money than Fantine's. No matter. She would tell Fantine to order one of the carriages from the stables and have one of the grooms drive her to the landing near Rhinebeck. She had enough money to pay her fare on the river steamer, at least.

But what about her arrival in New York? Would Rosalind help her? The woman was kind and had always been helpful, but Captain MacKay was, after all, Jason's employee. No matter. She would have to throw herself on Rosalind's mercy. Although it was distasteful to her, she would even tell Rosalind exactly what had happened here last night, if necessary; even show the bruises on her body to prove her story.

And anyway, she would not ask to stay with Rosalind long. Only until she could get a ticket on a packet boat to Charleston. Or a train ticket.

"I'll walk if I have to," Denise said to herself.

She went to the closet and searched until she found a small carpetbag. Still wearing her nightgown and robe, she began to pack the bag with such necessities as she might need for the trip home to Charleston.

She could not repress a wistful glance at the rows of dresses in the closet and at the drawer that held her jewel case. No. She would take no more than she needed; she would leave behind all those gifts from Jason, the emerald and diamond necklace, the sable-lined cloak—the cloak on which she had lain naked in his arms the first day he'd brought her here to Mooncliff.

A traitorous tide of warmth threatened to engulf her, but she fought it down. Probably he would bring other women here when she was gone, street women, the kind he was used to. Women who could be treated as he'd treated her last night.

She pushed the thought away and hurried to finish her packing. Then she rang for Fantine. What would the maid say when she realized Denise was leaving Mooncliff?

It didn't matter. Once she was away from here, she'd never see Fantine again. Denise waited impatiently for the maid. When nearly five minutes had passed, she rang again. She paced the room with growing irritation, feeling that her taut nerves would snap if she did not get away from here quickly.

Still no answer. She pulled her robe tightly about her and went out into the hall. It was deserted. She moved swiftly down the stairs, not stopping on the landing, where the feeble gray light filtered through the stained-glass panes. She was halfway down the flight of stairs that led directly to the main hall when she stopped. Her hand flew to her lips and her eyes widened in disbelief.

The front door was open, and just inside it stood Jason. Denise gasped as she saw that he was carrying a girl in his arms, her limp body wrapped in a cloak, her head lying back at a curious angle as if she were unconscious or—

"Jason!"

Denise ran down the rest of the stairs. She was at Jason's side before she could get a close look at the girl's face in the dimly lit hallway. Wide cheekbones, a narrow, pointed chin. And, where the wet cloak fell away from the limp body, the folds of tulle, once white, now stained with mud.

"Elspeth Buchanan—"

"That's right," Jason said. "I sent one of the grooms to find a doctor. Right now, we'd better get Elspeth upstairs."

"But what happened to her? Where did you—"

"I found her on the Cliff Road. There was an accident last night. Their carriage was wrecked—"

He had already started for the stairs, and Denise had to hurry to keep up with him. "And Doctor Buchanan?" she asked.

Jason paused for a moment. "He's dead. His neck was broken when the carriage overturned."

Denise clung to the wide railing of the stairway. Doctor Buchanan had said there was a curse on Mooncliff. And on the night of the housewarming he himself had become the first victim.

Chapter 9

Jason carried Elspeth upstairs to one of the guest rooms.

"Get one of your nightgowns—a warm one," he said to Denise. "Hurry; her clothes are soaked through."

Denise ran to obey. Jason was in control of the situation for the time being.

A short while later Elspeth had been put to bed, and Denise was arranging the blankets over her. Jason, who had been standing at the window, staring out at the rain, came to join Denise beside the bed.

"I thought for a moment she was about to regain consciousness, but— Jason, she's not going to die, is she?"

"I don't know. She was out there in the rain half the night." He looked toward the door. "Where's Fantine? I told her to bring bandages and spirits of ammonia."

"Fantine's new here," Denise reminded him. "She doesn't know where the household supplies are kept."

But when Fantine finally arrived, she wasn't carrying bandages or smelling salts. She had, however, brought a decanter of brandy and a glass.

"There are no old sheets to be torn up for bandages, Mr. Moreland," she explained. "I did not think you would wish that I should tear up new ones without permission."

"Tear up any damn sheet you can find, and be quick about it."

His angry tone sent the maid scurrying out of the room.

"I suppose if I asked her to help with the nursing, she'd be outraged."

"I'm perfectly capable of taking care of Elspeth. If necessary, I can tear up the sheets, too."

Jason raised an eyebrow.

"At Riverview," Denise explained, "Mama was responsible for the care of the sick servants. We girls were trained to do the same, when we should have homes of our own."

She broke off, seeing Elspeth's eyelids flutter.

The girl murmured something; then her eyes opened and she cried out in pain. Jason sat down beside the bed and took Elspeth's hands in his. "Lie still. Don't try to talk."

She gave him a dazed look. "Mr. Moreland, what—"

"You're at Mooncliff, Elspeth."

Her eyes widened, and a shudder ran through her. She tried to sit up, gave a strangled cry, and fell back against the pillows.

Jason pulled the blankets away. His fingers touched her body, moving carefully across the arc of the ribs. When she moaned, he took his hand away at once.

"It could be a broken rib," he said to Denise.

He covered Elspeth with the blankets again and brushed her damp hair back from her face. "Rest now," he said. "We've sent for a doctor. You'll be all right."

"I'm cold . . . so cold. . . ."

Jason motioned to Denise, who poured a glass of brandy. He held the glass to Elspeth's lips, supporting her head with his other hand. "Just take a little of this," he said.

Watching her husband, Denise found it hard to believe that this was the same man who had used her so cruelly last night and left her body bruised and aching. She thrust the memory away.

Elspeth was speaking now, her eyes fixed on Jason's face.

"My father was in no condition to drive home last night, Mr. Moreland. I should have stopped him."

"You couldn't have stopped him. Don't blame yourself."

She went on speaking, compelled to tell what had happaned.

"It was raining hard when we left. And it was so dark. I begged him to wait, but he—he was very drunk. We took the road that runs along the cliffs back of the estate. It was so narrow in places. . . . The horses were hard to handle. The wind frightened them, I think. A horrible sound, it was.

"Father said strange, crazy things, shouting above the wind. He said, 'They're dead! Why don't they stop screaming?' "

"Elspeth, don't."

But she ignored Jason, ignored the pain that made her lips go white. "Something ran across the path—a small animal. The horses shied. They reared up, and Father couldn't control them. The carriage turned over. I was flung out a little way down the side of the cliff, but Father was still inside when it went to the bottom. I remember climbing down to try to help him. There were sharp rocks. It seemed to take forever, climbing down there. But when I got to him I knew he was dead. I don't remember anything after that."

"A couple of fishermen found you lying on the beach. I was on my way to New York City, and they hailed my carriage."

"You should not have brought me here," Elspeth said. "Father would not have wanted me to return here."

"You'll be properly cared for here. At the moment, that's all that matters," Jason said.

Denise leaned over the bed. "Elspeth, is there anyone you want us to notify about the accident? A relative, perhaps? Or a friend?"

Elspeth shook her head. "There's no one," she said. "No one at all."

"It would seem from what that doctor says that Elspeth will be staying at Mooncliff for some time."

The doctor had just departed, and Denise had gone to

her bedroom. Jason had followed her, and he now paced the floor, his eyes troubled.

"Broken ribs, he said, and a high fever. I'm afraid she'll have to stay here, no matter how she feels about the place."

"If you hadn't let Andrew Buchanan leave here last night in his condition—"

"I had no way of knowing the drunken fool would lose control of the horses," Jason said.

"But you did know he was drunk. I suppose you were too concerned with the impression you wanted to make on your other guests to stop and think what might happen." Her voice rose. She was on the edge of hysteria. "Maybe you wanted him to die! After all, he was a reminder of—"

Jason turned on her. "That's enough! That kind of talk won't bring Buchanan back. And maybe he's better dead. No, not for my sake: for his. He was tortured by his memories, unable to live with them."

He broke off abruptly and stopped his pacing. "What's this?"

He picked up the carpetbag Denise had packed that morning and had left beside the bed.

She flushed and looked away.

"I asked you a question."

"It's mine. I packed it. I was leaving you, Jason."

"What the hell are you talking about?"

"Surely, after last night, you didn't imagine I'd stay."

"Last night?"

"I don't want to discuss it. But I haven't changed my mind. I'll remain here until Elspeth is out of danger; then I'll go."

"Supposing I were to allow you to leave here, where did you plan to go?"

"To Charleston, of course. To Papa."

"Your father won't take you back." He spoke flatly, with complete assurance.

"Papa loves me. When I tell him what you did to me, he—he'll probably kill you."

Jason threw back his head and laughed. "He'd challenge me to a duel—is that what you're saying?"

"It wouldn't be the first time he's fought a duel. And he's still an excellent shot. When Papa was a young man, he—"

Jason held up his hand. "Spare me the history of the ancient and noble Chevillon family. I know all about them and about the idiotic southern code of chivalry. I also know your father. A shrewd, practical man. I like him for it. It's about the only thing we have in common, he and I, and—"

"You have nothing in common with anyone in my family. You can't understand my father!"

"It's you who can't understand, because you don't want to. Your father gave his consent to our marriage because he needed money. He wanted to rebuild Riverview, to restore his fortune and live the way he had lived before the War. That's still his goal, and he still needs my money."

She tried desperately to shut out his words. "Papa won't turn me away. Not when I tell him the sort of man you really are."

"He won't believe you. Or he'll pretend not to. He'll tell you your place is with your husband. He'll lecture you on the duties of a good wife. Because he'll know that if he were foolish enough to take you back, he wouldn't get another penny from me."

"You'd use your money to hold me, even knowing how I feel about you?"

"Are you surprised? What else would you expect from a man like me?"

She forced herself to ignore his sarcasm as she tried to find another route of escape.

"I'll go to France. I'll stay with Mama and my sisters."

"Your sisters are in France in search of suitable husbands. The French are conservative people, my dear, at least where marriage is concerned. A divorce scandal would wreck your sisters' chances."

"And you'd see to it that there would be a scandal, even if you had to follow me to France."

"Now you're beginning to understand," Jason said calmly.

Denise sank into a chair, exhausted and confused, unable to find a weapon with which to combat her husband's cold assurance.

He came and stood over her, then took her chin in his hand, tilting her face upward. His eyes were unfathomable.

"I married you because I wanted you, Denise. From the first time I saw you there at Riverview, I knew I had to have you. I won't let you go. Not now. Not ever."

"But after last night, surely you can't—"

"If you're referring to the little episode that took place here, it's not unheard of. I was quite within my rights as your husband."

"Rights? Maybe in the slums of Liverpool or on the Ivory Coast a man has the right to behave like an animal. But I'm not one of your fancy women or some helpless slave on one of your ships."

"I don't think you know much about men, Denise. They sometimes behave like—animals—even in your precious Charleston. Where do you suppose all those mulatto and quadroon babies came from? And what about the southern gentlemen who paid fortunes to keep their whores in style on some of those Charleston streets nice ladies never went into? I'm sure your father and your sainted brother Louis had their quadroon girls."

Denise twisted away from him.

"You're low and vicious, so you'd like to believe every other man is, too. I don't care what you say, I won't stay at Mooncliff one day longer than I have to, and I won't live with you as your wife—"

"Oh, but you will. And you'll bear my sons, here at Mooncliff. And in time you'll forget last night."

"I can't."

His eyes held hers, so that she could not look away.

"You'll give me sons, Denise. Perhaps you're carrying my child now. It's possible, you know."

"I won't have your child. I won't—"

"That's hardly a matter you can control, my dear."

His complacency, his conviction that events must shape themselves according to his will, made her reckless.

"There are ways. Even after a woman's pregnant, there

are things she can do. Rosalind told me. There's a place in New York where lots of women go, when they—"

"Roselind MacKay dared to speak to you of such things?"

Although his voice was hard with anger, Denise sensed another, stronger emotion behind the outburst. Jason was afraid.

"Did you ever go to one of those harpies? Don't lie to me!"

"No, I haven't. I wanted your child, Jason. Only yesterday, I'd have been happy to think I was going to have a baby, but not now. Not after last night."

"Forget last night. You turned away from me, and I—" He took her in his arms. She did not try to free herself, but neither did she respond. She remained cold, unmoving.

"You wanted me before," he said. "You know it. That day in the conservatory, the first time I brought you here to Mooncliff. And last night, at the ball, when we were dancing together."

"That was before Doctor Buchanan showed me the kind of man you really are."

"Stop it!" His voice was harsh. "Don't ruin the rest of our lives because of one mistake I made. You can forget. I'll make you forget."

His hands caressed her, and a warm tide of feeling began to stir under the hurt and fear. For one moment she allowed herself to relax in his arms.

Then he released her. "You see, I'm right about you. You belong to me. You always will."

Because she feared that there might be some truth in what he said, because she hated the thought that he still had power to arouse her, she lashed out at him. "You'd like to believe that, wouldn't you? You'd like to think that I'm no different from the sluts you're used to, that you can make me want you enough to—to forget what you are. I'll prove you're wrong. I'll stay here only as long as I'm needed to look after Elspeth. When she is able to leave Mooncliff, I'll go, too."

Chapter 10

During the spring and summer of that year, Denise's words of defiance returned to mock her. For early in May she discovered that she was pregnant. As the days grew warmer and her body, now misshapen, began to be a burden to her, she felt the walls of Mooncliff closing around her like the walls of a prison.

Although Elspeth had recovered from her injuries and was making plans to find work, Jason persuaded her to stay on. He called her into the library one evening, shortly after Denise's pregnancy had been definitely confirmed, and offered her a position in his home.

"I know how you must feel about me," Jason said. "And about Mooncliff. But I'm prepared to pay you well, if you'll remain here as a companion to Denise."

Elspeth had already proved her capabilities during Denise's hysterical outburst when she'd found out she was pregnant. For two days she would let no one but Elspeth come near her.

"How long will you want me to stay?" Elspeth asked.

"Until the baby is born. I must have someone who'll

stay with Denise, someone who will be at her side constantly. Someone I can trust."

"I appreciate your offer," Elspeth began. "But I'm not sure—"

"You must know Denise doesn't want this baby. She'll come to accept her condition, of course. But in the meantime, she's just headstrong enough to try to—cause an accident."

"A miscarriage," Elspeth said calmly. "My father was a doctor. I know about such things. But I also know that it isn't so easy for a woman to miscarry simply because she wants to."

"Perhaps you're right, but I can't take any risks. And I can't permit my concern for Denise's emotional state to distract me from my business affairs. I have reason to believe that this country is heading for a financial crisis. I have to be sure— But business matters can be of no interest to a young woman like yourself."

Elspeth smiled faintly. "I do read the newspapers, Mr. Moreland. I know something about the Stock Exchange swindles, and the fact that the price of gold has been going up steadily, and much too fast."

Jason looked at her with surprise and unwilling respect. Most women confined their newspaper reading to social gossip and news of the latest Paris fashions. "You are most remarkable, Elspeth," he said. "I may call you that, now?"

"If you wish. However, about your offer—"

"You must accept. You may dislike me, but Denise has done you no harm."

"Dislike you? No, don't think that. I loved my father, but I knew his weaknesses. *They* destroyed him, not you. I don't think he ever knew a moment's peace after his voyage on your ship. He is at peace now."

Jason was impressed by her calm, matter-of-fact acceptance of the situation, her self-control and poise. Yes, she would surely be of help in seeing Denise through the difficult months ahead.

"Promise me you'll stay. Only until my son is born. After that, if you want to leave I'll use my influence to find you a position elsewhere."

Elspeth smiled. "You're very sure it will be a son, aren't you?"

"I must have sons," Jason said. "To carry on my name and hold on to the empire I will build for them." He moved his hand in an expansive gesture that took in not only the room but all of Mooncliff, and much more.

"You usually get what you want, don't you?"

"Usually. And at the moment, I want you to agree to stay and help Denise. You will, won't you?"

Elspeth did not answer at once.

"Perhaps you're afraid to stay. Do you believe there is a curse on Mooncliff, as your father said?"

She looked at him squarely. "I don't believe in curses. Do you, Captain Moreland?"

"I'm not sure," he said. Then, angered by his own admission, he demanded, "Tell me you're staying."

"Very well. I'll stay."

Although Denise was grateful for Elspeth's presence in the house, she was unable to shake off the dark forebodings that were now a constant part of her life. Her hysteria had passed, but at times she was gripped by nameless, overpowering terrors.

"Ladies in your condition are often overemotional," she was told by Doctor Frobisher, the fashionable practitioner Jason had insisted on engaging to see her through her confinement. "It is too bad you're all the way out there at Mooncliff. If you were here in the city, you would find suitable diversions to distract you."

The doctor was more concerned with her physical symptoms. Denise, who had never had a sick day in her life except for the usual childhood ailments, was racked with nausea, not only in the morning but often throughout the day. She found it difficult to sleep at night, and when she did drop off, she was awakened repeatedly by terrifying nightmares.

Jason had moved out of their bedroom and now slept in the adjoining room. Although Denise was unwilling to admit it, even to herself, there were nights when she would have been grateful for his presence beside her. But she would not tell him of fears or her nightmares. She hid her physical discomforts as much as possible, breakfasting in her bedroom and coming downstairs after he had left for the city. In that way she was spared the humiliation of having him see her during her frequent attacks of morning sickness.

But as her pregnancy went on the nausea abated, and she began to feel better and look better—except for the inevitable thickening of her once-slender waistline. Her skin bcame smooth and clear once more, and her appetite began to return.

One morning late in September she had asked Fantine to arrange her hair in a becoming chignon style. Then she put on a hunter-green cashmere dress with a full-cut jacket and joined Jason at breakfast.

He looked at her in surprise. "This is an unaccustomed pleasure, my dear," he said.

Ignoring his sardonic tone, she said, "I would like to drive into the city with you today."

"That is out of the question."

"I'll wear my new tartan shawl. I'm sure it's long and full enough to conceal—"

"That's not the point. You can't go into New York today. Next week, perhaps."

"If I can't drive in with you. I'll have one of the grooms take me to the landing, and I can take a steamer to the city from there."

"You won't. I'll leave orders to that effect."

"You're trying to keep me a prisoner here, aren't you?"

"Don't be ridiculous. You don't know what's been happening in New York during the past few weeks. The price of gold is soaring, and the bubble has to burst very soon now. Perhaps today."

"I have no intention of going to the Gold Exchange or anywhere near Wall Street."

Jason rose, pushing his chair back. "I'm sorry. Your excursion will have to wait."

He turned as Elspeth entered the room, neat and composed, in a simple blue-gray dress with a prim white lace collar.

"Elspeth, maybe you can talk some sense into my wife.

She has some idea of going into New York today. All hell could break loose there."

"How can you be sure anything will happen today?" Elspeth asked.

"I have my sources of information. At any rate, it's a chance I don't want her to take."

Then the lines of tension in his face relaxed. He came around to Denise's end of the table and put his hand on her arm.

"I'm sorry to spoil your plans, but I'm glad you are feeling well enough to want to make the trip. You are feeling better, aren't you?"

"I'm quite well, thank you."

"You look charming. That shade of green is most becoming."

He bent and his lips brushed hers. She felt a warm tingling sensation at his touch and hated him for being able to evoke such a response.

"No woman can possibly look charming in this condition," she said.

"That's a matter of opinion." He started for the door. "I'll be home late tonight. There is no need to wait dinner for me."

Denise wondered whether all Jason's talk of a possible financial disaster had been no more than a cover-up. Perhaps he had another reason for not wanting to take her into the city. And for planning to come home late, as he had done several nights during the past month.

He had not slept with her since the night of the ball, and Jason was not the kind of man to be without a woman so long. Had he been spending his evenings at one of the brownstone parlor houses on West Twenty-fifth Street? Or perhaps at some sailors' dive along Greene Street? Even respectable women like herself knew of the existence of such places.

She realized that Elspeth was looking at her with concern.

"You mustn't be angry with him," Elspeth said. "He's only thinking of your safety, and the baby's."

Denise bit back an angry retort. What did Elspeth know of Jason, or any man?

In spite of Elspeth's efforts to keep Denise occupied, the day dragged; by late afternoon the sun had disappeared, and the blue mountaintops to the west were lost in the haze as the air became heavy and sultry. There would be rain before morning.

Denise went to bed early that night, taking a novel with her to read in bed. But she found Charles Dickens's *Oliver Twist* most depressing. Propped up against her pillows, she felt a growing uneasiness as she read the vivid account of Oliver's mother dying in childbirth. She pushed the book away. Women did die giving birth, even in luxurious surroundings, with doctors in attendance. Suppose she were to die. What would become of her baby? For the first time, she thought of the baby as a living person, not an unwanted burden that was keeping her tied to Jason.

Her sleep was restless that night, broken by distorted, frightening dreams. In one of them she found herself driving the surrey through a rainstorm, out to the edge of the cliffs. It was difficult to control the horses because of the heavy rain, and because she held something in the crook of her arm. Looking down, she saw that it was a baby wrapped in a ragged, faded blanket. Her baby.

The horses reared and plunged, and as she fought to control them, the baby slipped from her arms. It was falling . . . falling into the fog at the edge of the cliff. . . .

Denise screamed and woke up, her heart hammering, her body so tense with fear that it was a few moments before she was able to move.

As she sat up in bed she saw the door of her room swing open.

"Denise, what's wrong?" Jason was beside her, leaning over her.

"The baby," she said.

He fumbled and lit the gaslight beside the bed. "The baby? But the doctor said not before December—"

She shook her head. "It was a dream—a nightmare." She took a deep breath as she fought to control her panic.

"I was just coming upstairs when I heard you screaming. I thought—" He shook his head. "You're sure it was only this nightmare? The pains haven't started yet—nothing like that?"

"I've just told you, it was a nightmare. And I'm perfectly all right now. I've had them before."

"You never told me." He put his arm around her, and she did not draw away. Then, as she rested her head against his chest, she realized that he was still wearing his street clothes.

"You're only just getting home?"

"That's right," he said.

"But it's late—"

"Close to three, I'd say," he agreed.

"I see." She pushed him away, hot with anger.

"Exactly what do you see, my dear?"

"Please leave me alone. How dare you come to me from one of those—"

A puzzled frown drew his brows together. Then he threw back his head and laughed. "You think I've been with another woman!"

"What do you expect me to think?"

He rose, went to the mahogany cabinet in the corner, and took out a decanter of brandy. "I think we both need a drink," he said, filling two glasses. "Here." He pushed a glass into her hand. "Go on, drink it. You're still shaking from that nightmare, whatever it was."

The brandy was comforting. Her taut muscles relaxed, and she felt a warming glow spread through her body.

"Now, as for my late return from the city—"

"You don't owe me an explanation," she said with what dignity she could muster.

"You're quite right. Still—" He grinned at her. "For a delicately bred lady, you have a fairly lurid imagination. I hate to disappoint you, but I wasn't with another woman tonight. Believe me, Denise, if the entire Lydia Thompson Burlesque Company had appeared at the Gold Exchange this evening, not a man in the place would have looked twice."

"Wall Street is deserted after six," she said.

"Jim Fisk and Jay Gould changed all that, my dear. At this moment, a thousand bookkeepers are down there wrestling with the Clearing House statements for tomorrow, trying to find out if anything can be salvaged from the wreckage."

"You make it sound like a national disaster."

"It is. Fisk was assaulted, and it took the police to protect him. There was talk of troops ready to march on Wall Street to restore order. Men will be ruined, families will go under, because of what happened today."

"I don't understand."

"Of course you don't. Quite simply, Fisk and Gould tried to corner gold. They even hoped to bring President Grant into the scheme, but— No matter. They'll make millions out of today's debacle, but others, thousands of others, will be destroyed."

For the first time, it occurred to her that Jason might be personally involved. "Did you—were you in on this?"

"Don't worry, my dear. We're not ruined. Far from it." He drained his glass and set it down. "In fact, our son will be the heir to a fortune because of what happened today."

"You made money on this—this swindle?"

"That's a harsh word for a successful business transaction." He leaned forward. "I did make a great deal of money, though; you're right about that. And I'm going to invest it in real estate and in shipping and—"

"I don't want to hear about your investments. Cheating innocent people, ruining them, and boasting about it—"

"Innocent perhaps, but greedy and shortsighted, too. At any rate, I plan to invest some of my ill-gotten gains in Charleston and in your precious Riverview. That, at least, should please you."

For a moment she looked beyond him, beyond the luxurious gas-lit bedroom with its ornately carved furniture, heavy hangings and somber stained-glass windows. She was seeing Riverview as it had been and might be again. The marshlands drained once more and the crops planted. And the house itself, tall, stately, its Greek Revival facade gleaming white through the shadows cast by the live-oak trees with their veils of gray-green moss. And the inside of the plantation house, with new furniture imported from Europe, furniture of fine gleaming mahogany and rich velvet. Sparkling chandeliers in the high-ceilinged rooms, candles gleaming in heavy silver candelabra.

"You mean it, Jason?" He came to sit by her side, and she did not draw away. "You'll make Riverview the way it was before—just to please me?"

He put his arm around her and held her against him. Pressing his mouth against her dark red hair, he said, "Give me a son, Denise, and there's nothing I won't do for you."

Chapter 11

On a day early in December, when the wind brought a shower of icy rain to Mooncliff, Denise went into labor. The first pains struck in midmorning. By the time Jason had dispatched one of the grooms to New York City to bring back Doctor Frobisher, the rain had changed to snow. The big white flakes fell slowly at first, then faster, carried on the rising wind. Soon everything outside the windows of Denise's room was blurred. By four in the afternoon, Elspeth had to turn up the gaslights.

Although Denise tried not to cry out, Elspeth could see that her pains were getting steadily worse. "It won't take much longer, will it?" Denise asked between clenched teeth.

Elspeth knew that first labors tended to be prolonged, but she only said, "The doctor will be here soon. He'll be able to help you."

"Suppose he can't get through. It's snowing so hard—the roads may be blocked!" She pushed back her hair, already soaked with sweat; her nightdress felt clammy against her pain-racked body.

Elspeth, too, had been concerned that the doctor might not be able to get through the snowstorm, but she said nothing. Instead, she wiped Denise's face with a damp cloth.

"I didn't know—it would be this bad—" Denise found it difficult to speak. Each pain seemed to start at the small of her back and then to encircle her body. Between pains she lapsed into a dazed numbness.

"Jason," she whispered.

"You want to see him?"

"No—his fault—the night of the ball—that horrible night—"

"Hush, now."

"No! Listen. That night, he forced me. I didn't want him to touch me—not after I found out. But I couldn't stop him—"

Elspeth looked away, hot with embarrassment. Her father had told her that women in childbirth often made the most shocking revelations, their reticence wiped out by the onslaught of pain.

"Jason always gets what he wants. Always!" She broke off and gripped Elspeth's hand. "Why doesn't the doctor get here?"

"Maybe he's coming now," Elspeth said soothingly.

"Go and see. Please."

Elspeth sent Fantine in to sit with Denise while she went downstairs. In the entrance hall she saw Jason, his face grim. "I should have made Denise stay in New York this last month," he said. "Now, if that damn doctor can't get through— Elspeth, can you— Do you know how to take care of her, if the baby comes before the doctor gets here?"

"I helped my father with deliveries a few times. Farm women, mostly. If it's a normal birth, I think I can manage."

Jason's face went dark with anger. "Why the devil shouldn't the birth be normal?"

Although Elspeth could speak bluntly when necessary, she could not bring herself to tell him what she had learned from Denise only a few moments ago. Whether or not the baby had been conceived on the night of the ball, when

Jason had taken her by force, wasn't important; what mattered was that Denise believed it to be true. A woman like Denise would be revolted at the idea of giving birth to a child conceived in rape, on a night of violence and terror.

"Answer me!" Jason insisted. "What reason have you to believe anything will go wrong?"

"I'm not sure; I'm not a doctor. Your wife is frightened. That could make the labor difficult."

"But you'll do what you can to help her?"

"You know I will. But maybe you could get a doctor—the one you called when I had my accident—Doctor Macauley. He doesn't have Doctor Frobisher's reputation, but—"

"Don't you suppose I thought of him? I went after him myself while you were up there with Denise. He'd left on calls early this morning and hadn't returned. Stranded somewhere along the road, I suppose." Jason took her hand, his eyes holding hers.

"It's asking a great deal, I know, but I have no choice. Help her, Elspeth. She's got to live, and my son, too."

There was desperation in his voice, and humility. Jason Moreland, always so sure of himself, able to take what he wanted, with money or by force. She found herself feeling a kind of pity for him now.

"Denise will be all right," she said, with far more assurance than she felt. "And the baby, too."

The ordeal went on and on through the long snowy night and into the following day. When, on the second day, the early December twilight fell and the gas lamps around the canopied bed flared up again, Denise's pains had stopped. Her face was drained of color, her eyes dull and apathetic. Her hands moved aimlessly on the sheet. She muttered about places and events unfamiliar to Elspeth, and from time to time she spoke to Mama, Lucille and Madelaine.

Elspeth went to the window and looked down at the drive. The action was automatic; the doctor would not be here tonight. No one could get through to Mooncliff until the roads had been cleared.

Hearing a strangled cry, she turned and hurried back to the bed. Denise reached for her hand and spoke clearly: "If I die, Jason must not have the baby! I want my child brought up away from his father—and away from Mooncliff. Promise me."

Elspeth saw her opportunity. In desperation she shook Denise as hard as she could. "Then you've got to fight," she said. "If you die, Jason will have complete charge of the child!" She shook Denise again, harder this time.

Denise cried out. Her body twisted as she tried to free herself. A few minutes later the pains began again.

Downstairs in the library, Jason drained another glass of brandy. The decanter was nearly empty, but he was still cold sober. He cursed Doctor Frobisher and Doctor Macauley. And the blizzard that that was still going on in full force after nearly two days. And the sound of the wind blowing from the river.

He cursed himself, too, for his shortsightedness. He should have sent Denise to stay in the city for these last few weeks. If she had been at Rosalind MacKay's home, Doctor Frobisher would have been able to get to her, to deliver the baby. But he had never quite forgiven Rosalind for having told Denise about the possibility of having an abortion. More important, he had wanted his son to be born here at Mooncliff. Now he might lose both Denise and the child.

He tried to forget the screams he'd heard from the bedroom earlier that day. Denise had been in labor nearly thirty hours now. She would not be able to stand much more.

"Captain Moreland."

He started violently. For a moment he thought that Andrew Buchanan had called his name. Turning, he saw Elspeth in the doorway. Her slender body was drooping with fatigue, and her face was drawn.

In two strides he was beside her. "Denise is dead?"

"Oh, no. She's sleeping now. She had a bad time, but she will recover. And you have a son. A fine, healthy boy."

"She'll live? You're sure? And my son, too?"

"Yes, Captain Moreland, I—"

"Don't ever call me that again!"

Elspeth drew back, her eyes wide.

"Forgive me. Father used to call you—"

"I know. Right up until the end. To make sure I wouldn't forget I'd given the orders on the *Nubian Queen*." He drew a long breath. "I'm sorry, Elspeth." He took her hand. She winced and pulled it away.

At first he thought she was angry with him for shouting at her, or perhaps for the implied criticism of her father. Then, looking down, he saw that her hand was bruised. She seemed to be having difficulty moving her fingers.

"Denise. She didn't know what she was doing toward the end. She needed someone to hold onto. She—"

"It was that bad, then."

Elspeth nodded. "No matter. It's over now."

He put an arm around Elspeth and led her to a comfortable sofa, close to the fireplace. "I'm so grateful to you. What can I do to repay you? How can I ever—"

"There's no need. You see, I won't be dependent on you much longer. I've found a position—"

"You've leaving Mooncliff?"

"Yes. I'm to be housekeeper at the school where I was a pupil. I'll get room and board and—"

"And work from dawn to midnight, and take the slights of a bunch of dried-up old maids who'll remind you of your change of circumstances."

"I'm not afraid of hard work. And my circumstances have changed since— Father wasn't very practical. He had a bit of money invested, but after Black Friday—"

"You don't have a cent to your name—is that it?"

"That's it, Mr. Moreland."

"Elspeth, don't take that job at the school. We need a housekeeper here. Mrs. Hackett tries, but she can't cope."

"You think I can?"

He looked at her thoughtfully, her calm, steady eyes, her poised manner.

"The staff might resent—I'm very young—"

"Damn the staff. I'm master here. Give the orders and I'll back you up." When she remained silent he said,

"That's settled, then." He stood up. "Now I want to see my wife—and my son."

During the early months of her reign as housekeeper at Mooncliff, Elspeth needed Jason's support, for a few members of the household staff were plainly taken aback when they learned that this inexperienced young woman had been given complete control. Fantine in particular made no secret of her disapproval. But as Jason had promised, he backed Elspeth and agreed to the changes she suggested.

Mrs. Hackett, the gatekeeper's wife, was sent back to the gatehouse, with Jason's thanks for her services as temporary housekeeper and a tidy bonus as well. Jason suspected that she might be secretly relieved to be free of responsibilities that had been beyond her capabilities.

Elspeth hired an excellent cook, a laundress, three housemaids, and a nursery maid, Katerina Van Houten, a stout, red-cheeked Dutch farm girl from the neighborhood. Katerina was overawed at finding herself in these new and splendid surroundings, but she proved to be hard-working and experienced with babies, having helped to raise six younger brothers and sisters on her father's farm.

Jason himself, however, went into the city to hire an English nanny, Miss Wilmot, to take charge of Stuart, keeping Katerina on to do the menial work in the nursery.

"Really, Jason, I can take care of Stuart, with Katerina to help me," Denise objected.

"Absolutely not," Jason told her. "Every important family in New York has an English nanny." He kissed Denise lightly on the cheek and added, "I have other plans for you, my dear."

She soon discovered that those plans included the entertaining of Jason's business associates and their wives at Mooncliff. During the two years following Stuart's birth, the house was filled with guests who attended the Moreland's cotillions, dinners, sleighing parties when the Hudson froze over, coaching parties along the Albany Post Road, and lavish picnics on the beach below the cliffs.

At Jason's instructions, Denise arranged musicales, engaging such artists as Clara Louise Kellogg, the first American opera singer to win national fame, and several foreign performers, among them Christine Nilsson and Pauline Lucca.

Jason made it plain that he expected his wife to be the best-dressed woman present and to be able to converse with the other guests on those topics suitable for ladies. There was little time left for her to take charge of Stuart's upbringing.

Although she gave in to Jason's wishes in these matters, she was less easily persuaded when, a few weeks after Stuart's birth, Jason insisted that she hire a woman from one of the nearby farms as a wet nurse.

"You're not a farmer's wife," he said. "I won't have you ruining your figure." His eyes lingered on the curve of her breasts, and she saw the reawakened desire in his look.

It did not surprise her, therefore, when he moved back into their bedroom a few weeks later. She found that his touch still stirred her senses, but now, mingled with her need was a tinge of fear.

Sensing this, he said, "It will be all right, love. I'll be gentle."

But although he restrained the violence of his need for her, she was unable to respond. She could not blot out the memory of that other night when he had ripped her nightgown from her body and taken her by force, hurting her, shaming her. Now, even though he was able to arouse her, he could not evoke complete surrender, and he knew it. He must know it, she thought unhappily.

For the next few months he went on trying to make their marriage what it had been during the early months; then, gradually losing patience, he began to take her quickly, automatically, satisfying his own needs before he turned away from her and fell asleep.

She tried to console herself with the thought that perhaps most marriages were like this after the first year, but there were times when she sensed that if she could take the initiative, could say, "I want you," they might be able to find their way back to the sweet, passionate closeness they had known so briefly. But her pride would not permit her to speak or to reach out to him, to make the first advances.

Instead, she let herself become caught up in the round of activities he had forced on her. When they were not entertaining guests at Mooncliff, they drove or took a riverboat into New York City to attend the operas at the Academy of Music, where Jason had taken one of the limited number of boxes, so sought after by those who wanted to see and be seen; like most members of New York society, the Morelands arrived late and left early. Jason made it obvious that he did not particularly enjoy the melodious Italian operas, but only attended them to make the right contacts. Now, with the birth of his first son, his interest in his business became, if possible, even more obsessive than before.

He told Denise of his plans for establishing new shipping routes, including one to the Far East, for with the growing wealth in New York, there was an ever-increasing demand for luxury goods from China: not only tea but silks, embroidered wall hangings, lacquered chests, inlaid screens. In order to get this new line started, he would have to negotiate with local government officials on the waterfront and at the Custom House, as well as with men higher up in the Treasury Department.

"Moreland ships will be loading tea and silks at Canton," he told her proudly. "And that's not all. I'll be bringing in coffee from Rio and textiles from Liverpool."

He cultivated politicians and entertained them at Mooncliff, ignoring Denise's objections that some of these men were the same ones who even now supported carpetbagger rule in the South.

"I wonder you don't ask me to entertain Ben Butler and General Sherman," she said bitterly.

"I would if I thought I needed their help right now," he said, shrugging off her displeasure. "And I know you would be the perfect hostess, as you always are."

"Is that all you want of me now?"

"Not quite all," he said. He put an arm around her and drew her close. "I want more sons, Denise. It's been over a year since Stuart was born."

She gave a little involuntary cry and tried to pull away.

"Don't," he said, and his voice was gentle now. "There's no great hurry about it. I know you had a bad time when Stuart came. I suppose it's natural that you're still afraid."

She longed to tell him that although she dreaded another birth as bad as the first, she would have undergone any amount of pain if only she could believe that she still mattered to him, not as a hostess for Mooncliff or as the means of getting more sons, but as a woman. Even now, as he held her against him and stroked her hair, she felt alone, afraid of the years that lay ahead for them.

Chapter 12

Stuart Moreland was nearly two years old that August of 1871; a strong, active child, he already showed a stubborn will of his own. On this sultry morning he played on the terrace, watched over by Miss Wilmot, the English nurse Jason had hired.

Because of the heat, Denise and Jason had breakfasted out on the terrace, which had now been extended so that it stretched across the whole length of the house. While Jason read the *New York Herald,* Denise smiled over a letter she had just received from Charleston.

"Good news, Denise?"

"Lucille is to be married next month. On the twentieth."

"And who is the lucky groom? Someone you know?"

"Not really. His name's Charles Wingate. He's from Savannah. But his family is one of the oldest in Georgia. He was a major in the War."

"Wealthy?"

"The Wingates used to be, but now— He's studied architecture."

"Has he had any commissions yet?"

"I'm sure I don't know. Lucille doesn't mention anything like that in her letter."

"Forgive me for being crass. How does he plan to support your sister?"

"They will live at Riverview until he gets established."

"At least that way he may be of some use in helping rebuild the place. Or has the rebuilding been completed?"

"Almost. Jason, we'll have to make plans to go to the wedding."

Jason shook his head. "I won't be there. I have business that will keep me here in New York until the end of September—those new ships to be fitted out for the China run."

"But surely someone else can attend to that—Captain MacKay, perhaps."

"Impossible. MacKay's a good man, but there are dozens of details I must handle personally."

"But my family—what will they say if I come to Lucille's wedding without you? And all our friends?"

"I'm sorry," he said. "I don't want to put you in an embarrassing position, but I can't go down to South Carolina right now. The first of the ships will be leaving for China in October. She's a clipper, four hundred and forty-eight tons. The Far East trade is one of the last in which the clipper can still hold her own. MacKay will be captain, but I must be on hand until the ship sails."

Denise knew from Jason's tone that it would be useless to protest. But now, on this warm August morning, she found that she was strangely uneasy at the thought of their coming separation.

"You want me to go to Charleston alone, then?"

"I can join you at the end of September, if you like. I want to have a look at Riverview—and the lumber mills."

"I see. My sister's wedding doesn't matter, but your investments do."

He threw down the newspaper, his brows drawing together in an angry frown. "I'll never understand you, Denise. You were ready enough to leave Mooncliff that day after the housewarming ball, after—"

"Jason, please." She glanced in the direction of Miss

Wilmot, Stuart's nurse; the sturdy middle-aged woman was following her charge at the far end of the terrace.

"She can't hear us," he said impatiently. Then, his voice tight with barely controlled anger, he went on, "You've never forgotten that night, and you never will. You've given me a son, and you haven't once refused me since then, but you've only submitted out of a sense of duty."

She wanted to tell him that he was wrong, but his anger was a barrier between them. "Are you afraid of what your relatives will think if you arrive in Charleston without me? Don't be. Your father's a shrewd enough businessman in his own way to understand why I have to remain here. And as for your sister and her husband, I'll send them a suitably impressive wedding gift."

He was watching her closely, and there was something in his eyes she did not understand, something that belied the cold anger of his words. Once before, he had looked at her this way, but when?

Then it came to her. It was the night of the ball, after he had told her about the *Nubian Queen*. He had come into the bedroom, he had sought her understanding, and she had turned away. If she had not repulsed him that night, would it have made a difference? Even now, if she could reach out to him, could humble herself, perhaps they would be able to find their way back to the kind of marriage she had once hoped for. But her pride made her hesitate.

Then a shrill cry from the far end of the terrace shattered the moment. Stuart, who had been trying to climb the stone wall separating the terrace from the cliffs, had been dragged back by Miss Wilmot.

Jason turned away from Denise and hurried to the child, lifting him and carrying him the length of the terrace. Stuart, red-faced and screaming, pounded Jason with his small fists. Miss Wilmot hurried after them. "Really, sir, these outbursts of temper cannot be allowed. Master Stuart must be taught—"

But Jason only laughed and lifted Stuart to the rough gray stones at the top of the wall. The child stopped crying, his good humor restored. He waved his arms and laughed, too.

"Higher!" he screamed. "Higher!"

Jason held him up so that his feet swung above the wall.

"Stop, Jason. You'll frighten him."

"Don't be foolish. He's not afraid of anything."

Miss Wilmot said, "Perhaps he should be taught to be afraid, sir."

"She's right, Jason," Denise agreed. "When Stuart runs into danger, he must be punished."

Jason's blue eyes went cold. "No. You know my orders."

Miss Wilmot was not easily cowed. "A child must be disciplined."

"If my son needs discipline, I'll take care of it. No one else."

"You?" Denise laughed. "You dote on the boy. You treat him as if he were a young prince—"

"He is, my dear. Look at him."

He was a beautiful child, with Jason's dark blue eyes and her own fair complexion and thick auburn hair. Even at his age he held himself in an imperious way, his chin tilted back, his small shoulders squared.

"He's a spoiled little boy," Denise said.

"And a hungry one," Miss Wilmot added. "It's nearly time for his lunch, sir."

Jason smiled as he surrendered Stuart to the nurse. Denise saw that he followed the child with his eyes until Stuart was out of sight. Only then did he turn back to Denise.

"Your whole family will be at Riverview for the wedding, I suppose. Every Chevillon from Atlanta to New Orleans."

Denise felt her throat tighten. "Madelaine won't be there."

A year before, the Franco-Prussian War had broken out, and Madelaine, just married to her Edouard, had refused to leave Paris. Mama and Lucille had returned to Charleston without her, and a few months later Paris lay under siege. For four months the Germans had shelled the city, and during one of the last attacks Madelaine had been killed.

"Forgive me," Jason said quickly. "I know how much your sister meant to you." He went to her and put his arms around her. She did not draw away, but rested her face against his shoulder, grateful for the comfort of his nearness.

Only three years before, Denise had come to New York aboard the *Enchantress,* the graceful three-masted schooner. Now she would be returning to Charleston on a coastwise steamer, one of Jason's own.

"More efficient and faster, of course," he said. "But without the matchless beauty of a sailing ship."

They were standing together in the downstairs hallway. Upstairs in the nursery, Miss Wilmot would be feeding Stuart his breakfast, and Fantine would be packing the last of the hand luggage to be carried on board the steamer.

"Do you remember the *Enchantress,* Denise?"

"I remember."

"That first evening out of Charleston, you stood on deck, with that white dress billowing out around you, clutching that foolish little hat with the ribbons."

"I didn't think you remembered."

"I haven't forgotten anything about that particular night. And neither have you."

She looked away, but he turned her to face him.

"You haven't forgotten," he said.

When she remained silent, he pulled her against him, and his mouth covered hers. His arms went around her, she felt the hard muscles of his body, and a treacherous rush of feeling overpowered her, taking her back, away from Mooncliff to the cabin of the *Enchantress.* Once again she felt that strange blending of fear and desire that had possessed her on her wedding night.

Her lips parted, and the kiss deepened. Her body, which had been stiff and unyielding, now molded itself to his. Her arms encircled him, and her hands moved with a will of their own.

His tongue explored her mouth, and she moaned softly.

His lips moved to her throat, and then to the taffeta that covered her breasts.

When they drew apart, she saw the naked desire in his eyes.

"Come with me, Jason. Right now. Your business can wait. The ships can wait. Come to Charleston with me today."

His voice was unsteady. "When you look at me that way, I could almost—" He shook his head. "I'm sorry, love. You know I can't leave today. And a few weeks won't matter."

She felt a surge of frustration. She told herself she was disappointed only because, if she went to the wedding alone, there would be the inevitable gossip, the speculation. But there was something more troubling her. A nameless foreboding brushed her consciousness like the touch of a dark wing.

"They *will* matter! Please, Jason."

"Surely it will not be so great a hardship for you to sleep alone for a few weeks."

"I didn't mean—"

His mouth went down at the corner. "I'd have thought you'd welcome my absence from your bed."

"I should have known you wouldn't understand. You'll never change."

"Neither will you." He took hold of her and shook her. "Damn it, if you want me, say so! Say it, Denise. Tell me you want me to go with you now, not because you're afraid of gossip if you appear at the wedding alone. Not for any stupid conventional reason. But because you need me. Like this—"

He kissed her again, holding her so tightly that the pearl buttons on her blue silk bodice cut into her breasts. When he took his mouth away, she felt weak and dizzy.

"Say it. Tell me you want me."

He would go with her, then. She'd won. A smile of triumph curved her lips. But before she could speak, he was lifting her in his arms.

"No—we haven't time now. The boat for Charleston—"

"To hell with the boat. Right now, I'm taking you

upstairs. I'm going to tear this damn dress off you and—"

Cold fury ripped through her, blotting out everything else.

"And then you'll rape me, so that I can breed another son for the Moreland dynasty—"

He set her down so suddenly that she had to clutch at the newel-post to keep from falling. Abruptly he turned away, but not before she had seen his face.

"Jason—I didn't mean—I—"

The muscles of his heavy shoulders stood out against the cambric shirt he wore. His hands, balled into fists, were jammed into his pockets. When he turned to face her again, his blue eyes were frosty.

"I'd better go out to the stables to see if they've finished loading your luggage."

She reached out her hand, then drew it back.

"Jason—"

"Yes—"

"You're still going to come to Charleston when you've finished your business here?"

"Why not? I have extensive investments in Charleston. Since it seems I'm supporting the whole Chevillon family, I may as well make sure my money's being spent wisely."

Chapter 13

All that afternoon the guests had been setting out from Charleston for Riverview, where Lucille Chevillon's wedding was to be held. Those who still owned their own carriages had offered rides to friends who were less prosperous. The two Chevillon carriages and the phaeton were filled with relatives.

Now, in the master bedroom of the townhouse, Mama was saying, "Denise, my love, I don't know how we're going to manage."

"There's the barge, Mama," Lucille pointed out. "I'm sure Gilbert Laussat will be happy to escort Denise." She turned to her sister. "You remember Mr. Laussat—Louis's friend. They enlisted at about the same time." Lucille looked at Mama's face and broke off abruptly.

"Of course I remember him," Denise said. "What has he been doing lately?"

"Didn't I write you? No, I guess not. He's managing the lumber mills for Papa."

Denise sighed as she remembered the tall, slender young man in his gold-braided gray uniform, with his sword at his side. Gilbert Laussat. Once his family had owned one of the richest stretches of rice land in the Carolina Low Country and had had hundreds of slaves to work the acreage. Gilbert had been trained to ride, to hunt, to drink like a gentleman. One day he was to have inherited the vast Laussat holdings, the great house, the fertile acres. Now he was managing Papa's mills, work that before the War would have been relegated to a transplanted New Englander or an Irish immigrant.

But if Gilbert Laussat had suffered a change in fortune, Denise would not have been able to guess it from his appearance on that September afternoon. He stood waiting for her at the foot of the wide staircase. His face was leaner and harder than she remembered, and there was something almost wary in the gray eyes. But he was as handsome as ever, she decided, with his blond hair and his long, graceful body.

He looked up, hearing the rustle of her taffeta skirt.

"Miss Chevillon—forgive me—Mrs. Moreland."

She was wearing one of the new dresses she had had made especially for her trip South. The bodice was of heavy cream-colored silk and was fitted close to her figure; the underskirt was full and made of the same material. There was an overskirt of deep yellow and brown striped taffeta, caught back with brown velvet ribbons to form a bustle in back. Her hair was gathered in a smooth chignon, and a tiny yellow straw chip hat with brown velvet ribbons sat saucily over one eye. Seeing the look of open admiration on Gilbert's face, she was pleased by her choice of costume; she found herself blushing under the scrutiny of this man who had last seen her when she was only thirteen.

"You were a pretty child when I saw you at Riverview," he was saying. "You have become a beautiful woman."

The flattery was conventional, but there was an intensity in his voice and his expression that made her slightly uneasy, even while it pleased her. He smiled and took her arm.

"We'll have to ride in a hired hack down to the river,"

he said, "But the barge is waiting there. A slow trip but a pleasant one, I hope."

The trip upriver was more than pleasant. For Denise, on that September afternoon, it was a voyage into an enchanted half-forgotten dream out of her girlhood.

Before the War, the Chevillons had often traveled to Riverview in one of their own barges, rowed by strong slaves, all wearing the traditional white straw hats, red flannel jackets and wide-bottomed cotton trousers. There were freed blacks manning the oars now, but nothing else had changed. Denise leaned back against the cushioned seat. After the white glare of the Charleston streets, the river, with its deep shadows cast by the great oaks that lined the banks, was a welcome change. When twilight fell and the shadows lengthened, one of the boatmen lit a torch at the bow.

By its flickering light, Denise studied Gilbert's face: the high-bridged aquiline nose, the thin-lipped mouth, the somber, brooding gray eyes.

"You're very quiet," she said. "What are you thinking about?"

"I was remembering the last ball I attended at Riverview, before Louis and I went off to join our regiment. You weren't allowed to dance, of course—you were too young. But I saw you sitting on the stairs. You wore your hair loose, falling over your shoulders. Your eyes looked golden, like a cat's, by candlelight."

"There were so many candles." In spite of herself, she was drawn back into the past, to share his memories. "The big chandelier in the ballroom was polished, and there were flowers. And all those girls in their beautiful new gowns. How I wished I could hurry and grow older and dance in a gown with yards and yards of silk and lace. . . ."

Gilbert put his hand over hers. "Would you, perhaps, have danced with me?"

She drew her hand away. The intensity in his eyes disturbed her. "Of course," she said, trying to make light of his question. "I'd have saved every space on my dance card just for you."

"You're laughing at me." He shrugged. "And why not? Our situations have changed. I work for your father and you— Oh, yes, even down here we hear of your husband's exploits, his great fortune. And the splendid house—the castle he has built for you."

"Mooncliff," she said.

"Are you chilly?" Gilbert picked up her shawl and put it around her shoulders. "You're shivering. One feels the dampness here in the marshes after nightfall."

Although the touch of his hands was light and fleeting, she was stirred with a sudden awareness of him and of their isolation from the rest of the world. The river mist rose around the barge, shutting out the memories that had come to mind when she had said the name "Mooncliff."

She relaxed and listened to the steady stroke of the oars and the small sounds from the marshes: the cries of the quail and the snipe, the wail of the plover as it brushed the boat canopy with one wing. A possum scrambled through the reeds.

"Do you still go hunting?" she asked.

"Rarely. My job doesn't give me much time for such pleasant diversions. Don't misunderstand," he added quickly. "You father is a most agreeable employer. But the mills are thriving and— Why, what's wrong, Denise?"

"It should all have been so different for you, and for me."

"I know," he said softly. "Except for the War, you would have remained here in Charleston. Both of us would have lived out the lives we were meant for. You would have been mistress of a house like Riverview, and I—" He broke off. "Enough of such talk. Tell me about Mooncliff. It must be a fine house."

"It's very large and impressive. But it's frightening, too. In winter, when the snow shuts off the roads, and the wind goes on and on— The wind is never silent. It drives the rain and the snow against the windows, until I— Please, don't let's talk about it. Tell me about Riverview. The crops are thriving, Mama says, and you tell me the lumber mills are doing well. But who does the work? The freed blacks, or—"

"We tried that at first, but the wages cut down on profits. We use convict labor now, leased from the state."

"You oversee convicts? Isn't that—dangerous?"

"It can be. I carry a knife, and there is a shotgun in my office. I haven't had to use either yet. And the mills are making money. We're able to ship the lumber and turpentine to the North, of course, on your husband's freighters."

"And you live in Charleston?"

"Sometimes. When I'm out at Riverview, I live in the overseer's house."

"Oh, Gilbert, but surely—"

"I prefer it. I am, after all, an employee, not a guest—even though your father was kind enough to invite me to your sister's wedding." He spoke lightly, but the brooding look was still there.

"Your sister—will she be at the wedding too?"

"I'm afraid not. Janine is in Boston, teaching French at a girls' school."

Frivolous Janine, with her blond curls and soft, easy laugh. Janine who had worn a new dress for every ball and had ridden a white Arabian mare at the hunts. Denise found that she was crying. She fumbled for her handkerchief.

"What's wrong? Surely you're not crying because of Janine?"

But she was crying for Janine, alone among strangers in the North; for Gilbert, who had gone off to war with Louis and had returned to find his world in ruins. For Louis, too, lying buried in a far-off grave outside the site of the prison camp where he had lived out the last terrible months of his life. And for Madelaine, the sister she had loved. . . .

"It could have been so different, if only—" She let herself give way to the luxury of tears, and then somehow she was in Gilbert's arms, her face pressed against his shoulder.

"I know," he said softly. "And I think I know why you married Jason Moreland. Not that I blame you; we all do what we must, to survive." He put a hand under her chin and tilted her face upward. In a moment he would kiss her.

"No—"

"Why not? You don't love your husband. You can't love a man like that. A man without family, without breeding, an ex–slave trader—"

"You've no right— How can anyone know how I feel about my husband?"

"He's not here with you."

"His business is keeping him in New York."

"And are you sorry? Would you rather he were here with you now?"

Denise could find no answer. Did she still love Jason? Was love possible after all that had happened between them? Her thoughts went back to that day when she had packed a bag and prepared to leave Mooncliff. Only Elspeth Buchanan's accident had kept her there. Then later she had discovered that she was carrying Jason's child. . . .

"You haven't answered me, Denise."

"I can't. I'm not sure."

"That isn't the answer I'd hoped for, but I can wait. And in the meantime . . ."

Then he kissed her on the cheek, a gentle kiss, without urgency or passion. She drew away but remained with her head resting against his arm until, a few minutes later, the barge rounded a curve in the stream and she saw Riverview, gleaming white through the trees.

She straightened up, smoothed her skirts and tucked a few strands of hair under her hat. The barge glided on to the landing, where torches burned to welcome the arriving guests.

Lucille Chevillon's wedding to Charles Wingate was a lavish affair; although he was of English rather that French descent and had not been born and bred in the Carolina Low Country, his background was acceptable. He'd been a major in the Confederate Army; his family's plantation had been part of a land grant dating back to Charles II. Yes, the Chevillon relatives and friends agreed that Lucille had made a good match, indeed.

Denise knew that those same relatives and friends were gossiping about the fact that she had arrived at Riverview without her husband. They had politely accepted her explanation that Jason's business was keeping him in New York but that he would join her at Riverview in a few weeks. They exclaimed over Stuart, and complimented Denise on her elegant ball gown, a dazzling creation of shimmering green satin lavishly trimmed with Alençon lace.

Denise suspected that behind her back those same people were saying that the wedding gift she and Jason had given the newly married pair was far too lavish, even vulgar. Privately Denise would have agreed, but Jason had insisted on the massively engraved solid silver dinner service for twenty.

"Jay Gould ordered one exactly like it," he had said.

There were so many things Jason could never understand about Charleston, about her family, and about her. Now, at the first notes of the waltz, she forgot Jason for the moment. When Gilbert Laussat asked her to dance, she rose and went into his arms.

"I've been waiting for this dance, ever since that night I saw you sitting up there on the landing, with your hair down around your face and your eyes like saucers."

Denise turned away. "Doesn't Lucille look pretty?"

"She's charming," he agreed. She felt the pressure of his fingers at her waist through the layers of satin and whalebone. She found herself remembering the way he'd held her last night on the river, the kiss he had given her.

"I'm a married woman," she told herself firmly. "I have a child sleeping upstairs."

But tonight she felt young and carefree. This dance, this evening had been owed to her all these years. During the War her world had been a grim, anxious one; then, during the last year of it, when Riverview had been occupied by the invading army . . .

She pushed the unwelcome memories to the back of her mind. Now at last the candles burned again at Riverview; the new imported chandeliers sparkled with rainbow colors; the ballroom floor was polished and waxed to a rich, brilliant sheen.

Some of the guests were a little less elegant than their surroundings, of course; few of the women had been able to afford new dresses. But with the help of seamstresses, old silks had been trimmed with new lace; satin gowns, taken from their wrappings, had been gored, and panniers had been added to follow the new fashions. In the soft glow of the candlelight, Denise let herself pretend that the old days had returned.

She even allowed herself to imagine that she was a young girl again and that the tall young man who held her was her beau. She tilted her head back and smiled up at him. The tempo of the waltz quickened, and she surrendered to its insistent rhythm.

A week had passed since Lucille's wedding; she and her husband had departed for New Orleans for their honeymoon. Mama and the wedding guests had returned to Charleston, but Papa was at Riverview, busy running the plantation, and Denise had remained there also.

She did not mind Papa's preoccupation with the harvest; growing rice was a complicated business, requiring constant supervision and a sound knowledge of hydraulics. During the first stages the rice crop was submerged in water drawn from ponds and streams and regulated by a complex arrangement of locks and dams. This year Riverview had produced the largest crop since the beginning of the War, and Papa spent much of his time supervising the harvest.

Denise gloried in the long, warm days spent watching the plantation return to life. It was as if something inside her were returning to life, too. She went for long walks, leaving Stuart in Miss Wilmot's care. She lay on the riverbank, staring up through the oaks at the sky, or watching the muddy yellow river.

The stables at Riverview had been restocked, and one afternoon Denise picked out a russet mare and went for a ride. The sky was overcast, and it looked as if it might rain by evening, but she decided there was plenty of time for a canter along the River Road.

The air was heavy and sultry, but even when she heard the distant rumblings of thunder, she was reluctant to turn back. The first few heavy drops soaked her riding habit, and then came the downpour. It was a long way back to the house, for she had ridden farther than she had realized.

She was about to turn the mare in the direction of the house when she saw a gleam of white through the trees: the overseer's cottage. She could take shelter there. These rainstorms often lasted no more than an hour.

As she rode nearer, she saw that the cottage had been freshly painted; there was a trim, well-kept look about it. The door swung open at her touch, and she looked about in surprise. She was sure that those paintings on the walls and the old but still beautiful carpet had not been there during the days when the Irish overseer had lived in the house. Then the inner door swung open, and Gilbert stood looking at her. His blond hair was plastered to his forehead, and his white shirt and dark gray trousers were soaking wet.

She looked away, but not before she saw the lines of his long, lean body, clearly visible under the rain-drenched clothes. She backed toward the outside door, but Gilbert said, "No, don't go."

"I must. I—"

"Get out of those wet things, and I'll light a fire."

He disappeared into the bedroom and returned with a dressing gown. "Put this on," he said.

He turned his back to her and knelt down to get the fire started. Although he wasn't looking at her, she felt oddly self-conscious as she stripped off the wet riding habit and put on the dressing gown. It smelled faintly of bay rum and good tobacco.

He gave her ample time to change, directing his attention to the lighting of the fire, until she crossed the room and asked, "Where can I dry this?"

He rose and laid the riding habit carefully over a straight-backed chair. He pulled a rattan settee over to the fire.

"Sit down, and I'll get you a glass of wine. You mustn't get chilled."

He poured a glass of sherry for her and another for himself and came to sit beside her on the settee.

"Tell me, what made you stay here after your mother went back to Charleston? I'm sure you have many friends in the city you've been wanting to visit."

"I don't think my friends approve of me any longer. After all, I married an outsider, a Yankee and—"

"An ex–slave trader. Yes, I know. Is that all?"

"At the wedding I had the feeling that perhaps they resented me because—well, you saw the gift Jason sent. It might have seemed to them that I was flaunting my money, that—"

"And those are your only reasons for remaining here alone?"

"I don't know what you mean."

"Yes, you do."

She could not meet his eyes. She tried to rise, but he held her. Then he was bending her back, kissing her. A soft, quivering sensation spread through her body as she lay across his arm. She felt his tongue between her parted lips.

The small room was quiet, except for the crackling of the logs in the fireplace and the soft, steady beating of the rain against the windows. They were together in an enchanted world of soft silvery rain that brought the rich scent of grass and oak and cypress and the heavy, disturbing odors from the marshes along the river.

He pushed the dressing gown away from her shoulders, and his tongue explored the soft, rounded curves. She was aware of a strange division between her mind and her body. While a part of her stood off, cold and disapproving, the flesh was not to be denied. The dressing gown came open as his hands dealt skillfully with buttons and fastenings.

He caught his breath, and she felt the need in him growing, stirring. "Beautiful," he said softly. "Beautiful. . . ."

Then he released her, stood up and, without taking his eyes from her, removed his clothes. She did not close her eyes, nor did she look away. Even before they stretched ou together on the carpet in front of the fire, she saw that he was ready to possess her. For a moment, she felt afraid. Her body went cold and rigid.

He put his arm beneath her head and kissed her very gently.

"We have the whole afternoon, love," he said. "I can wait until you're—"

He did not finish, but moved his head down and kissed her breasts until the fear she had felt ebbed away, until her nipples grew hard and erect between his lips, until she pulled him against her, her hips moving slowly at first, then faster, in the ancient rhythm of desire.

The rain had stopped, and the evening air was fragrant with the perfume of the tea olive and the banana shrubs that grew around the cottage. Denise lay in front of the fireplace with Gilbert beside her. He reached out, lifted a strand of her long hair, and looked at it.

"I should like to paint you this way. With the firelight on your hair, and your skin like pale gold."

"Do you paint?"

He smiled sadly. "Once I did, a little. Not anymore, of course. I have no time now." He shrugged. "But I am doing my part to restore Riverview. Do you know that this year's rice crop will bring more money than any that your father raised before the War? And as for the lumber mills—"

"Don't," she said. "You sound like—" She looked away. "You don't care about crops and lumber, not really. Besides, it isn't as if Riverview were yours."

"You're right, of course. Belle Fontaine, like your Riverview, was destroyed. But, unlike the Chevillons, we were not able to rebuild the house, and the land is going back to the swamps now."

His tone was matter-of-fact, but she felt her throat tighten with pity. "You have no home at all, then."

He shook his head. "That's not quite true. My family owns land on the island of Martinique. The slaves there were freed back in 1848, but the house still stands. I've sometimes thought of going to live there. I think such a life might suit me better than this."

"The South is your home. I think you would feel like an exile anywhere else."

"I feel like one here, since the end of the War. The

South we knew doesn't exist any longer. You know what has been happening here. Scalawags—poor white `trash —running our state. The very men who refused to fight for the South, now being rewarded by the Yankees. And carpetbaggers swarming in on us from the North, gangs of unprincipled adventurers. No, Denise, I have no place here in the new South. At least in Martinique— Come with me."

He drew her to him, and the touch of his body sent a wave of desire spreading through her. "Come with me and live in my house. I'll paint you, just as you are now, with your hair like living flame in the firelight. Or perhaps in a rain forest, with a waterfall behind you, and your arms filled with flowers."

Denise smiled. "And what would you do there? Besides paint, I mean?"

"I would make love to you. And we would swim in the sea, then lie on the beach together, and I would . . ."

He bent his head, and his lips touched the swell of her breast. She moved closer and shut her eyes. Her lips moved downward.

"No, Gilbert. No more, please. I'm expected for dinner, and it's late."

"You don't have to leave, Denise. Not yet—not yet. . . ."

Chapter 14

Jason Moreland had returned to Mooncliff very late that November evening, to find the house silent and chilly. He had told the staff not to wait up for him, but now, as he shrugged out of his heavy coat, shaking off the first snowflakes of the season, he found himself feeling depressed by the silence.

He went down the hall to the library. He would have a brandy, then go upstairs to bed. It had been a long and trying day.

When he reached the library, he saw that the gas jets were brightly lit, and there was a fire on the hearth. Elspeth rose to greet him.

"Good evening, Mr. Moreland, I've—"

"What are you doing still awake at this hour? I gave orders that no one was to wait up."

"I thought perhaps you might want something to eat—and hot coffee, too. It's here, all ready for you."

She reached for the coat he carried over his arm. "Give me that. I'll brush it and hang it up to dry."

"You'll do no such thing. You've been up since six this

morning. I've told you, with all the other servants we have here now, there's no need for you to work yourself into a state of exhaustion." His voice was harsh; then seeing the troubled look in Elspeth's eyes, he smiled. "It was kind of you to wait up this way," he said. "And I could do with something to eat."

"There's a letter from Mrs. Moreland," she said, holding out the envelope. "I thought perhaps you might miss it if I left it on your desk."

He tore open the envelope. "It's about time. I've been hoping I'd be able to get down there to join her, but this new shipping line has been more trouble than I'd expected."

He did not add that the shipping line was only one of the business affairs keeping him in New York. He was also involved in the battle for the Erie Railroad, a war of titans, with Jay Gould and Jim Fisk on one side and Commodore Vanderbilt on the other, a conflict that during the past few years had frequently erupted into open violence. There were even now rumors that Gould, a puritan in his personal life, was going to drop Fisk from the board of the Erie. Fisk, who had been betrayed by his beautiful dark-haired mistress, Josie Mansfield, was about to be taken to court by that lady and her new lover, and the scandal promised to be a juicy one. The New York newspapers had implied that in the course of the trial the crimes of Fisk, Gould and their confederates in connection with the Erie Railroad and the infamous Tammany Ring would be thoroughly aired.

Of course, such matters were not to be discussed with Elspeth. But Jason, whose business affairs were linked with those of Gould and Fisk, had no wish to leave the city during these hectic times.

He seated himself in a chair and read Denise's letter while Elspeth stood beside him, pouring the coffee. His mouth tightened into a hard, thin line.

"She wants to stay at Riverview through November," Jason said. "Her sister and brother-in-law will be returning from New Orleans, and there is to be a ball in their honor next week."

"Couldn't you go down there to join her?" Elspeth asked.

He took a sip of the strong black brew. "It wouldn't be practical, with all hell ready to break loose here in New York over this Erie business and the first ship in my Far East line scheduled to sail in February. There's the matter of harbor rights, too—" He put down his cup. "I'm sorry," he said. "You've enough to do without listening to my business problems. Although I must admit that you have an unusual grasp of such matters. For a woman."

She did not take offense at his last words, for she knew that he liked and respected her. But she could not resist saying, "Perhaps, given the right opportunities, I could become another Victoria Woodhull. Or Tennessee Claflin."

"Heaven forbid. Intelligence in a woman is desirable, but those two—"

Victoria Woodhull and her sister, Tennessee Claflin, had been scandalizing New York City since early in 1870, when they had rented a suite of offices on Broad Street and gone into business as "lady stockbrokers." Having first ingratiated themselves with Commodore Vanderbilt, they had received stock tips that enabled them to make more than half a million dollars on the market. They had also launched *Woodhull and Claflin's Weekly*, with headlines that screamed: "Progress! Free Thought! Untrammeled Lives!"

"How can you compare yourself to those trollops? Why, you've never even—"

"You're quite right, Mr. Moreland. I've never loved a man."

Jason looked at her in the soft light of the gas lamps. She wasn't beautiful like Denise. But she was oddly attractive, with her wide-set gray-blue eyes, her high cheekbones and pointed chin. There was character in that face, and strength. His eyes moved over her slender figure, too thin by the popular standards of the day, but trim and graceful.

Perhaps it was her utter lack of coquetry, the direct way she had of looking at a man or speaking to him, that had kept prospective suitors away from her.

"The man who wins your love will be fortunate indeed," he said. "Perhaps one day— But right now, I think this talk has gone far enough. Besides, you must be tired."

"I am," she said. "But, Mr. Moreland—"

"Yes?"

"Perhaps you should go down to South Carolina, if only for a few days. Surely Stuart misses you, and Mrs. Moreland—" She broke off and, after saying good night, left the library.

Jason wondered exactly how much she knew of his relationship with his wife. Could she have overheard the bitter exchange with Denise during their last hour together in this house?

Perhaps Denise was waiting for him to come down and bring her back. She had her pride. Maybe she was hoping he would make the first move toward reconciliation.

Why not go down to Riverview? He had missed her sister's wedding; at least he could be there for the ball that was to be held for her homecoming. If he applied pressure in the right quarters and settled the business of the new shipping line, it might be possible for him to get away.

And it would be a practical move, too, for he wanted to look Riverview over and see what progress had been made in its rebuilding. Three thousand acres of rich Low Country land was a solid investment. He might make other such investments while he was down there. A number of northern businessmen had told him of the money to be made in iron and in textile mills.

He slammed down his coffee cup. Why the devil should he go on lying to himself? He wanted to see Denise, to be near her. He wanted to hold her in his arms, to feel her body, warm and pliant, against him.

During the months of her absence, he had tried to lose himself in his work, but he had not entirely succeeded. One evening when he was more lonely and restless than usual, he had gone to Josephine Woods's parlor house on Clinton Place, an elegant establishment, to which, after he had been carefully inspected through a grille in the door, he had been admitted by a butler. He had waited in a parlor as elegant as any to be found in the mansions along Fifth Avenue, furnished with chairs of satin and brocade, Oriental rugs, crystal chandeliers and gilt-framed mirrors. The girls who had been paraded through the room for his inspection had been beautiful. And expensive. A far cry, he had thought, from the sailors' whorehouses in Liverpool and San Francisco, the shabby warrens on Greene Street here in New York, where gas lamps blazed in bowls of red-tinted glass.

But after a night with the statuesque brunette he had chosen, he was left with the familiar sense of depression. She had been skilled in her trade and had given a convincing imitation of a woman in the throes of passion. But although she had left Jason physically satisfied, something had been lacking.

Whether Denise had felt love for him or anger, she had responded to him as an individual. She might be ardent and yielding or cold and angry with him, but she was his. She belonged to him, and he needed her.

Now, sitting in the library and staring at the dying fire, he made his decision. He would go down to Charleston and bring her home. He would not even bother to send a letter. He would leave New York in a few days and arrive in time for Lucille's homecoming party.

The ball that had been planned to welcome the newlyweds back to Riverview was not so large as the one that had marked their wedding, but the stately house was crowded nonetheless, and more guests were arriving every moment. Torches blazed on the landing to greet those who were traveling by barge. Along the drive leading to the house, carriages moved in a slow procession, stopping to discharge their passengers.

Behind the house a feast had been set for the workers who had toiled to bring in a record harvest. Long trestle tables under the trees were laden with platters of ham, turkey, vegetables, biscuits and corn bread. Coachmen and bargemen had been invited to join the festivities.

Riverview had prospered, thanks to Jason's money; seeing the change, Denise felt a bittersweet satisfaction. She knew that for every Riverview rebuilt with money from the North there were a dozen Belle Fontaines falling into ruins. Gilbert had told her of the ruin of the Laussat plantation: the house, barns and fences burned; the cattle driven off; the fields returning to the surrounding marshland because there was no money to hire freedmen to keep the acres under cultivation.

Without Jason's money, Denise realized, she too would probably be up North, like Gilbert's sister, teaching in a boarding school or working as a governess for some wealthy family in New York or Boston. Jason's money had paid for everything, even the dress she was wearing tonight for Lucille's homecoming ball. It was a pale lilac creation, trimmed with ecru lace and purple velvet bows, and a glance in the mirror assured her that it was most becoming.

"Will Madame wear the amethyst earrings? Or perhaps the pearls?" Fantine was asking.

"I—I'm not sure. The pearls will do."

Ever since Lucille and Charles had returned to Riverview a week before, Denise had been nervous. With guests crowding into the house, it would be more difficult for her to seek out Gilbert. Indeed, she had not gone to his cottage since her sister and brother-in-law had come back from their honeymoon. She had tried to tell herself that she was only being discreet, but now, tonight, she was facing the truth. She would have to stop seeing Gilbert. But it would not be easy to give him up.

He was a wonderful lover, gentle and adoring, and in some ways she felt closer to him than she ever had to her husband. With Jason there was always that terrible, driving ambition. He was not satisfied with his business success, and she knew that he never would be; there would always be the need for more. A new shipping line to the Far East. More railroad stock. A mine in Colorado. Blocks of valuable real estate in New York City.

In his business dealings, Jason was completely ruthless. That did not surprise her as she remembered how his fortune had been founded, what he had done when he had been captain of the *Nubian Queen*. No matter how he tried to justify his actions, she knew that there could be no justification for cold-blooded murder. He had been equally ruthless in his treatment of her. The night that

Stuart had been conceived, there had been no pretense of love between them. No man who truly loved his wife could have hurt and humiliated her that way.

Yet she knew that she would go back to him. She had no choice. He would never give her a divorce. Jason was not a man to part with a valuable possession.

I am Stuart's mother and the mistress of Mooncliff, Denise thought, Jason won't give me up to anyone. And even if he would, what kind of life could I have with Gilbert? Life can't be all lovemaking and nothing more. There must be order, stability, a home in which to bring up children. Gilbert talks of taking me to Martinique, but that is only a dream. I have been brought up in a certain way; I live a certain kind of life. Mooncliff is a great house, and I have been trained to be mistress of such a house.

Maybe if I really loved Gilbert enough, it wouldn't matter. I'd follow him to that ruined plantation in Martinique, and I'd live in a shack on the grounds or a hut on the beach. I'd cook for him and wash his clothes.

"Madame, if you will hold your head still one moment more, I can complete your coiffure. These little ringlets—"

Denise realized that she had unconsciously shaken her head, interrupting the maid's careful work. "Never mind," she said. "Please stop fussing and leave me alone."

"As you wish, Madame." Fantine's lips curved in a knowing little smile. She put down the comb, curtseyed and left the room.

How much does she know? Denise wondered. My God, can she possibly know about Gilbert and me? And if she does, will she dare to use what she knows to hurt me?

Denise knew that Fantine had resented seeing Elspeth Buchanan installed as housekeeper at Mooncliff. An inexperienced girl put in charge of the house and given a staff of servants to direct. Fantine herself had had her eye on the position, and she had voiced her disappointment openly, until Denise had told her to accept Elspeth or to leave Mooncliff.

A knock at the bedroom door interrupted her troubled thoughts.

"Fantine, I thought I told you—"

"Forgive me, Madame. Mr. Laussat gave me this note to give to you. He said it was important."

Denise snatched the note from the maid's hand. It had been reckless of Gilbert to send her a note this way. But Gilbert was reckless and impulsive.

> Denise, my darling,
> I have not seen you alone this week. Meet me at the river, by the landing, after the ball has begun. You must come.

She crumpled the note in her hand. She would ignore it, pretend she had not received it. But if she did that, Gilbert might come storming into the ballroom to find her.

It would be better to meet him, to tell him that their affair would have to end. Even now it had gone on too long. If Fantine had read the note—

Looking directly at the maid, Denise tore the paper into tiny shreds and tossed them into the flames of the fireplace. Then she turned and took a look at herself in the mirror. The pale lilac skirt of her gown floated around her like a cloud at twilight. She touched her hand to her hair. In spite of Fantine's misgivings, the coiffure was perfect; her hair was piled high on her head, with tiny ringlets brushing her cheeks. She lifted her head so that the pearl earrings glowed in the candlelight like tiny twin moons, and walked slowly from the room and down the hall, careful not to betray her inner turmoil. She must be in the receiving line, but later, when the dancing had begun, she would slip away to meet Gilbert.

Why the boat landing? she wondered. Why not his cottage or the grove of pecan trees at the edge of the woods?

The music from the ballroom lingered in the air. The dancing was in full swing when Denise crossed the veranda and hurried down the path through the back garden. Heard at a distance, the waltz had a melancholy sound. The night was cool. A full moon touched the withered grass and leafless shrubbery with silver. Even here in the Carolinas there was a feeling of approaching winter.

Denise quickened her step; her enchanted autumn was over now, and a nameless fear touched her as she hurried through the night.

Jason Moreland paced up and down the deck of the *Buccaneer,* the sleek steam yacht that had carried him down the coast to Charleston. He had planned to arrive at Riverview a day or two before the ball, but business had delayed him longer than he had anticipated. No matter. Denise would be mollified when he appeared at the ball, and surely the yacht would please her.

Vanderbilt had bought a yacht, and so had Jay Gould. The *Buccaneer* had been a decided bargain, too, built in Jason's own shipyard and furnished in the elaborate style of the 1870s. The yacht had been ordered by a copper king from the West who had planned to crash Newport society. But the copper king had done some unwise speculating on the stock exchange and had returned to Arizona to recoup his fortunes. Jason had decided to take the yacht for himself.

He and Denise would return to Mooncliff aboard the yacht. Their cabin had been furnished with Turkish rugs, gilt-framed mirrors and a magnificent carved mahogany bed. Jason thought of the nights with Denise, of her body, pale golden against the white silk sheets. . . .

He walked to the rail, looked across the water, and watched the first faint outlines of Charleston take shape in the distance. Then he turned and went below to change his clothes. He would take a hired hack directly to Riverview.

"If she's not down there in the ballroom, where the devil is she?" Jason demanded.

Fantine looked away. "I'm not sure, sir. She—I believe Madame has gone down to the river landing."

"Why would she do that? Did she tell you she was going?"

"Oh, no, sir, but—"

Fantine broke off, realizing that she was about to trap herself. It would not do to admit to Mr. Moreland that she had read the note from Mr. Laussat before she delivered it.

"I was watching from the window. I saw Madame going in that direction."

Jason turned on his heel, hurried down the wide steps to the hall, and left the house.

When Denise reached the landing she looked around for Gilbert. Not seeing him at once, she called his name. He stepped out from the shadows of the live oaks and caught her in his arms, crushing her against him.

"My darling, it has been so long—"

"Only a week," she said. "With Lucille and Charles here, and all the guests, I could hardly get away."

His lips brushed her hair, her throat. "That's the only reason, Denise? You're sure? I was afraid—I thought—so many foolish things—"

She tried to draw away, but his arms held her. The billowing skirt of the lilac dress was pressed against her body.

"You should not have given that note to Fantine. She may have read it."

"What does it matter?" He laughed softly; there was a strange, feverish look in his gray eyes. "Forget Fantine. Forget all of them up there at the house. After tonight, it won't matter what they think. They'll know. And we won't care, will we, darling?"

"You're not making sense."

He took her wrist. "Come with me," he said. He led her down to the edge of the landing. Her full skirts trailed in the mud.

"Gilbert, be careful. When I go back to the ballroom—"

"You're not going back." His voice was soft and tender, but she caught an undertone of excitement.

"Look there," he said.

In the light from the torches that blazed on the landing she saw the outlines of a small, graceful skiff.

"Whose is it?"

"Ours. Denise, you're coming with me. First downriver

to Charleston, and from there to Martinique. I've booked our passage on a ship. It leaves at dawn."

He wasn't serious. He couldn't be. How could he imagine she would walk out of the ballroom at Riverview and disappear with him into the night? That she would turn her back on her son and her husband to run off like the heroine of an old ballad.

"Gilbert, I—I don't know what you thought, but surely you must see—"

"I see that you are beautiful, and that I love you. We must be together, always. Come with me, Denise. Now."

"I can't."

"You can. You must. Denise, you're not like other women. You don't make a game of love. Those hours together at the cottage, you gave yourself to me completely. There was a hunger in you, a passion I've never found in any woman—"

"Yes, but that kind of love—the kind you're talking about—we can't live on that for the rest of our lives. I have responsibilities. Commitments."

"To your parents? They sold you when you were too young to know the meaning of marriage."

"I know, but—"

"You owe your parents nothing."

"There's Jason. He'll never divorce me. You don't know what he's like."

"I can guess. Cruel, ruthless, possessive—"

"He's all those things, yes. But he—I—"

How could she ever make Gilbert understand her feelings about Jason? Cruel, ruthless, possessive—he was all those things, and worse. Ordering helpless slaves to their death to save his fortune. Taking her by force the night she had refused him. Using her to fulfill his ambition to found his own dynasty.

But there was another Jason Moreland. A man who had been gentle and understanding with her on their wedding night, who worshipped his young son, who had given a home and a position of authority to Elspeth Buchanan.

Gilbert looked at her face in the torchlight. "Surely you can't be in love with your husband." There was an edge to his voice, and with a shock of apprehension

Denise realized that under his polished, well-bred surface there was a streak of violence she had never seen before. He had fought in a long and bloody war; he knew how to hate and how to kill. Even now, he worked a crew of convicts for her father; he kept a loaded gun in the office of the mill and carried a knife. She knew that, like all the men in his family, he was skilled in the use of both weapons.

"You don't love Jason Moreland?" he persisted.

"I don't know. I'm not sure. But even if I left Jason, what about Stuart?"

"His father will take care of him. You've always said Jason adores the boy. There'll be governesses, the best schools. You needn't worry about Stuart."

Denise thought, I deserve this. During these past weeks I've never expressed the slightest concern for my son. I left him with Miss Wilmot. Some days I scarcely thought of him. I was playing at being a young girl again, without a husband or a child, without responsibilities.

"I can't leave Stuart. I love him as much as Jason does."

The words had come, unbidden, but she knew they were true. It no longer mattered how the child had been conceived. He was hers, he was innocent, and he needed her.

"We can have children of our own, Denise," Gilbert was saying. "We'll watch them grow up, barefoot and happy, on the beaches in Martinique. They can live in a world of sunshine and beauty."

She looked at Gilbert as if seeing him for the first time. He was unable to face reality. He could not understand that children needed more than sunshine and tropical beaches, that she herself could never be happy living in open sin with one man while married to another. Her Chevillon pride would not permit it.

She thought of her parents and Lucille, having to face the gossip and the condescension of their friends; of Stuart, growing up with the knowledge that his mother had abandoned him to run off with a lover.

"I can't go with you, Gilbert. Not tonight. Not ever."

"I don't believe you. You're confused, unsure of yourself. Afraid of the unknown. But you'll change your mind once we're away from Charleston. Come now, before they miss you back at the house."

He took her arm and forced her along the landing toward the flight of wooden stairs that led down to the river.

"Gilbert, let go of me!"

"You don't want me to let go. This is what you want!"

His mouth claimed hers, and the arms that held her were hard and unyielding. He was no longer using words alone to persuade her. Instead, his hands caressed her body. When she struggled to free herself she heard a sound of tearing fabric. The bodice of her gown was ripped open to the waist under his impatient fingers. His mouth burned against her bare flesh.

Then he released her with a suddenness that caused her to stagger back and clutch the wooden railing of the pier. He was looking past her, in the direction of the live oaks that edged the path leading to the landing. She followed the direction of his gaze.

"Jason!"

Her husband stepped from the shadow of the trees. He took a step forward, tore off his jacket and flung it away. Then, with the wordless roar of a maddened animal, he ran down to the pier and lunged at Gilbert.

Gilbert pushed Denise out of the way. "Jason—no!" she screamed. In her guilt, she saw him as an avenging apparition. But there was nothing unreal about the force with which Jason struck Gilbert. The blow caught him on the side of the head, and he staggered back. But Gilbert regained his balance, and the two were immediately grappling, panting. Denise heard the sound of fists on flesh and bone. She saw Jason's fist smash into Gilbert's face, saw Gilbert fall to his knees. Jason towered over him, his face bleeding, his lips drawn back from his teeth. Jason raised his arms, and Denise saw that his hands were joined, the fingers interlocked. She remembered that he had learned to fight on the docks of Liverpool and in the harbors along the Ivory Coast. Instinctively he would fight to kill, unless—

"Jason—don't! Stop!"

Jason shook his head like a dazed animal and turned

to look at her. In that moment she saw Gilbert make a swift motion with his hand, and the torchlight caught the gleam of a knife blade.

Gilbert was back on his feet, lunging for Jason, who moved aside, his feet slipping on the wet surface of the wooden pier. The knife thrust was deflected, but the blade had ripped through his shirt and glanced off his ribs, leaving a red streak where the edge had cut through skin and flesh.

Now her fear was all for Jason, and with an incoherent cry she flung herself at Gilbert, throwing her weight against his arm, giving Jason time to back off. Gilbert pushed her away.

Jason's back was to the river, and Gilbert was moving in on him again. The long knife blade glittered in the torchlight. Jason took a step, then another, until Gilbert had backed him to the head of the steps. Then Gilbert crouched, the knife held upward for the final thrust. As he sprang forward, Jason flung up an arm to protect himself and, quick as a cat, stepped to one side.

The weight of the thrust and the slippery surface of the pier threw Gilbert off balance. He grabbed for the rail as he hurtled past Jason. His hand gripped it for an instant, but Jason brought his open palm down in a short, chopping blow that caught Gilbert on the side of the head. The grip loosened. Still clutching the knife, Gilbert rolled over and over, down the stairs to the edge of the landing.

Denise ran to the head of the stairs and stood beside Jason, looking down. Gilbert lay motionless on the landing, face downward.

"Stay where you are," Jason said, but Denise followed him down the steps. Jason bent down and turned Gilbert over. The blade of the knife was buried deep in his chest; only the hilt could be seen, and the scarlet stain that spread across his shirt.

Slowly Jason got to his feet. For a moment they stood in silence. Denise, looking down into the dead white face of her lover, felt a coldness spreading through her. From somewhere along the river she heard the cry of a quail. The night wind rippled the sail of the skiff that was moored close by.

"Denise." Jason's voice was quiet and controlled, but his face was drawn. "Are you all right?" He looked at her torn bodice, and she drew it together with one hand. "Did he hurt you?"

She shook her head. "He didn't—"

"Did you know him?"

"His name is—was Gilbert Laussat. He managed Papa's lumber mills."

It came to Denise that Jason had no suspicion of what had happened. Not yet. He had seen her fighting off a man, and he had come to her defense.

"Listen to me," he was saying. "Do exactly as I tell you. Go back to the house, and go straight up to your room. Don't let anyone see you. Take off that dress and hide it."

"The dress? But why?"

"Look." She looked down and saw that the hem of the lilac gown was stained with blood. Gilbert's blood. She gasped. Jason steadied her. "You can't lose your head. You've got to control yourself."

"When you've changed, call Fantine and tell her you want to talk to your father. No one else. Tell him to come down here alone—and fast. Do you understand?"

"Yes, Jason."

"Then hurry. I'll join you at the house as soon as I can."

Chapter 15

It was dawn when Jason came to her. She had been lying awake, staring at the ceiling. Each time she had closed her eyes she had seen Gilbert's face, his gray eyes open, accusing.

Now Jason closed the door and came to sit beside the bed.

"Are you all right?" he asked.

"All right?"

"You don't have to be afraid. Your father and I have taken care of everything. I was within my rights; your father agreed with that. But he also agreed it would be better to avoid any hint of scandal."

"Scandal?" Jason knew, then, or had guessed, that Gilbert had been her lover. She looked away, fighting down the beginning of panic. But he went on:

"My dear, it was foolish of you to leave the ballroom alone and go strolling down by the river. I suppose the young fool saw you and was carried away. Been drinking, most likely."

Denise pressed her lips together. She should have

known that Jason's limitless self-assurance, his pride and arrogance, would make it impossible for him to think she had betrayed him with another man. She remembered that he had found her struggling with Gilbert, fighting him off. Her dress had been torn. That had been proof enough for Jason that she had been completely innocent.

"But the scandal you spoke of—"

"If the story were made public there would have to be some sort of an investigation. But there won't be. Your father will tell everyone that Laussat was dissatisfied with his job here and that he went out West to try to rebuild the family's fortunes. Many young southerners have been doing just that."

She felt the sickness begin to rise inside her. "But what about— What have you done with—"

"There's no need for you to know."

"Tell me."

Jason shrugged. "We took the body deep into the marshes. Then we stripped it and buried it."

There were living things in the marshes, predatory creatures with claws and teeth. . . .

Denise pushed the blanket away and flung herself out of bed. She made it to the washbasin in the dressing room, and then she was sick, horribly sick.

Later, when the last spasm had passed, Jason carried her back to bed and wrapped the blankets around her. He washed her face and smoothed back her damp hair. "I didn't want to tell you," he reminded her. He took her icy hands in his. "Put it out of your mind. We'll be leaving for home in a few days."

"Home?"

"Mooncliff," he said impatiently. "We'll be returning on the *Buccaneer*. A yacht. I wanted to surprise you. She's magnificent. And our cabin—wait until you see it."

She heard the words, but they had no meaning. She could only think: I will have to go back to Mooncliff. It will be winter when we get there. Snow and cold, and the wind never silent. The gray walls will close around me; they will crush me. . . .

"I can't go back. I won't!"

"Denise, what's wrong with you? Surely you don't blame me for what happened last night?"

"No, Jason."

The guilt was mine, she thought. And I will have to live with it.

"Then what's this talk about not going back to Mooncliff? Of course you're going back."

"I know. I—Jason, please leave me alone for a while. Please."

Jason stood up, his blue eyes hard. "As you wish. But get hold of yourself. Or all my efforts and your father's to prevent a scandal will come to nothing."

During the rest of her stay at Riverview, Denise could not sleep at night, even though Jason left her alone, taking the guest room adjoining hers.

But on their first night aboard the *Buccaneer*, when he had taken her to their sleeping quarters, she knew that she could not put him off any longer.

He stood in the center of the cabin. "How do you like it?" he asked, with obvious pride.

"It's splendid," she answered. Dutifully she looked at the mirrors, the deep red carpet, the tiger-skin rug beside the huge mahogany bed with its brocaded velvet canopy.

"I thought you'd be pleased," he said complacently.

"Yes, I—"

"You're feeling better now, aren't you?"

She nodded. Only that morning, she had had another violent attack of nausea, but Jason had been up on deck, and she had not told him about it. She had forced herself to eat the elaborate dinner he had ordered, had rocked Stuart to sleep before turning him over to Miss Wilmot. Now, although she felt numb and drained of all emotion, she hoped that she could at least pretend a response. She had to try. Perhaps, since she and Jason had been apart for so long, he would be too impatient to sense her lack of feeling.

But as soon as she was in bed beside him, the walls of the cabin began to close in. She lay perfectly still as his hands moved over her body.

She forced herself to turn to him. The cabin was oppressive; she felt that she was suffocating. She closed her eyes and saw again the flaring torches that had burned on the landing back at Riverview. And Gilbert's dead face. She heard again the lost cry of the quail out in the marshes.

We took him out into the marshes and buried him.

Jason's hand cupped her breast. She went rigid and cried out.

"Denise, what is it? Why did you—"

"It's nothing. Don't stop—"

Gilbert's hands, light and caressing on her body.

She jerked away and sat up, her back pressed against the carved headboard. She pressed her fist to her mouth to stifle the scream that rose in her throat.

"For God's sake, what's wrong? What have I done?"

"Nothing," she whispered.

"Are you feeling sick again?"

"No—not the way you mean." She looked away from him. "Jason, would you mind sleeping in the other cabin—"

"I damn well would mind. It's been more than two months since—"

"I know. And I'm sorry. I thought—I was sure I could force myself to—to—"

She put out a hand as if to hold him off. But he got up out of bed and put on his robe. "Don't worry," he said. "I won't force you. Not this time."

His hand doubled into a fist, and he slammed it against the heavy carved bedpost. Then he turned away quickly.

"I thought—I was so sure I could make you want me again. I took care of that business in New York as quickly as I could. I was down at the docks night and day. I came down in time for that damn party because I thought you'd be pleased. I bought this boat for you. I wanted the voyage back to Mooncliff to be like our honeymoon trip—only better."

"Jason, give me a little time. I'll try, truly I will."

"Don't bother. I don't want you to pretend with me. If I wanted that sort of performance I could get it from any girl in Josephine Woods's house. They can be most convincing."

She caught her breath as the implication became clear.

Of course she knew who Josephine Woods was. Everyone in New York recognized the dark-haired, expensively dressed woman who went driving in Central Park in the company of her "girls." Once she would have been furious with Jason over such a tacit admission of infidelity. But now there was no room for anger. Only cold despair.

He leaned over the bed. "I suppose I've shocked you."

"It doesn't matter."

He jammed his fists into the pockets of his robe. "I see. So long as I leave you alone, you don't care if I go to a brothel."

"Oh, no."

"Don't bother to lie."

"I'm not—I—" But she couldn't go on, couldn't say, "It doesn't matter, because I've done worse. I took a lover. And he's dead because of me."

Jason went to the door.

"Wait," she begged.

"For what?" He turned and his face was set in a cold, expressionless mask. "I won't force myself on you again. If you're ever ready to be a real wife, you'll have to come to me."

He slammed out of the cabin, and she heard him moving around in the one adjoining hers. She pulled the blankets around her and lay wide-eyed in the darkness.

The first rays of the sun turned the sky outside the porthole rose and crimson before sheer weariness brought her sleep.

Chapter 16

It was the first week of the new year, 1872. Denise, seated in Doctor Frobisher's office on the north side of Gramercy Park, looked past the doctor and out through the window. She kept her hands pressed together tightly and her eyes fixed on the branch of a tree outside; the sun made the icicles glitter.

"You were quite right, Mrs. Moreland," the doctor was saying. "The baby should arrive sometime in July. My congratulations."

She tried to look pleased, but the fingers of one hand dug into the back of the other. Doctor Frobisher gave her an understanding smile.

"Now, there's no need for you to be afraid, my dear. I'll be out to Mooncliff in plenty of time. Not likely to be a blizzard in July, is there?"

When she still could not find the words to answer him, he said, "Think how pleased Mr. Moreland will be."

Hysterical laughter bubbled up inside her. She pressed one hand against her lips.

"I've seen a great many proud fathers in my time, but

when I saw Mr. Moreland with little Stuart—the way he looked at that infant, the way he held him—yes, indeed, he will be pleased to hear there's another baby on the way. I can't guarantee that this one will be a boy, of course."

Somehow, Denise remained quiet until the doctor finished speaking. She even managed to force a smile and keep it in place until she reached the steps outside the house. She looked around her, as if seeking escape.

Then slowly she walked down the steps to the curb where her carriage was waiting.

Jason would know the child wasn't his. He had not slept with her since early September, and now, in January, she was two months pregnant.

In spite of the closed carriage and her sable greatcoat, she was shivering. She would have to tell him the truth. He would have to know that she and Gilbert had been lovers.

She had tried to put the memories behind her. The autumn days, the long afternoons in Gilbert's cottage, with the rain tracing patterns down the windows. She and Gilbert in each other's arms before the fire. Gilbert, lying at the foot of the steps leading down to the river. . . .

And she was carrying his child.

Since the first night aboard the *Buccaneer,* Jason had kept his word; he had not touched her. When they were out in public together or when they entertained guests at Mooncliff, he behaved toward her with formal courtesy.

Often he stayed out until dawn and did not tell her where he had been. Miss Woods's establishment, perhaps. Sometimes, when she woke alone in the vast bed, she wanted him beside her, his arms around her, to shut out the black terrors that assailed her night after night. But he had said that when she wanted him, she would have to make the first move, to offer herself willingly, and her pride would not permit her to do that.

During the long, sleepless nights at Mooncliff she had found some measure of escape by reading novels. Not the classics, for her exhausted mind would not fix itself on these; instead, she had turned to the romantic tales of

Mrs. E.D.E.N. Southworth, the serialized love stories in the newspapers.

On this particular morning in January, however, the papers had carried a front-page story more dramatic than any work of fiction. Jim Fisk, the flamboyant "Prince of Erie," had been shot to death on the stairway of the Grand Central Hotel by Ned Stokes, the young dandy who had cheated him in business and had stolen the affections of his mistress, the beautiful black-haired Josie Mansfield.

Denise and Jason had often entertained Fisk at Mooncliff, without Josie, of course, for while Jason had visited Fisk at Josie's West Twenty-third Street mansion, he would never have permitted a kept woman under the same roof with his wife.

Now, as her carriage turned onto Broadway, Denise could hear the newsboys shouting out the lurid details surrounding the death of Jim Fisk. She suspected that many New Yorkers secretly would miss Fisk, for his exploits had provided a wealth of juicy gossip. Even respectable ladies had turned to stare when he went out driving in his carriage, a six-in-hand drawn by three pairs of black and white horses with gold-plated harnesses. He had usually been seen in the company of Josie Mansfield or a group of the prettiest actresses from his Opera House. Denise remembered having danced with him on the night of the housewarming ball at Mooncliff. He had danced lightly for such a big man. Now he was dead.

She shivered and drew the carriage robe around her. The sunlight was bright along the snowy streets, and the chill in the air had not daunted the shoppers along the "Ladies' Mile," a stretch of Broadway whose shops drew the most fashionable women in the city.

Denise had told Jason that she was going into New York to buy new clothes; she had not dared to tell him of the suspicion that had driven her to Doctor Frobisher's office. She tried to imagine his reaction when she did tell him. She knew that his anger would be all the greater because he had trusted her so completely. Finding her with Gilbert on the landing at Riverview, he had immediately assumed that she had been the innocent victim of an assault. If Jim Fisk had been driven to fury by his mistress's infidelity, what would Jason feel on learning that his wife had betrayed him?

The carriage pulled up in front of the Fifth Avenue Hotel, where Denise had arranged to lunch with Rosalind MacKay. As she walked through the great lobby to the dining room, she was remembering the first time she had been here, with Jason.

"You're a beautiful woman," he had told her. "You'll have to get used to being stared at."

Now, crossing the lobby in her magnificent new sable greatcoat, with a hat of matching fur perched on her deep red hair, she was scarcely aware of the eyes that turned in her direction. She entered the dining room and was escorted to her table in a quiet corner sheltered by potted palms.

"Denise, my dear, how wonderful to see you," Rosalind said. "How was your trip? Tell me all about your sister's wedding."

But as always Rosalind gave her little chance to talk, breaking in frequently with choice bits of gossip of her own.

"Shocking about Jim Fisk, wasn't it? They say he's to be laid out in state in the foyer of the Grand Opera House. I wonder if that shameless Josie will be there. She did look perfectly dashing when she appeared in court over that blackmail business. She wore the most beautiful velvet mantle and a little Alpine hat. And that awful Ned Stokes—you'd have thought he was going for a stroll in the park, in his Alexis overcoat. Terribly handsome, of course. You wouldn't think he was capable of murder—" Rosalind broke off.

"My dear, what's wrong? Aren't you feeling well? I know Mr. Fisk was out at Mooncliff several times, but I had no idea his death would upset you so—"

Denise tried to speak, but the crowded dining room began to blur before his eyes. She fought to take a deep breath; her stays compressed her waist, cutting off the air.

Rosalind poured a glass of wine and held it to her lips.

"Drink this, my dear."

Obediently she swallowed. "Rosalind, I'm so afraid."

"Afraid? Of what, Denise?"

"Promise me you won't tell anyone. Not even Captain MacKay."

"I promise."

"I've just come from Doctor Frobisher's office. I'm going to have a baby. I'm two months pregnant."

"Oh, Denise—you mustn't be frightened. The second baby always comes more quickly."

"You don't understand. I can't have the baby. You told me there were ways. That woman, Madame Restell. You said she took care of women who—"

"But dear, I meant women who had a good reason for needing such services. You have only one child, and your husband adores him. Surely it wouldn't be such an ordeal to give him another son. Heaven knows, he can support a dozen."

"You said only country women had a dozen children anymore."

Rosalind looked down at her plate, but not before Denise saw the glint of tears. "I said a great many things."

"I don't understand. You have only those two girls by your first marriage. I thought—"

"I wanted to give Captain MacKay children," Rosalind said, so softly that Denise had to bend forward to catch the words. "He—it hasn't happened with him. He knows it's his fault, because of my girls. That's why I sent them away to school when they were so young. I didn't want him to be reminded that—"

"I'm sorry," Denise said. "I didn't know."

"So you see," Rosalind went on, "if you can give your husband more children, you should. Besides, Madame Restell's operations are dangerous. A woman can die or be left an invalid for the rest of her life." Rosalind looked at Denise closely. "I don't believe you want to—get rid of this baby."

Denise was silent. This child she carried was Gilbert's, conceived in passion and tenderness. She had brought about Gilbert's death. If she were to destroy the unborn child as well—

Rosalind was speaking, and Denise forced herself to listen.

"Go home to Mooncliff, and tell Jason about the baby."

Back at Mooncliff that evening Denise stood at her bedroom window. Jason had not returned from the city, but Elspeth had said he had left word that he would be home late. "He said to tell you not to wait up for him."

A familiar message, but this time Denise would have to ignore it. There was no use delaying their confrontation. He would have to know about the baby sooner or later, and she was afraid that if she put off the moment, she would lose her courage completely.

The snow had started to fall again, and the wind from the river drove the white flakes against the windows. Denise pulled her robe of soft brown velvet around her and waited for Jason to come home.

It was after midnight when Jason arrived at Mooncliff. Although the lamps still burned in the great, gloomy hall, the shadows were oppressive, and the only sound was that of the wind from outside, beyond the rocky cliffs.

Jason was aware that he was very tired, and yet he was too restless to go to bed at once. It had been a long and trying day. Fisk's death had created a double scandal, and while the gossips talked over the more personal details of the affair, businessmen like Jason, who had been involved in the Erie Ring, had remained closeted with their lawyers and accountants, discussing the financial implications.

Jason, still wearing his coat, walked slowly down the hall. He knew that Gould was seeking to reorganize the board of directors of the Erie; with Fisk gone, the organization could now have an outward semblance of respectability. If he were offered a seat on the board, it would mean an additional fortune. More servants for Mooncliff, more paintings to add to his growing collection, expensive new furniture imported from Europe. A summer place in Newport, perhaps.

He looked up into the blackness of the great staircase. Denise would be asleep now. Not that it mattered. Even if she had been awake she would not have wanted him to come and talk to her, to tell her about the events of the day. He continued down the hall, heading for the library. Before he could reach it, the door leading from the servants' hall swung open.

"Elspeth," he said. "I suppose it's no use telling you not to wait up."

"That's right," she said. "You'll find a fire in the library." She looked at him disapprovingly. "Let me take your coat—it's soaked through. There's brandy in the library, but if you want hot rum it will only take a minute."

"The brandy will do nicely. Stop fussing, Elspeth, and go to bed."

"You won't stay up too late, I hope."

"Damn it, girl, I don't need you to tell me—" He smiled apologetically and pressed her hand. He liked and respected Elspeth, but sometimes she made him feel uneasy. Maybe because her eyes were so like her father's. There were times when he felt that Andrew Buchanan was looking at him out of those gray-blue eyes.

But after she left him he felt very much alone. He went into the library, poured himself a drink and stood staring at the fire.

I was right, taking Elspeth in, he thought. I've been repaid many times over. The night Stuart was born she saved Denise, and Stuart, too. Doesn't look strong, but she is, inside, where it counts. Stronger than her father. . . . I should have known he wasn't fit for a slaving voyage. But I was young myself. I hadn't learned to judge a man, size him up at a glance. I was twenty-five. . . .

He drained his glass and refilled it. Stop it, he told himself. He walked to the tall, narrow window. It's not like me to look back. No profit in it. And there's so much to look ahead to. A seat on the board of the Erie. And next month, another of my ships on her way to the Far East. I'd like to be on board her. China. Japan.

What about Denise? She wouldn't care. Be relieved to be rid of me for a while.

There's Stuart to think about. He would miss me. At

least I hope he would. If it weren't for him— To stand on the deck of my own ship again.

The library was too close, too crowded, with its towering bookcases packed with rows of leather-bound books he had never had time to open. Oil paintings in ornate gilt frames. Moorish lamps, marble statues, Chinese screens.

He opened the windows. The icy wind felt good against his face. Great flakes of snow clung to his skin and melted. He could not see beyond the terrace. The wind howled around the stone walls of the house, driving downriver and striking with gale force against the jutting promontory on which Mooncliff had been built.

Tonight the wind was changed. There were variations in its tone that reminded him of . . . what? The deep vibrations of the shrouds, the once-familiar high-pitched singing of the wind in the rigging.

And now, something different. Voices in the wind. Voices crying from the waters below the cliffs.

In spite of the icy blast, Jason was sweating. He opened his shirt. At sea he had come to know every sound the wind could make. This was different, wrong. . . .

The voices grew louder. Words came, words he could not understand. The brandy glass slipped from his fingers. A strange yet familiar mixture of Portuguese and African, a dialect heard only on the Ivory Coast. Words and screams and another sound that brought the sweat to his face and a hoarse cry to his lips. The sound of an anchor chain dragging along a deck. The sun-bleached deck of the *Nubian Queen.*

I don't hear it. Not any of it. Only the wind, blowing in from the river.

But the voices grew louder, more distinct. Voices crazed with terror. Then a splash.

And once more, the only sound was that of the winter wind driving the snow against the house.

Jason closed the window. He rested his hands on the sill for support. He wanted to believe that what he had heard had been caused by the wind, his own weariness, the brandy he had drunk. But it was no good. He had heard the cries of the doomed slaves, the dragging of the anchor chain that had been used to weight them down, and the splash as they had struck the water.

But why? He had done the only possible thing he could have done that day long ago.

He found himself thinking of Andrew Buchanan, standing here, under the roof, accusing him before his guests. "You're not human, are you, Captain? . . . I took refuge in the cabin below, but you stayed on deck; you watched living human beings thrown into the sea, screaming for mercy—

"You'll come to share my madness in the years to come. You'll hear those cries, too. . . . You and your children and their children. . . ."

Buchanan had been right. Jason could not explain away what he had heard. He closed his eyes and rested his forehead against the windowpane.

All right, then, he had heard the voices. He might hear them again. But he wasn't weak like Buchanan. He wouldn't break, wouldn't turn to drink for escape. He would live with his guilt, and no one would ever know.

"Jason."

He started and turned from the window. He had not heard Denise open the library doors, but she was here, standing in the doorway, her red hair falling about her shoulders.

He wanted to speak and couldn't. His shirt clung to his body with the cold sweat of fear. He watched her cross the room to stand before him.

"Are you ill?"

He shook his head, as if to rouse himself from a heavy sleep. "What do you want?"

Until she had entered the library, Denise had been completely obsessed by her own terror. Prepared as she had been to face Jason and tell him about the baby, she was still afraid. Now, standing here beside him, her fear ebbed away. For this man looking down at her was a stranger.

The features were familiar to her: the mouth, full-lipped and sensual, the broad forehead and heavy dark brows. But there was something in his eyes that she had not seen before. The mockery was gone, even the self-assurance. Instead there was a kind of bewilderment. It was the look of a man who had lost his bearings, who struggled now to master himself and his surroundings.

"What do you want?" he repeated.

"I—I came down to talk to you."

"Not now," he said without inflection. "Go to bed. It's very late."

"But Jason, this is important. I must—"

He put out his hand as if to hold her off. "Please," he said. "Try to understand; I need to be alone for a while."

She took his hand in hers and led him to the small sofa next to the fireplace. "Something's happened. Tell me," she said. When he remained silent, she went on, "If it's something to do with business, I'll try to understand. I know I'm not clever about such things, but I'll try."

"Denise, once I told you that there were some things in a man's life he couldn't share, or speak of. You were very young then, and you didn't believe me."

She was silent. Whatever had happened to him tonight he had to keep to himself. Not because he did not love her, but perhaps because he loved her too much. Because he wanted to protect her from the nameless terror that had touched him.

And it came to her that she must protect him, too, that if she told him that she was carrying her dead lover's child, it would destroy him.

I can't do that to him, she thought. I can't hurt him that way, not now. Yet how can I keep it from him?

Her mind moved swiftly. It was possible. She would make it possible.

From their first meeting she had judged him by the rigid standards of her own pride and untested virtue. Now she saw him as he was. A man who had fought desperately to make a place in a world that had rejected him. He had seen her, a young girl looking down from the balcony at Riverview. To him she had been the living symbol of all he longed to attain. Now, with a few words, she could destroy that symbol forever. And with it she could destroy his pride in Mooncliff, in the success he had fought for all these years.

She shivered. The room was cold in spite of the fire.

"You'll get a chill sitting here," he said. "Go upstairs. Whatever you had to tell me can wait until morning."

"No, it can't." She put a hand on his arm. "Jason, you told me that night when we were coming back from Charleston that you would never force yourself on me again. That if I wanted you, I'd have to come to you and ask you to— I don't want to sleep alone tonight."

His eyes were still remote, clouded. She kept her hand on his arm, the other working at the belt of her robe. The velvet folds fell away from her body.

She heard the sharp intake of his breath. Then his arms were around her; his face was against her breasts.

"You're sure?"

She stroked his hair. "Very sure," she said. "Jason, I want another child."

If it was a sin, then the guilt would be hers, for she would never tell him the truth. There would be more children, the Moreland dynasty he had dreamed of. She could give him that.

She drew away at last, rose and held out her hand to him. After a moment he took it. Together they left the firelit room and went down the shadowy hall.

BOOK 2

Chapter 1

On an afternoon in mid-July, Denise Moreland lay on the great canopied bed in the master bedroom. Her dark red hair was loosened and tangled around her face, and her brown eyes were wide with pain. She was only dimly aware of heaviness of the air that warned of a coming thundershower.

Her thoughts and feelings were turned inward. She lay tense, rigid, in the grip of the pain that clutched at her body. She had gone into labor early that morning, but no one at Mooncliff knew what was happening. She had retired to her bedroom, having given orders that she was not to be disturbed. In this great house, with its full staff of servants, she had fought through he first stages of her labor alone. Soon, however, she knew she would have to ring for Elspeth.

The pain eased momentarily, and she was able to relax, to remember the winter day, three years before, when she had given birth to her first child. The doctor had been unable to get to Mooncliff through the blizzard but Elspeth had stayed with her and had helped bring Stuart into the world. Now, on this July afternoon, it would have been easy enough to get word to Doctor Frobisher in the city. But Denise did not want Doctor Frobisher here, for his presence might ruin her plans.

She caught her breath sharply as another pain struck. She pressed her lips together and tried not to remember those nightmare hours preceding Stuart's birth. A second labor is always easier and shorter than the first, she reminded herself. Rosalind MacKay had told her so. She pushed her fist against her mouth to stifle any cry of pain, and waited. The torment lessened, then stopped, and she relaxed, her body drenched with perspiration.

At least Jason wasn't here at Mooncliff. Although she had told him that his second child would not be born until September, she had had a hard time persuading him to go to Rhode Island on business, leaving her at Mooncliff.

"I want you to be in New York City when this baby arrives," he insisted. His heavy dark brows met in a scowl. "Nothing must go wrong this time."

"Nothing went wrong last time," she reminded him. "Stuart is a perfectly healthy child, and I'm none the worse for having had him without Doctor Frobisher on hand."

"We were lucky," Jason said. "I won't have you risking your life or the baby's this time."

"But there won't be any risk," she insisted. "The baby isn't due for two months. By then I'll be off to the city, and I'll stay there until after the delivery, if that's what you want."

"That's what I want," he told her. He put his arms around her and held her close, as if afraid of losing her. "Nothing must happen to you, my dear."

When she had said goodbye to Jason as he was preparing to leave for Rhode Island, where he planned to buy another shipyard, he had said, "As soon as I get back, I'll lease a townhouse in New York City. That way, you can wait in comfort until the baby comes."

But even as she had agreed, she had known that there would be no need for such an arrangement, that her second baby would be born not in September but in July.

She thought as she lay on the wide bed, waiting for the next pain to strike, that there were those who would have condemned her for her deception, who would have said that right now she was committing a second sin far worse than the first. Maybe she was. But Jason must never know the truth about her and Gilbert. She would make her husband believe that this child was his own, a Moreland, another heir to Mooncliff.

A pain started in the small of her back, encircled her body in a vise and drew a cry from her. She reached for the bell cord to summon Elspeth.

Elspeth would share her secret. Elspeth already shared the other secrets of the Morelands; her life had become inextricably interwoven with the lives of Denise and Jason on the night she had come to Mooncliff for the first time.

"Mrs. Moreland, what's wrong? Did you have an accident? A fall?"

Denise looked up from the damp pillow and forced a smile. "No, Elspeth. Nothing like that. I'm not having a miscarriage, if that's what you're thinking. Sit down. I have to tell you—"

"Not now. I'll tell Patrick to saddle the horses and get word to Doctor Frobisher—"

"No!"

"But the baby's not due for another two months, and a premature birth can be difficult."

Denise reached out and gripped Elspeth's hand. "This baby isn't premature."

"But you told Mr. Moreland—"

"I had to tell him that. He must never know anything different. Elspeth, swear to me you won't tell him, that you'll help me and keep my secret."

She broke off as she felt another pain encircling her with jaws of steel. Through the blur of agony that dimmed her vision she saw Elspeth's face, the bewilderment giving way to understanding.

"That's right," Denise whispered. "This baby was conceived when I was in South Carolina last fall."

"And Mr. Moreland was—here at Mooncliff."

Denise nodded. "You know Jason. The kind of man he is. His pride. You can understand why he mustn't know."

"I understand," Elspeth said quietly.

Elspeth knew the dark side of Jason's nature, the furies that possessed him, the twisted needs that could sometimes drive him to violence. But she knew, too, that it was not fear that was causing Denise to lie to Jason about this baby.

"You love him very much, don't you?" Elspeth said.

"Very much."

The heat grew more oppressive. Denise, writhing on the huge bed, longed for the first drops of rain against the window, for the cool breezes from the river. Her body, in its light cambric nightgown, was soaked with sweat, and her red hair clung to her forehead.

"Elspeth, help me," she moaned.

"I can still send for Doctor Frobisher."

"No. He'll know the baby's not premature. He'll know—"

"All right," Elspeth said soothingly. She dipped a cloth into a basin of water and wiped Denise's face.

What must Elspeth think of her? No matter. Elspeth would not ask, now or ever, what had driven her to take a lover, and if anyone did ask her, she was not sure she would be able to give an answer. Her mind was blurring now under the onslaught of pain, so that she could no longer think clearly. She reached out and Elspeth took her hand.

"I'm here, Mrs. Moreland," she said. "Don't be afraid. I'll take care of you."

"Elspeth, have you—"

"Yes, Mrs. Moreland?"

"Have you ever forgiven Jason? Have you never wanted to run away from Mooncliff? Or to curse this house as your father did?"

"Mooncliff is my home," Elspeth said evenly. "And Mr. Moreland has been kind to me."

"How can you say that? He destroyed your father."

"My father destroyed himself."

Denise clutched at Elspeth's hand. "Then you don't believe in the curse?"

"Of course not. And neither should you."

"But so many things have happened here since the night of that first ball—terrible things."

Denise fell silent. There were some things that even Elspeth must not know. Memories that only she and Jason shared. Elspeth might have heard much and guessed at more, but only Denise knew the whole terrible story of Jason's past, the shameful truth of how the Moreland fortune had been founded.

Dizzy and light-headed after the long, dragging hours of pain, Denise found her mind drifting back to the night of the housewarming ball. She heard again the strains of the waltz, saw Jason looking down at her as he whirled her around the polished floor, his blue eyes blazing with triumph, a triumph that had been shattered by the words of Elspeth's father. "What kind of life will you have here, you and your wife?" Andrew Buchanan had demanded of Jason. "You have built a house over the bodies of the dead. . . ."

Now, tortured with pain, Denise tried to forget those words. But she could not.

"Elspeth, suppose your father was right. Suppose there is a curse on Mooncliff. On our children."

Elspeth's calm face swam out of the blur, her gray eyes steady and reassuring. There was an inner serenity, a strength that lent beauty to the plain face under the neat, starched lace cap.

"You're exhausted. You're not thinking clearly," she said. "Please let me send for a doctor, any doctor. Mrs. Moreland, you need help. More help than I can give you."

"You delivered Stuart," Denise reminded her.

"I had no choice then. The blizzard—the doctor couldn't get through—"

"And you have no choice now."

"But Mrs. Moreland—"

"I forbid you to call a doctor."

Elspeth put her face close to Denise's. "Listen to me and try to understand. If Mr. Moreland finds out when he returns that I did not call a doctor, he's sure to suspect something."

"I hadn't thought of that. But what can we do?"

"There's a new young doctor in Rhinebeck. He's not been in practice long. He doesn't know you, and he won't know when the baby was expected. I'll send for him."

Denise tried to answer, but the words did not come. Another wave of pain engulfed her.

"This doctor from Rhinebeck may have his suspicions but he won't talk. I'll see to that."

"But how?" The words were scarcely more than a whisper. Denise's lips were cracked and dry and tasted of blood where she had bitten them. Elspeth's face blurred again, and there was a rushing sound that grew louder.

From a long way off she heard Elspeth saying, "Even if I send for him now, I think the baby may arrive before he does."

Denise, aware of the new sensations in her pain-racked body, the urge to bear down, sensed that Elspeth was right. The baby was coming now. Gilbert's child. The child that Jason must be made to believe was his own.

It might have been an hour or an eternity that passed before Denise heard Elspeth saying, "The labor was so short, there was no time to send for Doctor Frobisher. His office is in New York City."

"Premature labor is often short," a man's voice replied. "But the boy is exceptionally large for a seven-month baby. Are you sure the child was not due before September?"

"Positive, Doctor Underhill. It's not so unusual, really. Stuart, Mrs. Moreland's first child, was quite large at birth. After all, Mr. Moreland is a big man, at least six feet four, with a powerful physique."

"That would be a factor, of course, Miss Buchanan, but nevertheless—"

"What are you trying to say, Doctor?" There was a steely quality in Elspeth's voice that Denise had rarely heard before. An unspoken challenge.

"I—that is—"

"You are just beginning your career in Rhinebeck, are you not, Doctor Underhill?"

"That's right," the doctor said. "But I hardly see—"

"It must be difficult for a young man like you to get established in a new community, particularly when there are a few older doctors already practicing there."

Denise's hands closed into tight fists under the blanket. She was too weak, too exhausted to fight for herself, and Elspeth was doing battle for her, determined to save her reputation, to protect her marriage to Jason.

"Forgive me," Elspeth was saying. "My father was a country doctor, you see. He came here from Scotland, and he had some difficulty getting started over in Staatsburg. These farmers are often slow to accept a new man with new ideas. They're set in their ways."

"Yes, that's quite true, but—"

"If the Morelands were to have you for their doctor, your reputation would be made. Other prosperous families would follow their example."

The young doctor was silent. Denise closed her eyes and strained to hear his next remark.

"Well, of course, babies do vary in size. Even premature babies. And since Mr. Moreland is, as you say, a big man, why, I suppose—he should be pleased. A fine healthy boy. The second, you say?"

"That's right. And he'll be most grateful to you for coming out on such short notice and doing such a fine job."

"Really, Miss Buchanan, the baby was here when I arrived. I only cut the cord and—"

"And now, perhaps you wish to examine Mrs. Moreland?"

"To be sure," Doctor Underhill said.

Denise opened her eyes as the doctor crossed the room. Exhausted though she was, she studied his face intently. He was obviously impressed by the unfamiliar and lavish surroundings. He was a thin, sandy-haired young man, almost boyish looking, with a black suit that was shiny in places and a little too short in the sleeves. It had probably served him all through medical school. A farmer's son, perhaps, with intelligence and ambition, but without the right connections.

She saw him staring at the great bed with its hangings of jade-green velvet, at the Oriental rug, the oil paintings in their heavy gold frames. During the last year, Jason had had wood paneling imported from France and a pedimented mantel of agate and onyx marble brought from a palace in Italy; both were now installed in the master bedroom. She thought the effect was ostentatious, but now, seeing the doctor's reaction to these splendors, she was glad that Jason had insisted on them.

She endured the brief examination, her thoughts elsewhere. Yes, Doctor Underhill would go along with the fabrication about the premature birth. Jason would accept her second son as his own.

She loved Stuart, but she had never been able to forget that he had been conceived in anger and fear. This second child was born of love. Her mind drifted back to those stolen hours in the overseer's cottage at Riverview, to Gilbert. He had loved her, had possessed her with tenderness, almost with a kind of worship.

She would give Gilbert's child all the love of which she was capable, would cherish and protect him. But she would not let Jason spoil him as he had spoiled Stuart, who had grown so self-willed and headstrong that even now only Jason was able to control him.

Denise closed her eyes and sank into an exhausted sleep. Her last thought was of her newborn son, who would not, must not, be touched by the Moreland curse.

Chapter 2

Always before, when Jason Moreland returned to Mooncliff after a trip, he had felt a deep sense of satisfaction. Driving up the last curve of the road that led from the iron gates to the steps of the house, he usually had paused a moment to look with pride at the massive structure of gray stone. But on this particular July afternoon he was scarcely aware of the house itself, of the shadows that were beginning to fall across the towers of the east wing, or the sun that struck sparks of amethyst, ruby and topaz from the mullioned stained-glass windows of the second story.

In Jason's pocket was a telegram sent by Elspeth Buchanan, informing him that Mrs. Moreland had gone into labor prematurely and advising him to return as soon as possible.

Until now, he had always prized the isolation of Mooncliff, but today he had cursed the slowness of the return trip, the distance from the nearest railroad station. He had left the train at Rhinebeck and hired a surrey and team there; he had driven the horses at breakneck speed to reach home as quickly as possible. Now, drawing up before the house, he did not stop to return the greeting of the stableman who had hurried forward at the first sounds of wheels in the drive. He threw the reins to the man and ran up the steps of the house, to be admitted by Elspeth.

He stood towering over her in the front hallway. He took her by the shoulders and searched her face anxiously.

"Is Denise—is she—"

"Mrs. Moreland is recovering nicely. And the baby is fine. A boy." She gave him a strained little smile. "He's not as large as Stuart was when he was born, but that's natural."

Jason took a deep breath, released it. "She wasn't due until September. She told me so. You're sure the baby is going to live?"

She winced at the pressure of Jason's fingers on her shoulders. "Quite sure. Doctor Underhill said—"

"Doctor Underhill? Who the devil's he? Denise was supposed to have Frobisher." He saw then for the first time that her lips were pressed together tightly. "I'm sorry, Elspeth," he said, taking his hands away. "I didn't realize—"

"There was no time to get Doctor Frobisher all the way from the city. Mrs. Moreland's labor was very short."

"Even so—"

"Doctor Underhill is quite competent. He's the new young doctor at Rhinebeck. He was the nearest, and so I—"

"A country doctor just starting his practice. What the—what would he know? I wanted Denise to have the best this time." Then, realizing the meaning of his words, he added quickly: "You did very well when Stuart was born, Elspeth. I didn't mean to imply—you know I've always been grateful. But—"

"I understand," she said quietly. "Wouldn't you like to see your wife now? And the baby?"

He nodded and started from the stairway.

"Mr. Moreland, you must not tire her. She is exhausted."

"You said it was a short labor." Jason's brows drew together.

"Yes, but even so, Doctor Underhill did not arrive until afterward, and I—"

"You delivered the baby? Good Lord, Elspeth, what would the Morelands do without you? That first time with Stuart, and now again." Strange, he thought, that Elspeth Buchanan, who had first entered this house on a night of violence, who had been carried back unconscious the following morning, should have remained here to become the mainstay of the family.

"I owe you a great deal, Elspeth," he said. "What can I do to repay you? I'll give you—" He searched his mind, trying to hit upon a gift that would express his gratitude for her help in bringing his second son into the world. "What would you like?"

"You give me a generous salary, Mr. Moreland. And a comfortable home. What more could I want?"

He looked at the slender girl, no older than his wife, erect, composed, prim in her dove-gray dress with its white lace collar and cuffs. She never wore jewelry. He would buy her a brooch, perhaps. Simple but expensive. Worthy of her.

Pleased by the thought, he hurried upstairs to the master bedroom on the second floor. He opened the door, and then he forgot all about Elspeth, about everyone and everything, except Denise and his new son.

Denise's face was pale, and there were dark smudges under her eyes. Her hair had been brushed and tied back from her face with a satin ribbon. She raised her head as Jason came into the room.

He went to her and sat down very carefully on the side of the bed. She reached out to draw him closer, but her arms fell back on the quilt. Jason took her hand, pressed it against his cheek; he was afraid to put his arms around her, she looked so spent, so fragile. A short labor, Elspeth had told him. Too short to send for Doctor Frobisher, and yet it had left Denise drained of strength.

Seeing his look, she said quickly, "I'm all right, truly.

It was nothing like the first time, Jason. Doctor Underhill said I would be up and about in a few days."

"Doctor Underhill. Fresh out of his internship. Good enough for those farmers over at Rhinebeck, but—"

"Their wives have babies, too," Denise reminded him gently.

"That's different. You're different."

"I'm your wife. And the mistress of Mooncliff. But I assure you, my babies arrive in the usual way." Her lips curved in a smile.

"It's nothing to joke about," he said sternly. "Besides, Elspeth said this Doctor Underhill didn't even arrive until after the baby was born. I'm sending for Frobisher. I want him to examine you."

"No," Denise protested. "Jason, no. I don't need him. Please—"

"All right, dear, don't upset yourself."

"You haven't even seen the baby," Denise reminded him. "Elspeth put the bassinet in the dressing room." She turned her head in the direction of the half-open door that separated the bedroom from the small room adjoining. "He's asleep now," she said. "Try not to wake him."

In the dressing room, Jason bent over the bassinet with its lace and satin draperies. Denise watched as he gently drew back the blanket. When he returned to her, his face was filled with pride. She felt her throat tighten. If only this moment had not been shadowed by her knowledge of her deception. If only the infant lying in the bassinet had been Jason's son.

"He's a fine boy. And sturdy, too." He smiled down at her. "Another son for Mooncliff," he said.

"I hope you won't spoil him. Stuart is—"

"I have not spoiled Stuart, no matter what that damn nanny says. She's too strict. Set in her ways. Stuart has spirit, that's all."

"Too much spirit. Not four years old, and he's been trying to bully Patrick and the other stablemen into letting him ride."

"Has he, indeed?" Jason's smile deepened. "I'll buy him a pony of his own, then."

"You'll do no such thing. Not yet."

"Very well. We'll talk of it another time, when you're up and around. Right now, you had best get some sleep."

He bent and kissed her lightly on the forehead. She turned her face, and her lips found his; there was something urgent, almost desperate in her kiss.

The long July twilight was fading into evening, and Jason, standing at the library window, stared out at the terrace and the cliffs beyond. He was warmed by the memory of Denise's embrace, by the way she had clung to him until she had drifted into sleep.

Even after four years of marriage, he had never completely ceased to wonder that Denise had become his wife. True, he had used his fortune to bribe her father into consenting to the marriage. But afterward he had made her love him. During those first months of their marriage, he had overcome her resentment, her fear of him and of her own emotions. He had taught her what it was to be a woman, and she had gloried in the knowledge.

But if she had known happiness with him here at Mooncliff, she had known sorrow, too, and fear.

He turned away from the library window and paced the floor as he tried unsuccessfully to shut out the memory of that night, four years ago, when he had brought Denise to this room. Had she ever forgiven him for that night? Could a woman like Denise forgive that kind of violence?

He pushed the thought away. She had just borne him a second son, hadn't she? And there would be more children. Perhaps, next time, a girl. With two boys to carry on the Moreland name, he would not mind if the third child were a girl.

Denise would need time to recover her strength, of course. In spite of her assurances that she had had an easy labor, he could not forget her pallor, the dark circles under her eyes.

He should have been here. He should not have left her alone. But his trip to Rhode Island had been important, and the outcome had been as successful as he could have wished.

His newly acquired shipyard would provide his company with steam-powered vessels only. He regretted the passing of sailing ships, but he was enough of a realist to accept the fact that now, in 1872, steam had triumphed over sail, and there could be no turning back. Some diehard shipbuilders clung to the belief that sail would always have a place on the seas, and sailing ships were still being built with iron-clad hulls. Indeed, a few of the Moreland clippers were still doing a formidable trade in the Orient. But even that would not go on much longer, Jason knew. With his new steam-driven ships, he would establish regular routes between New England and the ports of the Caribbean and Central America. There were fortunes to be made in such a venture, particularly for a man who was willing to take a few risks.

That Cuban business, now. Jason knew Cuba, from those long-ago days when he had run illegal cargoes of slaves to the island's ports. Before the Civil War, the United States had made attempts to acquire Cuba. Southern expansionists, such as Denise's father, had favored the purchase of Cuba to add to the slave territory of the United States, and a hot debate on the Cuban question had continued almost until the first shots had been fired on Fort Sumter. Now, of course, the South had no further interest in Cuba, but there were northern businessmen, Jason among them, who were farsighted enough to see the importance of the island, so close to the American mainland.

Right now, a bloody revolution was raging in Cuba, and Jason, like other northern shipowners, had been approached by representatives of the rebel forces who were desperate to buy arms. Such trade was risky, but Jason had built his fortune by running such risks. His lips curved in a humorless smile as he looked around the library at the luxurious furnishings bought with the profits from his slave-trading ventures.

It was a somber, tastefully decorated room, with its Circassian walnut paneling, stamped in gold and decorated with bas-relief carvings in the style of the High Renaissance. The coffered ceiling, carrying out the theme of dark wood and gold, had been shipped here from

Europe; the magnificent antique fireplace had been taken from a sixteenth-century French chateau. And those rows of beautifully bound books he had never found time to read. No matter, his sons would read them. They would have the education and the leisure to enjoy books and paintings.

His thoughts were interrupted by a knock at the door. Elspeth came into the room, carrying a tray. "I was sure you would be hungry," she said. "If you would rather have dinner in the dining room, I can—"

"No, this is all right," he assured her. He laughed. "I'd forgotten about dinner."

"I thought you might have," she said, setting down the tray.

"Denise—she's asleep, I suppose?"

"Yes. And the baby, too. If you've a moment, Mr. Moreland, I did want to ask you—"

"The baby's well, isn't he?"

"Of course. I've told you. And you saw him for yourself."

"He looked perfect to me. A fine, big boy, considering—"

"It's about the baby I wanted to talk to you," Elspeth said quickly. "He'll be needing a nurse. If you want me to notify one of the agencies in New York City, I could do so, and then screen the applicants."

"Why can't Miss Wilmot look after the new baby, and Stuart, too?" Jason demanded. "At least for a while."

"I'm afraid Miss Wilmot has all she can do, chasing after young Master Stuart," Elspeth said.

Jason laughed. "He is a lively young man, isn't he?"

Elspeth looked at Jason squarely. "I'd call him spoiled," she said. "He's not so bad when you're here. He'll listen to you. But poor Miss Wilmot—"

"If Miss Wilmot can't cope with Sturat, perhaps we'll have to let her go."

"Forgive me, Mr. Moreland, but you're being unfair. If Stuart is unmanageable, it's because you have not allowed Miss Wilmot to discipline him properly. Why, she's afraid to raise a hand to the child—"

"Is she, indeed?"

"Yes, sir."

For a moment Jason stood looking down at Elspeth in silence, his dark brows drawn together, his blue eyes cold. Then, all at once, he smiled. "You're not afraid of me, though, are you?"

"Not when I know I'm right, sir," Elspeth said quietly.

"Very well," he said. "Here's what I'll do. Miss Wilmot can take charge of the new baby. And I'll hire someone else to care for Stuart. Not a nurse. A governess. Someone who is young enough not to be set in her ways."

"And active enough to run her legs off chasing after Stuart when he goes off to the stables."

"That's it, Elspeth." He laughed. "I understand he's picked up some choice language from Patrick and the other stablemen."

"He has. He—"

"Bring him down here, Elspeth. I haven't seen him since I got home."

"I certainly will not, sir. He's been asleep these two hours."

"Very well, then," Jason said. "But I'll have breakfast with him tomorrow. I want to hear some of this choice language he learned while I was gone. And, Elspeth, I'll see to finding a governess for him."

Chapter 3

The streets of New York City were bright with sunshine that September morning of 1874, but a brisk northeast wind brought a chill to the air, a hint of approaching winter. To those who were out on the streets looking for employment, the crisp, windy day held a feeling of uneasiness, of fear. For there were many men and women without jobs and without prospects of work. The city had not yet recovered from the financial panic that had begun the year before with the closing of Jay Cooke's banking house and the shutting down of the New York Stock Exchange.

Although President Grant had come in quickly from Long Branch to throw the influence of his office against the rising tide of panic, and although the government, the banks and certain western interests had supplied money, well-known firms had gone down to ruin. The Crédit Mobilier scandal had exploded, and faith in the government had been badly shaken when it became known that President Grant himself was involved.

To Lavinia Corbett, newly arrived in New York City

from England, the prospects were bleak and a little frightening. For the last two weeks she had trudged the crowded, unfamiliar streets, wearing out her only decent pair of shoes. She had become familiar with the horde of pale-faced, anxious-looking women who waited outside the employment agencies of Lower Broadway, jockeying for places on the hard wooden benches inside. Some had graying hair and lined faces, while others were as young as she.

Miss Fisher's Agency was like all the others, and Lavinia's interview with the stern woman in black bombazine was no more satisfactory than the other interviews she had had during the last few weeks. Miss Fisher, seated behind the heavy oak desk in her private office, eyed Lavinia coolly. "I'm afraid I have nothing for you right now," she said.

"But I'm an excellent teacher," Lavinia said. "I have a thorough knowledge of Latin and French. I can teach the pianoforte and the harp, sketching, watercolor, needlework—"

Miss Fisher looked over the paper in her hand. "I see all that," she said impatiently. "Most commendable. But there are no openings at the moment, not for someone with your lack of experience. If you had held a position as a teacher in a school or as a governess in a private home, it might be different."

Lavinia pressed her lips together and looked away. She had, in fact, been a governess in a private home, but she had no reference from her first and only post. Better therefore to present herself as a young woman just out of school, seeking her first position.

"I'm sorry," Miss Fisher said. "Without experience, there is little you can do, except— You have a neat appearance and are well spoken, and you say you can do good needlework. Perhaps I could find something for you as a lady's maid—"

"No," Lavinia interrupted. "I won't be a servant."

"That's up to you." Miss Fisher looked irritated. She handed back to Lavinia the sheet of paper with the engraved heading from Miss Chadwick's Academy for Young Ladies.

"It is a pity you came all the way from England without apprising yourself of the business prospects here. A rather rash thing for a young woman to do, Miss Corbett."

Lavinia did not answer. She folded Miss Chadwick's letter of recommendation and put it back into her reticule. The interview was definitely at an end. "Perhaps in a few weeks," Lavinia said as she stood up and smoothed the skirt of her olive-green poplin dress, "if I were to come back to see you—"

"You would be wasting your time and mine. You'd be wise to reconsider taking work as a maid. At least you would have a roof over your head this winter, and three meals a day."

Perhaps she was right, but Lavinia's stubborn pride kept her from giving in. She held her head high and walked to the door, then had to step aside swiftly to avoid being jostled by the man who strode briskly toward Miss Fisher's private office.

He was tall, with massive shoulders under the well-tailored black coat. He wore narrow, pale gray trousers and a fine embroidered waistcoat. Lavinia caught a glimpse of his face; his blue eyes were almost startling in contrast to his deep tan, and there was arrogance in the strong chin and wide mouth. He was surely not looking for work here.

Miss Fisher's voice, now soft and ingratiating, drifted through the door. "Why, Mr. Moreland. I wasn't expecting to see you again so soon. Do come in, please. You are seeking additional help, perhaps?"

"I'm seeking a new governess," he said. "Miss Armstrong did not do her work satisfactorily."

He closed the door behind him. Lavinia started for the street, but before she could take more than a few steps she felt giddy, suddenly light-headed. She sank down on the straight chair beside the inner office door. She knew well enough what was wrong with her: she had had only tea and crackers for dinner last night and nothing but tea this morning. She would have to sit here until she recovered, for it wouldn't do to walk out and faint in the street.

A fresh-faced young girl left the bench across the room

and hurried over to her. "You all right, dearie?" The girl had a heavy brogue, and Lavinia knew she must be one of the Irish immigrants who were still crowding into the city, seeking any kind of work they could get.

"I'm quite all right," Lavinia said stiffly.

"It's not easy finding work these days, now is it?"

"It seems not."

The girl sighed. "All those great, fine houses, like palaces, they are. You'd think they'd need dozens of servants, but—"

"I'm not a servant. I am a governess," Lavinia said.

The girl raised her pale eyebrows. "Well, pardon me, milady," she said. She shrugged and returned to the bench with the other waiting applicants. Lavinia heard her say something to the girl next to her, and then they both laughed. Lavinia turned away.

When she had arrived in New York two weeks ago, she, like the Irish girl, had been impressed by the city. She had walked along Fifth Avenue in the autumn sunlight and stared with admiration at the fine new mansions that lined the avenue. She had lingered before the shop windows farther downtown and had admired the gowns displayed there: dresses of soft velvet and gleaming satin. She had sighed over the taffeta hats trimmed with ostrich plumes, the elegant muffs of sealskin and ermine. She had watched girls no older than herself, alighting from carriages that sparkled with polished brass, and sweeping into the shops. The newspapers might tell of the national depression, but there were obviously people with money here in New York.

And for Lavinia there was a chance to make a fresh start in a new country. Her hopes were not easily crushed, in spite of all that had happened to her in the past. At twenty, she was sure to find work as a governess, perhaps in one of those Fifth Avenue mansions. But one agency after another had turned her away. Her training was excellent, but she had had no practical experience. A few of the women who had interviewed her at the agencies had spoken of her youth as if it were a handicap. Even in her drab dress, with its high round collar and long sleeves, and the prim, old-fashioned black bonnet, she had not found favor.

She had to get work, and soon. In a week her rent at the shabby rooming house on Vesey Street would be due again. That was why she had been skimping on food, why she had postponed having new heels put on her shoes.

The door of Miss Fisher's inner office swung open, and Lavinia looked at the tall man who stood there taking his leave.

"I'm afraid you don't have the sort of person I'm looking for, Miss Fisher."

"But it seemed to me that Miss Armstrong—"

"She had good references, but she was unable to care for my son properly. She was not suitable."

"I'm sure we can find the sort of person you want, Mr. Moreland. There is a lady who worked for a very fine Boston family. She should be coming to see me this afternoon—"

"I'm sorry, Miss Fisher, but I'm going out of town as soon as I leave here. I had hoped—" He shrugged. "Good day," he said. He turned on his heel and walked briskly past Lavinia, past the rows of waiting applicants and out into the street. He seemed a self-assured man, one who knew what he wanted and would not settle for less. He reminded Lavinia of the mill owners back in her native city of Manchester.

She took a long breath and stood up, ignoring the weakness of her legs, and hurried to the outer door. The man was getting into a high-wheeled carriage with gleaming brass trim and well-brushed seats of dark red plush.

"Mr. Moreland?"

He turned and looked down at her, and she was conscious of his height and his massive, heavily muscled body.

"Please, may I speak with you?"

His brows went up. "I don't believe I've had the pleasure, Miss—"

"Corbett. Lavinia Corbett. You—you don't know me, Mr. Moreland, but I must speak with you on a matter of business."

"I don't usually conduct my business out in the street.

Miss—Corbett." His blue eyes were remote, frosty. The arrogance in his look made her want to turn and lose herself in the crowd, but she stood her ground.

"You need a governess. I heard you tell Miss Fisher so. I think I might qualify."

"Indeed? What makes you think so?"

"If you'll look at my letter of recommendation—"

He glanced at his watch. "I haven't much time, Miss Corbett. I'm on my way downtown to my office."

"I could speak with you on the way—that is, if you'll let me." She glanced at the carriage. He looked at her sharply, and she flushed. What must this well-dressed, prosperous gentleman think of her for waylaying him here in the street? A governess was supposed to have impeccable manners, to behave on all occasions with a prim correctness.

"Very well, Miss Corbett," he said. "I'll listen to your qualifications on my trip downtown."

He helped her into the carriage, and she felt his easy strength. She was conscious, too, of his overpowering masculinity. It made her feel uneasy.

He leaned forward and ordered the liveried driver to start. "I'm leaving town this afternoon on business, and I had hoped to settle this matter of a new governess before I left."

"I know, Mr. Moreland. I heard you telling Miss Fisher—"

"You were eavesdropping, then?"

"No, sir, I was not. I—I was sitting outside her office door, and I couldn't help overhearing—"

"No matter. But if you have good qualifications, why didn't Miss Fisher recommend you for the position?"

"Because I haven't worked before." The lie came easily, for she had repeated it so often. "But I have an excellent education. If you'll just read this testimonial—it's from Miss Chadwick—I'm sure you'll—"

He took the letter of recommendation, which was now a little worn and dog-eared with handling. His eyes went over it quickly.

"You have had no practical experience teaching children, I see."

"That's not quite true. I tutored the younger girls at Miss Chadwick's to help pay for my tuition."

"You were a charity pupil?"

She winced, for his guess had come close to the truth.

"No, indeed, Mr. Moreland. My aunt paid my tuition until she was taken ill." She did not add that her aunt had not paid in cash, but through her services as a dressmaker and seamstress for Miss Chadwick's young ladies, and for the headmistress as well. "Only after my aunt's illness did I work to pay for my education." She looked at him squarely. "Do you find that disgraceful?" she asked.

He shook his head. "On the contrary," he said. "I find it admirable."

She let herself relax slightly then. But a moment later she was back on her guard as he asked her, "You come from England. What made you leave?"

"I lived in Manchester all my life. It was a very sheltered existence at Miss Chadwick's Academy. No one for company but the teachers and the other girls. I—I wanted to see something of the world outside. I had read so much about America—the accounts of Mr. Dickens were fascinating—and so—"

"And so you decided to pick up and leave. Quite adventurous for a young lady in your position. Have you no family back in England?"

His blue eyes, under the heavy black brows, held hers. There was a peculiar half-smile on his arrogant mouth. She realized that he was a mature man, in his late thirties at least, and a man of considerable experience, she judged. How could she hope to carry off her lies with him?

"There was only my aunt. She died."

"I see. But I confess I'm still curious. You say you had to work as a student-teacher after your aunt could no longer pay your tuition. Where, then, did you come by the passage money to bring you to New York?"

"My aunt owned a small cottage outside Manchester, and after she died I was able to dispose of the property. The money I received covered my passage." He nodded without comment.

"Well, then, if you were eavesdropping—pardon me—

if you overheard my conversation with Miss Fisher, you know that I have had four—no, five—governesses for my son in the last two years. What makes you think you can succeed where they have failed?"

"You've nothing to lose by giving me a chance. I'll do my best, Mr. Moreland."

"You're determined, at least. And your method of approaching me was an original one. But so far, you have taught only little girls. My son is a headstrong boy, willful. I'm not sure you have either the experience or the strength to cope with him."

"I had the strength to work in a cotton mill in Manchester when I was ten years old—"

Her hand flew to her lips. She had not meant to speak of her early life. Bad enough to have admitted she had been a charity pupil, but to add to that the confession that she had started as a factory hand—

"The cotton mills—I know something about them. You must have a stronger constitution than I would have thought to look at you." He studied her in silence as the carriage moved along the narrow, crowded streets leading to the South Street pier. "Perhaps—yes, it's possible," he said at last.

She looked up at the hard, deeply tanned face. She did not dare to hope that he would really hire her, not after her revelations about her humble beginnings. But she had wanted to convince him that she had enough stamina to cope with a dozen small spoiled boys, if necessary.

They were down at the waterfront now, and the wind from the wind from the harbor was cold and raw. She drew her thin black cloak around her and stared out at the pier, at the ships anchored here. There were some sailing ships, with tall masts and furled sails, and many steamers. She breathed the mingled odors of salt, fish, spices and coffee. The man at her side looked out over the harbor, too, his face thoughtful. For a moment, he appeared to have forgotten her presence.

"My wife tells me I should take a suite of offices farther uptown in a more fashionable part of the city. But I feel at home here, close to the sea. You see those ships over there?" He pointed to two steamers that were being loaded by longshoremen. "Those are Moreland ships, new ones. They'll go to the Caribbean."

She did not interrupt him. There was obvious pride in his voice as he spoke of his ships. "I sailed out of Liverpool at twelve," he said. "As a cabin boy, aboard a slaver. I kept sailing in the triangular trade as long as there was profit in it, until the risks outweighed the profits. Then I traded in slaves on land, in the South. The Civil War put an end to that, of course."

"And now?"

"Now, Miss Corbett, I deal in other cargoes. Sugar, tobacco, rum. Tea from the Orient. And there is quite a trade these days in Oriental works of art. You'll see some of those when you go to Mooncliff."

"Mooncliff?"

"My home. It's in Dutchess County, overlooking the Hudson."

"Then you—you will give me a chance."

"Yes, Miss Corbett. You are a rather unconventional young lady. Enterprising, even a little daring." His eyes met hers. "Desperate, too, aren't you? You don't have to answer. I know the signs of deprivation, of hunger."

She did not answer. She felt humiliated that he could guess at her desperation, but her shame gave way before her vast sense of relief. She had work. She would have a roof over her head, food to eat; and she would not have to work as a lady's maid. A governess was, of course, a paid dependent, but one who ranked above the ordinary servants.

"Since you've had no experience as a governess, you won't be set in your ways. You will deal with my son Stuart exactly as I tell you to."

"Oh, yes. Mr. Moreland."

"It isn't easy for a young woman like yourself, in a strange country, in search of work."

There was sympathy in his voice. She straightened her shoulders and raised her head. "I've managed."

"Not too well, I would guess." He reached into his coat pocket, took out his wallet and handed her a few bills. "Buy yourself a square meal. It's a long trip out to

Mooncliff, and I shouldn't want you to collapse on the train."

The following day the weather changed; the wind blowing in from the river brought rain, light at first, but glowing heavier as the day went on. Lavinia Corbett, peering through the window of the closed carriage that had brought her from the station, could scarcely see the huge iron gates of Mooncliff until the carriage was directly in front of them. The gatekeeper hurried out of his gray stone house to open the gates, the driver cracked his whip, and the horses trotted up the long, winding drive at a smart pace. Two rows of red maples, one on either side of the drive, made a tunnel of foliage, shutting out the rain-swept sky.

When they were nearly half a mile along the road, Lavinia saw the towers and chimneys of Mooncliff looming up ahead like those of a castle in a dream. The lower part of the house was veiled in the fog that drifted up from the river.

The Morelands' coachman helped her down and held an umbrella over her head as he accompanied her up to the door. Then he pulled at the bell. When the great door swung open, he left her and returned to the carriage.

The woman who answered the door was dressed in fine gray broadcloth. Her gown, despite its simple cut, had a certain elegance. On her smooth, dark hair she wore a starched white cap trimmed with Brussels lace. Lavinia handed the woman a note Jason Moreland had written.

"Oh, yes. You are Lavinia Corbett," the woman said, gleaming at the note. "The new governess." She stepped aside, and Lavinia entered the hallway. "I am the housekeeper," she went on. "My name is Miss Buchanan. Mrs. Moreland is rather busy this afternoon. We all are. But if you will wait here, I'll tell her that you have arrived."

Lavinia was painfully conscious of her new surroundings—rich, imposing, completely overpowering. The Selby house in Manchester, where she had worked, had been nothing like this. She stared at the heavy hanging bronze lamp overhead, at the black and white marble floor. Miss Buchanan had turned and disappeared into the shadows of the hallway that stretched ahead. Even with the gas lamps set at intervals in the walls, the hallway was dim. The tall, narrow windows with their panes of ruby, emerald and violet glass did little to admit light on this rainy autumn afternoon. Lavinia could make out the tall, carved newel-posts of the great stairway directly ahead, but not much more.

She found herself wishing that she had not come here to this great mansion under false pretenses, that she could have told Jason Moreland the whole truth about herself; but that, of course, would have ruined any possibility of her getting the position of governess. A governess had to be a person of unblemished respectability.

"As I was when I left Miss Chadwick's Academy," she thought. Her first position had been that of governess to two little girls, the daughters of Roger Selby, a prosperous millowner. She had done her work well and conscientiously, and her two young charges had been fond of her. After she had worked there for six months, Lieutenant Arthur Selby had come home to Manchester on holiday leave from the army. To Lavinia, whose only acquaintance with men had been limited to formal introductions to stout, balding businessmen like Mr. Roger Selby himself, young Arthur was a revelation. Tall and splendid in his red and gold uniform, he was like a figure out of one of the romantic novels Lavinia sometimes read in secret, after her charges had been put to bed.

Even now she could remember every detail of that Christmas week in Manchester. Her stolen meetings with the young lieutenant, their whispered conversations. And his promises. He would take her away to London, where his regiment was stationed. They would be married, and later she would go with him to India. Glowing promises. Fantastic dreams.

The reality had come later, after the trip to London. Reality had been a room in a London lodging house, a wide brass bed. He had taken her without tenderness, without the slightest consideration for her complete lack of experience. It had been a terrifying, painful interlude that she would never forget.

She had wanted to leave him the following day, but she could not have returned to her post in Manchester, and she had nowhere else to go. She could only hope that Arthur would marry her, although she had no illusions about being in love with him, not any longer. But she might still have the security of being Mrs. Arthur Selby. This, too, had been lost to her. When Arthur's regiment shipped out to India he said goodbye, leaving her with enough money to take care of her needs for a few months, a year if she was careful.

She had used that money to come to New York, steerage class.

Her thoughts were interrupted by the reappearance of the smartly dressed housekeeper. "Mrs. Moreland will see you now," said Miss Buchanan.

Lavinia followed the housekeeper down the long, high-ceilinged hallway, past what seemed like endless doors leading to the first-floor rooms. She caught fleeting glimpses of oil paintings in heavy gold frames, of antique weapons, tapestries from French chateaus, and rare embroidered silks from China.

Through one half-open door, Lavinia could see a group of servants scurrying about, polishing, dusting, moving furniture. A trim young maidservant was perched atop a ladder, shining prisms of the largest, most ornate chandelier Lavinia had ever seen.

"The ballroom," Miss Buchanan said as they hurried past. "The ball isn't until next week, but there are so many preparations to be made. "It's the first ball of the season here, and a very special one. President Grant himself will be the guest of honor."

Lavinia could not think of a suitable reply. The President of the United States here, under this very roof, where she would be living. Mr. Moreland was, then, not only wealthy but involved in the politics of this exciting country. A man of importance, of prestige. Of course, it wasn't like having Queen Victoria as guest of honor, but nevertheless Lavinia was deeply impressed.

She reminded herself that although Mr. Moreland had hired her, she would not remain long unless Mrs. Moreland approved his choice. She had to make a good impression on the mistress of Mooncliff.

"This is the library," Miss Buchanan was saying. She knocked, then opened the heavy sliding doors. "You may go in," she said. Then, to someone inside the room: "Miss Lavinia Corbett, Mrs. Moreland."

Lavinia crossed the threshold of the large book-lined room, looked at its dark walnut paneling, its coffered ceiling and heavy wine-red drapes.

"Come in, Miss Corbett." Mrs. Moreland had a soft voice with an unfamiliar inflection, unlike the quick, clipped speech of the New Yorkers Lavinia had heard these past weeks. "We're rather busy here right now, but since my husband sent you—and such a dreary day for a trip, too—I will look at your references."

Lavinia had been right, then. Mr. Moreland had hired her, but she would have to pass Mrs. Moreland's inspection, too. She studied the woman who for the moment controlled her fate.

The glowing firelight showed Mrs. Moreland to be a young woman, only a few years older than herself, and beautiful, with masses of dark red hair parted at the center and drawn back into a simple chignon. Brown eyes that turned to gold in the light of the leaping flames on the hearth.

It was not easy for Lavinia to keep the look of naked envy from her face, to compose her features into the respectful mask necessary for the interview. As she made her curtsey, then waited to be asked to take a seat, she had to struggle to hide her feelings. What must it be like to be Mrs. Jason Moreland, mistress of this splendid house where great balls were given, where dignitaries were entertained? To be waited on, pampered, loved?

That last, Lavinia did not envy. Remembering Arthur Selby's brutal caresses, knowing what love meant when it had been stripped of all the fine romantic trappings, she wanted no part of it. But perhaps it would still be worth submitting to those inexplicable masculine needs in exchange for a life like Mrs. Moreland's.

"Please sit down," Mrs. Moreland said. "No, not over there. Here by the fire. You must be chilled to the bone."

Lavinia sat down carefully on the edge of a high-backed leather chair, opposite the walnut and velvet love seat on which Mrs. Moreland was sitting. She kept her eyes cast down in the demure manner taught her at Miss Chadwick's Academy; from under her long lashes, she studied the red-haired, soft-spoken woman.

Mrs. Moreland wore a gown of pale yellow silk, cut in the latest fashion. The underskirt was trimmed with three wide folds of amber velvet, and the tunic, which emphasized her high, rounded breasts and small waist, was looped at the side with an amber rosette. The short peplum was trimmed with velvet of the same amber color. Lavinia had observed enough about clothes to realize that Mrs. Moreland had chosen the amber color to set off her gold-flecked eyes, slightly tilted under their delicately arched brows.

There were generations of good breeding in that face, Lavinia thought, in the fine bone structure, the delicate, creamy skin. Jason Moreland, despite his wealth and self-assurance, lacked that look of breeding. His manners were perfect when he wanted them to be, but Lavinia knew he did not come from the same background as his wife.

"May I look at your references?" Mrs. Moreland was asking.

Lavinia reached into her reticule and handed her the letter of recommendation from Miss Chadwick's Academy.

"You've never worked as a governess."

"No, but I—" Once more, Lavinia told the carefully concocted version of her story.

"I suppose Mr. Moreland had told you that we have had five governesses during the past two years. Not one has proved satisfactory."

"Yes, Mrs. Moreland. But I have a way with children. I get along with them, and they like me."

"Little girls, perhaps. But Stuart is an active boy, big for his age and—high-spirited."

Lavinia did not fail to catch the slight pause before the last word. Spoiled and willful was more like it, she thought. But she would succeed where those other governesses had failed. "If you will give me a chance, I'll do everything I can to please you—and Mr. Moreland."

"My husband has rather definite ideas as to how Stuart should be brought up. I don't agree completely, but . . . "

Jason Moreland was master of the house, then. Still, Lavinia was sure that he could not fail to be influenced by his wife's opinion in domestic matters. If she disapproved of the situation, she would find a way to rid herself of Lavinia in short order. Surely a woman like Mrs. Moreland would know how to use her beauty, her feminine wiles, to sway her husband. Lavinia repressed a slight shiver as she remembered her feelings about Jason Moreland during the short time they had sat side by side in his carriage during the drive along Broadway. She had feared him, his overpowering, almost brutal masculinity.

To live under the same roof with such a man would not be easy. But, she reminded herself, she would have little contact with Jason Moreland. She would see him only at a distance. Her world would be the nursery and the schoolroom. She would take her meals with her pupil, would live in the half-world of the governess: neither a servant nor a member of the family.

"I have a younger son, Phillip," Mrs. Moreland was saying. "But his nurse, Miss Wilmot, takes care of him."

"Then I would have charge of Master Stuart only."

"You will find that he will occupy all your time," Mrs. Moreland said dryly.

Lavinia held her breath. Had Mrs. Moreland made her decision? If Lavinia had been religious, she would have prayed. As it was, she pressed her hands together and tried to shut out thoughts of the cold wet streets of New York City, of the oncoming winter and of aching hunger such as she had known as a child.

"Personally, I think you are too young and inexperienced to cope with Stuart. But you may try. The position is yours, Miss Corbett. For the present."

"Thank you, Mrs. Moreland. I'll do my best."

"And now Miss Buchanan will show you to your room. We will speak again, another time. Today, I'm quite busy; we all are."

"Oh, yes," Lavinia said. "The ball. It is a great honor to have the President as a guest, is it not?"

Mrs. Moreland's full red lips tightened. "That is a matter of opinion. I am a southerner, Miss Corbett. I cannot be expected to share your obvious admiration for Ulysses Grant."

Lavinia silently cursed her luck. She had tried to flatter Mrs. Moreland and had instead offended her. "Of course, I know little of American politics, only what I have read."

As a matter of fact, Lavinia had always taken a keen interest in politics and had read extensively about the American Civil War. She knew, too, from her reading that President Grant had been a better general than he was a national leader. Almost from the outset of his first term in office, he had been implicated in the scandals that had rocked the nation. He had been accused, perhaps unfairly, of having been a party to the machinations of Gould and Fisk that had led to the disaster of Black Friday. He was blamed for not having taken action against the Custom House Ring until the abuses had been investigated by a congressional committee and the corruption brought to light. Money from the infamous "Whiskey Ring" had flowed freely into Grant's campaign chest in 1872. Even in England, Lavinia had read of these matters, for politics had always fascinated her, although she knew better than to discuss such unfeminine interests with others.

Now she found herself wondering what possible connections Jason Moreland might have with the great affairs of the nation. He obviously had important political connections; he was more than a prosaic businessman. She wondered, too, why Mrs. Moreland had agreed to be hostess to President Grant, feeling as she did about him. She supposed that, while Mrs. Moreland might be influential in the domestic sphere, her husband ran his business activities as he saw fit, and used his home for social affairs that would further his business interests, even if it meant forcing his wife to play unwilling hostess to a man she despised.

Mrs. Moreland stood up. The interview was at a close. Miss Buchanan led Lavinia upstairs to the third floor. She moved quickly, purposefully. Lavinia felt a thrill of excitement. Her employer was one of those Americans she had read about, one of the new movers and shapers of this post-War period; his ships traveled the globe, bringing wealth from far-flung ports she knew only as names in a geography book. And she was to be a part of this fascinating household, this Mooncliff.

Then she sighed, reminding herself that she must not dream of anything more than what she had already achieved. She was a governess. She would care for Jason Moreland's son and confine herself to the world of the schoolroom. She would live the quiet, isolated life of a governess, would try to ingratiate herself with her young pupil. That, she suspected, would be no easy task. The great events that touched on the life of Mooncliff had nothing to do with her.

Miss Buchanan opened the door of a handsomely furnished room, all maple and starched chintz. "I hope you will be comfortable," she said. "I'll have your trunk carried up directly. And one of the maids will bring you tea and sandwiches."

Lavinia murmured her thanks, but Miss Buchanan had already started off down the hall. She appeared to be always in a hurry, and no wonder, with a house the size of this one to run.

On the threshold of her new room Lavinia paused, savoring the comfort of her surroundings. This was quite unlike the dreary quarters she had had in the Selby home. This was a prim, virginal room, and the furniture was new, the draperies and hooked rugs bright and cheerful. No shoddy castoffs here at Mooncliff, not even for the governess.

She turned quickly as she heard a clicking of nails on the polished floor of the hallway. Then she stepped back to avoid something large and dark that came running at her. A long-haired black dog with a head like that of a shaggy lion. A huge dog with bright yellow eyes.

Behind the dog came a small boy wearing a sailor suit of dark blue flannel. He watched Lavinia as she pressed herself against the wall to avoid contact with the dog.

"Are you afraid of dogs?" he asked.

This had to be Stuart, a solidly built little boy of nearly

six, with dark red hair and bright blue eyes. A handsome child. "You are afraid, aren't you?"

He obviously hoped that she was. "No, not in the least," she lied. He looked disappointed.

"You're the new governess, aren't you?"

"That's right." She made herself reach out and pat the dog's gigantic head, with its mane of long, coarse fur. The animal licked her hand, leaving it wet and sticky.

"I'll bet Nelson's the biggest dog you ever saw," the boy said.

"No, he isn't, Master Stuart," she lied again. "Back in England I had two dogs, both larger than Nelson."

The boy's bright blue eyes grew round. Unwilling to give up so easily, he said, "I'll bet you're afraid of snakes, though. Ladies are always afraid of snakes."

"I'm not. I think they're pretty. Do you have a pet snake to show me?"

"Well, I—" His blue eyes searched her face, eyes that were curiously familiar. Of course. Jason Moreland's eyes, alert, missing little, judging her. "What *are* you afraid of, then?" he finally asked.

A strange question for a young child to ask. She looked at him squarely, and this time she spoke the truth. "I'm afraid of going hungry."

Stuart was genuinely bewildered. Then all at once he smiled, and Lavinia thought, "What a beautiful child."

"You won't go hungry here," he said. "There's lots of food down in the kitchen. I'll tell Elspeth."

"Thank you," Lavinia said, "but Miss Buchanan has already ordered a tray for me."

"All right, then," he said. He snapped his fingers, and the dog Nelson trotted after him along the hall and down the stairs.

It was still raining late that evening when Lavinia was getting ready for bed. She stripped off the dreary poplin dress and the petticoats beneath. Then, before she put on her nightgown, she paused in front of the pretty gilt-framed mirror and looked at her naked body. She ran her fingers lightly over the smooth, pale skin. Her breasts were beautiful, small and high, with rosy, pointed nipples. Her hips curved in a graceful line from her tiny waist. Without her ugly, badly cut clothes, she was a beautiful woman.

She took the pins from her hair and shook the blond waves down over her shoulders. She could not bear to cover herself with her cheap flannel nightgown, not yet. She turned this way and that, looking at herself with a mixture of pride and bitterness. She was as lovely, in her own way, as Denise Moreland. And yet, Denise Moreland had everything—money, position, a luxurious home, fine clothes, a husband like Jason Moreland.

At the memory of Jason Moreland Lavinia felt a curious excitement. Yesterday, when she had sat beside him in his carriage, he had seen her as a prim, plain young woman in shabby clothes, a woman desperate for work. But if he could see her now, pale and slender, her blond hair falling over her shoulders and the lush curves of her breasts . . .

Instinctively she reached for her nightgown and pulled it on, fastening the buttons up to her chin. Jason Moreland wasn't even in the house. He would not be back for several days, not until the day of the ball.

And even then, when they were living under the same roof, he would never see her as anything but the governess. And that only if she was fortunate enough to keep the position.

Five governesses in two years. How could she, young and relatively inexperienced, hope to succeed where all those others had failed?

Chapter 4

The great chandelier overhead sparkled in a rainbow of colors; the floor of the ballroom at Mooncliff had been polished until it gleamed like satin under the feet of the dancers. The scent of the hothouse roses blended with those of French perfumes.

Although the September evening was cold and windy, Denise Moreland knew that even if it had rained or snowed, even if a blizzard had swept down on Mooncliff, her guests would have found a way of getting there tonight. During the years she had been Jason Moreland's wife, the balls held at Mooncliff had become famous. Tomorrow, she knew, this one would be given prominence on the pages of the *New York Herald* and the *Globe*. President Grant was the guest of honor; that fact in itself made the affair newsworthy.

Denise danced the first dance with the quiet, stocky, bearded man who only a few years before had led the Yankee Army against her own Confederacy. Somehow she managed to make the politely formal conversation expected of her as the hostess, the mistress of Mooncliff.

But she was relieved when the last strains of the waltz died away, and she could go on to another partner.

She looked regal that night in a gown of black brocade, with diamonds sparkling at her throat and in her high-piled hair. Diamond earrings swung and glittered with cold fire as she went through the movements of the waltz, the polka, the German. She danced with senators and representatives, with businessmen who controlled great railroads and shipping lines and mining companies.

During the early part of the evening she caught sight of Jason, dancing with ladies as fashionably and expensively dressed as she. Their gowns billowed out around them in the intricately draped folds and panniers that were in style this season. Their jewels gleamed under the lights from the great chandelier and the wall sconces. The sound of their laughter rose above the music of the orchestra. Every one of them was having a marvelous evening.

Everyone except Denise.

She had danced only one dance with Jason, and he had appeared preoccupied and distant. He had not seen her for two weeks, and yet tonight, after he had complimented her on her gown and told her she looked lovely, he had lapsed into silence. She knew that his thoughts were not with her, and her attempts to make conversation faltered and died away.

Shortly before eleven o'clock he went into the library, accompanied by President Grant and several other men, including Senator Burgess and Congressman Marsh, both of whom Jason had invited to the house recently on several occasions.

Denise found herself dancing with one after another of her guests; she had no lack of partners. But there was only one man she wanted to dance with tonight, only one man whose arms she wanted around her. And he was closeted in the library talking business.

Now, as midnight approached, she was dancing with Captain MacKay. "It's nearly time for supper," he was saying. "I'm sure Mr. Moreland will join us then." He smiled down at her. "You may be sure he has important business; otherwise he wouldn't have left your side tonight—not with you looking so pretty."

She forced a smile to acknowledge his compliment. "Jason always has important business, Captain MacKay. But I wish he could confine it to his office and—" She broke off. It was improper to complain about her husband, even to one of his oldest friends. "Jason has been in Washington these last two weeks—something to do with his new Caribbean line."

"There you are, then," MacKay said. "He'll need political support for that. There are trade agreements to be worked out and—"

"Captain MacKay, tell me the truth. Jason's not involved in trade with Cuba, is he?"

MacKay looked away.

"Forgive me," she said quickly. "I did not mean to make you reveal anything Jason wants kept confidential. It's only that I've heard rumors about illegal trade in arms with the Cuban rebel forces. Now that they've started their war for independence again, they'll need arms, and Jason's new ships—"

"Don't worry yourself about such matters, I beg you. These are men's affairs." The sunburned, weather-lined face softened in a benevolent smile. "A charming young woman like yourself should not even know about these things. I'm sure my wife doesn't."

Denise knew perfectly well that Rosalind MacKay, the captain's blond wife, was far shrewder and better-informed than she pretended to be. If she chose to appear frivolous, light-minded, with no more serious thoughts than the arrival of her newest party gown or the angle of her bonnet, that was her affair.

"No, indeed, Mrs. Moreland," the captain was saying, "my wife doesn't concern herself with men's business, and neither should you. Why, with this great house to supervise and two fine young sons, I should think you would be busy enough. As for your husband, he can take care of himself. Look how far he has come these last few years."

The waltz came to an end. There was a movement in

the direction of the adjoining room, where a lavish supper had been spread. The staff had outdone itself tonight. Even the first ball at Mooncliff five years before had not been more impressive.

"There, you see, my dear," Captain MacKay was saying, "there's Mr. Moreland now. And from the look on his face, I should say he's scored another triumph."

Rosalind, who came to join them, laughed, the pink and rose plumes on her elaborately dressed hair swaying. "Leave it to a man, any man, to be right on time when supper is ready." She laughed again with that high-pitched, tinkling sound that had become so familiar to Denise over the years.

But Denise could not share her light-hearted mood. Jason was making his way over to them, but he was still accompanied by their guest of honor, President Grant, and by those others with whom he had been discussing business. She would not get a chance to speak to her husband alone until after the ball.

She had made such wonderful plans for tonight. She had hoped to draw Jason away into the conservatory or out onto the terrace to tell him her news. Now she would have to wait through the long lavish supper, and then more dancing.

It was nearly four o'clock in the morning. Having dismissed her maid, Denise sat at her dressing table. Her hair cascaded around her shoulders, the dark red masses freed from her high-piled coiffure. A pale green silk nightdress and matching lace-trimmed robe had replaced the black ball gown.

Jason came into the bedroom. His blue eyes were still bright with that look of triumph she'd seen when he had emerged from the library earlier that evening. Whatever business had been transacted, it had been favorable for him. He had the look of a conqueror.

He came to her swiftly and put his hands on her shoulders, and she felt the warmth of his fingers through the thin silk of her garments.

"What a night!" he said, laughing. "And you—you were magnificent. The perfect hostess. President Grant was charmed, and Mrs. Grant said you were—"

"May we talk about something else?"

Her tone was formal, even icy, although Jason's touch had stirred her as it always did. She wanted to turn to him, to raise her face for his kiss. Instead she forced herself to sit perfectly still, to ignore the warm current that had begun to move through her.

"I realize you did not particularly want President Grant under our roof," he said. "But the War has been over for some time now."

"Not for me. Not for my family and my friends in Charleston. How can you say the War is over, with carpetbaggers and thieves sitting in the legislature back home? With President Grant imposing martial law on nine counties in South Carolina? With the oldest families in the state penniless, having to sell their silver and their furniture to buy food—"

"At any rate, your family has escaped that humiliation."

"Thanks to you and the money you gave my father. You don't have to remind me, Jason."

"I have no wish to remind you, love. But neither do I wish to fight the War over again—not tonight." His hands moved from her shoulders and cupped her breasts. "I've been away for two weeks, and now I'm home. I want to forget everything except that you're my wife, and you're here, and I—"

He drew a long, ragged breath, and his hands caressed her breasts until the nipples hardened under his fingers.

She drew away and stood up quickly.

"Jason, I—I have something to tell you."

"It can wait." His arms went around her, and his lips were warm and eager. His tongue explored the moist softness of her mouth. She felt the hard pressure of his body against her, and she knew that he would not wait much longer. Still, she refused to respond.

He released her abruptly, his dark brows drawing together, the hard lines deepening around his mouth. "Damn it, you're not going to sulk like a spoiled child because I couldn't be with you all evening. I've explained—"

"You've explained nothing. These men you associate

with—Senator Burgess, Congressman Marsh—radical Republicans, all of them. Men who want to keep the South at the mercy of their carpetbagging friends, of the Freedman's Bureau and the black militia. Men who were involved in profiteering during the War and every kind of scandal since. They are upstarts, adventurers who—"

Jason's laugh was harsh, unpleasant. "Like me, Denise? Surely you haven't forgotten that I am an upstart and an adventurer, too." His eyes were cold and angry. "You haven't forgotten?" he repeated.

There was a coldness in her now, too. "No, Jason. I haven't forgotten."

Ever since that night when he had told her about the voyage of the *Nubian Queen,* she had tried to forget. She had tried to shut out those terrible visions that sometimes haunted her dreams. But that had been years ago, when Jason had been young and desperate to lift himself out of the squalor and misery of his early life. Now, surely, he had as much as he would ever need.

"There is no need for you to involve yourself with men like Marsh and Burgess, not now," she said. "You have Mooncliff, your ships. You have everything you've ever wanted."

"Everything?" His mouth twisted. "You know, Denise, I thought when I married you that you would belong to me completely. I knew you resented the means I had used to make you my wife. But I thought that in time you would forgive that, that you would realize how much I— Stupid of me, wasn't it, to think that a marriage ceremony would make you mine?"

"I am yours, Jason. How can you doubt that?"

"Then why do you torment me? You know I need you and yet you hold me at arm's length, because of far-fetched scruples, because of matters that have nothing to do with you. My business, my life away from Mooncliff—"

"I want to share your life, every part of it."

He looked down at her, his eyes alight with mockery now.

"Very well, my love. Shall we discuss my business, then? Shall we talk about the problems of a protective tariff, or about Cuban imports, or perhaps the possibility of building a canal through Panama one day, so that my ships can reach the Pacific without going around South America?"

"Don't, Jason. Please don't laugh at me. Perhaps the things you do would not seem wrong to me if you would take the time to explain."

"Once you forced me to tell you things about myself I didn't want you to know. And then you turned away from me, and you drove me to—"

"Jason!" Her voice rose in a cry of pain. "No! Please, I don't want to remember that night."

"Neither do I." His arms went around her and he pressed his face against her hair. "I want to cherish you, to protect you. To stand between you and anything that might hurt you. Isn't that enough?"

It wasn't enough, but she knew that she must forget the horror of that long-ago night, and make him forget, too. There was only one way to do that. She pressed herself against him, molded her body to his. His fingers shook as he opened the buttons of her robe.

He lifted her off her feet and held her against him, her long red hair sweeping down over his arm. He bent his head, and his mouth was hot against her breast. She felt herself surrendering to the hunger inside her.

Together on the bed, they clung to each other. He undressed her, then himself. At first he teased her with light touches on her bare flesh. Then she drew him down to her, and she felt the hard, urgent thrusts. She moved beneath him, her hands drawing him against her, until with a force that was close to violence he brought her hunger to its highest peak, then satisfied her completely. Even then she could not let him go, but held him against her, listening as his harsh, unsteady breathing resumed its normal rhythm.

"Was it good for you?" he asked.

"Need you ask? Can't you tell?"

He laughed, the warm, self-satisfied laugh she had come to know. "Of course," he said. "I like to hear you say it, though." He stroked the curve of her hip and her long, rounded thigh. Then, raising himself on one arm, he looked down at her, his face shadowed in the dim glow of the lamp beside the bed.

"The next time we have a ball here at Mooncliff, I shall dance every dance with you."

She smiled. "Perhaps that won't be possible."

"What do you mean?"

"I may not be able to dance for a while. That's what I wanted to tell you this evening. I'm going to have a baby."

"Why didn't you tell me as soon as I got home?"

"How could I? First you were down in the library alone, going over papers; then we had to get dressed, and then—"

"I'm sorry. Denise, I wasn't—I didn't hurt you just now, did I? If I'd known I wouldn't have—"

"I wanted you to. I'm not a china doll. I won't break."

He held her in his arms, tenderness taking the place of passion now. "You're sure about the baby?"

"Quite sure. It will arrive in the spring."

"You're not staying here at Mooncliff," he said firmly. "This time, we're taking no chances. You will move into New York City right after the first of the year. You can stay with Rosalind MacKay, if you like."

"But she wouldn't have space enough for the children and Miss Wilmot and Miss Corbett."

"The boys can remain here at Mooncliff. Miss Wilmot is good with Phillip. And as for Stuart, I think Miss Corbett can cope with him. How is she working out, by the way?"

"She seems efficient, and Stuart likes her, but—"

"What's wrong, then?"

"I'm not sure. She's very young, and she has had no previous experience. We don't really know very much about her."

"I suppose not. But if it will set your mind at ease, I'll check on her references."

"She comes from England."

"I have connections in Manchester. Leave it all to me." He smiled down at her. "I don't want anything worrying you, love. Not now." He drew her close. "You've made me very happy, Denise. You've given me two fine sons—"

She stiffened in his embrace. Two sons, but only one

of them his. So many times during the past years she had been tormented by the knowledge of her deceit. But she had lied for Jason's sake, to save his pride, to keep his illusions about her from being destroyed. This third child would be his, as Stuart was. That was all that mattered.

She relaxed in Jason's arms and closed her eyes. But her last conscious thought was of Lavinia Corbett. She did not like the idea of leaving Stuart in the care of this young woman whom she scarcely knew. There was something about Lavinia. . . .

Chapter 5

Stuart Moreland disappeared immediately after lunch, and Lavinia Corbett, who, after three months at Mooncliff knew his habits, went in search of her young charge, heading in the direction of the stables. She was crossing the terrace at the rear of the house when she was intercepted by Jason Moreland. Except for the customary formalities, he had not said a word to her since his return from his business trip.

Apparently, after hiring her, he had forgotten her existence. Now, as he came up to her on the terrace, she smiled politely and said, "Good afternoon, sir."

She would have moved on, but he put a hand on her arm to stop her. "Just a moment, if you please."

"Yes, sir?"

She realized that he was looking at her with more than a passing interest. Her appearance had changed, she knew, since that day in late September, when she had come up to him in the street to plead for a job. She was better dressed. Elspeth Buchanan had sent her to the seamstress who did the sewing for the staff of Mooncliff, and Lavinia had ordered a most becoming dress of pearl-gray silk, shot through with subtle undertones of blue and purple. It was a simple garment, without frills or decorations, but the skillful cut emphasized her small waist and her high, firm breasts. Her hair, no longer pulled back and hidden under an ugly, old-fashioned bonnet, was now curled around her face. A few blond ringlets could be seen under the hood of her dark gray cloak.

Perhaps Jason Moreland was noticing the change in her appearance for the first time. But then, something in his eyes told her that he had not stopped her here on the windswept terrace to admire the way she looked.

"May I speak with you for a few moments?" he asked. It was not really a question, of course, but a command.

"Of course. Only—I was on my way to the stables to look for Stuart. I was told that his pony would arrive this afternoon, and I did not want him to be there when it was brought in."

Jason stood quite still, looking down at her with a coldness that made her uneasy, that caused her to chatter in a way that was alien to her. "He's been looking forward to the pony. It's the perfect Christmas gift, and I know he'll be pleased when he sees it tomorrow morning."

"I'm sure he will. However, I don't wish to discuss Stuart's Christmas gifts at the moment."

Jason had planted himself in front of her, and she felt an odd, trapped sensation. The wind from the river beyond the terrace whipped her cloak about her.

"Mrs. Moreland tells me you are doing well with Stuart."

"I think so, sir."

"The boy likes you. And you know how to handle him. Commendable, since this is your first position as a governess."

"Thank you, sir. I've tried."

Jason did not raise his voice, but it took on a steely undertone. "Do you think I am a fool, Miss Corbett? A man who is easily deceived?"

Her heart began to hammer, and she found it difficult to take a deep breath. "No indeed, Mr. Moreland."

"Then why did you try to deceive me?"

"I don't understand."

"Don't you? As I recall, you told me you had been a pupil at Miss Chadwick's Academy in Manchester. That your only teaching experience was the tutoring of the younger girls there."

"Indeed, sir, my reference—"

"Your reference was accurate. So far as it went. But you also said your aunt had died and that you used your legacy from her to come to New York."

She looked out over the gray waters of the Hudson. She was not able to meet his eyes.

"You left out a few rather important facts, didn't you?"

He put his hands on her arms and swung her around. She was forced to look at the hard, tanned face; the alert eyes, icy and probing now; the wide, sensual mouth.

"You did not come to New York directly from Manchester at all."

"Well, no, but I don't see what—"

"In fact, you underrated your credentials, my dear Miss Corbett. You had six months of experience as a governess in a private home. The home of a Mr. Roger Selby, a Manchester millowner."

"Of course not. If I'd had experience, why would I have—"

"You did not remain long in Roger Selby's home." His voice took on a suave brutality that frightened her more than if he had shouted at her.

"You found—employment, shall we say—with another member of the Selby family. Lieutenant Arthur Selby. You went to London with him, and there you—"

"Oh, please—"

"There you lived with him as his mistress, until the regiment was ordered to India. Tell me, why did you decide to leave England then?" His cold blue eyes moved over her, appraising her face, then her body. "Surely a young woman with your charms could have found another officer to—"

"It wasn't like that. Arthur said he wanted to marry me, and I believed him."

"You really thought he'd marry you, a little nobody

who started out in a cotton mill, a charity pupil at Miss Chadwick's?"

He released her then, and she turned and looked past him, not at the river but at the gray stone towers and chimneys of Mooncliff. This house had been a sanctuary, and now she would have to leave it. Now, in December, when New York City was crowded with an army of the jobless, the homeless, she too would be without work, without shelter. Without even a reference. She would be turned away from Mooncliff this very afternoon, perhaps. To spend Christmas day in some wretched lodging house in the Five Points district of the city.

She squared her shoulders and looked directly at Jason Moreland. If he had expected her to beg, to dissolve into tears, he was mistaken. "Shall I pack my things now, sir?"

"We're not finished with our talk yet." He gave her a swift, impersonal glance. "You're shivering."

"It's cold. The wind from the river—"

"Of course. Let us go inside."

He opened the door leading into the conservatory and stood aside to allow her to enter the warm room, with its fantastic frieze of flowers, shrubs and vines. Then, closing the door behind them, he led her to a wrought-iron bench at one end; a potted Chinese wisteria overhung the bench, its pale purple blossoms perfuming the air with their delicate scent.

"Sit down."

It was warm and humid in here; her fingers, usually quick and deft, were clumsy as she fumbled with the fastenings of her cloak.

"Let me help you." He undid the fastenings, helped her off with the garment and laid it over the arm of the bench. She sat down on the brightly colored chintz cushions, knowing that her legs would not support her much longer.

Jason seated himself beside her. "You look quite pale, Miss Corbett. But most attractive. That gown is becoming. The color suits you. New, isn't it?"

She nodded, bewildered by this new tack he was taking.

"And you no longer have your hair pulled back in that ugly fashion." He looked at the pale blond ringlets that fell over her shoulders. "I suppose you learned to make yourself attractive, back there in London. As the mistress of Lieutenant Selby, you must have led a colorful life. Balls, fetes. . . ."

He was playing with her, tormenting her as the boys had done back in the Manchester cotton mill, when she had been a half-starved, overworked drudge at barely ten years old. Damn him! Wasn't it enough that he had discovered all her secrets, that he was about to turn her out of his house? Did he have to amuse himself by using sarcasm as a weapon against her?

"What do you know about my life in London?" For the moment, her fear of the future was pushed aside, and anger took its place. "I hated it. From that first night in that stuffy, overfurnished room, when I found out what Arthur was like, what you all are like."

He raised his brows and smiled. "All?"

"Men." All her long-suppressed rage and disgust were concentrated in that one word.

"Go on."

"You are coarse and cruel, all of you. Taking what pleases you, and then—"

"If you felt that way after your first night with Selby, why did you stay with him?"

"I've told you."

"You thought he meant to marry you. But surely, after that first night, you must have guessed he had other plans."

"It was a gamble. I thought I could make him change his mind."

"That was foolish of you. But if you found him so coarse and cruel, you must have suspected he would be no different even if he did marry you."

"I thought about that. But I didn't have much choice, did I?"

"No, I don't suppose you did. Mr. Roger Selby, the self-righteous and respectable millowner, would not have taken you back. And I'm sure his wife lost no time in informing Miss Chadwick of your fall from grace. But I'm told there are refuges for fallen women in England, charitable institutions—"

"I would rather have died."

She fumbled for her handkerchief, knowing that she could not hold back her tears much longer.

"Don't cry," he said. "I can't talk sensibly to a weeping woman. When I first met you that day on Broadway, I said you were a determined and unconventional young lady. I admire those traits. And a moment ago, when you flared up at me like an angry cat, I liked that, too."

"I don't give a damn what you like!" No need to play the prim, virginal governess now, and there was a measure of relief in giving vent to her real feelings.

"You should care. After all, I am your employer."

"Not anymore."

"You're planning to leave Mooncliff?"

A swift, impossible hope flared up within her. "I thought—surely you won't allow me to stay and take care of your son, now that you know about me."

"I hardly think Stuart is old enough to be corrupted. You get on well with him, and he likes you. Yes, Miss Corbett. You may stay on here at Mooncliff, if you want to."

The profound sense of relief that she felt was almost too great to be borne.

"Now that we understand each other, we should get along better."

What did he mean? Now that he knew she was not what she had pretended to be, would he expect, or demand— He was a sensual man; that much she could see in his face. And his wife, advanced in her third pregnancy, would be leaving Mooncliff to stay in the city after the first of the year. She drew away with a quick, involuntary movement.

He laughed. "You do have a poor opinion of men, don't you?"

She flushed, shocked and embarrassed that he had been able to interpret her movement so easily. "And why not?" she demanded. "No man ever meant anything but trouble for me."

"There were others after Lieutenant Selby?"

"No. He was the only one who— But there was my father. He deserted my mother before I was born. She had to go to work in the mill, and she put me to work there, too, when I was ten." She looked away, fixing her eyes on a long cluster of wisteria. She did not want to remember the past. Her mother dying, lungs rotted away by the dust of the mill. She did not want to think of herself, undersized, half-starved, working from five-thirty in the morning until seven-thirty at night, with two half-hour breaks. Girls as well as boys had been stripped and beaten for any infraction of the rules.

"It was bad in the cotton mills," Jason Moreland was saying. "I know something of conditions there."

"It was worse when the cotton mills closed down during your Civil War, when your southern planters could not get their cotton shipped because of the blockade. That was the really bad time."

"Yet you survived."

"My aunt took me in. She didn't want to at first. She had little enough for herself. Besides, she disapproved of my mother and of me. But I made myself helpful to her. She was getting old, and her sight was failing, so I helped with the sewing. She was a seamstress."

"And then you went to Miss Chadwick's Academy. That much of your story was true, I discovered."

"My aunt did sewing for Miss Chadwick. I wanted desperately to learn to read and write and—to be a lady. I sewed in exchange for my lessons. Then I found a position as governess with Mr. Roger Selby, and you know the rest. It must seem to you a sordid story."

"No more so than my own."

She remembered what he had told her of his beginnings. "You said you shipped out of Liverpool on a slaver when you were a boy."

"That's right."

"But all this—" She made a gesture that took in not only the glass-enclosed conservatory with its rare plants and brilliantly colored flowers, but the whole of Mooncliff.

He shrugged. "A man has more opportunities than a woman. You took what you believed to be the best chance open to you. You gambled and lost. But that's past now."

He turned and picked up a white china pot of violets.

"Here, Miss Corbett." He handed her the plant. "A small token of our new understanding of one another."

She looked down at the blue-purple flowers, unable to speak.

"They're not exotic like those orchids over there, or that scarlet lobelia. But they suit you. They are the same color as your eyes." Then, before she could find a suitable reply, he said, "I'll go down to the stables and bring Stuart back. No need for his afternoon lessons, though. It's the day before Christmas, after all. He'll be far too excited to learn anything."

Later, as she was climbing the stairs to her room, Lavinia was still brooding about their conversation. What were Jason Moreland's real reasons for keeping her on at Mooncliff? Did he feel some pity for her? Or did he believe that they were two of a kind, that there was some unspoken relationship between them?

Lavinia stopped halfway along the hall as she saw Denise Moreland coming toward her. Even now, well advanced in her pregnancy, Denise was beautiful. She wore a loose houserobe made of yards of creamy Brussels lace lined with tearose-colored satin. Her dark red hair was drawn back in an intricate chignon. There was a rich glow about her complexion, and her curiously colored eyes were placid, self-assured.

"Miss Corbett, where is Stuart? Shouldn't he be having his lessons?"

"I believe he's down at the stables. His father has gone to fetch him."

"I see." Denise looked down at the china pot that held the violets. Lavinia said quickly, "Mr. Moreland gave me the flowers. He—that is—"

"An early Christmas gift?"

"Yes, that's it."

"How nice," Denise Moreland said. Then, calm and unconcerned, she moved past Lavinia and down the wide stairway.

Lavinia's lips tightened. Denise was not particularly interested in the fact that her husband had given the governess a pot of flowers.

"And why should she be?" Lavinia thought, bitterly envious. "The whole conservatory is hers, built to please her. She has everything. This house, fine clothes, jewels—she has everything, and I have nothing. She probably doesn't even think of me as a woman, with the same feelings and desires as her own."

But then she remembered Jason's words. He had said the violets were the color of her eyes. He had seen her as a woman.

It was a pleasing thought, but a frightening one, too.

Chapter 6

Early in January, on a day when the sun came and went in an overcast sky, Denise, dressed in a new traveling costume of honey-colored taffeta, waited in the bedroom for Jason, who was to accompany her to Rosalind MacKay's house in the Murray Hill section of New York, after which he planned to leave for Washington. Denise did not fully understand what his business in the capital might be, but she knew that it was connected with his new Caribbean shipping line.

She paced the floor, restless and uneasy. If only Jason had not insisted that she leave Mooncliff to go to stay with the MacKays in the city. She paused before the mirror. What she saw reflected there should have raised her spirits, for her complexion was smooth and glowing, and the taffeta accented the golden lights in her brown eyes, turning them to warm amber. Her new coiffure, with its mass of curls, was most becoming. But her spirits did not rise; indeed, as she waited for Jason, her uneasiness grew into nameless panic. She felt a tightness in her chest, and her hands were damp and cold.

She was relieved when Elspeth came in. "You hardly touched your breakfast tray, Mrs. Moreland," Elspeth said, frowning slightly. "Let me bring you some coffee and toast, at least."

"I'm not hungry," Denise said, her voice dull and expressionless.

"Is anything wrong? If you aren't feeling well, perhaps you would want to postpone your trip. It's a long ride into the city."

"I don't want to go to New York at all. Oh, Elspeth, if only I could make Jason change his mind. I don't want to leave Mooncliff."

"But—why ever not? I should have thought you would welcome a visit to New York, particularly during winter. It is rather lonely at Mooncliff, and if the snow should make the roads impassable—"

"I don't want to go. I don't want to leave Jason. I'm afraid."

Elspeth took Denise's arm and led her to a chair. "Sit down here," she said. And, when Denise had obeyed, she added: "Do you want to tell me what's troubling you?"

"I don't know if you'll understand. I don't completely understand myself. It's a kind of feeling; a premonition, if you like. Elspeth, do you remember the last time I left Mooncliff, to go down to Charleston for my sister's wedding? Jason couldn't go with me. It was then, at Riverview, that I turned to another man."

"The man who was Phillip's father."

Denise looked away. "It must be hard for you to understand, Elspeth. You've never loved a man. If I could make you see how it happened—"

"There's no need."

"But there is. Jason and I were apart for the first time since our wedding, and there was a young man, someone I'd known before the War. We shared certain memories that Jason could never be a part of."

"Did you love him—Phillip's father?"

"Not as I love Jason, but—yes, I think I did love him, for a little while, that summer. . . ."

"But I still don't understand why you're afraid to leave

Mooncliff now. Surely nothing like that will happen this time."

Denise smiled. "Hardly," she agreed. "Even if I were not . . . as I am, I know that Jason is the only man I will ever want. He'll hurt me again; I know that, too. He'll be ruthess when he must. It is his nature. But it doesn't matter, because there can never be anyone else for me."

"Then surely you need not fear this separation. You know Mr. Moreland would not insist on it if he were not concerned for you. He wants you to be close to a doctor this time."

"I know, but I'm afraid. I don't want to leave him, to leave Mooncliff."

"I thought you hated Mooncliff. I've heard you say so many times."

"Yes, but even so, Elspeth, I—" Denise struggled to find the words in which to convey her feelings. "I'm a part of this house now. And I'm afraid that if I leave, something terrible will happen."

"Now, Mrs. Moreland," Elspeth said briskly, "you know perfectly well that a woman in your condition is sometimes low-spirited and has strange fancies. All the more reason you should go to stay with Mrs. MacKay. She is exactly the person to keep you busy and active. She'll plan small parties and outings. You can go shopping together and to the theater—yes, you can. For the next few months, at least."

"I suppose you're right," Denise said. "You're always so practical, so strong and sensible. I wish you were going to New York with me."

"I'm needed here," Elspeth said. "There's this house to run, and—"

Denise rose with a rustle of her taffeta skirt and said urgently, "Elspeth, I know running Mooncliff is a difficult job, but could you, at the same time, look out for the boys?"

"Miss Wilmot is absolutely trustworthy with Phillip, Mrs. Moreland."

"Yes, I know, but Miss Corbett—"

"She's doing well with young Stuart, from what I've seen. She might take a firmer hand with him, but Mr.

Moreland's forbidden that. Under the circumstances, she's more successful with Stuart than any other governess has been."

"I suppose so. But what do we know about her, really?"

"I don't understand, Mrs. Moreland. Surely, her references—"

"She brought a note from the headmistress of the academy for young ladies she attended, back in England. She's had no experience as a governess until now. Jason promised to check on her background, but I don't think he's had time to do it. He never said anything more about the matter to me."

"He's been very busy. The new shipping line, and now this trip to Washington."

"To curry favor with men like Senator Burgess and Congressman Marsh. Vulgar, corrupt politicians who want to see everything fine and decent in the South destroyed forever. Jason says he needs the help of such men, needs special concessions and subsidies for his business from them. The thought sickens me."

"He is doing what he thinks best, Mrs. Moreland. He's a man of limitless ambition. You must accept that, as you have come to accept—his other failings."

"I've tried, Elspeth. But I'm afraid sometimes, for him as well as for myself."

"You must take him as he is."

Denise smiled. "How wise you sound, and yet how can you understand? You've never loved a man. Elspeth—" She stopped, seeing a flicker of warmth in Elspeth's eyes, a flush on her cheeks. "You haven't, have you, my dear?"

"There is someone, Mrs. Moreland."

"Why haven't you told me?"

"Nothing can come of it."

"But why not? Who is the man, Elspeth? Please tell me."

"His name is Terry—Terence O'Connor. He's the captain of one of Mr. Moreland's new ships, the *Tropic Star*."

"Does my husband know?"

"Of course not. And you must not tell him. Oh, please,

Mrs. Moreland. Captain O'Connor is not—he would not want to settle down. He's young and reckless, not a marrying man at all."

"And handsome?"

Elspeth's flush deepened. "Oh, yes, Mrs. Moreland!"

"And where did you meet your young captain?"

"At the ball in honor of President Grant. And I've seen him a few times since then, when he's come here on business."

"Oh, yes," Denise said. "He's the tall, sandy-haired young man. He is handsome, Elspeth. And as for his not being the marrying kind, men do change their minds about such things."

"If a woman is beautiful, as you are, Mrs. Moreland." Elspeth spoke calmly, without self-pity. "I've always been plain, and lacking in— I don't know how to flirt with a man. I don't know what to say."

"You've always been able to talk to Jason."

"That's different. We talk about the running of the house."

"And about business matters, sometimes. Jason says you have as clear a grasp of such things as a man." Perhaps, she thought, that was a drawback in winning a husband. Almost certainly it was. Elspeth's crisp, straightforward manner of speaking might please Jason Moreland, but it would not win young Captain O'Connor.

"I should not have spoken about this," Elspeth said. "Nothing will ever come of it. I only wanted you to know that I do understand what it is to be in love."

Impulsively Denise put an arm around Elspeth. "Don't give up so easily, my dear. You deserve a life of your own, a home and children."

"Someday, perhaps. But now my place is here. I don't want you to worry about anything while you're away, Mrs. Moreland. When Mr. Moreland returns from Washington, I'll remind him to check on Miss Corbett's background. Meanwhile, I'll keep a sharp eye on her."

"Then you don't trust her either."

"I didn't say that."

Denise, who had resumed pacing the room, paused at the window overlooking the side lawn, now brown and withered and lightly covered with a sparkle of frost. She had caught sight of Stuart mounted on his new black and white pony. Miss Corbett was beside him, seated on a fine brown mare. As Denise watched, she saw Jason approach the two, saw him stop and remove his tall hat and linger to talk with the governess. Something he said caused her to throw back her head and laugh. The gesture, so uninhibited, disturbed Denise; inside the house Lavinia Corbett was quiet and demure, her every movement restrained. But there had been a certain boldness in the toss of her head. The wind whipped her ash-blond hair around her face. Denise noticed how handsome the young woman looked, slim and erect in the saddle, dressed in a fine pearl-gray broadcloth riding habit. The matching hat sported dashing black plumes. But while her costume was in good taste, it was, Denise decided, not suitable to her position.

That was unfair, however. Hadn't she herself given Lavinia permission to order a riding habit so she could accompany Stuart on his jaunts around the estate? Even so, she was troubled by a nameless uneasiness at the sight of the trio on the lawn below the window: Jason, tall, imposing in his dark gray broadcloth suit; Stuart, straddling his pony, his dark red hair glinting in the pale sunlight; and the young governess, Lavinia, elegant and striking in her smart new riding clothes.

Denise turned from the window abruptly.

"Elspeth, please go down and ask Mr. Moreland if the carriage is ready. I want to reach Rhinebeck in plenty of time to get the boat downriver."

"Yes, Mrs. Moreland. And please, don't trouble yourself about matters here at Mooncliff while you're away. I will see to it that nothing goes wrong."

But after Elspeth had left on her errand, Denise returned to the window. She saw Jason helping Lavinia down from the mare. His big, powerful hands encircled her waist, and her gloved hands rested on his shoulders for a moment before he put her down.

Denise, too impatient to wait for Elspeth's return, picked up her heavy, honey-gold velvet cloak lined with black fox and started down the stairs.

Chapter 7

The winter had been unusually severe, and Lavinia Corbett, reading in *Harper's Weekly* about the widespread unemployment and the terrible suffering of thousands in New York City, had marveled at her own good fortune. Seated before a leaping fire in the library at Mooncliff, she read of the hordes of homeless, starving men and women who had marched from Union Square to Tompkins Square in protest while the entire police force of the city had been kept on duty to prevent possible rioting.

The New York Central Council of Labor had asserted that "the recent alarming development and aggression of wealth . . . will inevitably lead to the pauperization and degradation of the toiling masses." When eight thousand jobless men met to hold a peaceable meeting, they were ordered to disperse, and when they stood their ground the police charged in with clubs.

Lavinia read of unemployment workers living on refuse, sleeping in station houses, trying to survive on thirty cents a day. She remembered the dark time when the Manchester mills had shut down and she had nearly starved before her aunt had taken her in. She was passionately grateful to Jason Moreland. He might so easily have turned her out of Mooncliff when he had learned the truth about her; instead, he had permitted her to remain.

During the short days of late winter, with the snow heavy on the broad lawns around Mooncliff, with the wind driving in across the river, she was warm and secure. She reveled in the unfamiliar pleasures of warm fires, delicious food, a bed with a goose-feather comforter. She marveled over the continual supply of freshly cut flowers from the conservatory. She was surrounded with velvet and mahogany, thick, deep Oriental rugs, and fine pictures.

But now, in early March, Lavinia was overcome with a peculiar restlessness that dulled her pleasure in her new environment. She realized that during these last months she had spoken to no one except Stuart and Miss Wilmot; Elspeth Buchanan, hurrying about the great house, had no time for idle conversation.

As for the master of Mooncliff, his trip to Washington had kept him away from the house since early in January. What was he doing there? Lavinia had always had a lively interest in politics, and, during the long winter evenings, she had passed the time by reading the newspapers and magazines in the library. She had learned that at present, business and politics were closely linked, and rarely in ways that would bear investigation.

She had read of the Crédit Mobilier scandal and the investigation that had revealed that Oakes Ames, Representative from Massachusetts and member of the House Committee which had authorized the Union Pacific Railroad to issue bonds to be redeemed by the government, was himself a director of the railroad. In an attempt to cover his involvement in the scandal, he had palmed off shares of railroad stock among other congressmen where "they would do the most good."

Closer to home was the scandal surrounding "Boss" Tweed of Tammany Hall, who had been convicted on two hundred and four charges of fraud. And the Custom House scandal, which had led to the wholesale looting of importers; implicated in the affair was Tom Murphy, a close friend of President Grant.

Lavinia also read of the colorful schemes for the annexation of Santo Domingo and Cuba: schemes that, although they were backed by certain businessmen and supported by Grant, had failed to win the approval of ordinary citizens.

Perhaps, Lavinia thought, Jason Moreland's business in Washington had to do with his newly established interest in the Caribbean. She remembered how he had shown her his new ships when he had driven her down to South Street on the day they had first met. How exciting to control such far-flung interests, to be a part of this new era—the "Gilded Age," as it was being called. To have a part in shaping the destiny of a nation.

Such matters did not concern women, of course. For Lavinia that winter, there were the lessons in the third-floor schoolroom. Stuart proved to be a bright child but difficult to control. Since his father had given him the new pony it was next to impossible to keep his attention on reading and sums. He spent most of his time in the stables, and when he was angry he would forget himself and use some of the more colorful language he had picked up from the coachmen and stablehands.

In spite of the frosty weather, Lavinia had enjoyed riding with Stuart on her brown mare. The icy wind from the river was invigorating, and she knew that she made a charming picture in her fine new riding habit with its dashing feathered hat. But lately that diversion had begun to pall, for Lavinia longed to ride alone along the Cliff Road. She had learned to ride in London during the months when she had lived with Arthur Selby. And here at Mooncliff her skill had improved under the tutelage of Patrick, the head coachman.

At twilight on an afternoon early in March, Lavinia moved restlessly about Stuart's room. He was recovering from a cold, but she had decided to keep him indoors an extra day, and it had been difficult to think of indoor activities to amuse the active child. Now that he was asleep she ached to be out of doors, if only for an hour.

Enlisting the cooperation of Miss Wilmot, she fled from the house, and a short while later she was riding briskly along the Cliff Road, her bright hair under her jaunty riding hat streaming behind her.

With the onset of evening, a heavy fog was rolling in from the river, shrouding the rocks that edged the road, transforming the wind-twisted trees into phantom shapes. But Lavinia did not want to turn back; instead, she spurred the horse, and the speed of movement gave her a sense of release from the restlessness that had possessed her these past weeks.

When she saw a movement out of the corner of her eye, she drew rein so suddenly that the brown mare reared, and she had to struggle frantically to keep from being thrown.

A man stood before her. He had seized the reins and gotten the mare under control before she realized that he was Jason Moreland.

"Easy, now—there now, girl—"

Only when the mare was quite still did Jason turn his attention to Lavinia. "Are you all right?"

"Yes, I think so. I didn't hear you coming up the cliff."

"The wind and waves play strange tricks. Here, let me help you down."

She put her hands on his heavy, powerfully muscled shoulders, and he lifted her from the saddle with an easy motion.

"What the devil are you doing out here at this hour? The Cliff Road is dangerous, particularly in fog like this."

"Dangerous?"

"There are sharp turns in the road, and places where the rocks are crumbling away. Elspeth's father was killed out here on the Cliff Road on a night like this one."

"I didn't know."

He spoke as if to himself. "It was after the first ball we ever held here at Mooncliff. Andrew Buchanan was somewhat the worse for drink, and he lost control of the horses. The buggy overturned—" Abruptly he fell silent.

"What happened?"

"He broke his neck," Jason said, without expression. "Elspeth was found, half-dead, the next morning. I brought her back to Mooncliff. She's been with us ever since."

"But surely you didn't give her charge of the whole staff simply because of an unlucky accident."

"There were other reasons." Jason stood looking out over the cliffs. Finally he turned back to Lavinia. "Don't ride on the Cliff Road again. There are safer paths."

He took the mare's reins, and for a few moments they walked together in silence. Feeling the need to say something, Lavinia remarked, "I trust your business in Washington was successful, Mr. Moreland."

"My business? Oh, yes. Better than even I could have hoped. But a young lady would not be interested in such dull matters."

"You're quite wrong. Politics has always interested me, and I've done a good deal of reading on the subject this winter."

Jason smiled indulgently. "You amaze me. Mrs. Moreland reads only Dickens and the works of Mrs. E.D.E.N. Southworth."

"I find Mrs. Southworth's work ridiculous," Lavinia said. "And as for Mr. Dickens—"

"Surely you don't find him ridiculous, too."

"Not always. But he's far too sentimental about poverty. There's nothing romantic about squalor and starvation. And in real life Oliver Twist would probably have been hanged or transported. And that silly prig David Copperfield would have spent the rest of his life in the bottle factory."

Jason threw back his head and laughed. "What a grim view of the world, for one so young. I'm afraid you're a very cynical young lady, Miss Corbett. What must you be teaching Stuart about the great world?"

"Oh, Mr. Moreland, please don't think—I would never speak this way to Stuart. Never!"

He dropped the reins and took her arm. "Good Lord, I was only teasing." His eyes searched her face. "You're still afraid, aren't you?" His voice was quiet and without a trace of its usual mockery. "What frightens you?"

"Being poor. Going hungry. Having no home."

"I think I can understand that. I can remember tramping the streets of Liverpool with my mother and my brothers. Turned out of some wretched lodging house, with no money for the night's dinner."

It was nearly dark now, and Jason's face was a blur above hers. She felt a closeness to him. "And your father?"

"He was a seaman in His Majesty's Navy. He died when I was very young. Flogged to death for striking an officer."

"How horrible."

"I hardly knew him. As for the rest, my mother died before I went off to sea. And my brothers—" He shrugged. "The workhouse, perhaps. Or the jail. I did better than that for myself, but I haven't forgotten those miserable years."

"Is that why you allowed me to stay on, even after you knew the truth about me? Because you felt sorry for me?"

"Partly, I suppose. But there were other reasons."

His hands cupped her face, turning it up to his. She was so close to him now that she could feel his warm breath against her cheek. "You said you thought all men were—how did you put it?—coarse and cruel."

"I had no right to say that."

"Why the devil not, if you feel that way? Maybe you're right. Maybe we are, sometimes. But not always, Lavinia."

He put his arms around her. "You're very lovely, do you know that, Lavinia?" His lips brushed her forehead, and she did not draw away. His embrace was light, almost tentative. But she made no move to break free. His mouth found hers, and he kissed her lips. She felt that her mounting restlessness had been a kind of searching, and now she knew what she had been searching for.

But almost as strong as her need was her fear of surrender. She remembered Lieutenant Selby. He had been gentle too during those first weeks in his brother's house in Manchester. But when he had taken her to London, to that ugly, stuffy room, had carried her to the wide bed with its dusty velvet hangings . . .

With a swift movement she wrenched free, lifted the long skirt of her riding habit, and fled back over the damp, fog-shrouded lawns to the house.

Jason Moreland made no move to follow her. Behind her she heard only the rising wind.

It was after midnight, but for the first time since she had come to live at Mooncliff Lavinia found it impossible to fall asleep; the soft bed, the warm goose-feather comforter, even the sound of the rain against the windows did not lull her tonight. She told herself to forget Jason's kiss, that it had meant nothing. He had let her go at once when she had pulled away. He had not tried to hold her there, although he could have done so easily. He could have taken her by force had he wanted to.

Perhaps he had been waiting for her to respond. But Arthur Selby had never demanded a response, had apparently never expected one. He had taken her to satisfy his own need, without regard for what she might be feeling. Why not? Hadn't she been taught that, except for prostitutes, women did not feel such desires?

She turned restlessly under the feather cover. How did Denise Moreland respond to Jason's lovemaking? Probably she did not respond at all. Perhaps she took some slight pleasure in the act because she wanted children. More likely she considered her surrender part of the marriage bargain. A woman gave herself; and in return, if she was as fortunate as Denise, she received a fine home, beautiful clothes, comfort and security.

If Lavinia were to give herself to Jason Moreland, what could she hope for in return?

She sat up and pushed away the cover. Not marriage, surely. Unless— Women sometimes died in childbirth. Denise had had two difficult deliveries and was now facing the ordeal for the third time. Suppose she were to die. Oh, no, she must not allow herself to think such a thing. She might envy Denise Moreland, might hate her for having everything, while she had so little, but she would not want Denise to die.

But suppose she did die? And Lavinia stayed on here at Mooncliff, to care for Stuart. Jason loved his eldest son, and if she could win the child's affection, wasn't it possible—

She saw herself as mistress of Mooncliff. Perhaps she did not have Denise Moreland's breeding, her background, but she was pretty, and she could pass for a lady. There were many women with no better origins than her own who were accepted into the finest circles in this free and easy society that had come into being at the end of the Civil War.

"Stop it," she told herself. "Denise Moreland is alive, and there is no reason she should not come through the birth of her third child, particularly since Jason has sent her to New York City to be close to her doctor this time." Knowing Jason, Lavinia was sure he had chosen the finest doctor in the city.

Divorce, then. Suppose she could make Jason love her, need her so much that he would divorce his wife. A decade ago it would have been unthinkable, but manners and morals were changing now. Hadn't the dashing beauty Miriam Folline Squier divorced her husband to marry Frank Leslie, the publisher? Now she edited her husband's fashion publications, and all the most important people flocked to her Fifth Avenue mansion. Lavinia had read, too, of her splendid home in Saratoga, with its stables, arbors, rustic summerhouses and terraced lawns. If a woman like Miriam Leslie could rise above the stigma of divorce, could hold a prominent place in New York society, why not Lavinia Corbett?

She told herself not to be a fool. Jason Moreland had spoken to her a few times and had kissed her once. That was all.

But when she had asked him why he kept her on, he hadn't answered. Perhaps he had pitied her, but there had been another reason. They were alike in a way that Denise Moreland could never understand. Even in the short time Lavinia had lived here at Mooncliff she had overheard enough to know that Mrs. Moreland did not approve of the way her husband had made his money or of his present associates, the conniving politicians and the rapacious businessmen. She might entertain them in her home, along with their wives, but she did not accept them as her equals. She did not understand Jason Moreland, although she had married him and borne his children. She could not understand him as Lavinia did.

Suppose I had stayed with him, out there on the cliffs? Lavinia thought. Would he have taken me, then and there? And if he had, would it have been like those times with Arthur Selby? Or would there have been something different, something more?

She pushed back the masses of her pale blond hair. Her face was damp. Impossible to sleep with these sensations coursing through her.

She needed a drink; that was it. During those nights after Arthur had sailed for India with his regiment and she had been left alone, she had learned that a glass of brandy was enough to allay her fears, to help her to sleep.

She rose, put her robe over her nightdress and slid her feet into her slippers, then hurried down the three flights of stairs to the first floor. The gaslights lining the hall had been turned low. Moving as quietly as she could, she headed for the dining room. One drink and back to bed.

Before she could open the dining room door, the huge double doors of the library opposite slid open. Jason Moreland stood in the doorway with another man, a tall sandy-haired young man wearing a heavy dark blue coat and carrying a visored cap. Lavinia pressed her slender body into a shallow alcove that held a potted plant on a stand. She hoped that the light from inside the library would not reveal her.

Jason was holding out his hand to the young man. "A safe voyage to you, Captain O'Connor."

The young man shook his hand. "And a profitable one, sir. I'll see to that."

"O'Connor, sometimes I think you're too damn reckless for your own good. This is no pleasure cruise, remember. If anything should go wrong, there's little I can do to save your neck."

"I wouldn't expect you to, sir," he said. "I knew what I was getting into when I took command of the *Tropic Star*."

"All right, then. You'd best get started now."

The young man nodded, said good night, and hurried down the hallway. He was swallowed up in the shadows, and there was a rush of cold, damp air as the door leading to the terrace shut behind him. Jason had turned to go back into the library when a small movement from Lavinia caused the plant stand to sway and thud against the marble side of the shallow alcove.

Jason whirled, strode to her hiding place and seized her by the arm. "What the devil are you doing down here?" he demanded. His hand tightened on her arm, and she cried out with pain, afraid of the man who loomed over her in the dark hallway.

Chapter 8

"In here!" he ordered, pushing her into the library ahead of him. "Do you make it a habit to prowl around the halls after midnight?"

She shook her head, unable to speak. He closed the doors. He looked huge and menacing in the firelight.

"I couldn't sleep. I came down to get a book, and when I saw you with Captain O'Connor—I'm not suitably dressed, as you can see."

"Your modesty is most edifying—most suitable for a young lady in your position." Then the mockery left his voice and he demanded, "Why did you need to come down here for a book? There must be plenty of them upstairs."

"Yes, but—"

"What do you know about Captain O'Connor?"

"I've seen him here before. I know he commands the *Tropic Star* for you—that's all."

"That's right. I came back to Mooncliff aboard her. She's moored down there at the foot of those cliffs. O'Connor will be weighing anchor in a few minutes now."

"That doesn't concern me," she said, regaining control of herself.

"You're quite right, my dear. But since you were eavesdropping, I wanted to satisfy your curiosity."

"I wasn't eavesdropping. I've told you—" His blue eyes were mocking again, and a corner of his mouth turned down.

"All right, then. I couldn't sleep—that much is true—and I wanted a drink. It's not proper, I know, but—"

He laughed softly. "I think there's a bottle of sherry in the morning room. But I recommend this." He took a decanter from the sideboard. "Unless you're too ladylike for rum."

"No," she said. "Anything to help me sleep." Her hand flew to her lips when she realized how brazen that sounded, but Jason only shrugged and poured a drink for her and one for himself. "Your hand is shaking. Here, sit down on the sofa, close to the fire and drink up."

The rum burned her throat. She coughed, her face flushed, and tears stung her eyes.

"A gift from Captain O'Connor. He got it on his last voyage. Havana rum. The *Tropic Star* is heading back there now."

"There's a revolution in Cuba," she said.

"That's right. And Captain O'Connor is risking his neck—and my ship—to get supplies to the revolutionary forces."

"And if he's caught?"

"The quarries on Isla de Piñas if he's lucky. If not, a firing squad."

"But surely your government would protect him."

"Not at this point, my dear. You said you were interested in politics. You should know, then, that those shortsighted fools in Washington can't see the importance of Cuba. We should have annexed it years ago. We might have done so now, if hidebound gentlemen like Hamilton Fish hadn't opposed it. There are fortunes to be made in Cuba as soon as the revolutionists break the grip of Spain."

"That's why you're helping the revolutionary forces."

"That's part of it. There's money to be made in smuggling arms right now, no matter which side wins this phase of the struggle. Surplus arms left over from the Civil War, for sale at rock-bottom prices—they're not in demand here any longer. But the revolutionists will use whatever they can get their hands on."

Once more she had a sense of the great forces controlled by this man sitting beside her. There were men at war and governments to be overthrown, and he played a part in all of it.

"Finish your drink," Jason was saying. "I should have diluted it with water, but from what you said, I assumed you were a hardened tippler."

"Indeed, I'm not. But after Arthur left me alone in London I used to take a drink sometimes—to help me sleep."

"You missed him then, coarse and cruel though he was?"

She wondered that he could not forget those words of hers. She took another sip. This time it did not make her cough, but she began to feel curiously lightheaded. The fire was pleasant, and she watched in silence the way the glow played over the wine-red draperies, the gold-embossed panels of the room. She rested her head against the back of the wide velvet sofa.

"You did miss him, didn't you?"

"Certainly not! I hated him."

"You're lying to me again," he said softly. "Or to yourself, Lavinia. No matter. I don't give a damn about Arthur Selby. But tell me why you couldn't sleep tonight."

"Please don't—"

"Was it because of what happened between us out there on the cliffs? I'd be flattered to think that was the reason."

"You may think what you please," she said, trying to keep her voice steady. "I'm going to bed now."

"Not yet." He moved closer, took the glass from her hand and set it down. Then he put his arms around her and kissed her. Her robe fell open, and his fingers caressed her through the thin nightdress. She felt naked, helpless before the surging tide of warmth that overwhelmed her. He bent her head back and his mouth, hard and demanding, parted her lips.

She turned her face away. "Please don't."

He released her, but she made no attempt to rise, for her body still trembled with the emotions he had aroused. "Please leave me now."

"Very well, if that's what you want. Go back to your empty bed. Take the bottle with you and drink yourself to sleep." He stood up, and she saw that his fists were thrust into the pockets of his coat. There were harsh lines in his face. "Tell yourself that you don't need a man. That you're finished with all that." His voice was not quite steady. "Go on—what are you waiting for? Don't be afraid. I won't take you by force."

"Why not?" she asked. "Because you're a gentleman? Or because it would hurt your male vanity to have to take me against my will? Or perhaps because you know that I'm not able to refuse you."

She saw that she had hurt him, but she could not stop herself. "I'm not able to refuse, you know. I'm not brave enough to face hunger and cold again, to sleep in the streets. I'm dependent on you for the clothes I wear and the food I eat, and I—"

"You'd like to believe that, wouldn't you? If I were to take you by force or threaten you with dismissal to get what I want, you could tell yourself that I am no different from Arthur Selby. You could tell yourself I mean nothing to you.

"Deceive yourself, Lavinia, if you must, but don't try to deceive me. I know women. I know you. I think you were not as revolted by Selby as you want to believe. Maybe he was coarse and cruel, but perhaps there's something in you that wants those things from a man."

She was on her feet now, facing him, her eyes blazing, her whole body shaking with anger. She lashed out at him with a movement swift as a cat's, but he caught her hand, then put both arms around her, holding her helpless against him.

"You know nothing about me. Nothing," she said.

He pressed his face against her pale golden hair. "You're wrong. We're very much alike, you and I. Both ambitious. And we don't care a damn about what the world calls morality. The only difference is that I'm honest with myself and you're not. If you were, you'd stay here with me; you'd let me—"

She clung to him, the room swimming around her, a blur of dark red and gold. The warmth of the fire, the heat of the rum in her blood made it impossible for her to think, to find the words that would free her from this man, from the hot dark tide that was sweeping her toward an unknown place.

She pressed herself against him, felt the hardness of him through her nightdress. Then he was unfastening the high collar of her garment, and moments later they were together in front of the fireplace.

He took her in silence, and although he was gentle with her at first, delaying long enough to arouse her fully, his restraint eventually gave way to a driving ferocity that took her to a place she had never known. A dark, secret place of total fulfillment.

That spring, it was as if the whole world had been created anew for her. Later she would remember those days, the broad lawns turning to deep velvety green, the forsythia flowering in golden profusion. She would remember evenings on the cliffs above the river when the sky was pale violet and the water was lost in purple mist.

Sometimes she met Jason in the summerhouse, where the wisteria and the early roses screened them from view, or in the library on rainy nights, with the sound of the river an accompaniment to their lovemaking.

Lavinia was obsessed with her passion for Jason. At times her need for him frightened her, for she could not imagine life without him. In a hidden part of her consciousness she knew that he used her in ways he would not have used his wife, without restraint, but the violence he offered her was a part of the closeness between them. Loving him, she had lost all modesty, all shame. She did not speculate any longer on their future together. So long as she could be a part of his life, nothing else mattered.

Sometimes, after making love they talked. More often he talked and she listened. He told her of his past, and she found many of his stories exciting: the close brushes with the British patrols when he was a crew member aboard one of the "blackbirders," the marches into the reeking swamps of the Ivory Coast, and the pitched battles with rival Spanish and Portuguese slavers. At other times he told her of his earliest voyages, when he was not yet in his teens. Even though she had known suffering during those early years when she had worked in the mills in Manchester, his accounts of his experiences aboard the slavers shook her.

"I suppose that's why you're so indulgent with Stuart," she remarked one afternoon, when they were walking along the cliffs.

"And you," he said. "I sometimes think you want to protcct him for the same reasons. He's very fond of you."

"Particularly when I give him his own way." She spoke lightly. She did not say everything she was feeling at the moment, such as the fact that she loved Stuart because he was Jason's son. She sensed that there were certain things that could not be said between them. For although Stuart was Jason's son, he also belonged to Denise.

She knew that there were times when Jason stayed in the city with his wife and returned to Mooncliff preoccupied, his thoughts remaining with Denise. At other times, business absorbed him. He would shut himself away in the library after making it plain he did not wish to be intruded upon.

One afternoon early in May they descended the path from the Cliff Road to the shore below. It was midafternoon, but Stuart was having a riding lesson with Patrick, and Lavinia was free to accompany Jason.

He held her hand, but he did not speak, and when she asked him what was wrong, he said, "The *Tropic Star* is overdue. Nothing to be concerned about as yet, but I had hoped O'Connor would make port before this."

"I'm sure he'll return safely," she said, hoping to soothe him and turn his attention back to her.

"What do you know about it?" he demanded. "He's risking his neck every time he makes a voyage."

She was startled by the anger in his voice. "You pride yourself on knowing so much about current affairs. Perhaps you read about the *Virginius* incident, two years ago?"

"No, I don't think so."

"The *Virginius* was an American steamer. She was captured by a Spanish gunboat while taking supplies to the Cuban revolutionaries. Eight members of her crew were executed in Cuba by the Spanish authorities."

"But Captain O'Connor knew that when he took command."

Jason made an impatient gesture. "O'Connor's twenty-four. At that age, a man's willing to take any kind of risk if there's money to be made. I was only a year older when I took command of the *Nubian Queen*."

He broke off abruptly and looked out at the river in moody silence. At times like this Lavinia felt shut out, and the old fear and loneliness welled up in her. She looked at the face of this man whom she loved so completely; at the full, sensual mouth, set in a hard line now; the jutting chin, the blue eyes under their dark heavy brows. "Forgive me," she said in a whisper. "Don't be angry." She put her hands on his arms. "Don't shut me out."

He did not reply, and she moved closer. She pressed her face against his shoulder. Then, after a moment, she felt his arms around her. "It's all right," he said. "It's unfair of me to expect you to share these concerns of mine."

"Oh, but I want to share everything with you. I want to understand everything that matters to you."

He laughed shortly. "Denise said that, too, a long time ago. I suppose she thought she meant it. Later, I saw her turn from me with loathing because of what I had told her."

"But I'm different. She's been sheltered all her life. She only cares about this house, the children, the luxuries you've given her—"

"That's enough! You know nothing about my wife."

"But you just said that when you tried to share your past life with her, she hated you for it."

"That's enough," he repeated. His voice was quiet, but there was an icy finality in his tone.

"All right, Jason. I won't mention her again. I'll do

anything, everything you want, only—" She was crying now, silently. "—don't stop loving me. I think I would die if you did."

"Stop it! What's happened to you, Lavinia? You used to be calm and controlled, and now—" But he held her against him, even as he spoke.

"It's only that I love you so much. I've never loved anyone before." She pressed her body against his, feeling the strength of him against her, hearing his breathing quicken.

Then he went tense and unmoving for an instant. He released her, pushing her away. "Up there," he said. "On the Cliff Road. There's someone coming. It's Elspeth Buchanan."

He started up the path that led from the beach to the top of the cliff, leaving Lavinia below, but Elspeth did not wait for him to reach her. She hurried down to meet him, her white apron billowing, her face flushed.

"Mr. Moreland, a message has come from Mrs. MacKay!"

"Tell me."

"Mrs. Moreland has given birth to the baby. Early this morning, it was."

"Is she all right?"

Elspeth had reached him now, and her eyes were bright.

"Your wife is quite well, and the baby, too." She hesitated. "It's a girl this time."

"A girl?"

"You're not displeased, I hope?"

Jason threw back his head and laughed, and there was triumph in the sound; even from where she stood, Lavinia could see the happiness in his face, and it struck her like a physical pain.

"I have two boys, Elspeth. It's about time I had a daughter, don't you think?" He put an arm around Elspeth and hugged her. "A daughter," he repeated. Then he said, "Go back to the house, Elspeth, and have a bag packed for me at once. And tell Patrick—no, I'll tell Patrick to hitch up the carriage myself. I'll be staying in the city until Mrs. Moreland and my daughter are ready to travel back with me."

Hearing the satisfaction, the joy in his voice, Lavinia was torn with anger and frustration. As long as Denise Moreland had remained in New York City, Lavinia had been able to forget, most of the time, that Jason had a wife. Now she could not shut out the unwelcome memory any longer.

Jason had slept with Denise in the big bed in the master bedroom; he had held her in his arms. A picture burned itself into Lavinia's brain with unholy clarity. She could see Denise, her burnished red hair spread on the pillow, and Jason, his limbs entwined with hers. And from that union a child had been born, a daughter.

"Hurry, Elspeth," Jason was saying. "I want to be in the city as quickly as possible. I want to see my daughter."

Only when Elspeth had gone back to the house did he return to Lavinia.

"I'll be away a few weeks, at least," he said. "Take care of Stuart. See that he doesn't get hurt riding that pony of his."

Then, as if at last sensing a little of her desolation, he said, "Lavinia, don't look that way. Nothing has changed for us."

She wanted to hurl angry words at him. How could nothing change when Denise would be coming back to Mooncliff, when she would preside over the house again? Suppose Denise sensed that Jason had turned to Stuart's governess in her absence. Denise was no fool, and she had too much pride to allow such a situation to go on under her own roof.

Lavinia felt that Jason was already slipping away from her. She put her arms around him and clung to him, but she felt the lack of response, the impatience to be on his way.

"You'd better get an early start," she said. Without another word or a backward look he turned and went up the path, leaving her alone.

The sky was still bright and blue and the waters of the Hudson sparkled silver in the spring sunlight, but the wind that swept across the river made her draw her shawl around her. She remained unmoving, looking out at the hazy purple outlines of the Catskill Mountains on the western shore.

Chapter 9

All that summer morning Denise Moreland had been borne along on a tide of joy. Now, seated on the terrace that looked out over the river, she gave a little sigh of pure satisfaction.

She knew she looked as beautiful as she ever had; that her waistline was scarcely wider than it had been before her marriage, that her skin was as smooth and fresh as a young girl's. Her dark red hair, arranged in the fashionable French twist, gleamed like satin. She wore a new dress of pale green silk trimmed with yards of lace and jade-green velvet ribbons.

She smiled to herself, remembering how only a few hours ago at breakfast she had told Jason that the doctor had pronounced her fully recovered from Vanessa's birth. "You won't have to sleep alone tonight," she had whispered. Once she would have gone hot with shame at the thought of speaking to her husband so boldly. Now, after seven years of marriage, there was no longer room for false modesty.

She looked over at Jason, seated across the terrace; as

if aware of her glance, he raised his eyes from his newspaper. The look he gave her and the smile that accompanied it made her blush a little. He had read her thoughts; she had never been able to conceal her need for him, not since that first night in the cabin on board the *Enchantress*. Even then he had seen through her fear of him, which had been real enough, to the elemental hunger that no man had awakened in her before.

She wanted to go to him now, to feel his arms around her, but she had to wait. If only he had not planned a dinner party for tonight. Still, the day would pass, and the evening, and then he would lie beside her again.

The sunlight had never been so bright, she thought, nor had she ever known Mooncliff to look so beautiful. The terrace was a riot of color, with red and pink geraniums in stone pots along the railing, white and crimson roses and the cool green of ferns. He had ordered new statuary for the terrace while she was away: a cupid bending his bow and a Greek maiden poised on one marble foot and chastely draped in a marble tunic.

At the far end of the terrace Miss Wilmot, Phillip's gray-haired nanny, was crocheting a lace collar for one of her charge's velvet suits: an unnecessary chore, but Denise knew Miss Wilmot was the product of an age that deplored a moment's idleness.

Lavinia Corbett held an embroidery hoop in her slim fingers, but she was not engrossed in her handiwork; she was watching for Stuart to return from his riding lesson. Although Denise had had her doubts about Miss Corbett's ability to handle the headstrong little boy, she was forced to admit that the young governess was devoted to Stuart. Indeed, since her return from New York City she had begun to think that there was something too intense about the bond between Miss Corbett and Stuart. It was bad enough that Jason indulged the boy and made excuses for him; Miss Corbett should not pamper him, too.

Her thoughts were interrupted when Lavinia Corbett got up so quickly that her embroidery slid to the flagstones of the terrace. A moment later Stuart bounded up the steps.

"How did it go today?" she asked. "Were you able to take the higher jump?"

"Of course I was." He swaggered a bit, and Denise had to repress a smile. He was such a handsome child, and determined to prove his manliness. "It was easy. Just wait 'til I get a big horse like Father's."

He ran to Jason, who dropped his newspaper and put an arm around the boy. "Nothing like that for you until you're nine or ten," Jason said. "Surely you've not outgrown your pony already."

"Ponies are for babies," Stuart said. He moved away from Jason and stood, legs apart, striking his riding crop against a polished boot.

He looked so like his father; even though he had Denise's dark red hair, the blue eyes under the straight, dark brows, the wide mouth and the square, determined chin were Jason's own. He was well built and tall for his age, and so active that Denise wondered how a slender young girl like Miss Corbett could keep up with him.

"I want a real horse," Stuart said, frowning.

"Even you can't have what you want all the time, son."

Stuart's dark brows drew together, as Jason's often did in moments of anger. He threw down his riding crop and turned his back on his father.

Phillip, who had been riding a painted rocking horse, a splendid beast with yellow glass eyes and a flowing purple mane, snatched up the crop and began pounding it against the toy horse.

"Give me that," Stuart said. "It's mine!"

Phillip would not surrender the riding crop; instead, he set up a wail that brought Miss Wilmot hurrying to his side.

"Now, Master Phillip, you mustn't—"

But Phillip continued to hold onto the riding crop until Stuart twisted his arm. "You're hurting him!" Miss Wilmot cried, but Stuart ignored her.

"Give it back, you little bastard!" Stuart's voice, shrill and clear, shattered the peace of the sunlit terrace, and with it the warm contentment Denise had felt all that morning. Her hand flew to her throat and she gave a little cry; a wave of nausea engulfed her, and the pink and red geraniums, the roses and ferns blurred together.

Stuart did not realize what he had said, and no one except Denise knew the full cruelty of it: that Phillip had no right to Jason's name.

Stuart, still determined to have his way, wrenched the riding crop out of Phillip's hand and brought it down across the younger boy's face. Denise got to her feet, but Miss Wilmot, who was closer, snatched Phillip into her arms. Swiftly she examined the cut. "His eye's not hurt," she said. She pressed a large white handkerchief against Phillip's face, making comforting sounds. In a moment Phillip's outraged screams subsided into quiet sobbing.

"Here, let me look at him," Jason said. Then, "It's all right, Phil." He turned to Miss Wilmot. "Take him down to the pantry—that's closest—and see to the cut. Then send for Doctor Underhill."

"I don't think he'll need a doctor, sir," Miss Wilmot said. "But I warned you. Master Stuart has never been disciplined. You wouldn't let me punish him, and you wouldn't do it yourself. You think I am old-fashioned, but I know children. And I know the Scripture. 'Who loveth his son, chasteneth him.' "

Denise expected Jason to make some retort, but to her surprise he remained silent. With a flurry of black poplin skirts, the stout nanny carried Phillip into the house.

Lavinia spoke quickly. "Stuart should not have— But I'm sure he learned such language from the stablehands."

"You're the one who is supposed to be educating my son," Denise snapped. "Not the stablehands!"

"Denise, that's unreasonable," Jason began, but she turned on him, her voice shaking with controlled anger.

"You'll find an excuse for Stuart, I'm sure. You always do. No doubt you feel what he's done to Phillip only proves he's high-spirited."

"No, Denise. Not this time."

He picked up the riding crop that was lying now on the flagstones of the terrace.

"Come with me, Stuart," he said. He did not raise his voice, but Stuart, after a look at his father's face, ran to take refuge behind Lavinia.

The governess held out a hand as if to defend the child. "It's my fault," she said.

Jason ignored her. "I've been too easy with you, Stuart." He struck the crop lightly against his palm. "When you've learned what this feels like, you won't use it so freely again."

"No, please. I'll punish him," Lavinia said. "I won't allow him to go near the stables for a week—for as long as you say."

Jason gave Lavinia Corbett a cold, warning look, and she said no more. Stuart's hand clutched at her skirt, and he buried his face in the billowing folds of pale gray muslin.

"Turn her loose and come here!" Never had Jason used such a tone of voice to his eldest son. The boy made a small, whimpering sound, but he let go of Lavinia and obeyed.

Stronger than Denise's pity for Stuart was her knowledge that the boy deserved to be punished. Better now, she thought, than later, when it would be harder to control him. She did not try to intervene but stood in silence, watching Stuart, head down, stumbling into the house in front of his father.

"Mrs. Moreland, stop him."

Denise could not believe that Lavinia Corbett would show such effrontery. "How dare you interfere? Mr. Moreland has every right—"

Lavinia grasped her arm. "No. Not when he's angry like this; you don't know what he's capable of."

Her words hung between them, revealing, outrageous. Then, a moment later, Lavinia lifted her skirts and ran into the house. Denise stood where she was, trying to steady herself, to still the turmoil inside her. What gave Lavinia the right to intimate that she knew Jason better than his own wife did? *You don't know what he's capable of.*

Slowly she walked across the terrace and into the cool shade of the long hallway.

Lavinia was at the closed doors of the library. "Jason —Jason, let me in, please—"

She was calling him Jason. Lavinia Corbett, a governess,

was calling the master of the house by his first name. Even Elspeth, who had worked at Mooncliff all these years, who had helped to bring both Stuart and Phillip into the world, had never called Jason by his first name. Worse still was the abandon with which she called him, hammering on the locked door with her fists.

"Miss Corbett! Stop that at once."

Lavinia turned. "He locked the door," she said, her voice unsteady. Denise saw that she was trembling.

A moment later, there was a piercing wail from inside the library.

"You've got to stop him!"

Stuart cried out again.

"Stuart deserves this. His father has every right—"

"But he's so angry!"

In spite of herself Denise could not help being moved. Whatever Stuart had said or done out there a few moments before, he was only a child. How could he understand why his father, who had indulged him and spoiled him all these years, had turned on him in anger?

While she stood there, not knowing what to do, the shrieks died away. A moment later Jason came to the door, his jacket off, his shirt clinging damply to his chest. His face was drawn. "Take the boy to his room," he said to Lavinia. "Don't look at me that way, Miss Corbett. You must see that he couldn't be allowed to go unpunished."

Denise went hot with anger. Why should Jason try to justify himself, not to her, but to Lavinia? Why did he feel that this outsider's opinion mattered?

A moment later Stuart came to the door, his face red and streaked with tears. Lavinia picked him up in her arms and, cradling him against her, carried him upstairs.

"She must leave the house at once."

It was early evening, and although Denise had finished dressing for dinner, she remained in a chair by the bedroom window.

"Denise, we'll discuss it another time. Our guests will be arriving soon. This dinner tonight is important."

Jason, composed and looking unusually handsome in a black broadcloth suit with a white ruffled shirt and an embroidered black and silver waistcoat, was making an effort to control his temper, to placate her.

"I want Miss Corbett out of this house," Denise said. She stood up and smoothed her intricately draped skirt of ice-blue taffeta.

"Stuart's been punished. He won't hurt his brother again." He forced a smile. "He won't be riding his pony for a day or so, either, I'd guess."

"I don't want him going to the stables again, ever."

"He's a boy. If he didn't pick up bad language in the stables, he'd pick it up somewhere else, as I did."

"How can you make such a comparison? Stuart hasn't —he isn't—"

Jason's mouth lifted at the corner: "Do go on." And when she remained silent, he added, "Surely you won't pass up an opportunity to remind me that I was brought up in the gutter."

"That has nothing to do with Stuart."

"I agree. And I believe I've convinced him that certain words are suitable for the stable but should not be used in the presence of ladies."

"That's not my point."

"Oh, for— Denise, we'll settle this later. Congressman Marsh will be here shortly, and Roscoe Conkling. I've told you these men are important to my business. And spare me your criticism. The War's been over nearly ten years, and it's of no interest to me that they were on the Yankee side."

"I'm afraid I can't forget so easily. It isn't only that I lost a brother in the War, but even now men like Marsh and Conkling would like to see the South humbled and degraded for as long as possible."

"When you speak of 'the South' I assume you mean people like your father, who used to own hundreds of slaves. You're not referring to farmers who had only one or two, or none at all."

"Poor white trash. And yet those are the ones your friends in Congress and the Senate have put in control."

"I don't give a damn what Marsh's policies toward the South are—or Conkling's or any of the others'. Not that I haven't profited well enough by my investment in Riverview. An investment that helped your family from going under, too."

"We were speaking of Miss Corbett," she reminded him.

"You were."

"I've not tried to interfere in your business, even when it means opening my home to men I despise. But Miss Corbett is part of the household staff, and that is my business. I never thought the girl was suitable. No references, except from her headmistress at that school in England. And her behavior today was outrageous."

"In what way?"

"She tried to interfere, to stop you from punishing Stuart."

"She's fond of the boy. Is that all you have to criticize her for?"

"When I came into the hall, she was pounding on the library doors, making a spectacle of herself. Anyone would have thought *she* was being beaten."

He put an arm around Denise. "Try to understand. Lavinia Corbett had the kind of childhood you cannot imagine, although I can. She worked in the Manchester cotton mills when she was only a few years older than Stuart is now."

"I didn't know."

"She suffered terribly. Starved, beaten—"

"I can't believe—"

"No, I suppose you can't, but it's true, all the same. I've had dealings with the Manchester millowners, and I know. That's why she may have forgotten her place. Because she cannot bear to see a child mistreated."

"You know a great deal about Miss Corbett's past, and about her feelings, too. Perhaps you can tell me why she presumed to call you by your first name, not once but over and over. And why she told me that I didn't know what you were capable of, implying that she did."

"I've told you, she was upset. Hysterical, if you wish. She won't forget her place again."

His arm was still around her, and his nearness made her long to forget everything that had happened that day. Later tonight, they would be together in bed. He would make love to her, and she would feel close to him again. It would be easy to yield to her hunger for him. Too easy.

"Jason, before I went to New York, you promised you would check into Miss Corbett's background."

"I did so. There was nothing in her background to make me feel she was not suitable as a governess for Stuart."

"Yet you've just told me she worked in a cotton mill."

"Good Lord, do you think she wanted to? Do you think she had any choice? I went to sea because I would have starved otherwise. I sailed on slaving ships, and she went to work in a mill. You were learning French and dancing and fine embroidering in the schoolroom at Riverview, while she—"

There was a knock at the door. Elspeth had come to tell them the first of the guests were arriving.

"Come along, Denise," Jason said.

"Not until we've settled the matter of Miss Corbett."

He took his arm from her shoulders. "Are you saying—? Damn it, Denise, this dinner is important to me! You have to be there."

She raised her head and looked him squarely in the eye. Her lips were a thin, tight line.

For a moment she was afraid, but she stood her ground. It was he who gave way. "All right, Denise," he said softly. "Miss Corbett will leave tomorrow. I'll tell her first thing in the morning. Now come along. Our guests are waiting."

Looking back on that evening, Denise could never remember how she had managed to get through it, to keep up the pleasant small talk that was expected of her, to make a pretense of eating a little of each of the seven courses. She found that it was difficult for her to swallow even a mouthful of the rich, heavy food.

She had to force herself to carry on a polite conversation with Congressman Thaddeus Marsh, a short, stocky man with muttonchop whiskers. Marsh, Jason had told her, was a leader in the Radical Republican faction, a virtual dictator who demanded complete obedience from party followers; he supported the use of black militiamen in

South Carolina and had been instrumental in filling the legislature of that state with ex-slaves and carpetbaggers.

But she managed to play the role Jason had demanded of her. She made herself smile at the flattery of Roscoe Conkling, the Radical senator from upstate New York who was a ladies' man and a dazzling orator. She could understand why most women were delighted with Conkling's attentions, for he was undeniably handsome, a bearded blond Adonis as tall as Jason, with broad shoulders and a fine profile. But Denise thought he had the mannerisms of an actor, and while others might find him charming, she disliked and distrusted him.

Jason had told her that both Conkling and Marsh had favored the annexation of the island of Santo Domingo by the United States, and had, indeed, persuaded President Grant to support the corrupt dictatorship on that island until such time as the island might become a possession of the United States. Santo Domingo, Jason insisted, was an important foothold for American business interests in the Caribbean and also a steppingstone toward control of the Isthmus of Panama. Like so many American shipowners, Jason was excited by the possibility of a canal across the isthmus. "Even the fastest clipper ships lost precious time going around South America. That's one reason they're being driven off the seas."

Not all the guests, were politicians. Denise recognized a few prominent journalists and some businessmen who had interests similar to Jason's. She also found herself looking at Captain Terence O'Connor and wondering why Jason had invited him to this particular gathering; the young man was quiet and a little shy, and Denise guessed that he would have been more at ease aboard the *Tropic Star*. She wondered, too, whether Elspeth was still attracted to him and whether the captain knew of her feelings.

It was a relief when the long dinner was finally over and she was able to retire with the other ladies to the sitting room, while the gentlemen were left to talk business.

The sitting room windows had been opened to admit the breezes from the river. The amber velvet draperies stirred slightly. Denise had chosen those draperies, knowing that they enhanced her own coloring.

It was easier for her to keep up her role as hostess out of the company of the men she so disliked and resented. She might have little in common with their wives, but it was possible to chatter about the new fashions without paying too much attention to every word. Mrs. Marsh, a plump brunette who tossed her head often so that her large emerald and diamond earrings would catch the light, was rattling on about the daring new swimming suits being worn at Long Branch this summer. "They have trousers gathered at the ankles. Like something out of a Turkish harem. And short-sleeved blouses. Don't you find that shocking, Mrs. Moreland?"

"Yes, indeed," Denise said automatically.

"Of course, I prefer the kilted skirts. They may be a bit heavy after one has been bathing, but they do conceal the figure."

"I suppose so," Denise agreed. Women like Mrs. Marsh, who had attained their social position through their husbands' election to high government office, made a special point of emphasizing their modesty and good breeding. Jason had told Denise that Eugenia Marsh had begun life as plain Jenny Higgens, and had waited on tables and done laundry in her mother's boardinghouse in Washington. Now she delighted in her role as arbiter of public morals.

From the discussion of fashion she went on to a rehashing of the Henry Ward Beecher scandal. "Imagine him, a man of the cloth, seducing one of his own parishioners. No one will ever be able to convince me that Elizabeth Tilton was not his mistress."

"The church committee found him innocent," Denise said.

"Oh, the man's a charmer, no doubt about it. But he was guilty all the same. Well, I'm not surprised. There isn't a man alive who won't stray if some woman puts temptation in his path."

Denise felt uncomfortable; she wished that Mrs. Marsh would change the subject. She was not thinking about Dr.

Beecher and Mrs. Tilton but remembering her quarrel with Jason earlier that evening and the excuses he had made for Lavinia Corbett. Still, he had agreed to fire her. That must mean she was not really important to him. But he had tried to defend her. What had happened between Jason and the governess during the time that Denise had been away from Mooncliff? She was not sure she wanted to know.

"And to think that a man like that—father of a family, with a good and dutiful wife—and brother of Mrs. Stowe, a fine Christian woman—"

"I don't know about Mrs. Stowe's personal life," Denise snapped. "However, I cannot forget how she maligned the South in that dreadful book of hers. Pure sensationalism."

"I am sorry, Mrs. Moreland," Mrs. Marsh fluttered. "Of course, being from the South as you are— But really, weren't some of those incidents based on fact? Don't be angry, my dear. I'm only asking."

"Ask your husband, Mrs. Marsh! He obviously believes the South should never stop paying for its supposed crimes."

The plump brunette looked flushed and uneasy. Like so many of the ladies here tonight, she had no wish to offend Mrs. Moreland, whose husband was as influential as her own. She was well aware of Denise's background and stood somewhat in awe of her.

Denise, for her part, was ashamed of having taken out her nervous tension on this silly, ill-bred but harmless woman. If only the evening would end and the guests would take their leave. If only she could be alone with Jason.

But when at last they were alone in the great hallway and the last of the carriages had rolled down the drive, she found Jason remote and preoccupied.

"It's long after midnight," he said. "Why don't you go upstairs, my dear?"

In spite of all that had happened today, Denise wanted him beside her in bed; her body hungered for him. "Come with me," she said.

"I must talk to Captain O'Connor. He's still in the library."

"But surely—"

"I have some private instructions I must give him before he leaves on his next voyage."

His lips brushed her cheek. "Sleep well, Denise," he said. There was a cool finality in his voice that told her he would not come to her tonight.

Her pride would not permit her to beg him to sleep with her. She went upstairs, her head held high. But inside their bedroom she threw herself down across the bed, heedless of the ruin of her taffeta dress. She let the tears come at last, pressing her face into the pillow so no one would hear her.

Chapter 10

Jason Moreland sat with Congressman Thaddeus Marsh in the parlor of the congressman's suite at the Astor House; the hotel was still fashionable, although New York City was moving steadily northward, and Marsh maintained quarters there when he was in the city. The two men had finished a long lunch of game pie, terrapin, and duckling in Burgundy. A heavy meal for a sultry August afternoon, but well cooked and served. They were starting their second bottle of wine and discussing the matter that had brought them together. "You feel strongly about our involvement in the Caribbean," Marsh was saying.

"I don't agree with Grant's policies there, if that's what you mean. Damned shortsighted."

Marsh shrugged, smoothed his heavy black whiskers and adjusted his vest. In spite of the fact that he had a short, stocky physique, he was addicted to flashy clothing. This afternoon he wore blue and white striped trousers and a white satin vest embroidered with bright blue cornflowers. A huge diamond glittered on his finger, and another adorned his stickpin.

"Grant did all he could to force through the annexation of Santo Domingo; you know that as well as I do," Marsh said. "Why, if it'd been up to him, we'd own that island today."

"He should have stood his ground," Jason said.

"Didn't he send Colonel Babcock down there to negotiate a secret deal with that puppet dictator of theirs—Baez?"

"True enough," Jason agreed. "But he backed down. He let himself be stopped cold by Sumner, an addle-headed idealist, and Hamilton Fish, a gentleman politician."

"I tell you, President Grant did all he could. He allotted one hundred and fifty thousand dollars out of Secret Service funds to support the Baez regime, didn't he? And what a stink that raised during the investigation by the Foreign Relations Committee."

"Committees." Jason's mouth twisted with contempt, and he poured himself another glass of wine. "Grant doesn't understand business. Never will. He can't begin to see the fortunes waiting to be picked up in the Caribbean. Not only in Santo Domingo, but in Cuba, in Panama. Listen to me, Thaddeus. Spain's day in the West Indies is past. She's losing her last foothold there. And when she's out of the picure, who's going to take control, answer me that?" He paused and leaned forward. "It has got to be us."

The congressman's small black eyes were unreadable. "Are you talking about Manifest Destiny?"

"If you want to call it that. With the Caribbean in our hands, a naval base in Santo Domingo, we can move on to Panama. A canal right across the isthmus."

"It would help your shipping—"

"Mine? Everyone's! What's good for us is good for the nation; remember that."

Marsh was silent for a moment. He studied Jason's face carefully. "Have you ever thought of going into politics yourself?"

"I'm a businessman."

"No reason you can't do both."

"Are you serious, Thaddeus?"

"I am. Tweed's out of the picture. The public is screaming for reform. Think about it. Jason Moreland, reform candidate for the State Senate in the next election. A beginning. From there, who knows?"

"I'll give it some thought," Jason said, pushing his chair back from the table. "But now—"

"I suppose you want to get started. Long drive out to Mooncliff."

"I don't know that I'll go out there tonight. I have some papers to go over down at my office."

"Hell, you can't work all the time. If you're spending the night here in the city, why not join me and a few of my friends? We're going to drop in at Josie Woods's place. There's a new girl there—Hungarian, she says. A blonde with skin likc—"

"I don't think so," Jason interrupted.

Marsh grinned. "With these new apartment buildings going up—French flats, they call them—maybe Josie and her kind will be on the way out soon."

"How do you figure that?" Jason asked.

"Why, you rent yourself a flat, tuck away a pretty little girl there, and you always have a place to sleep when you stay over in the city. A home away from home, you might say."

"It's a thought," Jason agreed. Then he rose, dismissing the subject from his mind.

On the drive downtown to South Street, he considered the pros and cons of a career in politics. So far he had been able to buy the political concessions he had needed, but the situation might change.

What would Denise think about such a move? Probably she would refuse to discuss it. She had made it plain how she felt about men like Marsh; her dislike and contempt for them had never been hidden. If he brought up the matter of a political alliance with the Radical Republicans, they would have another quarrel. She simply did not understand.

Lavinia might understand. But where was she? Had it been only a month since she had left Mooncliff, since he had sent her away with a reference and five hundred dollars to tide her over?

The look she had given him before she had turned to go. No tears, no recriminations. Only that look, her violet eyes dark with pain, with the agony of betrayal. A white line around her lips and a greenish pallor on her cheeks.

He had been fair with her, damn it. He hadn't seduced her. She had been another man's mistress before she had given herself to him. And she had been willing enough. He remembered with a swiftly rising hunger how she had lain in his arms that first night, straining against him, burying her face against his shoulder to stifle her cry at the climax.

But he had had to send her away. That had been a bad time for all of them. Stuart had been miserable for the first few days after Lavinia's departure and had made himself positively ill, crying until he was feverish, rejecting all attempts by his mother to comfort him. Had the boy sensed, in that uncanny way of children, that his mother had been responsible for Miss Corbett's departure? Or did he blame her for allowing his father to punish him? Whatever his feelings, Stuart was still not himself; after his hysterical outbursts had ceased, he had taken to moping around the house, refusing even to ride his pony.

Denise had been unable to find a suitable replacement for Lavinia Corbett, although she had made two trips into the city, to Miss Fisher's Agency. She had, however, returned with the information that Miss Fisher had found another position for Miss Corbett, teaching at an academy for young ladies on Gramercy Square.

Denise had offered this information to Jason in a conciliatory fashion; she knew—she could not help but know—how much he had resented her demand that he get rid of the governess. Perhaps, Jason thought, his wife hoped that he would feel better knowing Miss Corbett had found another haven.

But she was wrong. Jason was not a man to take orders gracefully, not from anyone, and certainly not from his wife. He looked out at the crowds passing by, moving slowly through the hazy August afternoon. Soft blue twilight shadows were beginning to blur the outlines of the buildings on either side of the street. Suddenly Jason knew that he had no desire to go down to his office, to spend an evening alone among his maps and ledgers.

Marsh's suggestion that he go into politics had set up a whole new line of thinking, and he wanted to speak his thoughts to someone. Not to ask advice, for that had never been his way, but to think out loud to a receptive second party.

He leaned forward on the seat of the open carriage and said to Patrick, "I've changed my mind. Drive to Gramercy Square."

In spite of the circumstances of their last parting, Jason knew that Lavinia would not turn away from him. No matter what pain he had caused her, he knew, with a certainty that had nothing of male vanity about it, that he would only have to hold out his hand and she would come to him. For Lavinia had none of his wife's stiff-necked pride, none of that sense of self-esteem that made Denise a constant challenge.

Perhaps, Jason thought, that was why, though he might have a need for Lavinia now, Denise was the only woman he had ever really loved.

In her small room on the third floor of Miss Wyndham's Academy, a room she shared with Mademoiselle Tourneur, the French teacher, Lavinia stood before the wavy mirror, arranging her hair. She parted it neatly in the center, braided the heavy, pale blond mass, and twisted the braid into a tight coil at the back of her neck. It was not a flattering style, but Miss Wyndham insisted on simplicity of appearance in her teachers.

Lavinia noticed that she had lost weight during the past month. Her cheekbones stood out sharply, and her collarbones were too prominent. There were dark smudges under her eyes.

Th heat, of course. Who wanted to eat, who could get a proper night's sleep during this sultry August weather?

She had opened the one narrow window in the room,

but no breeze came to her from the square, and although the rooms below were large and comfortable, those up on the third floor which were allotted to the teachers were hot and airless in summer.

Lavinia told herself sternly that she should be thankful to have found a position at all. At least, Denise Moreland had given her an excellent reference, explaining that the reason for Miss Corbett's dismissal was the Morelands' decision to hire a tutor for Stuart. With such a reference, Lavinia had had no difficulty in getting the position at Miss Wyndham's Academy, where one of the teachers had left unexpectedly to nurse an ailing parent, and a replacement had been needed at once.

But from her first day at Miss Wyndham's fashionable establishment Lavinia had hated the place. It was difficult to adjust to the hot, crowded city after the refreshing country air and cooling breezes of Mooncliff. It was difficult, too, to get used to the Spartan routine. The girls at Miss Wyndham's school rose at six and studied until seven, assisted by Lavinia and the other teachers. Then they breakfasted, attended interminable prayers, and walked outdoors until classes started at nine. At four in the afternoon they again paraded in double file around the square, under the dusty trees. After returning to the school they changed for dinner, and after that they had practice in French conversation. Then more study, evening prayers, and bedtime at eight.

Now it was the hour for French conversation, and Mademoiselle Tourneur was downstairs; Lavinia had the tiny room to herself. It was the only hour of the twenty-four that she had any privacy.

But now that she was alone, she found no solace in her thoughts. As she got into her high-necked black poplin dress and began to fasten the small jet buttons, her mood was grim and filled with self-reproach. She had been a fool, had allowed a man to deceive her for the second time. She had allowed herself to fall in love.

Even so, she might still be at Mooncliff if she had not lost control of herself that day when Jason had punished Stuart. If only she had not run after him, had not pounded on the locked door and called him by his first name. Lavinia did not blame Denise for having taken swift action. "I'd have done the same in her place," she thought.

But she did blame Jason for her being forced to leave Mooncliff; he had obviously been unwilling to intervene on her behalf. "If he had loved me at all, if I had meant anything to him, he would not have allowed her to turn me away." The thought was painful, but she had faced it and accepted it. He had not even relegated the dismissal to his wife, although he might easily have done so; instead, he had called her into the library and handed her the letter of reference and a check for five hundred dollars, the latter to ease his conscience, no doubt. He had spoken to her with formal courtesy, as if she had never been anything more to him than a household employee.

She had fought down the longing to throw herself into his arms, to plead with him to reconsider, for she had sensed that such behavior would have aroused only his contempt. Somewhere she had found the pride to give him an equally formal farewell, to wait while her trunk was put into a hired cab, to ignore the curious glances of the servants. Not until she was seated in the cab, the blinds drawn, had she given way to tears. Since that day, she had not cried again.

Now she smoothed her dress and prepared to go downstairs to face another evening of reviewing the girls in their lessons and attending evening prayers with them. After that, she would embroider or knit until her own bedtime. She would make formal, meaningless conversation with Mademoiselle Tourneur and the other teachers. Then she would come back up to this room and lie alone and sleepless in her narrow bed.

"I'll grow old here," she thought. "Old and lean and dried out."

She felt an ache across her temples, and her eyes began to sting, but the tears would not come. She pressed her lids down, and all at once she saw Jason, as she had seen him so many times before: his face was close to hers, and there was hunger in his eyes.

Not love. She knew that now. Only lust. The same

animal need that had driven Arthur Selby to make her his mistress. Jason, like Arthur, had used her and then turned her away.

No matter. She would stifle every feeling she had ever had for Jason Moreland, would make herself an automaton. She would be a competent teacher, and over the years she would watch the girls come and go, see them leave the school to go out into the world, to enter New York society. Perhaps a few of them would think of her from time to time. More likely they would forget her as soon as they took up their new lives, fell in love, married.

She started, hearing a knock on the door. Miss Wyndham's little parlormaid poked her head in. "You have a visitor, Miss Corbett. He's waiting for you in the parlor. Mr. Jason Moreland. He drove up in a fine carriage with a coachman and—"

Lavinia heard no more. She pressed her lips together and willed herself to show no emotion. She would send Jason away, of course. She would tell the maid that she did not wish to see the gentleman.

No, that would be a mistake. It was perfectly natural, from Miss Wyndham's point of view, that her ex-employer had dropped in to pay her a formal call, and if she refused to see him it would look odd and might provoke suspicion.

Besides, she would not give Jason the satisfaction of thinking that she felt anything for him any longer, that she was afraid to face him. She would be polite and formal and would terminate the visit as quickly as possible.

What could he have to say to her? Surely he was not about to ask her to return to Mooncliff.

"Tell Mr. Moreland I'll be right down," she said to the maid.

Jason was waiting for her in the parlor, and she noticed how he dominated his surroundings, the small, overfurnished room with its rosewood pianoforte, its embroidered velvet ottomans and potted plants, its china cabinets and crocheted doilies.

"You don't look well," he said, without preliminaries. "Have you been ill?"

"The city is hot in summer, particularly when I have become accustomed to—other surroundings."

"My carriage is outside. I'll take you for a drive around the square."

"That's quite impossible. I have my duties here. In a little while Miss Wyndham will be calling me for evening prayers."

"All right, then. But close the door."

"I can't. It would be most improper."

Jason shut the door, came to her side, and put a hand on her arm. "I can't talk to you with that old dragon and half a dozen girls listening."

"We have nothing to say to each other, in any case. I only came down here to avoid a scene."

"You're a poor liar, Lavinia. You always have been. But you should know by now that you can't hide your feelings from me. The day you left Mooncliff—"

"The day you dismissed me," she said, not bothering to keep the bitterness out of her voice.

"You can't think that was my idea."

"You allowed your wife to turn me away. You didn't take the trouble to defend me. I was fired like a parlor-maid who had failed to give satisfaction."

"I didn't come here to talk about that," he interrupted.

"Then what did you come to talk about? Say what you have to say, and go. Leave me in peace."

He turned her around so that she faced him, and put his hands on her shoulders. His eyes held hers. "You haven't known much peace since you left Mooncliff."

"But I will again, in time. I got over Arthur Selby, and I can—"

"You're not comparing me with him, damn it!"

"Why not? Both of you took what you wanted and then left me with nothing." She stopped. "No, that's not quite true. You gave me five hundred dollars. That was most generous of you, all things considered. You could have bought a dozen women for such a handsome sum."

"Be quiet. You know, you must know, that you were more to me than that."

"I only know you sent me away. And that, having done so, you come back now, you walk in here as if— Why did you come here, Jason?"

He remained silent, but she read her answer in his eyes.

He put his arms around her and drew her to him, and her body came alive, but she did not let herself respond; she forced herself to remain unyielding in his embrace. Even when his mouth came down over hers, she did not part her lips.

He released her. "Now," she said evenly, "if you have what you came for, please go."

"I have to talk to you. Not here. I can't talk to you here."

"Would you like me in one of those places where they rent rooms by the hour, no questions asked? Oh, yes, even I have heard about them. Is that what you have in mind?"

"No, damn it! Lavinia, I want you to leave this place. I'll find a flat in one of those new apartment buildings. I'll give you anything you want. Clothes, jewels, a maid. You won't have to work. You can have a carriage—anything—"

His arrogance did not surprise her, for she knew him well. That he had dismissed her from Mooncliff, left her to suffer through the lonely nights this summer, and had come back to ask her to become his mistress—this was to be expected. Even now he was not pleading. He was making her an offer, sure she would accept.

Anything she wanted. If only she could muster the pride to make terms, to say to him, "I want to be your wife, Jason. I want to be mistress of Mooncliff. Nothing less will satisfy me."

Some women would take such a gamble, risk everything, and perhaps win. But she could not. Suppose he refused. Suppose he walked out of the room, out of the house, and never returned. Never to see his face again, never to lie in his arms. . . .

"I want you, Lavinia," he said.

Not "I love you." Not even that. "I want you."

The pain of it hardened her voice. "What you want from me you can find down on Greene Street or in one of those plush parlor houses uptown. Why come to me for—"

"Stop it," he said. He put a hand on her arm. "It's not like that. I need you to talk to. Only this afternoon something happened that could make a big change in my life, and I knew that I had to tell you about it. That you would understand. A man needs that, Lavinia." He drew her closer. "Please don't turn away from me."

She wanted to yield completely, but she heard a small, warning voice in the back of her mind. "Jason, what if—if Denise should find out? You sent me away once because she wanted you to."

"This time it will be different. We'll be discreet. No one need know about us." When she remained silent he drew her closer. "Do you want me to humble myself—is that it? I hurt you when I sent you away from Mooncliff. And now you want to hear me beg. Is that what you're waiting for?"

"No, you mustn't think that. It's only—a woman wants to know she's loved. Especially when that's all she has."

"There are different kinds of love, Lavinia. What I feel for you—the need to have you with me—a part of my life—isn't that enough?"

Outside the closed door, she heard the footsteps of the girls as they filed down the hall to evening prayer. She heard Miss Wyndham's crisp voice giving orders.

But those sounds were meaningless, unimportant. Only Jason's last question had any meaning for her. Enough? It would have to be enough.

Jason pressed her hand against his cheek, then turned it and kissed her palm. She raised her eyes to his face. "I'll go with you, Jason," she heard herself say. "I'll be whatever you want me to be."

She knew that she had turned her back on security, on respectability, forever. She would never have those things again. Nor would she have any pride, not where Jason was concerned. And even so she might lose him. She had no claim on him, as Denise had.

Then he put his arms around her, and she felt the warmth of his body through the thin cambric shirt he wore, felt the rise and fall of his chest, the quickening of his breath.

"Find a place for us, Jason," she said softly. "Soon. Please make it soon."

Chapter 11

The sound of carriage wheels in the street brought Lavinia to the front window of her apartment. She pushed aside the heavy purple velvet draperies and peered out into the darkness of the autumn night. Then she sighed when she saw the carriage roll on, moving west toward the Hudson River. Slowly she returned to the sofa near the fireplace and settled herself on the soft cushions, smoothing the folds of her silk wrapper. She heard the little white and gold china clock on the mantel strike eleven-thirty.

Perhaps Jason wasn't coming to see her tonight. He might have decided to return home to Mooncliff. She felt the familiar ache inside at the thought, but then she reminded herself that it was enough—more than enough—to be part of his life again; she must ask for nothing more.

The apartment Jason had rented for Lavinia was new and luxurious, five rooms on the third-floor front, overlooking a quiet, treelined street. He had given her a free hand in the furnishing of the place, and she had enjoyed creating a home of her own.

The first time she lay in Jason's arms in the huge brass bed, she told him, "If you had not come for me, I should have died."

"Don't talk such damn nonsense. No one dies for love."

She knew that she had displeased him, although she wasn't quite sure why, but she warned herself to be more careful in the future. She must never again do or say anything that might cause him to put her out of his life. She had been on guard since that first night, giving way to her feelings only in the wordless ecstasy of their physical union.

At other times, she was content to listen to his talk of business, of his possible future in politics. She encouraged him in the latter, learning all she could about the subject during the long hours when he was away. She dared not ask him, each time he took his leave of her, when she would see him again, nor did she risk any mention of his life at Mooncliff. She had even made herself wait until he volunteered news about Stuart.

"He cried himself to sleep for several nights after you left."

"And you?"

He laughed. "I haven't cried myself to sleep since I was six years old, and then it was because I was so damn hungry. After a while, of course, I developed a certain skill in stealing food from the vendors' stalls."

He would not admit that he had missed her during the month they had been apart, but he had. Otherwise he would not have come for her and set her up here in the apartment.

"Stuart's quite all right now, though, isn't he?" she asked.

"He's quieter, but he's well enough." He smiled at Lavinia. "You're fond of the boy, aren't you? I sometimes think you care for him more than—" He broke off, but she knew what he had been about to say. She thought for a moment of how it would be to be Stuart's mother, Jason's wife. Mistress of Mooncliff. Foolish, worse than foolish, to think about such things. She should be grateful for what she had.

But now, as she watched the hands of the clock move

toward midnight, she felt a growing depression. If Jason did not come soon he would not come at all, and she would have to get through the slow, dark hours alone in the wide brass bed.

He spent few enough nights with her at best: no more than two a week. But he had said that tonight he would be staying late in the city and might come to her when he had completed his business. He must have changed his mind, or . . .

Once more the sound of carriage wheels in the quiet street sent her flying to the window. A hired hansom stopped in front of the house. She closed her eyes for a moment, and when she opened them, she saw Jason standing in the street, in the soft glow of the gaslight. Although too far away to make out his features, she knew it could be no one else: the arrogant set of his shoulders, his long stride as he approached the house. Her mind supplied the details of his face: the wide, sensual mouth; the heavy, dark brows; and the square, hard line of the jaw. She could have wept with joy, but she dared not; he must find her composed, pleasant, and enticingly pretty. She looked quickly and unnecessarily into the hand mirror she kept in the table drawer beside the sofa. She had already brushed and curled her ash-blond hair, and it shone in the firelight. Her blue silk wrapper matched her eyes and outlined her body; she wore nothing underneath it.

She hurried to the door to let him in. His eyes were bright with excitement, his face animated. "I've done it," he said. "And you're responsible."

Tossing his coat across a small gilt and velvet chair, he lifted her into his arms and pressed her against him.

"What have you done?" she asked. "And why am I—"

He stopped her questions with a long kiss. Then he set her down and hurried her to the sofa. "I told him my decision."

"Who?"

"Congressman Thaddeus Marsh." He searched her face. "Did I wake you, love? I do believe you're half-asleep still."

She made herself keep silent. For hours she had been waiting for his arrival, running to the window at every sound. But she must not tell him so, for he might sense a veiled reproach.

"I met with Marsh and Burgess and Conkling, and I gave them my answer. Told them I would accept the Republican nomination for the State Legislature. As you told me to."

"I'm so pleased," she said. "Jason, think of it: the State Legislature. And after that, Washington, and—"

"You sound like Thaddeus Marsh. But you're much more agreeable to look at." Then he said, "Get me a drink and one for yourself. We'll celebrate."

He had sent over a case of Havana rum, and she hurried to get the decanter. She poured him a glass, then hesitated, for she was tired, and at such times a potent drink had an immediate effect on her. "Go on," he urged. "You do agree a celebration's in order, don't you? It was you who told me to do this, after all."

"As if anyone could make you do anything unless you wanted to." But she poured a second glass, and they toasted his success in the coming campaign. Then, as the rum began to relax her senses, she rested her head against his shoulder and listened while he told her all that had been said that night at Marsh's suite in the Astor House.

"It will mean a good deal of traveling, of course, and entertaining, too."

"But what will—"

"Go on," he said.

"I only thought, there might be problems at home. Mrs. Moreland won't be pleased. Her feelings about these people, Marsh and Conkling and Burgess—she hasn't made any secret of them."

"Let me worry about that," he said. "I think she will get used to the idea." At her look of doubt, he said brusquely, "My wife will do as I tell her."

"And if she refuses? Jason, the first day I came to Mooncliff, I complimented her on the fact that she was having such important guests as President Grant and his supporters. She made it perfectly plain that she did not feel honored by their presence in her home."

He moved away from her. "My wife's attitudes are no concern of yours." Although he did not raise his voice, she sensed his annoyance. But for once she could not stop herself.

She put her arms around him and tilted her head back to look into his eyes. "Oh, but you're wrong, my love. Don't you see? If you are to be successful in politics, you must have a wife who understands your ambitions and is in sympathy with them. One who is completely loyal to you."

"Are you saying Mrs. Moreland is not?"

"I understand her feelings. Her family were slave owners before the War. All her friends were members of the plantation aristocracy. But you are her husband. You should come first. Surely you deserve that much. And you would have it, my darling, if only you—if we—"

He set down his glass. "Exactly what are you trying to say?"

"I love you, Jason. If I were your wife, there is nothing I would not do for you." She searched his face, seeking a sign that he agreed. She was right for him. They were alike, he had said so himself, and she had more to offer than Denise: passion and loyalty and unquestioning acceptance of everything he was.

"Jason—"

He seized her arms and thrust her from him. "Denise is my wife and will remain so! You know nothing about her, and nothing of my feelings for her. You may have what opinions you wish, but you will not speak of her again!"

"Why? Because I'm not fit to? Because she is a great lady and I began life as a mill girl?" She felt afraid, but could not stop herself. "And what are you, Jason Moreland? You've told me enough of your early life to prove you're no better than I am."

"Maybe I told you too damn much."

The fear grew, spread until she heard a dull pounding in her head. "I didn't mean that. When a woman loves a man as I love you, she wants to know everything about him, to share everything, the bad as well as the good."

To her shock, he threw back his head and laughed. But there was no laughter in his eyes, and a moment later, when he leaned forward to pour himself another drink, she saw that his blue eyes were bleak and distant, and that the lines around his mouth had deepened.

"She said that once, when we were first married. She probably believed it, too. But afterward she had reason to change her mind."

"Tell me, Jason. Nothing you could have done would change my feelings for you."

"You sound very sure of yourself, my dear."

She shook her head. "I'm sure of my love for you, that's all. I know there are women who sit in judgment on a man, who have led such narrow, sheltered lives that they set impossible standards, and then—" She broke off, for she had caught the warning look in Jason's eyes. She knew better than to criticize Denise, even if she did not mention her by name.

Perhaps she should stop her probing now, should rise and lead Jason into the bedroom. But she could not, for the need to share every part of his life was too strong.

"The first day we met, when I drove down to South Street with you, you told me you had been in the slave trade, that you had started your fortune that way. But the trade was outlawed in England long before you would have been old enough to have captained a slaver—legally, that is."

"You're right." His voice was harsh. "Now, let's drop the matter, shall we?"

"But why? Oh, Jason, I never thought you were a law-abiding citizen. I know all about Captain O'Connor running guns to Cuba for you right now. I'm not shocked. A man has to bend the law to make a fortune—maybe even break it. You told me once that I was important to you because I could understand you. That meant a great deal to me. It's all I have to give you, except for—"

"All right, then. You won't be satisfied until I've told you all of it."

He did not look at her, and his words came slowly. "Remember that day back at Mooncliff when we spoke of Captain O'Connor? I said a young man of twenty-four will do anything, risk anything, without weighing the consequences, when he is determined to make a fortune."

She nodded. "But what has that to do with you?"

"When I was a year older than he is now, I took command of a slaver, the *Nubian Queen.*"

"Yes, I remember your telling me that. Elspeth's father sailed with you as ship's doctor."

"That's right. It was he who discovered, during the Middle Passage between Africa and Cuba, that some of the slaves, the cargo, were infected with typhus. Do you know about typhus? But of course you do. There was enough of it in the slums of Manchester, wasn't there?"

"I know," Lavinia said. "I remember."

"I was in command of a ship for the first time. Captain at twenty-five. I had taken that ship into hell to get my cargo. Dodged British patrol boats. Risked arrest, prison—even hanging. I couldn't sail into Havana with a cargo of dead blacks, and there was no way—no way at all—to stop the spread of the disease. Except—"

She turned away from him.

"You wanted to know, didn't you?" He seized her and turned her around to face him. "Didn't you?" he repeated.

"Tell me," she said quietly.

She forced herself to keep looking at him as he told her how he had ordered the diseased slaves to be thrown alive into the sea. How Andrew Buchanan had taken refuge in the cabin below and had drunk himself into insensibility. "But I stayed on deck to see my orders carried out. I watched while the crew chained the blacks together and weighted the chains and threw those living human beings, screaming and pleading, into the sea."

Jason took a long breath. "Buchanan said, just before he died, that there was a curse on Mooncliff. Perhaps he was right."

"You did what you had to do," Lavinia said. Then she put a hand on either side of his face and kissed him. "You must never think of it again. You must forget." She pressed closer to him. "I can make you forget. . . ."

She was not unaffected by what he had told her, but she knew that she must not let him know, not now, not ever. She must prove to him that her love was stronger than the love of his wife. She led him into the bedroom and made herself keep looking at him as she unfastened the buttons of her wrapper and let it slide to the thick rug beside the bed.

Usually he was the one who began their lovemaking, but now he stood before her, unmoving, until she began to unbutton his shirt. He looked down at her, studying her face as if he were seeing her for the first time.

"What kind of a woman are you, that you can—"

"One who loves you," she said. She pressed her naked body against him and put her mouth to his, and somehow they were on the bed together. But he lay beside her, still remote, withdrawn, until she reached out and began caressing his body, the wide chest, the hard-muscled abdomen and thighs, first with her fingers and then with her lips. She heard his breathing quicken, deepen.

Still lying on his back, he reached up and grasped her around the waist, drawing her down to him, penetrating her so swiftly and with such violence that she cried out. He brought her face down to his, twisting a hand in her long blond hair, and stifled her cry with his mouth.

Later, when it was over and she lay in his arms, bruised, spent and completely satisfied, she closed her eyes for a moment. She fell into a curious state between sleep and waking in which she saw, behind her closed lids, a blazing tropical sky and a sailing ship, black men and women huddled against the side of the deck, chained together, and Jason, looking down at them, giving the command that would send them to their deaths. . . .

She made a small, wordless, whimpering sound and opened her eyes. Jason, his mood changed, held her gently now, stroking her hair, her bare breasts. As his hands went on caressing her, she felt once again the rising tide of his passion and her answering need for him. He had asked what kind of woman she was, and now she asked herself that same question. Perhaps she should have turned away from him, withheld herself from his love-making tonight.

With a twinge of fear she wondered whether in giving herself to him without reservation she had lowered herself in his esteem. Perhaps if she had been more like his wife. . . .

But his hands were still moving over her, more urgent now, and he was whispering endearments, his face pressed against her breasts. She could no longer think of right or wrong. She knew only that he needed her, and she came to him on a tide of desire that rose, then ebbed away, leaving them both satiated.

But long after he had fallen asleep she lay awake, staring into the darkness. Jason had said that he would never leave his wife, but Lavinia could not accept that. She knew that it would be impossible for her to go on sharing him with another woman. Perhaps he would not divorce Denise, but there were other possibilities. When he told his wife that he was going into politics, supported by the men she hated so bitterly, was it not conceivable that she might leave him, return to her precious Riverview, her parents' home? A separation would not be as satisfactory as a divorce, but it might mean that if he were elected to the State Legislature, she, and not his wife, would accompany him to Albany. Later, perhaps, a quiet divorce could be arranged. Divorces were not common, of course, but they were not unheard of.

She moved closer to Jason; his head rested on his arm, and he was breathing evenly. She reached out and stroked his hair lightly. She had to have him to herself; she had to. Why shouldn't she be mistress of Mooncliff one day, instead of Denise?

Jason had said there was a curse on Mooncliff, and she thought that perhaps he was right. It was a house built on violence and cruelty—and death. "Let it be so, then," she whispered. Whatever was part of Jason's life was part of her own, and she was willing to share it all and take the consequences.

Chapter 12

The November afternoon was gray and cold, and a raw wind blew in from the East River, but South Street was busy as always, and Jason had to shoulder a path through the familiar crowd. There were sailors, staggering out of grogshop doors toward the docks where their outgoing ships lay at anchor; blue-coated captains and mates moving through the piles of cargo, dodging teams of horses that pulled huge iron-wheeled wagons; pallid-faced, immigrants who had somehow survived the brutal steerage voyage from Liverpool or Hamburg; cargo thieves; pickpockets; crimpers, whose job it was to supply sailors for any ship that might be short of a few crew members; whores in faded shawls, with skirts held up to avoid contact with the wet cobblestones, while they kept on the lookout for prospective customers. Occasionally Jason saw a respectable, well-dressed couple searching for the ship on which they had booked passage and that would carry them, in the relative comfort of a first-class cabin, across the Atlantic.

And a hell of a time it was to make such a crossing,

he thought. Even in first class, a spell of rough weather would reduce them to seasick, shivering wrecks in a few days. It was no time to sail for Europe, but Jason had felt a stir of envy on leaving the *Tropic Star* a short time before. She was bound for the West Indies, for Cuba.

He reminded himself that Terence O'Connor would have little opportunity to enjoy the soft air of the island, the translucent green of the water, the sugar-white beaches. His work was dangerous, and getting more so with each voyage, for the Spanish patrols were tightening their hold around that revolution-torn island. A few more runs and Jason would, he decided, give O'Connor command of another ship, one of the remaining sailing ships bound for the Far East, perhaps.

He wondered whether O'Connor would be content to go from a steamer to a sailing vessel. There were still sailing ships here on South Street, of course, but always fewer and fewer; Jason could remember when, standing where he stood now, he had seen a forest of masts, with yards and rigging making fantastic patterns against the sky, and towering hulls pointing their long bowsprits into the street itself.

Now, with property values rising in New York, Jason had abandoned his shipyards here and bought others along the New England coast. At the same time, he was investing in real estate in lower Manhattan, as well as in acreage farther north. It was necessary to anticipate the coming trends, but there were times when the present crowded in too closely, and a man needed to pause, to think, to take stock. That was why, instead of returning directly to his office after leaving the *Tropic Star,* he had spent nearly an hour walking along South Street, breathing in the familiar smells of spices, coffee, fish, and clammy salt air. Now he would get back to business for an hour, and after that perhaps he would visit Lavinia.

It had been nearly two weeks since he had seen her; between his business activities and his meetings with Marsh and Conkling, he had been too busy for her. But she would be waiting for him, her body naked and pliant under one of those soft silk wrappers she wore, her ash-blond hair shining white-gold in the firelight. . . .

His thoughts were interrupted when he caught sight of a familiar figure rounding a pile of crates, a young woman in a dark cloak, her head bent against the raw wind from the river. She did not see him until he was directly in front of her, and then she caught her breath in surprise.

"Elspeth! What on earth are you doing down here?"

"Mr. Moreland! I thought you would be back in your office by now."

Her face was pink, and she looked thoroughly flustered, not her usual calm and unruffled self. Her gray-blue eyes were bright, and there was an unusual, unguarded look about her face. "Terence said you had left the *Tropic Star* would be back at your office before—"

Thoroughly surprised, Jason asked, "You went to see Captain O'Connor on board his ship? What business did you have there?" He had not known she was acquainted with Terence O'Connor, let alone on such friendly terms with him.

"I was going to tell you about it, but—" The rest of her words were drowned out as a team of horses bore down on them, pulling a wagon laden with heavy casks. He put an arm around her and drew her out of the way. "Come along," he said. "We can't talk here."

He took her to the red brick building that housed his offices, and not until they were inside his private office and seated in front of the fire did he question her further. "Now, what have you been up to, Elspeth?" His voice was half-teasing, but it elicited no answering smile from her; she was still a little breathless, and she looked afraid. Not of him, surely.

"Is something wrong?" he asked.

She smoothed her dress, and one hand adjusted a piece of jewelry at the neck of her bodice. The brooch he had given her after she had delivered his second son, Phillip, more than two years before: seed pearls set in silver. This was the first time he had ever seen her wear it.

"I don't know quite how to begin," she said.

He hitched his chair closer to hers. "Come now," he said, "if you are in any sort of trouble, I want to know about it."

"No. Quite the contrary, Mr. Moreland, I—" He could see that it was difficult for her to look straight at him when she spoke, but she did it. "Terence—Captain O'Connor and I are going to be married."

He stared at her. "The hell you are," he said, his voice loud and harsh in the quiet room. No way to talk to a lady, but sheer amazement overcame the proprieties.

"I love him, and he loves me, and I am going to be his wife."

"And when was this decided?"

"Terence doesn't know yet. I mean, he loves me—he told me so—but he hasn't asked me to marry him yet. He will, though." Her eyes were soft under the dark lashes, and her small face with its too-wide cheekbones and its pointed little chin seemed almost to glow. He was deeply fond of Elspeth, and had sometimes thought she should one day marry. A sober widower with children perhaps, or a steady, settled businessman. She seemed older than her twenty-five years, sensible, self-controlled. She would perhaps appeal to a man who appreciated such qualities.

But not Terence O'Connor. A year younger than she, reckless, a born adventurer, willing to risk his skin for quick profits, to break the law. Jason knew that he was more than willing; danger appealed to him.

"No, damn it! Elspeth, I don't know how this could have happened without my getting wind of it, but now that I know, I'll see that you and O'Connor never meet again."

"Mr. Moreland, it is true you are my employer, but that does not give you right to forbid me to marry the man I love."

"Your employer? And nothing more?"

"You have been a good friend to me always, and I do not want to go against your wishes, but surely you must see—"

"I see that O'Connor has a way with women, and that one as level-headed as yourself is not immune to his charms, whatever they may be. But I tell you here and now, he won't marry you. And even if he did, he would make you miserable. Believe me, Elspeth, I know what I'm talking about."

"But surely, if you have entrusted him with one of your ships, with valuable cargoes, not once but many times over, you must approve of him—"

"As a captain, yes. But it's one thing to trust a man with a ship and a cargo, and another to hand over to him a young woman like yourself, with no knowledge of the world. Don't interrupt. What do you know of life outside of Mooncliff? What other men have you known?" Then he went on more gently, "I have no wish to hurt you. It is your right to marry, and had you chosen a suitable man, I would have given you my blessing—although no one could replace you at Mooncliff. But I will not permit you to marry Terence O'Connor."

"But I will marry him, all the same. He is the only man I shall ever love."

"Romantic nonsense!" he exploded. Then, seeing the hurt look in her eyes, he said, "The man hasn't even asked you to marry him. Perhaps he doesn't guess how you feel about him. Surely, you can't have seen him more than a few times—"

"I met him at Mooncliff on the night of the ball you gave for President Grant. I was out on the terrace, and I was not wearing a cap or apron. He thought I was one of your guests, for I was dressed in my best. He asked me to dance. Of course, I told him who I was then, but he insisted on dancing with me all the same. We could hear the music from the ballroom out there and—"

"And after that?"

"He sought me out when he came to Mooncliff. We met on the riverbank sometimes." Her eyes softened, and two pink spots glowed on her cheeks. "And we—"

Jason got to his feet so swiftly that his chair swayed and nearly toppled over. He seized her and pulled her to her feet.

"You *what?* Damn it, Elspeth, do you *have* to get married? Don't look at me that way, I want to know if you're going to have a baby."

"Suppose I were?"

"In that case," he said evenly, "I would see to it that Captain O'Connor married you. Afterward I'd make sure he was in no condition to enjoy the honeymoon."

"I'm not pregnant," she said. Then, with a quiet dignity he had seen in few women, she added, "I'd have given myself to him if he had asked me to. Down on the riverbank at Mooncliff, or even today in his cabin. But he respects me too much to ask such a thing."

"Perhaps he has a little decency about him, then. No matter. Since you don't have to marry him, I'll see to it that the marriage doesn't take place."

"I'm not a minor, Mr. Moreland. And even if I were, why should you feel any responsibility for me?"

"You know why. If your father had not sailed with me aboard the *Nubian Queen,* if I had not involved him in an act so repellent to him that it left him sick in his mind—"

"My father chose to sail with you. He knew what he was doing."

"No one could have known unless he had made a slaving voyage before."

She put a hand on his arm. "I don't blame you for what happened to my father. Why do you blame yourself? Why can't you forget?"

"Forget that your father put a curse on Mooncliff? I didn't believe in it at first."

"And now?"

"I'm not sure." He stood quite close to her now and looked down into her upturned face. Impossible to tell her, to tell anyone of that night more than three years before when he had stood alone in the library at Mooncliff and had heard those sounds from beyond the cliffs, sounds he had never been able to forget completely. He had not been drunk. Or mad. But he had heard the dragging of chains along the sun-dried planks of a ship's deck, the frantic cries of the drowning slaves. . . .

Now he heard Elsepth's quiet voice. "You are not the sort of man to believe in curses, 'the sins of the fathers,' and the rest of it."

"I know that good and evil exist. And I know that what I did that day on that ship was evil."

"But if you had it to do all over again, you would make the same choice," she said.

He did not bother to deny what she had said; she knew him far too well for that. Instead he said, "If I feel a certain responsibility for you, perhaps it is because I am trying, in some small measure, to undo the wrong I did your father. Also, you must know I am fond of you, grateful to you for all you have done. So if I ask you now to consider my wishes—"

"I can't," she said simply. Then added, with a little smile, "Could anyone have persuaded you not to marry Mrs. Moreland?"

"I must say I fail to see the slightest connection."

"You love her. I love Terence. I always will."

Jason made an impatient gesture. "If I can't reason with you, perhaps Mrs. Moreland can. When I tell her of this madness of yours, perhaps she'll be able to get through to you."

"She knows," Elspeth said calmly. "I told her myself, some time ago. And she understood."

Denise had known and had said nothing to him. How dare she keep him in ignorance? True, since the day they had quarreled over Lavinia's dismissal, he had been distant with his wife. He had bitterly resented her forcing him to send Lavinia away, refusing to entertain his political supporters that night unless he first agreed to get rid of the governess. He had made it difficult for her to talk to him, but nevertheless, she should have told him about Elspeth and O'Connor.

"Fortunately, Captain O'Connor is due to sail in a week," Jason told Elspeth.

"He won't be gone long this time, will he? He would not tell me his exact destination, only that he was sailing to the Caribbean. When will he come back?"

"A month—a little longer, maybe. Hard to say, this time of year. Don't look so worried: he's been lucky so far."

But he thought, watching her leave his office, that it might be better for her if O'Connor's luck failed this time, and he never returned from Cuba.

* * *

"But, Jason, why shouldn't Elspeth marry Captain O'Connor?"

Jason had returned unusually early and was now confronting his wife in the gray and gold sitting room. Although she was taken aback by his anger, she was relieved to see him. Since he had become involved in politics, he had spent little enough time at home, and even less talking with her.

"If she loves this Captain O'Connor—" Denise said, but Jason cut her off.

"That's not the point. You had no right keeping this a secret from me."

"You haven't been easy to talk to, these last months," Denise said quietly, "And if this is your attitude, I'm glad I didn't tell you, in any case. Elspeth has a right to fall in love with anyone she chooses, and Captain O'Connor—"

"He's no good for her. He's looking for quick money and excitement. He's an adventurer, the kind of man—"

"The kind of man you were that first time you came to Riverview." She could not repress a smile, remembering. She saw herself as she had been, a girl of fifteen, standing on the second-story balcony of the plantation house, looking down at the tall, wide-shouldered man until the boldness of his eyes drove her back into her room.

"That's got nothing to do with Elspeth and O'Connor," he said, but she could tell from his expression that he was remembering, too.

"Sit down, Jason, please." She moved to make room for him on the sofa. "You weren't a sterling character in those days, but you made up your mind you were going to marry me."

"But you had to be forced into the marriage."

She shook her head. "No one, not even Papa, could have forced me into marriage, unless I—"

"Surely you're not going to tell me you married me for love. We both knew better. If the War hadn't wiped out your father's fortune and destroyed his home, I would not have had a chance."

She wanted to feel anger, but could not. Perhaps she had not loved him when she had married him, but there had been something there from the beginning: he had stirred her passions, had aroused feelings she had not known she possessed. He had terrified her, but he had fascinated her, too.

"It's true, isn't it?" he demanded. "You've always reminded me that you disapprove of my origins, my past activities, the way I make my money, and now that I've decided to go into politics, you see that as a betrayal. A blow against your family, against the South—"

"No, Jason." She put a hand on his arm to stem his words. "I—can't say I approve of Congressman Marsh or your other supporters, but I know you feel strongly about this, and I am trying to understand."

His dark brows went up, and he looked disbelieving. "That's most generous. May I ask the reason for your sudden interest in my political career?"

"It's not your career, it's—"

"Go on."

"Do I have to say it? Since last summer you have been cold and distant. You spend so many nights away from home, and even when you are here, even when you come to my bed, I feel as if we were strangers."

He looked at her uneasily and made a move as if to rise, but she took his hands in hers. "Jason, I don't want you to shut me out. I want—"

"I've given you what you wanted. Mooncliff. The full charge of the children's upbringing."

"That's not enough. I want to be a part of your new life."

"How can you be, when you dislike my new associates and all they stand for? You've made excuses not to attend political rallies, to avoid Mrs. Marsh's dinners. Don't you think these people know your attitude? Don't you realize that your lack of cooperation could weaken my campaign?"

"Are you saying you need my help?"

"Of course. But I won't bargain for it, not this time."

She understood what he meant. And she saw how wrong she had been in making Lavinia's departure a condition and then, even after the governess was gone, refusing her wholehearted support. Jason was not a man to submit to domination by his wife. But perhaps it was not too late to undo her mistake. "You don't have to bargain—not now or ever again," she said. "I will do what I can to help you win the election, since it means so much to you. I'll attend rallies, and I'll be pleasant to Mrs. Marsh and the others."

"I hope you mean what you say. I didn't want to ask you before, but now— Next Saturday evening, there is to be a rally in the city, at Cooper Institute. I've been asked to speak, and Thaddeus Marsh thinks it would look good if you attended."

A political rally in support of the Radical Republicans, who, after all these years, still hoped to keep the South in a state of submission, who wanted the carpetbagger rule to go on indefinitely. She tried to hide her distaste, but Jason said, "If you don't want to go through with it, I won't force you, of course."

She saw the beginnings of disillusionment in his face, and she knew that she could not refuse; she had to prove that the promise she had given him had not been an empty one.

"Of course, I shall attend. I'll wear my new green velvet. It is dignified, but most fetching. And the green bonnet. I want you to be proud of me."

"I've always been proud of you," he said. His lips brushed her cheek, and then his arms were around her, and she knew that he was hers again.

Chapter 13

The streets around the Cooper Institute were crowded with carriages and hired hansom cabs. Icy winds and snow had failed to keep New Yorkers from attending the rally.

Lavinia Corbett, who stood beside the gas-lit entrance to the auditorium, shivered in her smart French blue walking suit and thrust her hands deeper into her sable muff; she knew she should have dressed more warmly, but she had only decided to attend the rally at the last minute, and had chosen whatever clothing came to hand. She was aware that she was not thinking too clearly, but she told herself it was not because of the rum: two—or had it been three?—glasses of Jason's Havana rum, from the bottle that she kept in the bureau drawer.

She had needed the rum to steady her, that was all. She had been lonely, afraid. For three weeks Jason had not come to see her and had sent no word.

She had not dared approach him in his South Street office, and it would have been unthinkable for her to have gone out to Mooncliff. But this morning she had read about the political rally in the *New York Herald,* and it had occurred to her that there, in the midst of a crowd of supporters and well-wishers, she could approach him. She could at least exchange a few words with him. She would be discreet, and perhaps he would be pleased to see her.

Of course he would. He had only stayed away so long because of his involvement in the coming campaign. That, in addition to his regular business affairs, explained his absence. She would go to the rally, and perhaps afterward he would escort her home to her apartment. Then she would talk to him, make him see how much she had missed him. Tell him he must never stay away so long again.

Now, pressing back against the entranceway of the Cooper Institute, her eyes searching the crowd, she felt her confidence begin to ebb away. It was snowing harder, and the wind drove the large, wet flakes against her face, but she would not go inside. The long line of carriages and cabs continued to move down the street, stopping to discharge their passengers. The majority were men, but there were a surprising number of ladies as well.

She caught her breath sharply, for there it was, the Morelands' closed carriage, a large dark green vehicle drawn by four black horses; she recognized Patrick, in green and white livery, up on the box, handling the horses with his usual skill.

The carriage drew to a stop in front of the entrance, and a stocky man with black muttonchop whiskers got out and assisted a female companion. Not Denise. Of course not. Lavinia knew how Denise felt about Jason's political activities and was sure she would not be here tonight. The lady must be Thaddeus Marsh's wife.

Lavinia took a few steps forward, and now she saw Jason. She would go to him only for a moment, and she would say—What would she say? No matter. Only to be close to him, to talk to him, to see his face again.

Then she froze, her hands closing into hard fists inside the sable muff, so that her fingernails cut into her palms. For Denise Moreland, with a flurry of green velvet and satin, was alighting from the carriage. How beautiful she looked, holding Jason's arm, her face upturned to his. There was an air of serenity about her, poise and self-assurance in her smallest gesture.

But why had she come? If Jason had forced her to be here, she showed no sign. She turned her head to listen to something Mrs. Marsh was saying, and then she smiled and nodded, and the two ladies hurried into the entrance of the building. Denise passed so close that Lavinia caught the scent of her perfume on the frosty air. The men started to follow, but were halted by the arrival of a third man in a fine dark blue cashmere coat and a tall hat. He had to be Roscoe Conkling; Lavinia had seen his picture in the papers many times. A tall, blond-bearded giant of a man and a favorite with the ladies, from what she had heard. She also knew that, like Marsh, Conkling wielded tremendous power within the party structure.

In a moment Jason would be inside the hall, and with Denise there, Lavinia would have no chance to speak to him. But she could not let him go without a word.

She lifted her skirts so they would not drag on the snowy pavement and hurried to his side.

"Mr. Moreland—"

He turned, looked at her, and drew back involuntarily. His eyes were hard, but he gave her a polite, impersonal smile. "Miss Corbett, isn't it? I'm pleased that you could come—and in such inclement weather. I trust you will find the rally interesting."

He started to turn back to Marsh and Conkling, but she took his arm; she could not restrain herself. "I must talk to you. Now."

Through her giddiness, through the pain caused by his impersonal manner of speaking—surely he could have given her some sign that he was pleased to see her—she sensed his controlled fury.

"Just for a moment—" she said.

"We'll wait here," Thaddeus Marsh said quietly, but she was aware that his shrewd black eyes were moving over her, from the plumes on her silk bonnet to the elaborate ruffles that edged the French blue walking suit. If only she had taken time to find a more conservative costume, one of those dark gray dresses she had worn when she had worked at Mooncliff.

Jason took her arm and drew her aside, while all around them the crowd pushed forward, and from inside the auditorium she could hear a brass band striking up "The Battle-Cry of Freedom" with a brisk marching beat.

"You should not have come here tonight."

"I did not know that your wife—"

"No matter. It was most indiscreet."

"Indiscreet? Jason, I haven't seen you for nearly three weeks. I waited for you; I hardly left the apartment. I could not go to you, for I knew you would not want me to come to your office—"

"You showed a little sense there," he said coldly. Then he added, "Go back to the apartment, Lavinia."

"But when will I see you?" And when he did not reply, she hurried on, "Couldn't you send Denise home in the carriage tonight? Make some excuse, and come to me." When he remained silent, she seized his arm and pulled him against her. "Please say you will. I know you need me as much as—"

She fell silent, seeing a look of disgust in his cold blue eyes. His dark brows drew together. "You've been drinking. Don't try to deny it."

"What else could I do?" she cried, so loudly that people turned to stare at her. "All those nights, waiting for you, wanting you! How else could I have gotten through those nights; how else—"

"That's enough," he said. "Control yourself. I'll get a cab for you. Wait here."

"No, Jason. Don't send me away—"

But he left her alone, standing there with the snow swirling about her, the brassy music from inside the auditorium beating in her head. She swayed and reached out blindly.

"You had better go inside." She saw Roscoe Conkling, hat in hand, standing at her side.

"No, thank you," she managed to say. "Jason—Mr. Moreland—has gone to find a cab for me."

"He—I've changed my mind—" If only he would leave her alone. If only the snowflakes would stop their dizzying dance in front of her eyes and the band would not play so loudly.

Then somehow Jason had returned and was hurrying her into a hansom cab. She sank back on the worn leather seat and watched as Jason, accompanied by Marsh and Conkling, headed for the Cooper Institute's auditorium.

Something had gone wrong, terribly wrong, with her plans. She should have been the one with him when he made his first speech, for hadn't she urged him to go into politics; hadn't she been sure that Denise would oppose him, and that he would turn to her for support? But now she was returning alone to the apartment. She would lie alone in the wide brass bed, needing him, aching for his touch. And he would not come to her tonight. After the rally there would be a supper, no doubt, and then he would go home with his wife, home to Mooncliff and the second-floor bedroom with its great canopied bed. Denise would lie in his arms, her dark red hair spread over the pillows, and he would . . .

Lavinia drew her hand from her sable muff and pressed it to her mouth, sinking her teeth into her own flesh, and feeling no pain in her hand.

She did not see Jason again until two nights after the rally, when he came to the apartment. She had spent the intervening hours in a kind of daze, pacing the floor of the small, ornately decorated parlor with its purple velvet draperies, its plush and mahogany furniture. She had not gone outside, even though the snow had stopped. There was little food in the apartment, but that wasn't important. A cup of tea, a few biscuits. The bottle of Havana rum on top of the bureau remained untouched, for she knew she had to be in complete control when Jason came to see her.

He would come. Of course he would. He had been angry with her before, but his need for her had always brought him back. She was prepared for his anger, and she knew that somehow she would placate him.

But when he arrived at last, bringing the cold of the street into the perfumed warmth of the parlor, he did not appear to be angry.

"Sit down, Lavinia," he said quietly. Then going to the fireplace, he leaned an arm on the mantel. "I would have written, but I thought I owed you something more than that."

"Written what? Jason, has Denise found out?"

"I don't know," he said. "It doesn't matter. Even if she knows nothing about us, I—I won't be seeing you again. No, wait and let me say what I must. It isn't easy for me; I want you to believe that. You have given me so much—"

"I want to give you everything," she said, trying to stem the rising tide of fear inside her. "And I can. More than Denise—"

"Stop it!" His voice was harsh, not with anger but with pain. "After the rally, I had a talk with Marsh and Conkling. They will not back me in the campaign unless I stop seeing you."

"Those miserable hypocrites! How dare they?"

"I'm running for office on the reform ticket, and there has been more than enough scandal within the party these last few years."

"But other men in politics—Marsh and Conkling—are they trying to pretend they've never—"

"Of course not. But you are unstable, indiscreet. They are unwilling to risk another scene of the kind you made at the Cooper Institute."

"But nothing like that will happen again."

"They can't take that chance."

"Then forget them. Withdraw from the campaign."

"I have no wish to withdraw," he said. Then he added, "I want to be fair with you." He drew out an envelope and placed it on the desk beside the sofa. "This check will pay your passage back to England."

"I don't want your money." She pressed herself against him. "Once I was afraid of being without money, but now I'm only afraid of losing you." But he freed himself from her embrace and started toward the door.

She knew that she had lost him. When he had to choose between giving her up and forgetting his ambition, his choice was inevitable. She was no more important to him than those black slaves he had condemned to death aboard the *Nubian Queen* years ago.

After watching his carriage disappear into the darkness, she turned from the window and went into the bedroom. No reason to stay sober now. She poured rum into a delicate Venetian goblet and swallowed it. She would drink only enough to make her sleep. She had to sleep.

But when the goblet was empty and she lay across the bed, her whole body remained taut, all her senses painfully acute.

Tomorrow she would go to the steamship office and book passage to England. She would find another man, perhaps on board the ship, perhaps in London. A man of wealth and substance. She would invent a past for herself, say she was a widow, without friends or family.

"No, it won't happen like that. Not for me." She sat up in bed and reached for the goblet. Empty. Her fingers closed around it, and the fragile glass cracked in her clenched hand; she had cut her fingers, but there was hardly any pain at all.

She lay back on the bed again. Jason had shared this bed with her, had held her and kissed her and made love to her with that curious blending of violence and tenderness she had never known before—would never know again—never—

She watched through narrowed eyes as the gaslight glinted along the edges of the broken goblet, and she smiled.

Every light was blazing at Mooncliff, and the guests began arriving at eight, in carriages, landaus and hired cabs. The curving drive leading to the house was crowded with the slow-moving vehicles. Ladies alighting in front of the door had to hold their cloaks around them and smooth their elaborate coiffures, for the November evening was unusually windy, although the sky was clear, and frosty stars blazed above the turrets and chimneys.

Captain MacKay and Rosalind alighted from their carriage and hurried up the steps. To keep her black velvet hood from being whipped away by the wind, Rosalind held it against one side of her face. "I wonder if Denise is really content, living all the way out here, so far from the city," she said to her husband as he escorted her up to the door.

"Hm? Happy? I should suppose so: a fine house like this and Jason Moreland for a husband."

Rosalind glanced up at the gray stone facade. She had always found it cold and forbidding, like its master.

"I prefer our brownstone," she said. "It's not so grand, to be sure, but—"

MacKay laughed. "All the same, my love, you've gotten yourself decked out in your finest feathers and frills to attend this ball, haven't you?"

She smiled back. She was pleased with her new gown, a rose-colored taffeta glittering with silver embroidery and trimmed with silver lace. But she knew that every other woman here tonight, the wives of congressmen and senators, of important businessmen, too, would be as well turned out as she.

Jason, standing on one side of the ballroom, felt a quiet complacency, for he knew the ball was a success. Thaddeus Marsh had advised him to invite not only politicians and businessmen but several leading journalists as well. The journalists had questioned him about his stand on the various issues of the day: the nationwide recession, the possibility of a Democratic resurgence in the South, the Temperance movement, the protective tariff. He had explained his stand on these and other issues and had agreed to interviews in the near future.

The visiting journalists were obviously impressed by Mooncliff and charmed by Mrs. Moreland, stately yet gracious in a Worth gown of amber velvet embroidered with gold and seed pearls and complete with a train embossed with gold arabesques.

Jason was careful to be flattering to the lady journalists present and to dance at least once with each of them, including the dashing and notorious Mrs. Frank Leslie and with Miss Sophia Cameron, a contributor to several of the popular ladies' journals. Miss Cameron, a sharp-featured spinster in her forties, questioned Jason on his opinions about education for women as well as on conditions in the New York City slums; he thought she was remarkably well informed as to the red-light district of the city. Marsh had stressed that while women could not vote, they could and did influence the males in their households, and so were worth cultivating.

Tonight would be a triumph, Jason thought, the first of many. His election to the New York State Legislature would be only the beginning for him.

Supper was served at midnight, and while the guests refreshed themselves with oysters stewed in cream, broiled venison with port wine sauce, trout in sherry, and roasted pheasant. Thaddeus Marsh drew Jason aside. "Let us go into the library," he said. "I've a little matter to discuss, and this is as good a time as any."

Inside the library, before the fire, the two men seated themselves, and Marsh began without preamble, "You have interests in Cuba, Jason. A complicated situation there, and likely to grow more so—but profitable, I believe. There's some risk, of course. The *Tropic Star* is already overdue, isn't she?" Then he laughed. "Don't be surprised. I make it my business to know everything about the men I'm backing."

"So it would seem," Jason said shortly, remembering Lavinia; althought he had acceded to Marsh's demand that he break off the liaison, he had resented the congressman's interference in his private affairs. His relationship with Lavinia could not have lasted, in any case; her instability, her obsessive demands would have caused them to separate sooner or later. But Jason disliked the notion of taking orders from another man in such a matter. Still, he was realistic enough to accept that, for the time being, he needed the support of men like Thaddeus Marsh.

"Very well, you know the destination of the *Tropic Star*. Now, if you are going to tell me I must stop arms shipments to the Cuban rebels, forget it. Unless you're willing to reimburse me for the profits I've been making."

Marsh laughed. "On the contrary. I too am interested in Cuba. What sources do you have for the arms you've been selling the rebels?"

"I'm surprised you don't already know," Jason said, "since you are so well informed about every other aspect of my affairs."

"Don't get your back up, Jason. I'm prepared to make you a profitable offer. Many of our western army posts are going to be supplied with new weapons shortly. Through certain connections, I can offer you a good deal on surplus guns, ammunition, explosives—"

"And what do you want in return?"

"A percentage of the profits from every voyage."

"How large a percentage? And what will I save by dealing with your sources? I've been doing pretty well on my own."

Marsh smoothed his black whiskers, smiled, and drew out a long, narrow envelope. "Here are the figures," he said. "I think you'll find them satisfactory. Perhaps you might glance over them now and give me your answer by the end of the evening."

"You don't believe in wasting time, do you?" Jason tapped the envelope against his palm. "Very well," he said. "Why don't you go back to supper, and I'll join you shortly."

"I've no wish to keep you from an excellent supper," Marsh began, but Jason laughed.

"No matter. When I go out there again, Sophia Cameron will be ready with a new barrage of questions about the number of brothels on Greene Street and the number of beds in each." He shook his head. "For a maiden lady, she has a most unwholesome curiosity about such things."

Once Marsh had left and he was alone in the library, he seated himself in a chair near the window and turned up the lamp. He tried to shut out the strident shrieking of the wind from beyond the cliffs. One would have thought Mooncliff was in the mid-Atlantic from the way the wind sounded tonight.

He opened the long envelope, and his eyes ran down

the sets of figures on the paper Marsh had given him. The cost of these surplus weapons was appreciably lower than that of other shipments he had made to Cuba. Perhaps he should fit out a few more small, fast steamers for the Cuban run. It would not be easy to find more men like Terence O'Connor, however; men willing to risk imprisonment or death for a fast profit. He had been such a captain in his twenties, but—

His body tensed and his fingers closed around the sheet of paper, crumpling it into a ball.

The sound of the wind filled the room, filled his brain until everything else was driven out. The paper dropped from his nerveless fingers. He stood up, as if to confront an unseen enemy. For the second time since he had built Mooncliff and taken possession of the house, he was hearing—what?

Voices, blending with the wind, rising above it. Anguished, tortured voices wailing their despair. Broken words in the curious dialect of the Ivory Coast. The sound of bare feet shuffling along the sun-dried planks of a ship's deck. Chains used to weigh down the bodies so that they would sink more quickly.

The sweat poured from his body, as it had that day long ago on the deck of the *Nubian Queen,* but now it was not the moist heat of the tropics that made his shirt cling to his back. He felt a tightness in the pit of his stomach.

It was happening again. He could not stop it. With his last shred of reason he thought that it was fortunate Marsh had left him alone here. If Marsh, if anyone, had seen him this way . . . had seen his hands start to shake and a muscle at the side of his jaw begin to twitch uncontrollably . . .

He bent and picked up the sheet of figures Marsh had given him, smoothed the crumpled paper, and put it into a desk drawer. Then he took out a handkerchief and wiped his face.

He tried to explain away what had happened. Mooncliff, jutting out over the curve of the river, caught the wind from three sides. And the chunks of ice that had already formed along the river bank were breaking, shifting, with every change in the weather—these things could account for the sounds, *had* to account for them.

He made himself leave the library and go back to the ballroom, where a waltz was being played and men and women were dancing beneath the great chandelier.

Denise came to his side, her face flushed and radiant. He put an arm around her to lead her out among the dancers, then stopped. Elspeth Buchanan, neat and inconspicuous in her gray silk, was signaling to him from the entrance of the ballroom.

In the hallway Elspeth said softly, "There are some gentlemen to see you, sir. I told them you were entertaining, but they were most insistent." She glanced anxiously at Denise. "They would like to see you, too, Mrs. Moreland."

"Now what the devil—"

"I showed them into the library and told them you would both be there directly."

"Why did you do that?" Jason demanded.

"I had no choice, Mr. Moreland." Elspeth spoke very quietly. "They are from the police."

There were two of them, a heavyset man as tall as Jason himself, and a short, thin man with alert dark brown eyes. The short man spoke first. "This is most distressing, Mr. Moreland, but in a case like this one, we have no choice." He stopped, cleared his throat and asked, "You know a Miss Lavinia Corbett?"

"She worked here as a governess," Denise said. "But we have not seen or heard from her since she left Mooncliff. I believe you can find her at her new place of employment—a girls' school on Gramercy Square."

The police detective shook his head. "Lavinia Corbett is dead. She took her own life two days ago in her apartment on West Forty-fourth Street."

"How did she—" Jason began.

The police detective glanced at Denise. Jason thought he saw a flicker of compassion in the officer's dark eyes.

"She slashed her wrists with a broken glass," the detective said. Then he added, "A check was found in her apartment, signed by you, Mr. Moreland. In the sum of ten thousand dollars. It was dated with the same date as the suicide."

"The check. Of course," Jason said half aloud.

"And you rented the apartment last summer. That is correct, isn't it?"

Jason watched the color drain from his wife's face and saw the swift, terrible comprehension come into her eyes.

Chapter 14

Outside the library, Denise stopped and looked from side to side, like a hunted thing seeking refuge. Then she picked up the train of her amber velvet dress and ran along the hall. As she passed the ballroom, she heard the lively rhythm of a polka and the sound of laughter. She knew she must get away, as far away as possible.

She opened the door leading to the terrace, indifferent to the blast of frigid air that enveloped her. She went on across the terrace and down the steps, heading blindly for the Cliff Road. She stumbled on a fallen branch and regained her balance with difficulty. The wind from the river moaned eerily, like a lost creature.

Denise turned and looked back at the house. Jason would still be in the library with the two police officers. She had not asked permission to go, but had simply risen and run out of the room, and no one had tried to stop her.

She could not have borne any more. Now she knew what she had only suspected before and had tried to bury at the back of her mind. Lavinia had been Jason's mistress. Even after she had left Mooncliff Jason had gone on seeing her. He had rented an apartment where he could be alone with her. And now she was dead, in that horrible, ugly way. A wave of nausea rose up inside Denise, and she sank down on the frozen ground. She could go no farther.

Once before she had tried to run away from Jason, from Mooncliff. When had it been? Yes, of course—the night he had told her about the murder of the slaves on board the *Nubian Queen*. But she had had to stay then, for she had learned that she was carrying his child. She turned her head and looked back at the house. There were three children in the nursery at Mooncliff now: Stuart and Vanessa, Jason's children, and Phillip, the son of her dead lover, Gilbert Laussat.

If Jason had sinned, so had she; if he had broken his marriage vows, she had done so, too. But Jason had never found out what she had done; that was the only difference.

She got to her feet, shivering with the cold, and retraced her steps to the house. Later she would think of Lavinia. Later she would try to understand, even to forgive him.

But she must take one step at a time. First, go back to the house, repair her coiffure, smooth her wind-disheveled dress, appear calm and self-possessed before her guests.

Inside the hallway, Jason stood looking down at her. "The officers are with Thaddeus Marsh now," he said. "He'll use his influence to keep the affair as quiet as possible. There is still the risk of scandal. Something like this is difficult to keep out of the papers, of course." Then, he said, "Denise, are you all right?"

She swayed slightly, and he took her arm. "Do you want to go upstairs? I can get Elspeth to look after you."

She shook her head. "You are forgetting our guests."

"To hell with our guests!"

As if she had not heard his last remark, she said, "Give me a few minutes to fix my hair, and then we will return to the ballroom."

"You're so pale—you can't possibly—"

"I'll borrow some rouge from Rosalind MacKay."

"Denise, I don't expect you to carry on as if nothing had happened."

"If I leave the party now, people will talk, and later it will be remembered. You don't want a scandal; you said so yourself. So we must both stay with our guests until they have all gone. It won't be more than an hour or two."

"You're right, of course. But are you sure you'll be able—"

"I'll do what must be done," she said.

It was late the following afternoon, and Denise was having tea in the sitting room. Jason stood looking out the window at the overcast sky.

He turned when Denise said, "I think we might have a musicale here in a few weeks. The gentlemen may not be overly fond of music, some of them, but the ladies will enjoy it, and we can invite Mrs. Frank Leslie and that other journalist—Miss Cameron."

"What the devil are you talking about?"

"A musicale. Part of the entertaining you've said we must do in the interest of your campaign. I promised I would do all I could to help, and I thought that a musicale—"

"Denise, there is no need to pretend now. The guests are gone. There is no one to hear us. Say what you've been thinking ever since last night. Cry or smash something or demand an explanation. You've earned the right."

"There is nothing to explain. You were in love with Lavinia Corbett; she was your mistress. And now she is dead."

"I wasn't in love with her. Not the way you mean."

He was obviously about to say more, but Denise interrupted. She did not want to know the nature of Jason's feelings for Lavinia, not now, not ever.

"We won't speak of it, now or in the future. We must plan ahead. I think we should be seen together in the city as often as possible. We might attend the opera next week, and then the theater."

"You're not going to leave me, Denise?"

"I can't. Not now."

"Because of the children?"

"That's part of it."

He went to her and took her hands in his. "Tell me the rest. I have to know."

"I'm not sure I can make you understand. I don't know that I understand completely. We—have a marriage.

"It won't be easy for us now. People will talk, but if they see that I am with you, that I do not believe the gossip about—Lavinia Corbett—they will find new scandals to amuse themselves with."

"And when we are alone? I did not try to share your bed last night, Denise. It would have been unthinkable. But will it ever be possible for you to—"

"Yes, Jason. Not right away, but soon, I think. Quite soon."

She ached to tell him everything then, to confess her own sin. But she had made her decision before Phillip's birth, that for Jason's sake and for the sake of the child she must never speak of her affair with Gilbert Laussat. So she said, "Jason, we can't change the past; we can only try to forgive each other and go on."

His arms went around her, and he held her so tightly that she could feel the buttons of his coat cutting into her breast through the soft silk of her bodice. At last he spoke, his face pressed against her hair: "You are the best wife any man ever had. Last night I was proud of you, knowing what it must have taken for you to go on that way, for my sake. If only I could— Denise, there is nothing I would not do for you."

She was silent for a moment, there in his arms. Then she asked softly, "Do you mean that?"

"Whatever you ask of me."

"There is something. Not for me. For Elspeth."

Jason took his arms away and looked down at her. "She wants to marry Captain O'Connor. But there are reasons why I am opposed to the match."

"I know she loves him. That's all that matters, but she says you refuse to give your consent."

"She doesn't need my consent."

"Elspeth is afraid of you, Jason. If you were to take command of the *Tropic Star* away from O'Connor and use your influence to prevent his getting another ship, you would destroy him."

"I've no intention of doing any such thing. But O'Connor is wrong for her. He won't make her happy."

"Let her decide that. You cannot control other people's lives. You can't be sure you know what's best for them."

"I know Terence O'Connor. Why shouldn't I? He's not so different from what I was at his age."

Denise took his arm, trying to communicate the importance of what she felt. "Please, Jason. Elspeth is not a woman to give her love casually. If you keep her from marrying Captain O'Connor, she may never marry at all. She may never love any other man." She looked up at him, her eyes pleading. "Even if he makes her unhappy, at least she will have known some joy, too, some measure of fulfillment, married to a man she loves."

"As you have?"

She put a hand on either side of his face. "As I have," she said softly. "I did not know I loved you when I married you. Indeed, I thought I hated you. And I was certainly afraid of you."

For the first time in their conversation, he managed a smile.

"How can I forget? That night aboard the *Enchantress*. You were different from any other woman I'd ever— And I wanted to make you love me."

"Then isn't it possible that Captain O'Connor, whatever his past life may have been—and I can imagine a little of it, I think—might be different with Elspeth?"

Jason did not answer at once, and Denise waited, conscious of the small sounds in the room: the crackling of a log in the fireplace, the hissing of sleet against the oriel window. Then: "Very well, Denise. I'll give Elspeth my blessing and assure her that O'Connor won't lose command of his ship. But only because that is the way you want it."

When Elspeth came into the morning room a few hours later, she was calm and composed, but Jason saw that her face looked drawn. As long as she worked efficiently, he took little interest in her thoughts or emotions. She was his housekeeper, an important part of his household; she saw to it that meals were served on time, that the ever-growing staff of servants performed their duties properly, that those who failed to give satisfaction were replaced. Now, as he looked at her closely for the first time since that day she had come to his office on South Street, he noticed the shadows under her eyes and the hollows in her pale cheeks.

"I had a talk with Mrs. Moreland a little while ago," he said. "She tells me you're still pining away for Captain O'Connor."

"Have you had any word? Has the *Tropic Star* returned yet?" The composure had slipped away, revealing the fear beneath.

"Not yet, Elspeth, but—"

"You said he would be back in a month, maybe a little more, but it has been three months, and there has been no word."

Jason had to choose, then, between a kind lie and the unpleasant truth that O'Connor's ship was indeed overdue.

He chose the lie. "The *Tropic Star* is not in the Caribbean. After I discovered your feelings about O'Connor, I changed his sailing orders. I sent him around the Cape and out to the Far East. I thought if he was gone long enough you would get over your infatuation for him." He looked at her stricken face. "I see that I was wrong." He took her arm and drew her down on the sofa beside him. "When he returns, if you still want to marry him, I won't stand in the way. I won't dismiss him, or destroy his career. I would not have done that in any case."

But when O'Connor returned from Cuba, he would put him on a different run; Elspeth's husband would not be permitted to risk his life again.

He saw that she was making an effort to regain her self-control, and he went on speaking quietly. "I'll give you a wedding here at Mooncliff, if you like."

He had expected tears or grateful protestations, but instead Elspeth started to laugh. She pressed a hand to her lips but could not stop. Hysteria, he thought, and who could blame her? "I know you mean well, and I'm thankful, truly. But Terence and I were married before he sailed. I tried to get your consent, and when I could not, I—we—"

Damn Terence O'Connor! He had known he was sailing into danger, and had married Elspeth on impulse.

"There is something else. You would have had to know soon, in any case. I'm going to have a baby. Don't look like that, please. I didn't lie to you that day in your office. We did wait until after we were married." She straightened her shoulders. "If you want me to leave Mooncliff, say so, Mr. Moreland."

"Don't be foolish. What I want you to do is to hire extra help. Get all the rest you need. You want to give O'Connor a fine, healthy son, don't you?"

She nodded. "I wish he could be with me when the baby is born. That will be next summer. Do you think he will be back by then?"

"Of course he will." And why shouldn't he be? Jason asked himself. O'Connor was reckless, but he was competent, and perhaps he would not take unnecessary risks with a new bride waiting for him. He had always come back before, and he would again.

When Jason left home that December morning two weeks later, it was with sense of relief, for the whole house was in turmoil, with Denise making preparations for her musicale and the staff decorating the place for the Christmas holidays. They were fastening wreaths to the walls and looping swags of greenery over mantelpieces and the arches of doorways. Jason looked forward to his meeting with Thaddeus Marsh in the suite at the Astor House, an oasis of masculine peace and quiet.

But when he entered the parlor of the suite, he sensed that he had been overoptimistic. Marsh made a show of heartiness while the lunch and drinks were being served, but when the hotel waiter withdrew, he leaned across the small table and said, "Jason, I regret being the one to bear such tidings, but in my position I feel it incumbent upon me—"

"You're not addressing your constituents at the moment, Thaddeus. Get to the point, damn it!"

"As you wish. The fact is, a police reporter has gotten hold of that business about Lavinia Corbett's suicide."

Jason got to his feet. "You said you'd hush that up! What the hell went wrong?"

Thaddeus Marsh smoothed his whiskers. "I said I would try. And I did my best, as you did. And your wife, too. A great lady, Jason. As well as a beautiful one."

"Never mind my wife. Where did you slip up?"

"Now, really, Jason, you know the power of the press these days. Didn't those cartoons of Nast's help to destroy Boss Tweed? I can't silence every reporter in New York."

"You can silence this one. And you will! The only thing that definitely links me to—Miss Corbett—is that check. The police have that."

"They have it, but the reporter got word of its existence. He may even have seen it."

"So long as he doesn't have it in his possession. I want that check destroyed, Thaddeus. At once."

"Now, Jason, that won't be easy."

"You have your connections in the department. Use them. I'll pay whatever I have to, but that check must be destroyed at once."

"Very well. But this reporter may keep digging—"

"Bribe him. You've done it before."

"Look here—" Marsh began, but Jason moved around the table and stood over him, thrusting his head forward like a bull about to charge, and he saw a flicker of fear in the congressman's eyes.

"I'm going to stay in this race," Jason said. "And you and Conkling are going to square it with the party. It's the least you can do."

"Good Lord, you can't blame me for—for that girl's death."

"Let's drop the subject, shall we? You know what you have to do. Do it. And now, if that's all, let's get on with lunch."

"It's not all, Jason. There's something more you'll have to know. It's confidential, but you've done me a number of favors, and I wanted you to have the facts. Damned unpleasant facts they are, but—"

"Go on."

"I've received word from certain sources in Washington. The *Tropic Star* won't be coming back to New York. She was captured by a Spanish blockade vessel. The story won't be released. Grant's administration has had enough international incidents to want to avoid another, especially with the presidential election coming up. Not that Grant stands a chance of being reelected, but he has his hopes."

"This is a private matter, Thaddeus."

"Not when it involves the internal affairs of another sovereign power."

Jason nodded, unable to deny the logic of Marsh's words. "The crew?" he asked. "What happened to them?"

"They're in a Spanish prison in Cuba."

"The captain, too?"

Marsh shrugged. "I suppose so." He helped himself to an oyster from the heaping plate in front of him. "They captured him along with the crew. The important thing is our arrangements about those surplus weapons from the western army posts. We had a nice deal worked out there, but in view of what's happened, I can't—"

"Forget the weapons for now. What are you going to do about getting my crew released? I'll pay off anyone in the government who can pull the right strings."

"Oh, now, Jason. Bribing a reporter is one thing, but getting involved in a ruckus with the Spanish government is something else entirely."

"Nevertheless, you've got to get involved. And this time, Thaddeus, see that you do the job without any slip-ups."

"Damn it, Jason, you can't talk to me as if I were one of your clerks!"

Jason's voice was quiet, deadly. "You've done a good deal of business with me, Thaddeus. And profited handsomely by it, as I'm sure you'll agree."

"Well, yes, certainly. But even so—"

"If you want to keep on making profits, you'll see to it that Captain O'Connor comes back unharmed."

"O'Connor? What about the rest of the crew?"

"Try to have them all released, if you can. But O'Connor has to come back. And soon!"

"What's O'Connor to you?"

"That's my business." He leaned across the table and smiled with mirthless satisfaction when he saw Marsh start and draw back involuntarily. "See that you carry out your end of it. Fast."

"All right. I'll do what I can. Your—your loyalty to those who work for you is most commendable." Marsh was plainly cowed, and Jason was sure he would do what he could to get O'Connor out of Cuba. It would be a tricky business, however, and Jason could only hope, for Elspeth's sake, that Marsh would succeed.

Chapter 15

On a sultry afternoon late in June, Rosalind MacKay, recently returned from the Centennial Exposition in Philadelphia, came calling on Denise. The two ladies sat on the terrace overlooking the river, and Denise listened to Rosalind's chatter, trying to push away her own troubling thoughts. During the last few weeks Denise had felt a growing concern for Elspeth; the housekeeper's baby would arrive soon, and Captain O'Connor had not yet returned. When Denise questioned Jason about the matter, his answers had been brief and uninformative.

It was a relief now to listen to Rosalind's glowing descriptions of the Exposition.

"You and Jason must go, my dear. I saw President Grant there, and General Sheridan. And Dom Pedro, the Emperor of Brazil. And Mrs. Frank Leslie was preening like a peacock, making sure everyone knew the emperor was to be a guest at her summer home in Saratoga."

"Of course," Rosalind went on, "Captain MacKay

spent most of his time among the exhibits in the Machinery Hall. I couldn't have cared less for all those mechanical things, any more than you will. But there are so many exhibits you would enjoy. The Queen of Belgium's lace, Italian mosaics, the finest needlework. And the Demorests have a special exhibit of their paper dress patterns—"

Denise interrupted her: "I don't know if Jason will be able to go. This campaign has taken so much of his time lately."

"All the more reason he should get away for a few days, and you, too. You won't have much time alone together when the campaign goes into the final stretch this fall, you know. Besides, if you don't mind my saying so, dear, you've looked a little tired lately. But then, you've been contributing so much of your time and energy to the campaign, too. It's only natural you'd be tired, and a little vacation—"

Denise did not tell Rosalind that it was not weariness that troubled her, but something far more disturbing. The memory of Lavinia Corbett had been haunting her since that night when she had learned of the girl's death. She had kept her word and had not spoken to Jason of Lavinia again, but she had not been able to forget.

"Perhaps you're right," Denise conceded. "It might do both of us good to get away for a while."

"Why, certainly it would. And you must have a new wardrobe. The gowns I saw there were quite splendid. Primrose and salmon are the most popular colors, and bows are being worn everywhere, on bustles and flounces and in rows down the front of skirts. And some ladies are wearing two bracelets on one arm, one at the wrist and one below the elbow."

Denise pretended to listen as Rosalind chattered about the new fashions she had seen at the Exposition, but her thoughts were far away. Perhaps Jason too would benefit from a change of scene. She did not know what he was thinking and feeling these days. Had he loved Lavinia, and did he grieve for her, or had he already forgotten her? No, Jason could not be so callous. Perhaps he thought of Lavinia as she had been during her time at Mooncliff; perhaps he remembered how she had looked riding with Stuart, her pale bond curls gleaming under her dashing plumed hat.

She broached the subject of a visit to the Exposition to Jason when he came home from the city, and after a little persuasion he agreed to take her there.

"Stuart can come with us," he said. "He's old enough to enjoy some of the exhibits."

That evening, when Jason told Stuart that he was to accompany them to the Exposition, he was delighted, but his small face darkened when Denise explained that he could not take his dog, Nelson.

"He wants to come," Stuart said, putting an arm around thc huge, shambling Newfoundland.

"He'd be miserable, chained up in a hotel room," Denise said.

Stuart stood up and set his legs apart, resistance in every line of his sturdy little body. Nelson, the object of conflict, began circling around Phillip's kitten, a small gray-striped creature. Phillip, seated on his bed, looked uneasy. He had been given the kitten only a week before by Patrick the coachman, whose stable cat had recently had another litter.

The kitten bristled and spat at Nelson, then backed off, stiff-legged and wary, her ears flattened against her head. Phillip reached down to get the kitten out of harm's way, but Stuart, infuriated by his mother's refusal to let him takc Nelson along to the Exposition, had found an outlet for his frustration. He grabbed the kitten, thrust her at Nelson and shouted, "Get her, boy! Go on, get her!"

The dog lunged for the kitten, who clawed at Stuart's hand. Stuart let her fall, and she scampered across the room and halfway up the window curtain, clinging there with her sharp claws.

Phillip hesitated, then flung himself on Stuart, and the two boys instantly locked together, rolling on the floor, wrestling and panting. Phillip put up a good fight, but Stuart soon had him down on his back. He struck at Phillip's face and chest with his fists.

"Jason, make them stop!" Denise said.

"It's time Phillip learned to fight," Jason replied calmly. Denise started forward, and Jason said, "All right, then." He had some difficulty hauling Stuart off his brother. As soon as he let Stuart go, the boy ran out into the hall, Nelson at his heels.

Phillip was shaking, his face white. "Tiger," he said. "Stuart tried to kill Tiger." Then he began to sob, and Denise reached out to take him in her arms, but Jason stopped her with a gesture.

"Come here, son," he said, and Phillip obeyed. "Stop that noise. You're not badly hurt, are you?"

"No, sir," Phillip choked out the words.

"Then why are you taking on that way?"

"Tiger—"

"The cat's all right," Jason said. "But you'd better give her back to Patrick. She's no match for that hound, not yet."

Phillip tried to speak, but he was crying too hard to get the words out. Once again Denise tried to take the child in her arms, but Jason prevented her. "Leave him alone. Don't coddle him. Wash your face, son, and then take the kitten to the stables. You can play with her there if you want to."

Then, dismissing the matter, Jason turned and left the room. Denise lingered behind. "Come, Denise," Jason said impatiently. She sighed and went out into the hall, closing the door behind her. "Jason, you're being unfair. Why should Phillip have to give up his pet when Stuart—"

"Denise, don't make so much of this. And don't act as if Stuart had done something terrible. All boys fight. My brothers and I—"

"Phillip's smaller than Stuart. You can't possibly expect him to hold his own against his brother."

"It looked to me as if he were doing pretty well. I'll give him a few pointers when I have the time."

"No. You mustn't. I don't want him to fight. Can't you see, he's not like Stuart. He's sensitive; he—"

"No son of mine is going to be a coward, if that's what you mean."

She wanted to cry out that Phillip was not Jason's son,

that he had no right to expect the boy to be a small replica of himself.

"You may raise Vanessa as you see fit," Jason told her. "But leave the boys to me." He put an arm around her waist. "Don't worry about Phillip. He'll be all right. I'll bring him a special present from the Exposition. What do you think he'd like? Shall I go back and ask him, or would it be better to surprise him?"

How like Jason, to think that an expensive gift would make anything right.

"Surprise him," she said. For she was sure that if Jason went back to the nursery now he would find Phillip in tears and would be angry with him.

Although she wanted to see the sights at the Exposition, Denise was more concerned with the desire to provide a change of scene for Jason. She had ordered a new wardrobe, not so much for her own pleasure as in the hope that Jason, who always took pride in seeing her beautifully dressed, might be pleased.

A few weeks after Rosalind MacKay's visit Denise was in her bedroom, trying on one of the new dresses. The warm scents of early summer came to her on the breeze that ruffled the curtains: the first roses from the garden beyond the terrace, the new grass, the freshly turned earth where the gardener was setting a row of ornamental shrubs.

"If you will stand still only a moment longer, Madame," Fantine said, "I will adjust the underskirt, so—"

Denise was pleased with the walking dress, with its pale yellow underskirt and its fitted tunic of brown and yellow striped satin. She smiled a little smugly, seeing how the dress outlined her breasts and trim waist. Then she started, surprised to hear Jason's footsteps in the hallway.

"I was not expecting you home from the city so early," she said as he entered the room. "But since you're here, tell me how you like my dress. I shall wear it on the trip to Philadelphia, and then, on our first day at the Exposition, I'll wear my pearl-gray satin." She fell silent.

Jason's mouth was set in a hard line, and his eyes were troubled.

"Please leave us, Fantine," she said quickly.

After the maid had gone, Jason said, "We won't be going to Philadelphia after all."

"But you promised Stuart—"

"That can't be helped."

"Jason, what has happened?"

"Elspeth's baby will be born within a few weeks, maybe sooner. You must be with her at that time." It was not a suggestion but a command.

"But we all agreed that Doctor Underhill would be on call, and there are plenty of female servants to—"

"You must be with her. As she was with you when Stuart was born, and Phillip, too."

"There's no need to remind me. I know how much I owe her. But she insists she does not want us to stay home on her account, and besides, she's sure her husband will be returning any day now."

"She's wrong."

"She says you told her he'd be home in time for the baby's arrival."

"I know what I told her. I lied; I had to. Terence O'Connor never sailed to the Far East. There was no last-minute change of orders."

"Then where is he?"

"I sent him to Cuba. To run the blockade and deliver arms to the rebels."

But if Terence O'Connor had gone to Cuba, Denise thought, fear rising inside her, he should have returned months ago.

"The *Tropic Star* was captured by a Spanish patrol ship. Terence O'Connor and the others were taken prisoner."

"But surely there is something you can do to get them freed."

"No, Denise."

There was a terrible finality in his voice. "What happened to Elspeth's husband?" she demanded.

Jason did not answer at once. He kept his eyes fixed

on the open window, as if he had never seen the view before.

"Jason, tell me—"

"He was shot by a Spanish firing squad."

She sat down on the bed, knowing her legs would not support her. What would happen to Elspeth, so near her time, when she learned that her husband was dead? And she remembered O'Connor, handsome and carefree. And young.

"He was only twenty four," she said shakily.

"He knew what he was getting into. He took a risk, and he lost." Although Jason spoke with harsh indifference, Denise did not want to believe that he was completely unmoved.

Then she remembered how strongly he had opposed Elspeth's marriage. "You sent him to Cuba. It was your responsibility. You could have saved him, couldn't you?"

"I tried—"

"Did you? You told me that you had connections with Thaddeus Marsh and Roscoe Conkling. You could have gone to them for help. To President Grant himself."

Jason's face was unreadable, his eyes cold.

She sprang to her feet and seized his arm. "Why didn't you save Captain O'Connor? Because you wanted to punish him for marrying Elspeth without your permission? Because you were angry with her for defying you?"

As soon as the words were out, she wanted to call them back, but it was too late.

"Damn it, if you were a man, I'd kill you for even suggesting— You think I didn't try? I used bribery, persuasion, threats, everything. I put pressure on Thaddeus, on all of them. It was hopeless." Then, regaining control, he spoke very quietly. "Believe what you want to about me."

He turned on his heel and started for the bedroom door.

"Jason, please wait."

"For what?"

It would be futile now to say she was sorry, but she could not let him leave her this way.

"We have to talk about Elspeth," she said. "She will have to be told."

"Not until after her baby is born," Jason said.

"And then?"

"I'll tell her, Denise, when the time comes. Perhaps she too will accuse me of killing her husband."

"I did not say you killed him."

"It was about the same, wasn't it?" His face darkened. "Maybe I can't blame you for thinking I'd be capable of such an act. But somehow I had hoped— Whatever you think, I'm fond of Elspeth. Always have been. Didn't I try to keep her from marrying O'Connor? And when I found out that he had married her before he sailed, knowing what might happen, I was angry with him. Why not? It was a selfish, irresponsible action. But all the same, I would not have let him die if I could have prevented it."

She knew in that moment that he was speaking the truth, and she wanted to go to him, to put her arms around him and ask him to forgive her for suspecting otherwise; but his eyes were icy and remote, and she dared not try to bridge the barrier she had placed between them.

Elspeth's daughter was born on a rain-drenched day late in July. Denise remained in the room throughout the labor, although Elspeth told her, "This is no place for you, Mrs. Moreland. What would Mr. Moreland say?"

"He would want me to be here."

"If only Terence would return! I was so sure he would be home in time for the baby's birth." She reached out and her fingers closed around Denise's hand. "He'll be home soon, though. Mr. Moreland told me."

Denise had to turn her face away, afraid her eyes would betray her.

Elspeth forced a smile. "Maybe it's better this way. By the time he gets home, I'll be recovered, and he'll be so pleased to see the baby. Imagine—he doesn't even know he's about to become a father—"

Denise rose and busied herself with dipping a fresh

cloth in a basin of water. When she came back to wipe Elspeth's forehead, she had regained a measure of control.

Doctor Underhill came into the room and made a brief examination, using the sense of touch alone, not lifting the sheet that covered Elspeth's misshapen body; no decent woman would permit anything else.

"It won't be long now," he said calmly. "Perhaps you ought to leave the room now, Mrs. Moreland. You might send up one of the female servants."

"I've borne three children of my own," Denise said, pushing a loose strand of hair back from her forehead and looking the young doctor in the eye. "I'm not about to make a nuisance of myself. My place is here."

Only after the baby had arrived and Elspeth had fallen into an exhausted sleep did Denise go downstairs. She sat on the terrace, waiting for Jason to return from the city.

She stared out over the cliffs and remembered Elspeth's words when the baby was placed in her arms. "I will name her Fiona. It was my mother's name. I hope Terence will approve." Then, looking up at Denise, she added, "You don't think he'll be too disappointed because his first child was not a son?"

Denise had shaken her head.

"I will give him a son next time," Elspeth had whispered, her eyes closing, a smile on her lips.

Chapter 16

During the weeks following the birth of Elspeth's baby, Denise found it increasingly difficult to conceal the truth about Terence O'Connor's death; sooner or later, Elspeth would have to know.

Early in August, Elspeth came inot the morning room after breakfast and announced to Denise that she was preparing to leave Mooncliff. "I've heard of a little house that's for rent in New York City," she said. "It's not far from the waterfront, but it's on a clean, quiet street. It was Patrick who told me about it; his sister lives close by there."

"You must not think of leaving yet," Denise said.

"I want a home ready and waiting for Terence when he returns. I have a bit of money put by, and Terence's share from this voyage will be ample."

In spite of the sultry summer weather, the morning room seemed chilly to Denise. "You cannot think of living alone and caring for Fiona. It's out of the question."

"I thought you would surely understand, Mrs. Moreland. After all these months at sea, Terence will welcome the change. I'm sure that he will want what I can give him: curtains at the windows, carpets on the floors—a home of his own. He's never really had one, you know. And, if you can, please try to get Mr. Moreland not to send him off on another long voyage. Not for a little while, at least." Elspeth's eyes were warm and urgent. "I've missed him so much."

"Stop it!" Denise cried, her voice too loud in the quiet, pleasant room.

Elspeth stared at her, obviously startled by her outburst. Then, with characteristic composure, she said, "Perhaps I did not choose a suitable time to discuss my plans. I'm sorry if I've disturbed you. If you will look over the dinner menu, I will take it down to the kitchen."

"No. Don't go." Denise could not look at Elspeth. "Please sit down here beside me." Elspeth obeyed, and in the silence that followed, Denise found herself listening to the endless surge of the water against the cliffs behind the house, the sighing of the wind. Soft sounds on this summer day, but they filled the room.

Jason had promised to tell Elspeth when the time came, but he was off in the city. She must delay the confrontation until he returned.

"Listen, Elspeth. If you will put off this plan to leave right away, perhaps later—"

"But this little house I was telling you about is perfect for the three of us, and if I wait, someone else may rent it. I do not wish to appear ungrateful, and I can never forget all you have done for me, you and Mr. Moreland. But I am Terence O'Connor's wife now, and I must put his needs first."

"Elspeth, listen. I wanted to wait. I tried to wait until you were strong enough to be told. But now you leave me no choice."

"I am quite well," Elspeth said, but Denise saw the color drain from her face, her eyes cloud with fear.

Denise put an arm around Elspeth.

"Terence," Elspeth said. "Something has happened to him. You must tell me!"

"Oh, my dear, if only—"

"Tell me!"

"You won't be needing a house now. Terence isn't coming back."

"But that's not possible! I know the *Tropic Star* is late returning to New York, but Mr. Moreland told me that is not uncommon, on such long voyages. He said perhaps a storm—"

"Your husband is dead, Elspeth."

Elspeth drew a long, shuddering breath, and Denise felt the spasm that shook her body. Then Elspeth went limp, and for a moment Denise thought she might have fainted. Then she heard Elspeth ask, in a strange, tight voice, "How did he—how did it happen?"

"The *Tropic Star* was not in the Far East, as you thought. Mr. Moreland lied to you. After he discovered you had married Captain O'Connor and were going to have a baby, he did not want you to know the truth. The *Tropic Star* was overdue even then, but he hoped the ship would return. Then Congressman Marsh got word that the ship had been captured by a Spanish patrol boat off the coast of Cuba, and—"

"Cuba? There's fighting in Cuba. Why did Mr. Moreland send my husband there?"

"Captain O'Connor was running guns to the rebels. After his ship was captured, he and his crew were imprisoned. And then—"

Denise tried to draw Elspeth's head down against her shoulder, to stroke the smooth dark brown hair, but Elspeth pulled away. "And then?"

"I can't—" She needed Jason at this moment. He could have dealt with this. He could have put the truth into hard, blunt words. But it did not matter, really, for there was no way to tell Elspeth except as Jason would have done.

"Captain O'Connor was shot by a firing squad. He and his crew. As a warning to other gunrunners, Jason said." Then, speaking more quickly, desperate to fill the agonizing silence, she went on, "He did everything possible to get your husband freed, Elspeth. He told me so. He used all his influence in Washington, but it was hopeless."

If only Elspeth would cry or scream or faint. If only

she would not sit there, her gray-blue eyes enormous in her white face. Denise went on, "He meant to take Captain O'Connor off the Cuban run after this voyage."

"Do you believe that?"

"Why, yes, of course."

"I don't. Not so long as there was money to be made. You know Mr. Moreland better than that."

"Elspeth, please, you must not—"

"No one matters to Jason Moreland unless he can serve his ambition. He gave me a fine position here at Mooncliff, after I had helped to bring Stuart safely into the world. A son for the Moreland dynasty. Don't look at me like that! He used you, too."

"That's not true."

"You think I've forgotten those things you told me the night Stuart was born? You were half out of your mind with pain after all those hours of labor, Mrs. Moreland, and I tried to forget your words. I thought I had, until now."

Denise looked away. Elspeth went on, quietly now. "I know he has his good side, Mrs. Moreland. He has been kind to me, surely. But when he has to choose between honor and ambition, he always makes the same choice."

"Not this time. My dear, you must believe me, he—"

"That day I went to see him at South Street. I asked him whether, if he had another chance to make the choice he had to make on board the *Nubian Queen*, he would do the same thing again—kill all those people to insure a profitable voyage. And he said he would."

"But he didn't mean it. He couldn't have meant it! It's only that he has too much pride and stubbornness to admit a mistake."

Elspeth stood up. "You are his wife, and I suppose you love him enough to overlook anything, but I cannot forgive what he has done to me. I cannot forgive him for sending Terence to his death." Her voice shook, but she managed to control it. "I am leaving Mooncliff. At once."

"Elspeth, no! I won't let you."

"You cannot stop me, Mrs. Moreland. I will not spend another night in this house." Her eyes looked haunted, shadows moving in their depths. "My father said there was a curse on Mooncliff, that it had been built on the bodies of the dead. For the first time I think perhaps I believe him."

"She will not change her mind," Denise told Jason that evening as they stood together on the terrace. The sun had set, but heavy low-lying clouds hid the stars. The rising wind caught at the skirt of Denise's dress and whipped a few strands of hair across her face. "We must not let her go, not this way. She is still too weak; she hasn't recovered from Fiona's birth. And now, this news about her husband—"

"I would have told her myself. I thought I had made that clear, Denise."

"But she was talking about renting a house for herself and Terence and the baby. I couldn't let her go on planning."

"I suppose not. And now she's set on leaving Mooncliff."

"But we can't let her! Jason, persuade her to stay."

"She blames me for O'Connor's death. Why would she listen to anything I might say?" He turned from Denise and looked out across the river.

"Don't you understand what I've been telling you? Or don't you care what happens to Elspeth and the baby?"

"I care," he said, but there was no feeling in his voice.

"Ask her, beg her to forgive you," Denise persisted.

He turned on her. "Forgive me? For what? I didn't force O'Connor to sail. I told him from the first that if the Spanish captured him, there was little chance I'd be able to help him. He knew the odds, and he took them. And he went right ahead and married Elspeth, knowing damn well he might never come back!"

"None of that matters now," Denise interrupted. "I want Elspeth to stay. I need her here. We all do. And now, she needs us. Promise me you'll talk to her."

"All right," he said at last. "But I won't ask her to forgive me. I refuse to take the responsibility for O'Connor's death."

He turned and went back into the house and into the

library. Denise followed him, hoping to convince him that Elspeth's welfare was more important than his own stubborn pride. But before she could speak, Elspeth was there, standing on the threshold. She was dressed in a traveling costume, a plain black walking suit, a black-veiled bonnet and a heavy shawl.

She looked past Jason and spoke to Denise. "I'll be leaving now, Mrs. Moreland. I've come to ask you to write a reference for me."

Chapter 17

Denise looked helplessly from Elspeth to Jason, who stood before the fireplace. "You promised," she reminded him softly. "Oh, Jason, please."

He appeared not to have heard her words, but he crossed the room and motioned Elspeth inside, then closed the heavy doors behind her. "So you're leaving," he said. "And you want a reference. Tell me, what do you plan to do with your reference?"

Her face was controlled, her voice steady. "I will seek employment as a housekeeper in New York City," she said.

"And what about Fiona? If you do find work as a housekeeper you won't be able to keep the baby with you. Such an arrangement would be out of the question in any other household. You know that, don't you?"

He was taking a high-handed approach, as Denise had feared he would, trying to bully Elspeth. Didn't he know that Elspeth was as stubborn, in her own way, as he was?

"If I cannot keep Fiona with me I will have to make

other arrangements. There are places in the city where babies can be boarded, I suppose."

"A baby farm? What do you know about such places? I know about them because of this campaign I've been engaged in. They're a disgrace. Babies fed laudanum to keep them from crying, left filthy and neglected by the harridans who run these places for profit. And if a girl does manage to grow up there, and she's pretty, she may disappear when she is no more than seven or eight."

Elspeth made a harsh, choking sound. "You've led a rather sheltered life here at Mooncliff," Jason went on. "I could tell you things about New York City—"

"It doesn't matter. I'm leaving. Patrick has hitched up the team. He will drive me to the landing near Rhinebeck, and I will take the night boat from there. I will not spend another night under this roof."

"Elspeth, listen to me," he said. "You want to keep Fiona safe with you, to give her a decent start in life. You can do that here. Think about it. She'll have fresh air, good food. When she's older, I'll see she gets a fine education. She can study along with my own children, and later—"

"It's no use, Mr. Moreland." She turned away and spoke to Denise. "If I can have my reference," she began.

"Wait," Jason said. "I suppose I can't stop you, if you're set on leaving, but at least I won't have you going off without money."

"I've saved a little."

"No matter. I'll give you enough so you can stay at home with Fiona, so that you won't have to work, at least until she's older. You owe that much to her, at least. And to Terence. He'd want his child properly cared for."

"How dare you speak to me of Terence?" For the first time since she had entered the library, she lost her control. Her eyes were hot with fury, and her small, slender body quivered. "You, who let him die when you might have saved him!"

"That's a lie," Jason said. "I won't have you go from this house believing that." He put a hand under her chin and tilted her head back so that she could not look away. "I've always admired your strength and your honesty,

Elspeth. Be honest now. You knew what Terence O'Connor was like—not the kind of man to seek a safe, peaceful life, ever. He took command of the *Tropic Star* because he wanted fast money, but also because he courted danger."

"I won't listen. Let go of me."

"There are men like that," Jason continued, as if he had not heard her. "I tried to tell you about him that day you came to my office on South Street, remember. But you wouldn't listen, because you were in love. And maybe O'Connor's recklessness was one of the things you loved in him."

He released her now, and she looked away. "No. That's not true. You mustn't say such things."

"Why not? You know I'm right, don't you?"

Denise wanted to intervene, seeing how Jason's words hurt Elspeth. But she sensed that Jason, for all his harshness, was reaching Elspeth as she herself had not been able to do. For now Elspeth was crying, stripped at last of her unnatural calm. Some of the tension went out of her, and she allowed Jason to put an arm around her shoulders. "I loved him—I loved him so. We only had that little time together. And now I'll never see him again—"

"You have his child," Jason said. He handed her a handkerchief, and she wiped her eyes and straightened her bonnet.

"I'm not blameless in all this," he went on. "I sent him on that voyage, and I was thinking about my own profits. But whatever you believe about me, I did use every source of influence I had to get him freed. I tried and I failed. That's the truth."

Elspeth searched his face, then said softly, "I believe you, Mr. Moreland."

"Then you'll stay on here? For Fiona's sake?"

"I can't."

There was a long silence in the room, while Denise listened to the wind from the river. The open windows cooled the big, high-ceilinged room after the heat of the day. The sound of carriage wheels and the clopping of horse's hooves on the drive came to her faintly.

"Stay for my sake, then," he said. Denise looked at him

with disbelief. "Stay because we need you, all of us here in this house. You know what kind of a house it is. You remember your father's words, the night he died. I can't blame you for being afraid." He paused and looked over at the windows and at the heavy draperies that billowed in the night wind. "There have been times when I've been afraid here, too." He stopped and shook his head as if to drive away an unwelcome memory. "But you are strong, Elspeth. We need your strength, all of us. Whatever happens here, in the years to come, we'll need you."

Before he could say anything more, Fantine came into the library to announce that Patrick was waiting at the front door with the carriage. "You must leave now," Fantine said, "or you will miss the night boat."

Elspeth stood quite still, her eyes unreadable.

"You are a part of Mooncliff," Jason said quickly, urgently. "You may hate the thought, but it's true. Please don't go."

Elspeth smiled then, an infinite sadness in her face. She looked past Jason, at Denise. Both women knew Jason well, each in her own way; both knew what it had cost him to make that plea.

"A part of Mooncliff. Yes, I suppose I am," Elspeth said.

She turned to Fantine. "Please tell Patrick to take the carriage back to the stables," she said.

When Jason and Denise were alone in the library, she turned to him and said, "Thank you." She put a hand on his arm, but he drew away and went to the window. He was obviously preoccupied. Or perhaps, Denise thought, he was embarrassed that she had been present to see him humble himself to Elspeth.

"We do need her," Denise said, forcing a light tone. "We'll be doing a great deal of entertaining this fall, with the campaign in full swing, and I don't know how I would have managed without her."

Jason turned, his eyes dark with anger. "You need not worry about the campaign," he said. "I'm not going to be running for the State Legislature after all."

"What did you say?" Ever since last winter he had

spoken of little else, and she knew what the election meant to him.

"You heard me."

"But what's happened?"

"I don't want to talk about it. Go upstairs and say good night to the boys now. Then get some rest yourself. You've had a difficult day."

"I won't leave you until you tell me what's gone wrong."

"Nothing's wrong. My business takes up too much of my time and energy, that's all. I should have realized that when Marsh first suggested my running for office. Now, with the loss of the *Tropic Star,* I'll have to make changes in the Caribbean routes. There's money to be made in Jamaica and Barbados, but it will take time."

Denise shook her head. "There's something more, something you're not telling me."

"All right, then. There is more to it. Now please go up to bed. I'll be along after a while."

"No, Jason. I thought you were disturbed by Elspeth's plans to leave, but I see now it was something else. I must know. Surely I have the right."

There was a curious emptiness in his voice. "Not this time," he said. Then, seeing her baffled look, he said impatiently, "Have you forgotten? Right here, in this room, the night of the housewarming ball. I told you certain things then, things you never should have known, and after that—everything changed for us."

"Oh, but surely whatever is making you think of giving up the campaign, it can't be like—like—"

"Let me drop out of the campaign, and don't ask me why."

"If you really wanted to drop out, I couldn't stop you, but you don't want that. Jason, look at me. Can't you see I'm not the girl you married, that I'm a woman now? Won't you trust me enough to tell me what's troubling you?"

He led her to the sofa and drew her down beside him. "Very well. It's Lavinia's suicide. You remember that night the police came here. They said they had found a check, signed by me, in her apartment."

"I remember."

"All right, then. Marsh used his influence to have that check destroyed. I thought it was the only tangible link between Lavinia and me. But a police reporter had learned of the existence of the check."

"I don't see what difference that makes now."

"He wasn't willing to let the matter drop. He's gone on digging, prying into the matter, all these months. And now—I don't suppose you've seen the *World* today."

"No."

"There's a column—most unpleasant."

"Not about you and Lavinia? But they wouldn't dare! That reporter has no proof—"

"It is possible to blacken a man's name without making open accusations. Not that I care, but you can be hurt by this kind of thing. I can't allow that to happen."

"And it won't. I don't know what this reporter has written, but if I keep on as I have, going to rallies with you, entertaining your political associates here at Mooncliff, surely no one will believe him."

"You couldn't stand it," he said. "I know you, Denise. You couldn't face the looks, the whispers. Besides, you didn't want me to go into politics at all. My election to office means nothing to you."

"It means a great deal to you, though, and if you give up your chance now, you'll hate yourself later on, and me, too."

"You're making too much of this," he said. "I have money, power. What more could I get out of a career in politics?"

"Is that all a political office means to you? Money and power?"

"What else is there?" he asked.

"You would have a chance to do a great deal of good, if you wanted to."

"Come now, Denise. You surely haven't been carried away by my speeches, have you? You can't possibly see me as a crusader, like Horace Greeley or Carl Schurz?"

"No, I suppose not. You'd use your office to further your business interests and those of your supporters. But you could do more than that."

"What would you expect me to do?" There was a hint of mockery in his voice, but she sensed that she had caught his attention and she went on quickly:

"I don't pretend to know much about such things. That's my fault. I've been shut off here at Mooncliff, wrapped up in the running of the house, in caring for the children. But I did spend some time in New York City while I was waiting for Vanessa to be born. I saw and heard such dreadful things, about the poverty in the Five Points, the living conditions of the immigrants there."

"Go on," he said quietly.

"Jason, there are hundreds of homeless children sleeping in alleys, in cellars, on the docks. As you did, back in Liverpool, before you went to sea. You told me about that, remember?" He did not answer, and there was no scorn in his eyes now. "I know you can't be completely indifferent to these conditions," she said.

"No," he agreed, "I can't. But you don't know politics, Denise. I couldn't act on my own. I'd have to follow the dictates of the party, at least in the beginning."

Her heart lifted, for although he was placing objections in her way, he was no longer refusing to consider the possibility of remaining in the campaign.

"You could make your influence felt gradually. I know you, Jason. If you go into politics, you won't be content to take orders indefinitely, and you won't stop with the State Legislature, either."

"Suppose that's all true. Aren't you forgetting something? That reporter. There could be others, as well."

She hesitated, then said, "You haven't told me exactly what was in his column. I can get hold of it and read it for myself, you know."

He turned away from her, and she felt a swift pang of fear. Had she pushed him too far, probed too deeply into those things he wanted to keep hidden?

Then he was speaking slowly, painfully, his eyes fixed on the fireplace.

"I thought, after the check was destroyed, that there was nothing more the reporter could use against me. But he found out that Lavinia had been a governess here at

Mooncliff, that she and I were—together—while you were staying with Rosalind in New York."

"But how—"

"Servants can be persuaded to talk. Not Elspeth or Miss Wilmot. But we have grooms, kitchen maids—it would take only one of them to give out all the information the man was looking for. He did his work thoroughly. I'm not sure, even now, how much he did dig up. The evening I went to visit Lavinia at the girls' school, to ask her to—"

Denise pressed her fist against her lips. Until this moment, even though she had known the truth, that Jason and Lavinia had been lovers, she had not allowed herself to think about the significance of that fact. Burdened with her own guilt about Gilbert Laussat, about Phillip, she had accepted Jason's adultery. Or had she?

No, not really. She had only accepted the fact that Jason had turned to another woman, but she had never asked herself why.

"I thought when I forced you to send her away, that would be the end of it," she said. "I thought she meant no more to you than one of those girls at Josephine Woods's parlor house—I had to believe that, you see. But she must have meant more, because you weren't able to forget her, were you? What made you go and seek her out after she'd left here? What made you set her up in an apartment? What was she able to give you that I could not?"

"Denise, stop this. For the love of God, while we still have something left—"

"No. I have to know it all, or we have nothing left, nothing except a life of polite evasions, a charade to be performed for the outside world. You loved Lavinia. All these months since her death, even when we've been together, even when you've made love to me, you haven't been able to forget her."

"That's not true."

"It is. Until the day she died you loved her, and even now—"

"No, damn it! If you want the truth, you'll have it, all of it. I've thought of her, yes, but not because I still love her. That was over before she died. Denise, haven't you ever wondered about the reason for her suicide?"

"I didn't want to think about it."

"From the time I entered this campaign, I began to lose interest in her. Then, that night when you came to the rally at the Cooper Institute with me, she was outside, waiting for me. Conkling saw her, and Marsh. She was drunk and hysterical. Afterward they told me I had to break off with her completely if I wanted party support."

"And you did that? You wanted to win this election so badly?"

"Yes, I did. I suppose I still do."

"Yet you're willing to give up your chance to be State Senator, for my sake."

"That's different. You're my wife. You're a part of me. . . ."

He put out his hand, then drew it back, as if fearing a rebuff. Was he remembering how once she had fled from him, out of this room, had tried to shut him out of their bedroom? She had never forgotten that night and never would, but somehow it was not important now.

She moved closer to him and rested her head against his shoulder.

"I won't change, Denise. You must know that by now. I'll try, for your sake, but I don't want you to deceive yourself."

She lifted her face and smiled, a little sadly, "I could hardly do that after all these years, could I? You're a ruthless man, Jason, and a hard one. You're ambitious and unscrupulous. You'll hurt me again."

"Then why not run away? Why risk your future with me?"

"Because you need me. I suppose I'll always be a little afraid of you. But I'll never leave you."

He took her in his arms then and held her against him, and she felt the strength in him, and the hunger. In a moment she would respond, but now, it was as if she found herself in a place beyond time, as if she could look ahead down all their years that were to come.

There would be tragedy in this house again, but there would be love and joy, too. She thought of Stuart, headstrong and willful, like Jason. He would need to be protected from himself. And Phillip, shy, sensitive, shadowed by the secret of his birth. Vanessa, who even now showed signs of becoming a beauty, with Jason's dark hair and brilliant blue eyes.

There would be more children, Denise thought, a faint smile curving her lips. She wanted more children, for Jason and for Mooncliff.

She felt a touch of fear, remembering Andrew Buchanan and the words he had spoken about Mooncliff. But she put the fear aside and told herself that a house was only a thing of stones and wood and mortar. The generations who lived in the house, who made it their own—they shaped its destiny.